PRAISE FOR DONNA GRANT'S
BEST-SELLING ROMANCE NOVELS

"Grant's ability to quickly convey complicated
backstory makes this jam-packed love story accessible
even to new or periodic readers."
–*Publishers' Weekly*

"Donna Grant has given the paranormal genre
a burst of fresh air…"
–*San Francisco Book Review*

"The premise is dramatic and heartbreaking;
the characters are colorful and engaging;
the romance is spirited and seductive."
–*The Reading Cafe*

"The central romance, fueled by a hostage drama, plays
out in glorious detail against a backdrop of multiple ongoing
issues in the "Dark Kings" books. This seemingly penultimate
installment creates a nice segue to a climactic end."
–*Library Journal*

"…intense romance amid the growing war between
the Dragons and the Dark Fae is scorching hot."
–*Booklist*

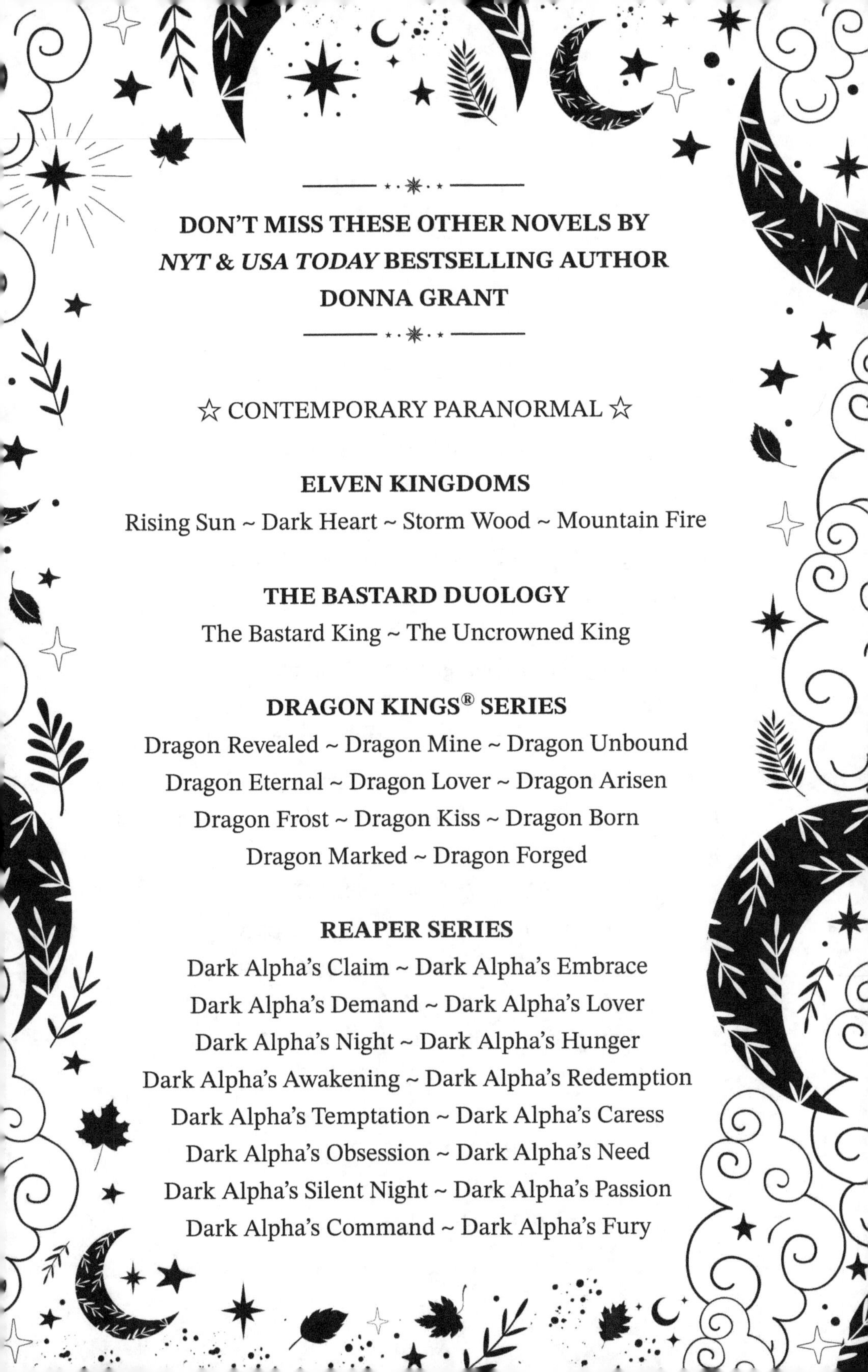

SKYE DRUIDS SERIES

Iron Ember ~ Shoulder the Skye ~ Heart of Glass
Endless Skye ~ Still of the Night ~ Blood Skye
After Midnight

DARK KINGS SERIES

Dark Heat ~ Darkest Flame ~ Fire Rising
Burning Desire ~ Hot Blooded ~ Night's Blaze
Soul Scorched ~ Dragon King ~ Passion Ignites
Smoldering Hunger ~ Smoke and Fire
Dragon Fever ~ Firestorm ~ Blaze ~ Dragon Burn
Constantine: A History, Parts 1-3 ~ Heat ~ Torched
Dragon Night ~ Dragonfire ~ Dragon Claimed
Ignite ~ Fever ~ Dragon Lost ~ Flame ~ Inferno
A Dragon's Tale (Whisky and Wishes: *A Holiday Novella*,
Heart of Gold: *A Valentine's Novella*, & Of Fire and Flame)
My Fiery Valentine ~ The Dragon King Coloring Book
Dragon King Special Edition Character Coloring Book: Rhi

DARK WARRIORS SERIES

Midnight's Master ~ Midnight's Lover
Midnight's Seduction ~ Midnight's Warrior
Midnight's Kiss ~ Midnight's Captive
Midnight's Temptation ~ Midnight's Promise
Midnight's Surrender ~ A Warrior for Christmas

CHIASSON SERIES

Wild Fever ~ Wild Dream ~ Wild Need
Wild Flame ~ Wild Rapture

LARUE SERIES

Moon Kissed ~ Moon Thrall

Moon Struck ~ Moon Bound

WICKED TREASURES

Seized by Passion ~ Enticed by Ecstasy

Captured by Desire

Books 1-3: Wicked Treasures Box Set

☆₊°˙⋆☽⋆⁺₊✧

☆ HISTORICAL PARANORMAL ☆

THE KINDRED SERIES

Everkin ~ Eversong ~ Everwylde

Everbound ~ Evernight ~ Everspell

KINDRED: THE FATED SERIES

Rage ~ Ruin ~ Reign

DARK SWORD SERIES

Dangerous Highlander ~ Forbidden Highlander

Wicked Highlander ~ Untamed Highlander

Shadow Highlander ~ Darkest Highlander

ROGUES OF SCOTLAND SERIES

The Craving ~ The Hunger

The Tempted ~ The Seduced

Books 1-4: Rogues of Scotland Box Set

THE SHIELDS SERIES

A Dark Guardian ~ A Kind of Magic

A Dark Seduction ~ A Forbidden Temptation

A Warrior's Heart

Mystic Trinity (a series connecting novel)

DRUIDS GLEN SERIES

Highland Mist ~ Highland Nights ~ Highland Dawn

Highland Fires ~ Highland Magic

Mystic Trinity (a series connecting novel)

SISTERS OF MAGIC TRILOGY

Shadow Magic ~ Echoes of Magic ~ Dangerous Magic

Books 1-3: Sisters of Magic Box Set

THE ROYAL CHRONICLES NOVELLA SERIES

Prince of Desire ~ Prince of Seduction

Prince of Love ~ Prince of Passion

Books 1-4: The Royal Chronicles Box Set

Mystic Trinity (a series connecting novel)

DARK BEGINNINGS: A FIRST IN SERIES BOXSET

Chiasson Series, Book 1: Wild Fever

LaRue Series, Book 1: Moon Kissed

The Royal Chronicles Series, Book 1:
Prince of Desire

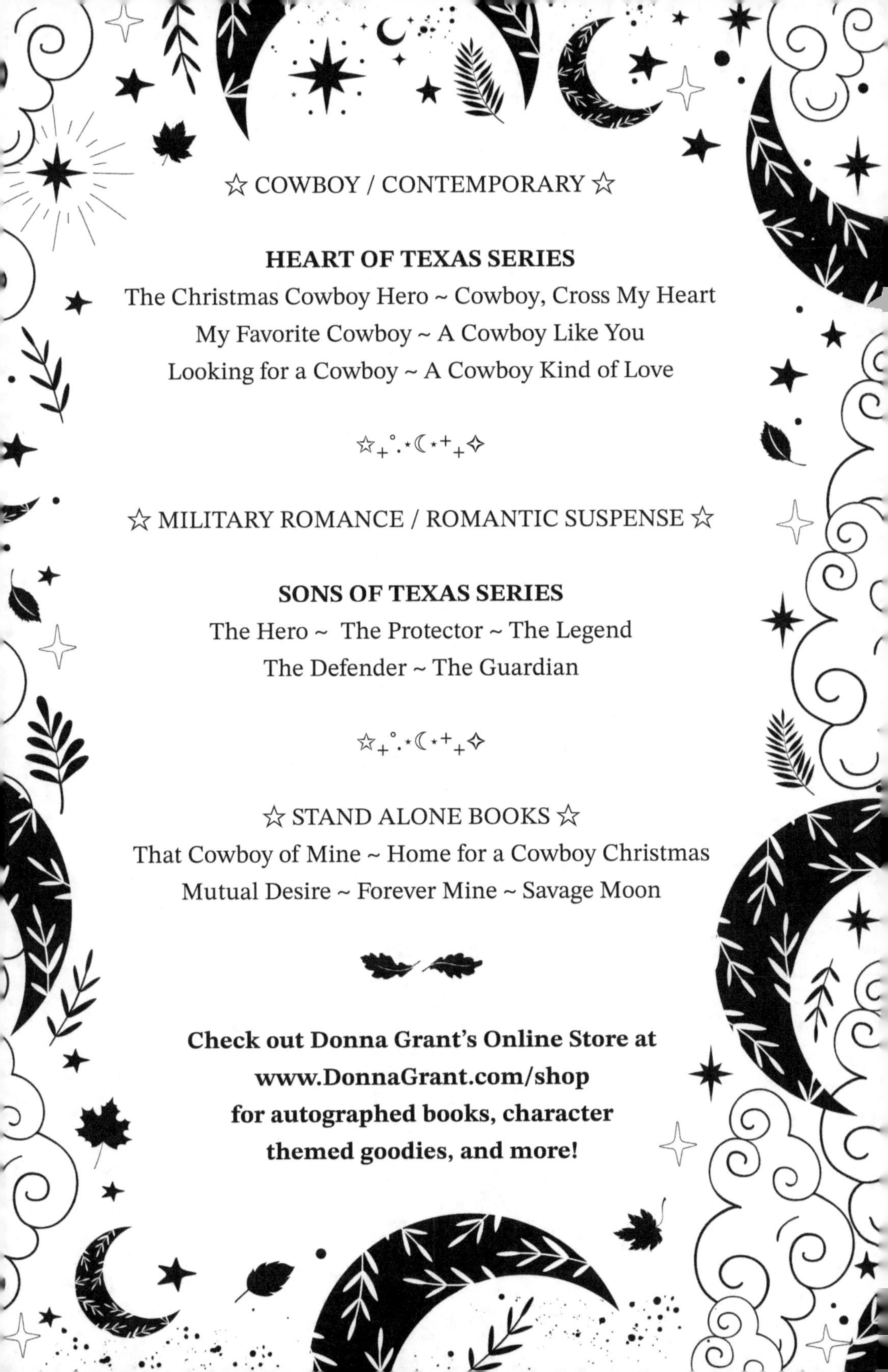

☆ COWBOY / CONTEMPORARY ☆

HEART OF TEXAS SERIES
The Christmas Cowboy Hero ~ Cowboy, Cross My Heart
My Favorite Cowboy ~ A Cowboy Like You
Looking for a Cowboy ~ A Cowboy Kind of Love

☆ MILITARY ROMANCE / ROMANTIC SUSPENSE ☆

SONS OF TEXAS SERIES
The Hero ~ The Protector ~ The Legend
The Defender ~ The Guardian

☆ STAND ALONE BOOKS ☆
That Cowboy of Mine ~ Home for a Cowboy Christmas
Mutual Desire ~ Forever Mine ~ Savage Moon

**Check out Donna Grant's Online Store at
www.DonnaGrant.com/shop
for autographed books, character
themed goodies, and more!**

STORM WOOD

ELVEN KINGDOMS
BOOK THREE

DONNA GRANT

SHECRISH
HUMAN LAND
DRAGON LAND
ZORA
Stonemore
Orgate
Iron Hall
Cairnkeep
Belanore
Flamefall
Rannora
N
S
E
W

7 RACES OF ELVES

SUN ELVES (GOLD ELVES)

– recognized by their golden complexions.
Known for their levelheadedness, think things through.
Have long memories. Maintain a love of
freedom and personal expression.

Skin: golden brown
Eyes: amber, copper, gold
Hair: golden blond, tawny
Ability: Readers
Magic Color: yellow/golden

MOON ELVES (AKA SILVER ELVES)

– Isolated race who prefer only themselves.
Moon elf society values individual
accomplishment and rights.

Skin: very fair, silver tint
Eyes: various shades of blue (icy blue)
Hair: blue, silvery white
Magic Color: silver

STAR ELVES (AKA PEWTER ELVES)

– Nomadic, often interacting with other elves.
Have a knack for perceiving inner beauty.
Curious and adventurous. Can be focused and relentless.

Skin: fair skin
Eyes: violet/shades of purple
Hair: lavender, purple, silver
Homeland: nomadic
Ability: Healers
Magic Color: purple

.. — .❋. — ..

SEA ELVES (AKA BLUE ELVES)

– Have webbed fingers and toes. Gills hidden behind
their ears. AKA as mermaids without the tails.
Among their own, delight in song, dance, and magic.
Toward others they are slow to bestow the gift of
their voice/artistry.

Skin: Blueish/greenish
Eyes: iridescent blue to silver white
Hair: bluish-black or greenish-black (oil slick)
Homeland: bodies of water
Ability: animals in the water
Magic Color: blue

WOOD ELVES (AKA COPPER ELVES)

– guardians of all things in the forest.
They live in complete harmony with the woods and
its inhabitants. Can be judgmental, but take time to
consider everything before passing judgment.
Once won, a Wood Elf's friendship is deep and lasting.
Some of the best fighters.

Skin: coppery skin
Eyes: Green or Hazel
Hair: Brown or Red
Homeland: forests/woods
Ability: good with animals; can sense truth/lies
Magic Color: green or copper

. . — .❀. — . .

MOUNTAIN ELVES (AKA BRONZE ELVES)

– prefer the highest peaks. Rarest of the elves.
Cautious and aloof. Understand the importance of
community. Suspicious of strangers. Best weapon crafters.

Skin: white or brown
Eyes: Black
Hair: Black, Dark Brown
Homeland: mountains
Magic Color: bronze

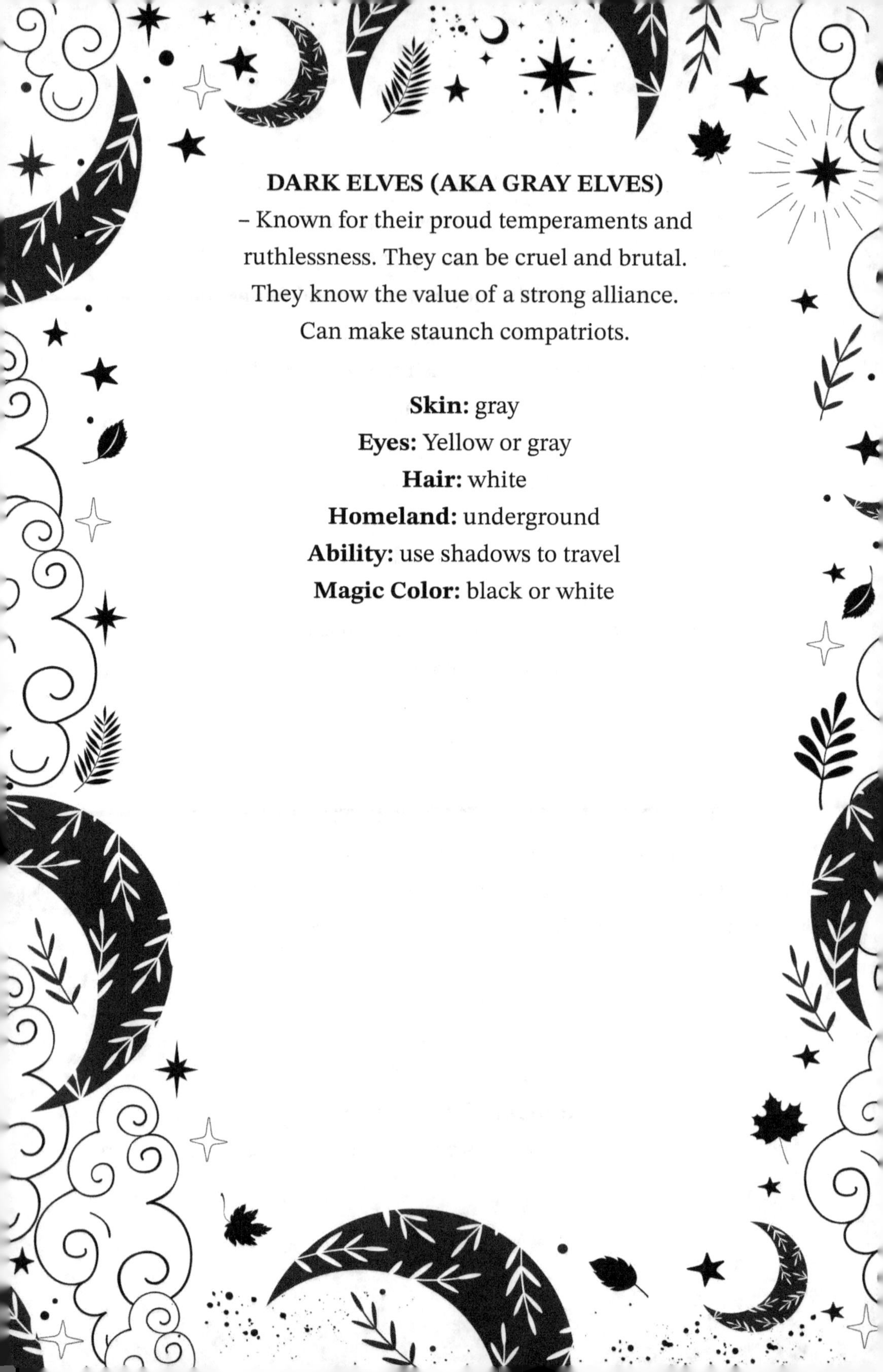

DARK ELVES (AKA GRAY ELVES)

– Known for their proud temperaments and ruthlessness. They can be cruel and brutal. They know the value of a strong alliance. Can make staunch compatriots.

Skin: gray
Eyes: Yellow or gray
Hair: white
Homeland: underground
Ability: use shadows to travel
Magic Color: black or white

STORM WOOD

ELVEN KINGDOMS
BOOK THREE

1

The metallic scent of blood hung in the air around her, heavy and oppressive. Farah blinked, her eyes focusing on the rough-hewn stone walls beaded with water, before her gaze lowered to the human who lay on her side in a fetal position, trembling.

The woman's terror-filled eyes locked on Farah.

Farah lifted her hands to find them covered in blood. Bile rose in her throat as she stepped back in dismay. Her brain refused to believe what she saw, but there was no denying she had crossed a line—one she had skirted since she'd stepped into the Mortham compound. And there was no going back.

Farah had to leave the room and get away from the two Dark Elves watching her. She needed some air. When had she last seen the sun? Felt the wind on her face? Touched the trees? It seemed a lifetime ago. When she was someone else. Before she went undercover.

She turned, looking for the exit, and saw her two chaperones blocking the door, watching her raptly. Golshan was the taller of the two. He had white hair trimmed short and perpetually narrowed yellow eyes as if he knew she was hiding something. Amarjeet was the follower. Stocky and on the shorter side, he kept his head shaved, highlighting the long scar on the right side. And his gray eyes saw everything.

They had taken her under their wing when she first arrived, but she wasn't fooled. They had long suspected her. After all, what was a Wood Elf doing underground? She had been determined, though. The problem was that to remain in Mortham, she had to become the very thing she was fighting against.

Each day had become a little easier. Now, it was hard to know which version of herself she was. She looked at her hands again. She had no memory of what had occurred with the woman. She couldn't remember anything after they led her into the room. Her mind was blank.

"I knew you had it in you," Golshan said, slapping her on the shoulder.

Farah forced a smile she didn't feel and swallowed more bile. Amarjeet opened the door as he and Golshan conversed. She didn't pay them any mind as she started out of the room. But her feet halted at the doorway—as if some invisible force kept her there. Farah made the mistake of looking back. She saw the blood on the human, the walls, the floor.

She stalked away, horrified by the evidence of the depths she had sunk. Farah had been underground for so long that she couldn't even recall the blue shade of the sky. There was nothing but shadows and darkness everywhere she turned. The flickering light of the torches on the walls reminded her that she wasn't outside where a Wood Elf belonged. The underground was for the Dark.

And the depraved.

It was a place where someone could hide. Where the shadows diminished the true depths of corruption. Here, in the fort, her sins were nothing compared to others. Here, she was urged to embrace debauchery and decadence. To seek out immorality. To give in to the wantonness.

Sin was everywhere. There was no need to look for it.

It found you.

Farah heard Amarjeet say something behind her. She kept walking. The mask she wore was close to slipping, and she hadn't spent months immersed in such horrors, only to be found out now.

Her steps quickened as she rushed to find somewhere to wash off the blood. Her chambers were three stories up on the other side of the compound. That was too far away. Sweat broke out on her skin. Her chest ached, and her breaths came quick and hard. She tried not to look down at her arms, but the red stood out. It kept drawing her eye, showing her—reminding her—of the line she had crossed.

Someone shouted her name. She stumbled against a wall and burst through a door. Wrong room. She spun and shoved her way out, leaving blood on the wall where she had touched it. She recoiled but kept walking. Someone's shoulder rammed into her. She mumbled an apology and tried to remember where the washroom was. Had she gotten turned around? There were so many hallways, so many doors.

Relief filled her when she saw the door for the toilet. She busted through it and started toward the sink when she spotted a male Sun Elf washing his hands. He gave her a side-eye before he left.

Her hands shook as she turned on the faucet. A heartbeat later, the sound of a toilet flushing filled the room. A female Dark Elf walked from one of the stalls. Farah kept her gaze down as she scrubbed off the blood. The Dark said nothing before walking out.

Farah had maybe two seconds to herself before Golshan and Amarjeet entered the room.

"You left the door to the cell open," Golshan reprimanded as he strode up to her side, putting himself so close she felt his breath on her cheek.

Farah's emotions were spinning out of control. If she didn't pull herself together, she would end up shut away in one of the many rooms around her. She fell back on her all-too-brief training and locked down her rampant feelings, before lifting her head to look at him. "The human wasn't going anywhere."

There was a stretch of silence before a wide smile spread across Golshan's face, and he started laughing. Many would think him handsome with his fine features that tipped more toward feminine. It was rare for him *not* to have some female on his arm—the prettier, the better.

She, however, had never been one of them. Golshan had tried to get her into his bed, but she had kept him at arm's length. Unfortunately, that had only intrigued him more. Women didn't reject his advances.

Farah joined in the laughter, her gaze moving to Amarjeet. He was the more muscular of the two, but his features were angular. There was nothing pretty about Amarjeet. Nor did he want there to be. He was the muscle to Golshan's brains.

"Ah," Golshan said, his laughter dying. "For a moment there, I thought you were running from me."

"Why would I do that?" she asked.

His yellow gaze was probing as he stared. "I asked myself the same question."

The running water was the only sound in the room as she held his gaze. Farah shifted to face him. "We're scheduled to do a pickup. If you have a problem, then say it now."

"No problem," Golshan said as he backed up a step and shook his head. One side of his lips curved downward. "No problem at all."

Farah looked at Amarjeet, who stood as silent as a statue. He appeared relaxed, but his sharp gaze searched her face and body as if he were waiting for her to show weakness. Golshan dusted off his hands and whistled as he left the room. Amarjeet remained a heartbeat longer before he followed.

She wanted to collapse. Perhaps rush to the toilet and vomit. But she didn't dare. She didn't even throw water on her face. They were listening. Always listening. Once she had washed off the blood, she dried her hands and turned away, all without looking in the mirror. She feared what she might see if she looked at her reflection. When she finally left Mortham, would there be anything left of the elf she had been?

Golshan and Amarjeet were long gone when she emerged from the restroom. She smoothed her hands over her hair and down her single braid as she headed for the delivery area. It was a set of rooms where the captains brought their cargo. That's what everyone called the abducted humans and elves. *Cargo.*

Her knees had knocked so badly the first time she walked these corridors, she'd been sure others could hear. Now, she didn't even notice the hundreds of doors or the unnatural silence. She didn't look through the small, square windows set in the doors. Which meant she didn't see the confusion and fear on the faces of the cargo-turned-slaves within, how their minds shut down, leaving them almost comatose. Shells of who they had once been.

All for profit and power.

For her to complete her mission, she had to shut out all sympathy for the victims and ignore the horror she felt at those taking part in the kidnappings. Her sister was among those taken. And Farah had no idea what had happened to Nitya. While not part of her mission, she hoped to find answers and give herself and her parents some closure. But given everything Farah had witnessed—and participated in—she wasn't so sure she wanted to know anymore.

Chills ran down her arms as she swung them while walking. She didn't look closely at the dark clothing she wore in case there were drops of blood on the fabric. She knew it was there. She just didn't wish to see it.

She walked through a set of doors and then took the stairs to her left, hurrying down both flights. Another door was ahead, this one with guards on either side. They were hidden but necessary. At least one of the kidnapped inevitably attempted to run. But they never got far.

Farah used to silently cheer for those who had the courage to make a break for it. She hadn't understood the excitement of those working at the fort when such individuals arrived. Not until she saw the delight everyone got in breaking those people. She had seen a side of elfkind that had only been reserved for her nightmares.

A foul, ugly side she would never be able to forget.

Farah strode through the final set of doors and walked to the dock, where Amarjeet and Golshan stood with several others. She watched the first of the newly captured make their way along the long, winding path from the Lotus River to their new home. And leading this load of new cargo was another Wood Elf who didn't belong in the Below. Salil—her handler.

And her only contact to the outside world.

Tall and broad-shouldered, Salil was an imposing figure, even among the Dark. He'd cast aside the traditional green-and-brown-colored clothes of the Wood Elves for dark gray. The tunic and trousers, as well as the sash around his waist, were simple, befitting the slave he pretended to be. He kept his thick, wavy brown hair short. He halted and stroked a hand over his beard as he inspected the faces of those around him with his intense, hazel gaze.

Both he and Farah worked for the Defense Intelligence Agency. Salil had brought her to Mortham on his ship. He was also her way out. All she had to do was get to him before he departed, and he would stow her away in the secret compartment.

Salil was a seasoned DIA agent, who held himself with calm, cool resolve. They were both undercover, but he did it effortlessly while she struggled every second of every hour. Which was even more challenging with so many eyes watching her, waiting for her to make a wrong move.

She should slip away to Salil's ship and get as far away from Mortham as possible. While she hadn't found what she had come to Mortham for, she *did* have vital intel about a new Shaldorn the DIA needed immediately. She didn't dare write down what she had discovered, though. And it would take more than a few whispered words to explain things to Salil so he could pass on the information for her.

But if she abandoned her undercover persona now, she wouldn't be able to return—unless it was as a slave herself. And if she couldn't return, then she wouldn't be able to uncover what had happened to her sister. All Farah needed was a little more time.

The Masters controlled the slave trade, Mortham, and many other outposts. They were furious that Shaldorn had been discovered and shut down. It had been their playground, a place for their friends and special guests to live out every fantasy imaginable. The Masters were so incensed that flyers circulated with images of the four responsible for Shaldorn's closure. A Sun Elf named Ravi, a human called Yasmin, a male Dark Elf, Dain, and a female Dark, Arya.

The details of how Shaldorn had been brought to heel sounded exactly like something the DIA was involved in, but there was no way to know for sure unless Farah returned to headquarters and checked in with her supervisor, Durga.

Salil's hazel gaze met hers. It was common for them to share a few words, so no one thought twice about her walking over to him. He returned his attention to the people being hauled in.

"You're pale," he murmured when she reached him.

She stood shoulder to shoulder with him. "I'm fine."

"Hardly. It's time."

Two words. That was all it took to end her time at Mortham. The code words weren't up for debate. She thought about the blood on her hands, and the woman huddled in fear in the corner. Then she thought of the information she'd gathered about the new Shaldorn. What she knew might save hundreds—maybe thousands—of lives. But what about Nitya? Farah hadn't spent over a year in the Below mingling with such a violent group to give up now.

"Not yet."

"Farah," Salil warned in a low voice.

She looked at him. "Give me until your next drop-off."

"There is such a thing as going too deep."

He was right about that. Too bad she hadn't realized it until it was too late.

Salil blew out a breath and looked over her head. "I won't return for two months. A lot can happen in that time."

"I know what I'm doing."

It was a lie, and they both knew it.

This was her first undercover assignment, and she was making all the wrong decisions. She'd be lucky if they ever let her go undercover again. *If* she survived. It had taken far too long to convince Durga to train her. Only Farah's threat of going on her own had finally made Durga relent. Farah's training had been hard and fast, and she thought she had all she needed to succeed—a false confidence instantly knocked away in the first hour she was at Mortham.

"Be safe," Salil murmured under his breath after the last abductee walked past them.

He pivoted to begin the trek back to his ship, and Farah followed the slaves up the steps into the next room, where they would be separated and sorted. Her job was to help divvy up this new group into smaller ones. It was hard to watch as those abducted bitterly accepted their fate. Would she do the same if she were in their position? Even knowing what she did about what happened to those who fought back, she still wouldn't submit.

Golshan barked orders, directing others where to go. Everything was business as usual. Farah couldn't focus, though. She kept thinking about her decision to stay. After her reaction—and actions—earlier, she should be grasping for any means of escape. Common sense dictated that. But she had gone too long without answers about Nitya.

Her parents assumed she was dead, but her sister was too strong to give up without a fight. Nitya was alive, and Farah would find her.

Golshan shouted her name. Farah looked up to discover everyone watching her. Amarjeet took a menacing step toward her. She inwardly shook herself and scanned the crowd as she should have been doing.

The human man made her do a double take. His shirt was torn, exposing a thick chest and wide shoulders rippling with muscle. Even in the dim light, she noticed his tan skin that spoke of days beneath the sun. He stood tall, his back straight. Rich, deep brown hair fell to his shoulders, with the top half gathered at the back of his head. A beard covered his face, but it was trimmed short along his sharp jawline and chin. Her eyes lingered there before dropping to his lips and then moving up his cheek to his forehead and dark brows. But it was his eyes that caught her notice. They scanned the room and those within it as if searching for something.

Or someone.

There was no fear in his gaze, no dejection. No panic, either. He was calm. Too calm.

She shook herself for admiring his handsome face. This human was exactly who she needed to alert the others about. She called out to Golshan, but an explosion snatched her voice and sent her soaring.

Farah came to on her stomach with bits of debris still falling around her. She was dazed and tried to see through the cloud of dust. A loud ringing in her ears prevented her from hearing anything. Still, she tried to get up, only to find something heavy on top of her leg. A scream ripped from her when she attempted to move her leg. The pain was so great, she nearly blacked out.

Suddenly, hands were moving away stone to free her. She tried to tell them that she was hurt, but the words wouldn't come. She screamed again as fresh pain rolled through her when whatever had trapped her leg was removed. Something warm and wet oozed down her calf as she succumbed to the darkness again.

She woke screaming, the agony in her leg unbearable. Someone held her shoulders down as someone else clamped a hand over her mouth to stifle her cries. But it was the person tending to her leg that she focused on. She tried to see their face as she thrashed, but those holding her were in the way. It wasn't a Star Elf tending to her—their healing magic didn't call for them to shove their fingers into her wound. But why wasn't a Star Elf here?

Nothing she did dislodged those holding her. The more she struggled, the weaker she became. She heard hushed, panicked voices and fought to breathe through the ever-growing waves of pain. It became impossible to keep her eyes open. Her last thought was that she would likely die before she saw the sun again.

Except she didn't perish, though the throbbing in her leg made her wish she had. When she became aware of her surroundings again, she was on a stretcher. The jostling aggravated her injury and kept her in constant pain. To retreat from the agony, she slipped back to oblivion where nothing could touch her.

The next time she came to, she clawed at her coverings. Fire lanced through her body. She had never been so hot. Someone held her down again. She looked up at Nitya, but when Farah blinked, it became Golshan's face.

Someone held her head, and another forced her lips open to pour something down her throat. She choked and coughed as it dribbled out of the corner of her mouth. The taste was horrid as it slid down her throat. Almost immediately her pain began to diminish. Sleep pulled at her, and she went willingly, even as she reached out for her sister.

2

"This was a mistake," Kalyani said.

Rohan lowered the elf's head to the pillow and looked at his younger sister. Her deep brown curls were kept away from her face by a strip of gray cloth. She had always hated her hair. When they were younger, he would chase her around, tugging on the ringlets just to get a rise out of her.

But they weren't children anymore. There was no time for playing such games.

He looked into her brown eyes, so dark they were almost black, and said, "It was our only option."

"You should've told me what you planned."

"You would've stopped me."

She clenched the bowl in her hand and bit out, "Aye. I would have. Because it was foolish. What were you thinking to purposefully get taken?"

"It was the only way."

"Stop saying that," Kalyani said angrily. She rose stiffly from the stool and walked to the table, her back to him. "What if it hadn't worked? Then you *and* Lata would've been taken from me."

Rohan watched her shoulders droop. She was as frazzled and worried as he was. The difference between them was that everyone in their village looked to *him* to fix problems. He had to act, and there hadn't been time for a debate. "But it *did* work."

She turned to him, her face set in hard lines. "I want your word that you'll tell me about any such reckless plans in the future."

Rohan looked down at his clasped hands and sighed. Then he met Kalyani's gaze. "You have it. I'm sorry. I thought it would be easier if you didn't worry."

"You were wrong," she snapped.

He nodded. "I see that."

All the anger left her then. She jerked her chin to the Wood Elf. "And if she doesn't live? Her fever is high."

"She'll live." He'd damned well make sure of it.

"You always take on too much, brother. Usually, you find your way out of it, but I'm not so sure this time."

"Because you don't believe me capable?"

She rolled her eyes. "Because there are forces at work you can't stand against. Your strength and conviction won't bend the type of wickedness that has pervaded Shecrish."

"We're not part of Shecrish."

"Ugh," she said, throwing a towel on the table. "You sound just like Dad. I hate to break it to you, but you can say that all you want. It doesn't change the facts."

"We live separate from them."

Kalyani put her hands on her hips and looked out the window to the ocean. "That hasn't kept our people from being taken, has it?"

Rohan was silent as she walked out the door. He didn't have an answer. He hadn't had one for the last two years. The abductions had begun slowly: one or two of their people disappearing at a time. Then, things ramped up, and groups were taken.

Their village was difficult to get to, but it didn't stop the kidnappings. It didn't matter what protocols he put in place, the guards stationed day and night, or even the walking patrols. People still went missing.

Rohan had been vigilant about his sisters. They didn't go anywhere if he wasn't there to watch over them. Lata had chafed at such measures. It was expected of adolescents. Still, he believed she understood why such methods were necessary. He trusted her. Yet she and a few others had snuck away in the middle of the night to go to the beach.

He only knew that because one of the guards had woken him. By the time Rohan got to them, Lata and her friends were gone—five more taken from their rapidly dwindling village. He eyed the Wood Elf. Her red hair was tangled and limp from illness. She would survive. She had to. Because without her, he might not get to Lata in time.

Rohan rose and walked around the narrow bed to the table. He didn't want to waste time healing the elf. Her kind was the reason his village lived as they did. And yet, her life was in his hands. He could let her die. She was close. All he had to do was stop tending to her. It would be easy. He never would've taken her at all if she weren't the key to finding his sister. But the elf had to live, whether he liked it or not.

He gathered more dried leaves from a jar and crushed them with a mortar and pestle, pulverizing them until they were powder. Then he added water to make a paste. Rohan walked back to the bed and sat on the stool. He looked down to find the elf's face turned toward him. Her skin was ashen. In the sunlight, he knew it would have a coppery sheen. What would make a Wood Elf leave the forests for the Dark Elves' underworld?

Rohan studied her face. She had delicate features that drew the eye. Her lips were full, her cheekbones high. Eyebrows that matched her fiery hair curved gently over her eyes. Long, curled lashes rested against her face. Freckles ran across her nose, along her cheeks, and even on her forehead.

If he hadn't seen her in Mortham himself, he never would've thought someone who looked so innocent could be so depraved as to take part in the abduction and enslavement of others. It didn't matter why she was there. She had made her decision—and fate had chosen her for his pursuit.

Rohan moved aside the blanket covering the elf's left leg to reveal her bandaged thigh. Her writhing had made blood soak through the dressing again. He set aside the bowl and carefully unwound the wrap to inspect the wound. The stitches were holding nicely. The wound had been jagged and deep, bleeding profusely. If he hadn't sutured the injury immediately, she probably would've bled out. Her fever had begun on the way to the village. He'd had no choice but to open the infected wound and tend to it. That's when he found the bits of rock he'd dug out of her.

He tested the flesh around the gash. Everything was healing nicely now. Why, then, did the fever still rage? Rohan spread the paste along the lesion and put on fresh bandages. Once finished, he rinsed the bowl and turned to look at his patient as he wiped his hands.

The elf wasn't the only one he had gotten out of Mortham.

Nearly everyone who had been on the ship with him had escaped. He hadn't expected the fort to be as large as it was. There hadn't been time for him to search the different corridors for Lata, much less the various floors. He'd freed the ones he could. He'd saved lives. That should be enough.

But it wasn't. Because he'd had to leave others behind.

They wouldn't be able to hit the compound like that again. The Masters would make sure of that. It was why the Wood Elf was so important.

"Well, elf, I'll sit by your bedside day and night, nursing you back to health if I have to," he promised her.

3

bright light shining in her eyes dragged her from sleep. Farah turned her head the other way to escape it, but the light was brighter there. She tried to swallow and found her mouth dry. Then she made the mistake of trying to lick her lips. Her tongue got stuck on them, making her wince. She lifted a hand to shield her face from the blinding light and cracked open her eyes.

She couldn't remember a time when she had felt so miserable. It took great effort just to keep her arm raised. The longer the light shone on her, the angrier she got. Who was pointing the light directly at her face? And why?

Her eyes were out of focus as she glanced around, looking for someone. Farah blinked to see better. That's when it became perfectly clear that she was no longer in Mortham. Or in the Below.

The area wasn't lit by a light but by sunlight pouring through an open window near her feet. The breeze brought in the fresh scent of salty air. She lifted her head to look outside at the cobalt ocean, the waves curling to foam white as they rolled onto the shore.

She lowered her arm and dropped her head back onto the pillow. That little bit of movement had exhausted her. She took stock of her surroundings: a narrow bed that sat close to the floor, the tall, hollow-stemmed stalks of the shrava plant tied together to make a window with a flat covering held open by another stalk.

She looked to the side and found a wall of rock. Farah rolled her head to the other side and saw more rock. A door and another window covering farther down had also been crafted from stalks. When it appeared no one was about, she pushed herself into a sitting position. She wasn't strong enough to remain sitting and had to brace an arm behind her. The ocean drew her gaze once more, but she forced herself to look at the rest of the room. The sides and back looked like a cave.

There was a table and stool to the side, and some elaborate water delivery system made of shrava stalks cut in half lengthwise that fed into a sink. A couple of shelves lined the wall with tableware upon them. A glance up showed another bed angled to the side above her. But the woven rugs on the floor pulled it all together. This was someone's home.

Farah didn't remember getting there. She didn't know how long she had been in this place or how she had left Mortham. In fact, she didn't remember anything since seeing Salil. She frowned as a memory teased her.

Something had happened. She squeezed her eyes closed and thought back to that day. When her recollections led to her washing the blood off her hands, she shook her head and jumped over those memories. There. She had watched the new slaves being brought in. Salil had wanted her to leave. She had decided to remain and get more information. Salil walked away, and she followed the last of the abductees into the next chamber. Everything had been normal. Right up until...the explosion.

Her eyes flew open. Had someone attacked the fort? She looked at the door. There was only one reason someone would have taken her from Mortham. She needed to leave. Immediately.

She threw off the blanket and discovered her clothes had been removed. But it was her heavily bandaged thigh that drew her up short—a reminder that she had been injured. No Star Elf had healed her. Nor had she been given any magical herbs. That could only mean she was with humans.

Unease iced her blood. Whatever they wanted with her couldn't be good. Farah swung her legs over the side of the bed, gritting through the pain that shot up her leg. The world spun around her, but she pushed through it. If they believed her still unconscious, it would give her the time she needed to get out and find her way to Rannora and the DIA.

The moment she tried to stand, her wounded leg protested and buckled. She fell to the floor in a heap—right onto her injury. Farah clasped her lips together and bit back the cry that nearly escaped. She put her hand on her leg and rocked back and forth in an attempt to lessen the pain, but the throbbing only intensified.

The door banged open, and a woman rushed in, followed by a man. Farah tried to get to her knees, but even that was impossible. The woman hurried to her and wrapped the blanket around her front. As if Farah cared about shielding her body now. She was caught. There was no escape.

"You shouldn't have done that," the female chided. "Your leg isn't healed enough yet."

The man stood at the door, his arms folded over his chest. Farah only spared him a glance. No doubt he was the guard meant to ensure she didn't use her magic on the female. If only she *had* her magic. She'd used it up in Mortham. A Wood Elf without the woods was as weak as any human.

To her surprise, the woman helped her back into bed. Farah wanted to sit up, but she had used the meager reserves of her energy trying to stand. And she was paying for it now as her body throbbed with every beat of her heart. The pain intensified. Sweat beaded her brow as she fought against showing how badly everything hurt.

What she wouldn't do for a Star Elf right then.

"That was stupid."

The deep voice cut through her as sharp as any blade. Her attention shifted from her injury to the other occupant in the room. Farah slowly rolled her head to look at him. She gave the male a long perusal this time.

Pale eyes scrutinized her with disdain. His clothes were made of thin, washed-out gray material. His loose-fitting shirt hung to mid-thigh with a V neckline that displayed his impressive chest. The sleeves were long and rolled up to his elbows. Wrapped around his waist was a wide leather belt. His trousers were tucked into brown knee-high boots.

He dominated the room without moving a muscle. He was so tall, his head nearly brushed the ceiling. Everything about him was hard and unyielding. His tan skin emphasized his fair eyes. His face was pleasing with its hard lines and full lips.

Her thoughts halted. Recognition flared. Her stomach dropped to her feet as she realized he had been at Mortham.

"I see you're putting it together," he replied. "I was beginning to think you'd taken a blow to the head."

The woman jerked her head to him. "Rohan," she admonished.

He didn't look away from Farah. There was aversion in his unusual eyes. Was it because she was an elf? Or because she had been at Mortham?

Both?

"What do you want?" Her voice was hoarse and scratchy, and it came out sounding as frightened as she felt. Not at all what she'd intended.

Rohan's lips curved into a smile. Not a nice, pleasant beam, but one filled with resolve and purpose. It was a cold smile. The kind charged with promise—and death. "You're going to help me find my sister and my people."

He was insane. That was the only explanation. The longer Farah stared into his unwavering gaze, the more convinced she was that he was unhinged. "That isn't possible."

"I got out," he stated.

She swallowed and curled her hand into a fist beneath the blanket. Not a day went by that someone didn't try to escape Mortham, but it had never happened. Not once. The only way he'd gotten out was with help.

Rohan dropped his arms to his sides and took a step toward her. "And I took others with me."

"Then you should be glad you have your life," Farah said. "No one has escaped before."

"More are being held. You know this," the woman said.

Farah turned her attention to the female. She was tall and curvy with a wealth of dark curls held back by a strip of faded gray cloth the same color as her clothes. Her attire was similar to

Rohan's, except her tunic was shorter, her pants fit tighter, and her boots only came to her calves. She even had a belt at her waist.

Rohan snorted. "Don't bother playing on her sympathies. She doesn't have any."

"You don't know anything about me," Farah stated.

The woman pointed to the door and told Rohan, "Out."

To Farah's surprise, he listened. Then, she was alone with the female. Farah eyed the door. No doubt Rohan was nearby. Even if she managed to get to her feet and remain standing, she would have to get past the woman to reach the door, and she had no idea what awaited her on the other side. Her injury made her too weak to do more than lay there.

The woman moved behind her. Farah heard water and craned her neck to see the human using the water system to fill a cup. Farah yearned for a taste of the cool liquid to ease her parched lips.

"You must forgive my brother," the woman said as she returned to Farah's bedside. She lowered herself onto a stool and leaned forward.

Farah inched back until she realized the human was moving the cup to her lips. She put her hand behind Farah's head, and when she lifted it, helped hold her as she drank. Farah's eyes closed as she savored the sweet taste of the water. She drank it all, already feeling its effects.

"Our village has been hit particularly hard," the female continued. "He is only looking for a way to return our people."

Farah looked into the woman's dark eyes and shook her head. "It's doubtful you could find them. Even if you did, they wouldn't be the same."

"Maybe." She rose and filled the cup again. When she returned, she said, "My name's Kalyani. What is yours?"

"Farah."

Kalyani held the cup in her hand and looked out the open window. "I didn't know Rohan's plans. I probably would've stopped him had I known. But he won't back away from this, and if I want to keep my brother alive, I must help him." Her dark gaze slid back to Farah. "You were gravely injured. You almost died."

Farah recalled someone digging in her leg.

"Twice," Kalyani added. "Your fever only broke earlier this morning."

So, the image of Nitya that Farah saw was nothing more than a delusion. That was a blow.

"We kept you alive. Please, help us find our sister."

Kalyani had no idea what she was asking. They would look through the rubble at Mortham for her, and when her body wasn't found, they would assume she had helped Rohan and the others. All those months of living and working at Mortham had been destroyed by one explosion. There was no going back, no matter how much she wanted to. Her duty now was to get to Rannora and hand over the intel she had.

"I wish I could," Farah finally answered.

Kalyani's lips flattened. "Rohan said you wouldn't help. He said your heart was too dark to see the evil you were a part of."

Oh, she saw it all right. It's why she'd nearly gotten sick the day of the explosion. But still, she had intended to stay. Maybe Rohan was right. Perhaps her heart was dark, and she just didn't know it yet.

4

Rohan stood upon the slender bridge that hung between dwellings and stared out at the horizon where the sky met the ocean. There was more land out there. He was certain of it. Convincing everyone else of that was more difficult. No one wanted to leave what they knew to face uncertainty and unknown dangers. People preferred stability. They knew they could live in relative peace—as they had for generations. Even the increase in abductions didn't seem to persuade them to leave.

Even Kalyani protested his suggestion to find a new home. She clung to the hope that Lata and the others would return. As long as she held on to that, she wouldn't go anywhere.

But freedom from magic and the kidnappings was just over the horizon for him. He could set out on his own. He'd even considered it a time or two. In the end, however, he decided he couldn't leave his family. So, he was stuck in a place he both loved and hated.

Shecrish was beautiful and offered much, but his kind would

always be second-class as long as the elves outnumbered the humans. Looked down upon. Denied the same rights and opportunities. He was tired of being treated as if his life meant less than an elf's. He was responsible for Siguk and those who lived there. It wasn't a position he wanted, but a responsibility placed upon him. And he took it seriously.

Generations ago, a small group of humans had struck out on their own after unsuccessfully trying to find a place among the elves. They traveled all over Shecrish, looking for a spot of their own before heading south. They built their homes along the southern cliffs of the mesa, far from the troubles throughout Shecrish, and cut themselves off from everyone—even for trade.

His people had struggled. They had nearly starved before learning how to take what the ocean provided. When they couldn't live atop the mesa or along the shore, they carved out spots within the cliffs and built homes.

That labor had continued. They had good years and bad ones. The winter storms that came were destructive, some forcing them to rebuild homes—and burn their dead. But they had never yielded. Many saw his wish to leave as giving up. The first Siguks hadn't quit when they searched for a new place. This generation didn't want to, either.

Kalyani's approach yanked Rohan from his thoughts. He looked at her as she came to stand beside him. She remained silent, her gaze focused out over the water. When they were younger, it was all their father could do to keep her out of the ocean. They had teased her that she should've been born a Sea Elf.

"She won't willingly help," Kalyani said.

Rohan drew in a breath and released it. Whether to leave or

not was once more cast aside as he focused on thoughts of the Wood Elf. "As I figured."

"I don't know how I feel about this. She'll double-cross you."

"It's a chance I'm willing to take."

Kalyani turned her head to him. "You're all I have left. I can't lose you, too."

He put an arm around her and pulled her against his side. "I don't know what else to do. We can't fight the abductors when we've not heard or seen anyone. One moment, our people were here. The next, they were gone. I don't have magic, Kal. But I do have a few other skills I can use."

"I know." She rested her head against his shoulder. "All the empty huts are a constant reminder of those missing."

"At the rate our people are being taken, we won't last until next year."

"I don't understand *why*. Who needs that many enslaved people?"

He squeezed her against him. "They must be selling them to others outside of Shecrish."

She lifted her head to look at him. "You don't think it's for the dragons, do you?"

"Nay," he said, scrunching up his face. "What do they need with humans? They're dragons. They can't communicate."

Kalyani lifted her face to the sun and closed her eyes. He watched her for a long moment. How long until they took her, too? How long until they came for him? Would he even be able to carry out his wild plan before then? Their village had been hit so hard that there weren't enough people left to keep sentries on patrol. And that left them vulnerable.

"They're going to return soon to take more of us," Kalyani said.

Rohan watched a sunhead with its distinctive white feathers and bright yellow head dive from the sky into the ocean, before resurfacing with its meal. "What do you want to do?"

"Live in peace, but that isn't an option." She opened her eyes and lowered her head. "We either remain and wait to be taken, or we leave as you've wanted to for years. The third option is fighting back."

"I don't want you anywhere near a battle."

She shrugged and shifted to face him. "Too bad. If you're in this, then so am I."

Rohan dropped his arm to his side. He knew it was pointless to argue with her when she had made up her mind. It was easier to accept the new turn of events and try to find a way to keep Kalyani out of harm's way.

She observed him, her dark eyes daring him to deny her. She knew him as well as he knew her. She was just as capable of leading their people—more so, in his opinion. She should've taken over after their father.

"Let's finish our discussion about Farah," Kalyani stated.

Rohan glanced at the door to the hut containing the elf. "What did she say?"

"Not much. I asked her to help, and she said she couldn't. She's still weak, but with the fever now broken, she should be back on her feet soon."

"We can't wait."

Kalyani's brow furrowed. "You want to head out before she's fully healed?"

"I wasn't supposed to leave Mortham so quickly. Her injury forced my hand."

"They'll be on high alert now."

"The elf will get us in."

Kalyani's lips twisted. "If she isn't healed, travel will be more difficult."

"It won't matter when we leave or what we do. She's going to make things as difficult as possible. Besides, if she's concentrating on her injury, maybe she won't be looking for a way to recharge her magic."

"Good point. She'll need clothes."

Unbidden, the image of Farah's bare back flashed in his mind. He hadn't meant to look when Kalyani helped her into bed, but his gaze lingered anyway. As long as he didn't see her pointed ears, he could almost imagine her as a human. *Almost.*

Between being soaked with blood and cut away so he could tend to her wound, her clothes hadn't been salvageable. He had burned them, erasing any evidence that she was with them. He doubted anyone would look for her She was one of many at the compound.

"I'm sure we can find some," he answered.

Kalyani nodded. "I'll take care of it. How are you going to convince her to help us?"

"I have a way."

"I take it you won't share it with me?"

Rohan tore his eyes from her and looked at the ocean, begging to be explored. "That's right."

"There's no way you can travel without entering the rainwood. And that will return her magic."

"Sadly, there's no getting around that."

Kalyani gaped at him. "Once she has her magic, she definitely won't help."

"Leave that to me."

"Please don't turn into the thing you're fighting against."

He would do whatever was necessary to return those who'd been taken. Even if it meant becoming that which he loathed. "I won't," he lied.

"I see this was pointless. I'm going to find some clothes for Farah. She needs to at least be able to sit up if we're leaving soon."

"*We?*" he repeated.

"What did you think I meant when I said we're in this together?"

"Kalyani," he began.

She simply skirted past him on the narrow gangplank and strode away. He leaned forward, bracing his hands on the rope. His plan was reckless, but when backed into a corner, the only way out was to strike. He'd already landed his first blow. The Masters and their followers were chasing their tails right now. If he had been able to remain in Mortham, he might have located Lata by now.

But his pivot could still work. No one had dared what he had. Yet he hadn't done it alone. Not that he was worried his ally would turn on him. His associate's help was over, however. Whatever else Rohan planned would have to be done alone.

He looked at the door again. He didn't relish going inside and trying to tend to Farah's wound. If he didn't need her to walk, he wouldn't bother trying. He sighed as he looked down at the empty huts around him. The dwellings hung in the middle of the cliff and expanded outward in either direction.

Few came south of the mesa. Fewer dared to look down and notice the huts if they visited. They only saw the occasional Sea Elf, and they paid them no mind. The Siguks weren't hidden. They could be found. Yet so few knew of them or their location. Perhaps that's what made abducting them so easy. Who would complain?

Rohan straightened and ran a hand down his face. He'd spent sleepless nights, the same thoughts going around and around. He couldn't find an answer. There probably wasn't one—at least none that he liked. And while he hadn't said it, he didn't expect to make the journey back. There would be casualties in this mission.

Just not Kalyani. She would lead their people when all this was finished.

He squared his shoulders and walked to the door of his hut. His hand rested on the handle for a long moment as he readied himself to face the enemy. The lives of his people—their very futures—rested on him. He wouldn't let them down.

Rohan opened the door and stepped inside. Farah was up on one elbow, looking out the window. She didn't seem to hear him enter, which allowed him to see her enjoying the same ocean he had been staring at. He wondered what could have forced her to leave her home. What had sent her away from the Wood Elves and into the bowels of the earth to mingle with the most abhorrent of them all?

He wouldn't ask.

She wouldn't answer even if he did.

And it didn't matter. He had a plan for the elf. It was the only reason she was still alive. He closed the door hard to announce himself. She jumped but didn't look at him. She kept an arm over her chest as if fearing the blanket would slip down. He almost told her she had nothing he wanted. Kalyani expected him to be charming to persuade her, but he didn't need to be. He had knowledge about her that she wouldn't want getting out.

5

Farah couldn't stop watching the ocean. She managed to brace herself on one elbow and push upright. The sun glittered upon its waves as if beckoning her. The smell of the salty air and the sight of the crashing surf took her back to another time when she and Nitya had snuck away from their community—breaking dozens of rules and disobeying their parents—to travel south for a glimpse of the sea.

She jumped at the sound of the door shutting abnormally hard but couldn't look away. The past had her in its grip.

Every step that led her away from home was debilitating. She had expected her father and archers to jump out at any moment to stop them. But while fear had hindered her, Nitya had been jubilant. She had raced ahead, leaping from limb to limb, while Farah constantly fought the need to return home. Nitya doubled back for her and spun a tale of grand adventure.

They traversed other Wood Elf territories, skirted human

outposts, and ventured into sections of the rainwood Farah had never viewed before. Soon, Nitya's excitement became hers. Emboldened, it wasn't long before Farah was racing through the trees with Nitya, ready to embrace the experience.

The smell of the sea air and the crash of waves reached them before they ever saw the water. When Nitya drew to a halt and had pushed aside a giant frond to gaze out, they were both out of breath. Farah had been too intent on the wonder on her sister's face to see anything else for a full minute, but then she took in the sight of the magnificent blue water.

"It's the most beautiful thing I've ever seen," Nitya had whispered reverently.

It was pretty, but Farah preferred the dense woods around her to the wide-open expanse of the sea. Yet Nitya's veneration of the water pulled Farah with her. As it usually did. She would do anything and go anywhere her sister asked.

"One day, I'm going to sail those waters," Nitya proclaimed.

Farah had pulled her eyes from the ocean to look at her sister. The thought of Nitya leaving not just their community, but also the rainwood, made her panic. Nitya wasn't just her sister. They were best friends. Where one was, so was the other. How could she face a future without Nitya?

Farah shut off the memories when they became too painful. She lowered onto the pillow and stared up at the ceiling, trying to recall specifics about Nitya's face, but the details had begun to blur long ago. It was becoming harder and harder for Farah to remember her sister. She could no longer describe the shade of Nitya's green eyes, but she could still hear her sister's laugh, could still remember her exuberance and thirst for life.

And how it had all been cut short with her disappearance.

Farah winced when her leg throbbed. She wanted to get out of bed. Being ill wasn't something elves endured. If a Star Elf wasn't nearby, they usually had magical herbs readily available. To be stuck in bed, at the mercy of enemies, was galling. And she stank. She wanted a bath so badly she ached for it.

She felt a presence next to her and looked over to find Rohan. He sat on a stool, holding a bowl with a blank stare. When he reached for the edge of the covers near her leg, she slapped his hand.

His nostrils flared, and they glared at each other. He tried again, and once again she smacked his hand away.

His eyes blazed with anger. "I need to tend to your wound."

"You aren't touching me," she stated. "I'll do it."

He contemptuously raked his eyes over her. "You can't even hold yourself up."

"I'll manage."

Suddenly, Kalyani was there. She waved her brother away. For several tense moments, Rohan didn't move. Finally, he jerked to his feet and walked to another part of the space.

Then Kalyani turned her dark eyes to Farah. "We are trying to heal you," she said calmly.

Farah sighed and looked away. "I can do it."

"You can't. And you know it."

The moment the infernal weakness vanished, Farah would be gone. No one would be able to hold her. Especially not humans.

"I brought you some clothes," Kalyani continued. "I thought you might enjoy a bath and then food."

"I would," Farah said hastily as she swung her gaze back to the woman.

Kalyani lifted a single brow. "Then you require assistance."

Farah glanced at Rohan, but his back was to them.

"He will leave," Kalyani replied.

A moment later, Rohan stalked out, though he closed the door softly this time. Kalyani wasn't paying attention to any of it. She was busy filling a large bowl with water. Farah twisted her neck to see what she was doing, but it began to hurt. Kalyani didn't try to fill the silence with conversation. Why should she? Farah was nothing more than a prisoner.

The image of the human covered in blood filled Farah's mind. She turned her head away and shut her eyes, but the woman's face remained. As did the memory of the blood. She could tell herself she had been playing a role, but she wasn't as convinced of that as she had once been. Was it a blessing that she had been taken from Mortham? Maybe there was something of her soul left to be salvaged.

The cloth on her shoulder startled her so badly she jerked away and then bit back a cry from the pain that shot from her leg.

"Apologies," Kalyani said in a soft voice. "I thought you knew I was there."

Farah tensed, the pain swelling within her.

"Breathe. Slow and steady."

She tried, but her lungs had seized.

"Breathe, Farah," Kalyani said loudly. She put a hand on Farah's wrist. "Your breath will draw the pain away. Do it. Now."

Farah looked at the human as she exaggerated drawing in a breath and releasing it. She motioned for Farah to follow suit. The longer she remained tense, the more her leg hurt. Farah drew in her first shaky breath, mimicking Kalyani as she breathed. To her surprise, the pain started to ebb. So, this was how humans dealt with discomfort. Breathing.

"Good," Kalyani said with a nod. "Stay focused on your breath."

Bit by bit, Farah relaxed into the bed. Kalyani gently lifted her arm softly wiped a warm, damp cloth along her skin. It felt heavenly to have the traces of her fever cleansed away. When Kalyani had finished Farah's front, she helped her sit up to wash her back. Farah's eyes were getting heavy. She fought against the pull of sleep as Kalyani helped her into a faded gray tunic.

Pants didn't follow, but she hadn't expected it with her injury. Kalyani gathered her hair and helped her lie back down, spreading the length behind her across the pillow. To Farah's surprise, the human began combing through the tangles. It wasn't long before Farah was completely relaxed, her mind drifting.

The comb reminded Farah of how Nitya used to run her fingers through her hair. It was the only way Farah would go to sleep when they were children. Nitya had done it so often, it had become a habit. After her sister vanished, Farah had gone weeks without sleeping. Her heart ached with a longing that could only be quenched if she discovered what had happened to her sister.

Kalyani moved the blanket away from her leg. She didn't exactly trust the woman, but she was right. They were trying to make her better. If they wanted to hurt her, they would've let her die. So, she grudgingly allowed Kalyani to tend to her.

Farah didn't protest when a hand slid under her knee and raised her leg so the bandages could be removed. The human's touch was light and tender, even when testing the area near the wound. Her leg was returned to the bed. The sea breeze brushed over her skin and along the exposed wound, causing it to sting. She winced and started to pull her leg away.

A soft hand landed on her thigh before something cool and wet was spread over the lesion. It immediately stopped the stinging and eased the pain that lingered. Once more, her knee was lifted, and more bandages were wound around her thigh. Kalyani didn't have to be courteous. The bath, the clothes, and brushing her hair were—

Farah's thoughts froze. Kalyani was still brushing her hair. So, if the female was doing that, then... She opened her eyes, instantly awake, and saw Rohan beside the bed. Farah lay frozen, watching as he quickly tended to her. The man she saw was so at odds with the one from earlier that she could only stare.

He finished and covered her leg with the blanket before glancing in her direction. Their eyes met, and she saw him stiffen, returning to the obstinate human she had encountered earlier. A muscle moved in his jaw.

"Don't worry. Your leg is still there," he mocked.

"Rohan," Kalyani said before speaking in their human language.

Farah had never learned it. Never had a need. Now, she wished she knew what they were saying. Rohan didn't look at her again as he got to his feet and walked out of sight. Farah could hear him moving things about, but she didn't know what he was doing.

Kalyani followed him to continue their discussion, leaving Farah alone. She focused on the clouds drifting across the sky so her mind wouldn't conjure imaginary conversations they were having about her. Because they *were* talking about her.

Farah willed her leg to heal. She needed to be able to stand so she could look out the window and find a way out. Quickly.

Soft footsteps announced Kalyani's approach. She held out a cup and nodded to it. "It's simple broth. You've been too long without food."

The moment she mentioned sustenance, Farah's stomach growled. She was starving. With her pain under control, she was able to think of other things. She tried to sit up. Kalyani helped her raise her head while bringing the cup to Farah's lips. When Farah smelled the fish, she almost pulled away. She hated fish. But her hunger got the better of her.

The taste was surprisingly pleasant. She had expected to hate it, not be delighted by the mild flavors that both soothed and nourished. Farah drank the entire cup of warm broth. The bath had done wonders to make her feel better, but having something in her stomach would go a long way to regaining her strength.

Rohan and Kalyani were talking again. Farah hadn't heard Kalyani get up. She was lulled by the food and the diminishing pain. When she heard Rohan start toward her, Farah almost pretended to sleep. She decided against it at the last moment. He came to stand at the foot of the bed, his tall form blocking a large section of the window and a perfectly good view.

"We leave tomorrow," he announced.

She waited for him to continue. When he didn't, she frowned. "I can barely sit up. How am I supposed to get around?"

"You'll manage."

"Nay."

He glanced over her, likely to Kalyani, before saying, "You don't have a choice."

"Where are we going?"

"Mortham."

It was the last place Farah wanted to be. Ever again. "You've lost your mind."

"I told you why I took you. I meant every word. If you aren't helping me, you're hindering me. And that means I toss you in the ocean."

He was bluffing. He had to be.

But the longer Farah stared at him, the more she realized he meant every word.

6

Rannora

The congested, noisy streets of Rannora didn't usually bother Salil, but they chafed his nerves that day. Shecrish had two major cities. Rannora was south, and Belanore was north. Neither was a place he'd choose to live. He longed for the quiet of the rainwood, to walk among the trees and be one with nature again.

Tragedy had pulled him from his beloved woods, forcing him to take steps he wouldn't have otherwise. It was why he mingled with the other elven races and among humans who struggled to eke out a living in places neither the land nor the residents wanted them.

Salil had always seen the cities for what they were: filthy, crowded, and polluted. Even in the upscale Geggin Square District, where he strolled now. Yet today, it seemed to press in all around him, suffocating and stifling. Someone ran into his shoulder. He fisted his hands and fought to control his swiftly unraveling anger. Salil walked on, making a beeline for the doors of *Twilight*.

The moment he entered, he unclenched his hands and drew in a deep breath. The tavern was continuously packed. Day or night, it was *the* place to be. There was always some form of entertainment on the stage. Today, it was a male Sun Elf reading what sounded like a poem.

Salil tuned him out and slid his gaze to the bar on the left. He nodded to the older female Star Elf who watched him. She dipped her head in return. It was the DIA's signal that things were good— at least, in their eyes. To Salil, *nothing* was right about Shecrish and hadn't been for a very long time.

He kept to the wall and headed for the side. The elf guarding the access opened the door as he approached. Salil strode down the hall and saw that some of the doors were open, but he didn't bother to look inside. None of it was his business, and the less he knew about others, the better.

Instead, he was headed to a meeting he'd hoped never to have. He rounded the corner and drew to a halt at seeing Durga headed in his direction. He didn't know her exact title. She claimed that titles didn't matter, but they must because she had her fingers in everything—and always knew what was going on. Her hazel eyes met his before she pivoted to enter the room.

Salil squared his shoulders before following his superior through the doorway. Durga was one of the few Wood Elves who seemed to thrive within the city. Perhaps it was her position and the success she wielded like a weapon. Either way, Durga was all city now.

Tall and thin, she cut an imposing figure in a ruby gown accented with gold thread. The color enhanced her coppery skin, and she kept her brown hair slicked away from her face into a tidy bun at the back of her head. Rubies swathed in gold adorned the tips of her ears. More rubies dangled from her lobes. A single, thick gold strand wound around her neck, and gold bangles were stacked on each wrist.

Durga never traveled alone. There was always at least one muscle-bound elf at her side and another dozen no one ever saw. Not even Salil—and he was trained to find them. But they were the elite of the DIA. They didn't have names, at least none he knew. No one knew how someone found their way to that team or the requirements. They chose you to join them, not the other way around.

Durga stood in the middle of the room with her arms crossed as he entered. Her face was tight, worry lines creasing her brow. It seemed someone had beat him to delivering the news. "I guess you already know, then."

"I just heard. Did you see the explosion?" Durga asked.

He shook his head as the bodyguard closed the door. "I heard it. Everyone heard it, but I had just set sail."

"How big was it?"

Salil lifted a shoulder in a shrug. "Hard to tell. As I said, I never saw it, but it had to be significant for the sound to reach us all the way at the river."

"Was there any indication that anything was wrong?"

"Something wasn't right with Farah."

Durga's frown deepened as she dropped her arms to her sides, her gaze intent. "Explain."

"She looked…unsettled. She was pale and couldn't focus. The two Dark, always with her, kept staring. I made the decision to pull her out. She refused."

"Did she say why?"

He shook his head. "I didn't get a chance to ask her. She just requested a little time. I told her to be ready when I returned. Then, I left."

"She must be trying to uncover something."

"Farah has been in for too long. I barely recognized the elf staring back at me."

Durga shot him a scathing look and turned to the side. "You know very well what undercover work does to someone."

"And I'm telling you, she's been in too long."

Durga walked to the wall and leaned against it. "You're right. You saw her. I didn't." She swallowed and fiddled with the bracelets on one wrist. "Do you think she caused the explosion?"

"Anything is possible. She's in the thick of things much more than I am."

"Did she pass on any intel?"

"That's what you're thinking about now? Not her life? Do you not care?"

Durga surged away from the wall, fury in her bearing and blazing in her eyes. It dripped from her words as she said, "Of course, I care. But in case you've forgotten, this is a job. We're fighting against an enemy we know little about." She stalked toward him. "Do you think it's easy for me to send individuals out on missions, knowing they may not return? Do you think I don't see the faces of the dead every time I close my eyes?"

It was rare to see her lose control like this. Salil kept quiet as she whirled around and paced a few steps away. She drew in a deep breath.

He looked at the floor, hating what he was about to pass on.

"What is it?" she demanded.

Salil lifted his head to find that she faced him once more. "Word is, her body hasn't been recovered."

"So, she was either killed in the blast, and there's nothing left. Or...she caused it."

"I don't think she would do that."

Durga looked away, her bracelets clinking when she bent her elbow. "I'd almost rather it be that than her death. There has to be a third option."

"I don't know what that could be. She wouldn't turn on us. Her need to find answers about her sister is too strong."

"Like you said, she's in deeper than you."

He twisted his lips. "I'm not sure if any of that matters now. They're hunting for her. The Masters want answers, and she's the only member of her crew who's missing."

"More of my people being pursued by these...these..." She threw up her arms, searching for a word.

"Fuckers," he offered.

Durga nodded. "Aye, those fuckers." She squeezed her eyes closed for a heartbeat. "I can't give up on Farah. Not until it's been confirmed that she's dead. Wait. Are others missing?"

"From what I've heard, six of those I brought in were killed in the explosion, which we both know is a blessing. Another eight were so scared they didn't move and were quickly locked away. The remaining thirty-six are missing."

"Farah could be with them."

"If she is, and the Masters' people find her, she's as good as dead."

Durga nodded absently and turned thoughtful. "That means we need to beat them to her. Are you being looked into?"

"It was my cargo."

She nodded to his wrist. "And the bracelet?"

He lifted his right hand to look at the silver cuff. It was an exact replica of what the Masters put on those they allowed to command the ships along the Lotus River. There was a high turn-around of captains and sailors, making it easy for him to infiltrate the group. "No one is the wiser."

"Perhaps your time as captain is done."

"If I disappear now, they'll believe I had something to do with it." When Durga tried to argue, he lifted his hand. "I can handle things. If I can't, that's on me."

She stared at him for a long moment. "I have no doubt you can, but—"

"You need me on the inside to know what's going on."

"Don't get cocky," she retorted. "You and Farah aren't the only ones who are undercover."

Salil had suspected as much. "And you know they have their own covert people."

"I'm aware. That doesn't change the fact that I need you to help look for Farah. Have an accident. Do whatever has to be done, but your captain's disguise needs to die."

Salil didn't reply as she strode past him.

When Durga reached the door, she paused and said, "You have two days."

She knew him entirely too well. He would have continued carrying on if she hadn't put a time limit on things. The only way he would know if they captured Farah was to maintain his disguise.

"Are we clear?"

He turned to face her. "Crystal."

"Good," she replied and walked out.

Salil listened to the sound of her bootheels on the floor fading as she walked away. His thoughts shifted to Farah. Something had been off when they spoke, but no matter how many times he went over their exchange, he couldn't pinpoint what was going on.

Golshan and Amarjeet watched her every move. One of them had their eye on her at all times. The scrutiny had been difficult for her, and he couldn't imagine it had gotten any easier. She had seen the worst of their kind doing unspeakable things. It had hardened her, sure, but it wasn't anything that would have caused her to look so detached.

Salil had two days to learn what he could about the explosion, clear his name so he wasn't brought before the Masters, and stage his death. The latter would be the easiest of them to arrange. And he knew exactly the place to do it, too. But first, he needed to get back to his ship.

He walked out of the room, proceeded out a hidden side entrance, and blended with the swarms of people. A cat darted out in front of him, holding its next meal in its mouth. He looked at the faces of those he passed. Any of them could be a servant of the Masters. Or the DIA. Or another organization he didn't know about.

And he had thought the politics in his village had been unbearable. That seemed like child's play compared to what he dealt with now. If the fate of Shecrish didn't hang in the balance, he might be tempted to walk away from it all and disappear deep into the rainwood where no one could ever find him. Not even other Wood Elves.

He had left his home to create change and make things better. He couldn't return until he had done that.

7

The pink sand squished between Rohan's toes. Waves crashed, the foamy water stretching for his feet. Autumn's cool temperatures made the water chillier, though it wouldn't keep him out of the ocean. The sea was their main food source, but fishing wasn't on his mind.

He paused and looked toward the horizon and the distant dark clouds. The winter storms didn't usually hit for another few weeks, but they had been known to strike sooner. The winds were calm, but the waves were cresting. He made out the flash of lightning amid the approaching storm.

Kalyani came up beside him, her arms crossed as she faced the sea. Annoyance rolled off her. "She's not ready for travel."

"I lost days bringing her here to recover. The longer she's away, the harder it'll be for her to return without suspicion." He jerked his chin toward the storm. "And there's that to consider."

"Shite," she mumbled. "It's too early."

Rohan turned his head to her. "It's rare, but it does happen. We can't afford to lose any more time. If that storm hits, we'll be stuck here for days, and everything I've done will have been a waste."

Kalyani shook her head and looked at the sky. "She needs more time."

"She has tonight."

His sister faced him, her arms dropping to her sides. Her gaze darted toward the water before returning to him. "There isn't any more left. You told me that the last time you dove."

"There is no more *within reach*."

"Nay. Absolutely not." Kalyani shook her head. "You can't possibly think to go into the cave."

Rohan looked at the rolling sea. He had already encountered the giant, speckled kythi once and barely came away with his life. The first Siguks to settle had accidentally discovered the red seaweed's healing properties and used it for anything and everything after that. Until they realized it took generations for it to grow. By then, his people had almost completely wiped out the stores in the cove.

Now, the seaweed was only used in the direst of circumstances. Rohan had dove for it when their father fell and hit his head. He'd found some, but it wasn't quite enough. He had dove for more and spotted it in the cave of a coral mound. When he swam closer to get a better look, he saw large clusters of it just inside the opening. When he went to cut some, the kythi charged him from the back of the cave, its elongated, dark-green-speckled body slicing through the water.

There were many predators in the ocean. Rohan knew better than to enter a cave without checking first, but he hadn't been thinking about any of that at the time. He'd been surprised at the sight of the kythi and lost what little of the seaweed he'd gathered while trying to stay alive.

Searching the coral for the bits he had dropped had taken hours. Ultimately, he kept the cave and the seaweed a secret from everyone except Kalyani until he could round up enough divers to go after the kythi.

But that time had never come. His father died, and Rohan found himself trying to navigate the task of being a leader. He'd been grieving his father and settling into his new role when the abductions increased. Then, he'd focused on that. Now, he was back figuring out how to get into the cave without being killed by the eel.

He ran a hand down his face and blew out a breath. "I need her healthy, Kal. I can get our people back. I can find Lata."

"You hope."

The wind caught Kalyani's words, snatching them away. But he still heard them. "It's all I have right now. Without it, I…" He looked away, fighting against a threatening swell of despair. He knew the impossibility of what he was attempting, but he had to try.

Kalyani touched his arm and moved closer. "What do you need from me?"

"Keep the elf company. I don't trust her alone."

"Things might go better if you called her by her name."

He gave his sister a hard glare.

She rolled her eyes. "Fine. I'll do that once we get the seaweed."

"We?"

"You don't actually think I'm letting you go alone, do you?"

"Kal," he began.

This time, she was the one who shot *him* a look. "End of discussion. We do this together or not at all."

"Then we need to do it now before the light fades."

She removed her shoes. Rohan let out a shrill whistle to catch the attention of a sentry at the bottom of the cliff. The guard whistled back, indicating that he understood Rohan was getting in the water. Rohan bent and grabbed the pole spear lying next to him. He straightened and found Kalyani without her headscarf, tying her curls back.

Once she nodded that she was ready, they walked into the water together. When the water hit her upper thighs, she dove beneath its depths. Rohan had seen her smile before she vanished under the sea. She broke the surface after a moment, wiping the water from her face as she turned to him. Kal was a better swimmer than he was. She was quick and agile and knew how to work the waves and currents like nothing he had ever seen before. He could mimic her, but he wasn't nearly as good. It didn't matter how many times she tried to teach him, it just wasn't as natural for him as it was for her.

Rohan glanced at the storm once more. It looked bigger, the clouds angrier. He dove. The chilly water was like a slap to his face as he submerged himself. His body quickly grew accustomed as he swam deeper to look for predators.

Kalyani swam ahead of him, her arms at her sides as she fluidly kicked her legs behind her. She rolled onto her back to look at the surface before flipping again. His eyes scanned the ocean floor. The surface was kicking up and stirring the shallows, but it hadn't reached the deeper depths so far. Brightly colored fish darted around him. Some small, a few large. The seabed dropped off quickly from the shore. It made for some dramatic waves and a diverse ecosystem, but it also meant the predators got closer than they would have if it had been a gradual slope.

His lungs burned. Rohan shot to the surface and sucked in a huge mouthful of air. He shook his head and slung hair from his face as he treaded water. Kalyani appeared a few moments later.

"All clear," she said.

He nodded. "Same."

"Ready?"

Rohan was far from ready, but that hadn't stopped him before. "See you down there."

"I have your back."

He curved inward, going beneath the waves and using his arms to swim deeper. Usually, he had the pole spear strapped around him, but he wanted to be prepared. He looked to the side and saw that Kalyani was already below him. He headed toward the outer edge of the cove and swam faster, but he couldn't catch her.

She reached it first. He shouted her name, but Kalyani couldn't hear him. Thankfully, she didn't go inside, only swam around it. He kicked his legs harder to reach her faster, his gaze locked on the entrance. Rohan tensed as he waited for the kythi to charge his sister. But nothing happened.

He was so worried about Kalyani that he swam straight into a rip current. It snatched him, dragging him away. Within moments, it flung him into the depths. When the current finally spit him out, he was far from shore. Rohan turned in a circle until he caught sight of the cliffs. He started swimming toward it, remaining parallel to the current so as not to get dragged back in.

Kalyani wouldn't have seen what happened. She wouldn't

know that he wasn't there. Nor did she have a weapon to fight the eel if it attacked. Rohan kept a steady rhythm of arm over arm as he swam. He might not be as quick as his sister, but he had endurance. That's what he fell back on now.

He looked up every ten strokes to ensure that he was still headed in the right direction. He told himself not to worry. Kalyani was smart. And fast. Yet his mind played through his encounter with the eel, leaving a pit in his stomach.

He gauged his distance to the shore. He was still too far out. Kalyani would have to come up for air. She would look for him, surely. She would see him swimming back to her.

Please. Please. Please.

First their mother, then their father, then Lata's abduction. Not Kalyani, too. Not yet.

He had never dealt with death well. His dad had counseled him on it after their mother's passing, but it hadn't done much good.

"Death isn't a personal assault on you, son. It is the way of things. There is a beginning, a middle, and an end. To a bird, a tree. And us. Even the sun."

But this was personal. Too much had been taken from him. Everyone had their breaking point. He was barely standing under the weight of it all as it was. One more thing, one more person taken, and he knew he would break.

Leaders were supposed to bend, not break. He was grasping at anything, desperate to find answers to his ever-mounting problems. Even though he knew there weren't any answers. Few cared about the humans. And *no one* cared about the Siguks. He was on his own to find solutions in a world he didn't fit into, with beings more powerful than him. The Wood Elf was that solution.

Rohan looked up and treaded water. He had covered a good distance without even knowing it, but he had swum slightly off course. He altered direction and swam to his right, getting closer to the outskirts of the cove. Then, he dove.

He scanned the area as he swam down, looking for Kalyani. Panic seized him when he couldn't find her. He stopped, suspended in the water as he turned in a frantic circle. Something caught his attention out of the corner of his eye. He spun and saw his sister along the slope of the ocean floor. Beside her was the enormous kythi, moving in tandem with her.

Rohan readied the pole spear and took aim. That's when he saw Kalyani's hand resting on the kythi. He blinked hard to make sure he was seeing what he thought he saw. His sister turned in a wide circle with the kythi and then spotted him. She flashed Rohan a smile and pointed to the cave. The kythi looked his way but did nothing.

A million questions buzzed through Rohan's head. He lowered the spear and swam to the cave. The red leaves of the seaweed plant swayed in the water as if beckoning him. His lungs were starting to hurt, and the pressure against his body was intense. He used the hand holding the pole to brace himself before leaning in and grabbing hold of a clump of the seaweed. He yanked, careful not to take too much.

He held his harvest firmly in his hand and turned to leave. Rohan saw his sister and the kythi to his right. He hesitated, but his lungs burned. He had no choice but to head to the surface. There, he waited for Kalyani. Minutes ticked by as he treaded water. Then he put his face under to look for her. He found her swimming toward him. Thankfully, the kythi was no longer with her.

"What was that?" he asked when she surfaced.

"I simply asked it to let us have some of the seaweed."

He frowned. "You what?"

"I asked," she repeated before swimming toward shore.

Rohan watched her for a heartbeat before following.

8

Farah had been happy to wake from her nap to find herself alone. There had been more broth waiting, and she hadn't even minded that it was cold. Sitting up seemed easier. Her muscles protested from lack of use, and she had to be careful about how she moved her leg, but she propped herself up.

Her gaze was pulled outside again. She saw a man standing at the shore with his shirt removed. Kalyani, with her distinctive curls, walked up. That's when Farah realized the bare back she stared at was likely Rohan's. The siblings exchanged words before he bent to retrieve something. She squinted and realized it was a spear of sorts. They walked into the sea together.

She looked at the cup of broth in her hand. Of course, they would fish. Farah looked up in time to see both go beneath the waves. She leaned toward the window to see how far down the ground was. It had been a long time since she'd stood atop the cliff with Nitya. She couldn't see much, so she attempted to scoot forward. She sucked in a quick breath as pain radiated from her injury. She decided to stay put for the moment.

Farah searched the waves for any signs of Kalyani and Rohan. Just when she was about to get worried, she saw their heads bobbing in the waves. Then they were gone again. She scanned the rolling water as she finished the broth and set aside the cup. It would be the perfect time to get a good look at the space she was occupying, but she couldn't turn away from the ocean. She sat straighter, hoping it would give her a better angle. When that didn't work, she cautiously lifted her injured leg with both hands and placed it in a different place before carefully scooting forward. She made little progress, but it was something she could do while examining the sea.

Farah managed to move about four inches when she saw Kalyani come up for air. Rohan didn't. The female gave a frenzied look around before she saw something in the distance. Farah tried to see what it was, but she couldn't make out anything. Whatever Kalyani saw seemed to calm her because she dove again.

It wasn't uncommon for elves to swim. The mesa had hundreds of lakes and numerous rivers running through it. But they swam only on the plateau. The only ones who dared to venture into the ocean were the Sea Elves. Was that who Kalyani and Rohan were seeking? Farah could've told them that Sea Elves stayed far from humans.

Not that she knew any Sea Elves very well. They could be found in the many waterways throughout Shecrish, but she had always kept her distance. She didn't know why. Maybe it was something she'd heard as a child. Perhaps it was just who she was. Nitya had been the only one who could bring her out of her shell.

Once her sister vanished, Farah became more reserved, closed off. Guarded.

Durga had told her that trait made her a good candidate for undercover work. Some naturally opened themselves and their lives up to others, telling them everything. She chose what to share.

Farah scanned the water again. That's when she saw what looked like someone swimming. She watched until they got close enough to see the person's arms moving. Then, they stopped. Even at a distance, she knew it was Rohan. A current must have swept him back.

"Too bad it didn't take him farther," she muttered.

She blinked, and then he was beneath the surface. She once more waited for him and his sister to come up for air. It felt like an eternity before Rohan and Kalyani appeared again. Then they started for shore. She continued to observe them until they walked out of the water. Rohan still held the weapon, but he had something red in his other hand.

Farah angled herself to the side to see when they headed toward the cliff, but she lost sight of them. Since she had no intention of going anywhere with Rohan—tomorrow or otherwise—Farah returned to her original position. She didn't know how long it would take them to reach her, and she moved slowly. When the minutes ticked by, she began to wonder if they were coming back at all. Maybe they were just out for a swim. Could be they'd retrieved that red stuff for someone. She was just getting stretched out when the door opened.

Water beaded Rohan's bare chest and dripped from his wet hair. He didn't look her way as he walked to the table at the back of the space. He left the door open, and Kalyani entered behind him. She, too, still wore her wet clothes. Brother and sister didn't speak. Kalyani briefly smiled at Farah as she checked the cup and found it empty. She seemed pleased that Farah had drunk the broth.

She went to the kitchen and returned with some water. Farah rose on an elbow and took it gratefully. As she drank, she looked at Rohan, wondering if the red stuff was meant to cause her pain to force her to comply with his plan.

The pain part was senseless. She already had that. It seemed more plausible that it was meant to somehow bend her to his wishes. She might not be able to stand yet, but she could still fight him. And she would.

Farah handed Kalyani the empty cup. She kept her gaze on Rohan, uncaring that his sister saw. Rohan took some deep red leaves twice the length of his forearm and wider than his hand and stacked them. When he finished, he gathered them and started toward the bed. He still didn't look at her. In Farah's mind, that meant nothing good was coming.

He sat on the stool but didn't immediately reach for the blanket. He carefully laid the leaves over his knee and took a deep breath. Then, he met her eyes. "We can do this the easy way or the hard way."

"And what is it we'll be doing?" she asked.

Rohan simply stared.

Kalyani sighed and nudged him in the shoulder with her elbow. "The leaves have healing properties. We need to lay them over your wound."

Farah looked from Kalyani to the leaves to Rohan. "Why not just tell me that?"

"The leaves heal," he replied.

He didn't like her. That much was obvious. But he also didn't know her. And he never would. Why should she care if he believed her to be something she wasn't? He was holding her against her will, which made him the enemy.

"You can travel tomorrow healed or limping," Rohan stated. "The choice is yours."

All this time, she had been thinking she would have to wait to heal to escape. Farah hid a smile. Now, he was giving her exactly what she wanted. She held his gaze as she pulled the blanket away from her left leg.

If she expected him to be rough, she was wrong. Rohan surprised her with his light touch as he removed the bandages. She pushed herself up, bracing her hands behind her back, and got her first look at the wound. The jagged laceration went from the outside of her thigh, across the top, and ended near the inside of her knee. Now, she fully understood why the pain was so horrendous.

It wasn't because she had a low threshold. It was because the wound was severe.

"I have to remove the stitches."

She saw the gray thread of the neat stitches. Farah had seen them on humans, but she had never known an elf to have them. There usually wasn't a need.

"Ready?"

She swallowed and glanced at Rohan. His eyes were on her. Farah nodded.

Kalyani walked around to the other side of the bed. "Maybe it would be better if you lay down."

Farah looked at Rohan again. He hadn't moved. His expression was unreadable. Perhaps he wanted her to feel the pain just as she had wished the current would've tossed him farther out into the ocean. She needed to forget everything and everyone and concentrate on healing so she could make her escape.

She lowered herself onto her elbows and then down to the pillow. Farah looked at the stone ceiling above her. Rohan's fingers touched her leg near the wound. At nearly the exact moment, he cut the first stitch. Farah relaxed when she didn't feel anything. She had been worried for nothing.

It wasn't until Rohan finished and Kalyani leaned over her that they began pulling out the stitches. Again, she was surprised that it didn't hurt. She could feel the thread moving through her skin, and it was odd, but it wasn't painful.

With the laceration being as long as it was, it took the pair some time to remove all the thread. Rohan inspected the injury once more. Farah found herself watching him. Or rather the top of his head. He bent low over her, and locks of his dark, wet hair fell forward and came within a hair's breadth of brushing her leg.

Her eyes lowered to his shoulders. The water had dried on his tan skin, leaving nothing but corded muscle. He had a light dusting of hair on his chest and down his stomach. He lifted his arm, causing the thick sinew to bunch and flex. When he turned his head, she saw the color of his eyes: a pale grayish green with a hint of yellow undertone so light it was almost without color and a band of deep gray encircling his irises. Such an unusual and beautiful color for such a ruthless man.

Rohan straightened before he began laying the cold, wet leaves across her thigh to cover the entire injury. She didn't like the feeling of the leaves clinging to her and tried to move one, but a look from him stopped her in her tracks.

Farah bit back some choice words when he wrapped a bandage

around her leg, most likely to keep the leaves in place so she didn't move them. When he finished, he stared at her leg for a moment and then lifted his gaze to Kalyani. Farah looked between them, but the wordless exchange was something only the two of them understood.

"Don't touch it," Rohan told her, then got to his feet and walked out.

Kalyani straightened the blanket over her leg. "He's a good healer. He knows what he's doing."

"It's not his healing skills I take exception with," Farah retorted.

Kalyani's dark eyes met hers. "How would you act in his place? Tell me what you would do to find your missing sister."

What hadn't she done? Farah looked away as she thought about the blood on her hands.

"You may not understand us or even agree with what we're doing, but we're just trying to find our people."

"This plan of his won't work. We'll never get inside Mortham."

"Rohan has thought this plan through. I trust him."

Farah turned her head to Kalyani. "But I don't."

"I wouldn't do you the disservice of asking you to even try." Kalyani drew in a breath and released it with a sigh.

"Yet you ask me to risk my life for a cause that isn't mine." That wasn't exactly true, but no one needed to know that.

Kalyani's lips twisted wryly. "I ask you to do what's right."

"You know I was in Mortham. That I worked with the Masters. How can you ask me that?"

"A hunch."

9

Rohan stood in the middle of his hut, unmoving. The voices and laughter of his people used to mix with the wind to make a pleasant babble. Now, there was nothing but the wind. He looked over at Lata's bed. They had fought endlessly, and she had chafed at everything. No matter what he asked of her, it angered her.

Lata and Kalyani had once lived together, but Kalyani couldn't control their younger sister. That's why Rohan had stepped in. At first, he'd been excited to have one of his sisters back under his roof. But that hadn't lasted long.

He'd believed Kalyani had exaggerated her difficulties with their youngest sibling because he remembered Lata as a sweet, gregarious child. Rohan soon learned Kalyani had actually down-played Lata's rebelliousness. She wasn't just defiant. She had become impudent. He tried every tactic he knew, but nothing had helped. In fact, he was sure he'd made things worse.

Their relationship had become strained and fractured, just as hers and Kalyani's had. But Rohan thought he had time to figure it out. All too soon, Lata was gone. He should've done more to ensure she couldn't sneak out. The fear and dread running through the village hadn't been enough to keep her and the others inside. His stark warnings hadn't penetrated her thick skull.

He scrubbed his hands down his face. Looking into the past didn't do any good. All it did was show him the many ways he had failed as Lata's guardian. Kalyani had entrusted him with her welfare, and he hadn't been able to keep her safe. He hadn't been able to keep anyone safe.

There was no magic running through his veins. He didn't have an army behind him. All he had was himself. Rohan was more than willing to give up his life if it meant Lata's and the Siguks' freedom. But he didn't have that choice. All he had was a reckless plan that might just be crazy enough to work.

He removed his wet pants and laid them across the open window to dry as he walked to the back, where a half-moon formation had been chiseled out of the bedrock. He stood beneath a spout that angled out of the wall toward him and tugged the string. Heated water liberally sprayed him before shutting off. He lathered his hands with soap and scrubbed his body and hair. When he finished, he pulled the string again. It took three tugs before the soap was rinsed away completely.

Rohan dried off and returned to the front. He dressed and combed his hair before tying the top portion at the back of his head. Then, he walked barefoot into the kitchen. The thought of food turned his stomach at the moment. He was too wrapped up in what he had set into motion and the ramifications that could befall those he loved.

He tugged on his boots and exited his hut. He looked left to where the elf slept, only a short bridge away. They would have a long trip together. And she was testy now. The moment she realized what he had on her, she would become downright hostile. Despite what Kalyani thought, his sister wasn't going with them. Rohan would have to watch his back every second because Farah would likely try something the moment she had access to her magic again. But he was prepared for that—or as prepared as he could be.

Rohan headed toward the elf, his hands skimming the ropes that held the bridge. He crossed and stood outside the dwelling, listening for any movement inside. He heard nothing. He'd never used the red seaweed on an elf before. There was a chance it wouldn't work. Then what? Did he force her to travel with such an injury? Did he carry her?

Time was running out. He could feel it. He had to act, and he had to do it *now*. His accomplice had found him. Rohan had no way of contacting him, so he couldn't ask for additional aid. And the first plan hadn't gone as Rohan had hoped. He hadn't been prepared for the sheer size of Mortham or Farah's injury. This second attempt had to work. There wasn't another option.

Rohan silently opened the door and peered inside. Farah was propped up with pillows, her head lolling to the side and her eyes closed. There was no sign of his sister. He quietly shut the door and retraced his steps across the bridge, moving past his house and over another bridge. He climbed a ladder up two levels and then crossed one more bridge before standing at his sister's door.

It was open, as it often was. Kalyani was kind and welcoming, with an inner strength he admired. A few had mistaken her gentleness for weakness, but she'd promptly set them straight. He found her weaving a basket from the shrava plant that grew so plentifully at the top of the mesa. Kalyani's skill was unmatched.

"I figured you'd find your way here," she said by way of greeting. "Have you eaten? I can make you something."

He waved away her words as he entered. "We need to talk."

"About?"

"Tomorrow."

She sighed and set aside the basket before motioning to the chair beside her. "Then you'd best sit."

Rohan lowered himself onto the chair and rested his forearms on his knees, clasping his hands. "I know we agreed that you would make the journey with us, but I need you to remain behind." When she started to object, he held up a hand. "Please. Hear me out."

Kalyani clamped her mouth shut and gathered her hands in her lap. Anger sparked from her dark eyes, but she dipped her head, urging him to continue.

"There are less than fifty of us left. Whoever is responsible for the abductions has targeted us. There's no other explanation. I don't know if my plan is the answer, but it's the only one I have. We're scared and anxious. You've always known what to say to evoke calm. I'm asking you to keep our people mollified while I'm away. Because nobody else can."

Her expression softened a fraction.

He glanced at the floor. "And if things go badly for me, you will lead them."

"Rohan—" she began.

He spoke over her. He had thought this through and needed to get the words out. "Even if everything goes as planned and I return with Lata and the rest of our missing, we'll have to leave. This place isn't safe anymore."

"I doubt any place in Shecrish is."

"Then we'll find something elsewhere. Maybe we can head to the mountains. Or sail to find more land. If we remain, they'll continue to pick us off one by one." Rohan dropped his chin to his chest. "Father would've known what to do."

Kalyani leaned forward and put her hand atop his. "He wasn't all-knowing. He was flawed like the rest of us. I trust you. We all do. Try trusting yourself."

He looked up and met her gaze. He hadn't known until that moment how much he needed those words. "I'll do everything in my power to find Lata and the others."

"No one doubts that."

"And what I'm asking of you?"

She briefly looked away, her lips turned down at the corners. "I'd rather be with you. You're going to need someone you can trust. However, I must also admit to the wisdom of your words, regardless of whether I like them or not. "

"Does that mean you'll stay?"

She sighed loudly. "Aye, I'll stay behind."

Relief coursed through him, easing some of the tension in his shoulders. "Thank you."

"You may end up regretting it, though," she teased. "I might have us living with the Sea Elves when you return."

Her comment made him think of what he had seen with the kythi earlier. He wasn't the only one with secrets. "What happened in the water earlier?"

"Nothing," she said, dropping her hand and sitting back.

"I know what I saw, Kal. The kythi tried to kill me, but it was swimming with you."

She sighed, looking bored. "I told you. I asked him to let us take some seaweed."

"How, exactly?"

"How do you scale the cliffs as quickly as you do?"

He frowned, taken aback by her question. "I just do."

"Precisely my point. I just did it. It's the same as how you're able to climb like no one else."

Rohan studied his sister for a long moment. "Nothing you could tell me would ever make me stop loving you. We're family."

"I know."

"Then explain it to me. Please."

Kalyani turned her head to the side and looked out the window. "Do you remember how I used to get in the water every chance I had?"

"Vividly."

"When I'm swimming, particularly when I'm underwater, everything makes sense. Not like here with all the chaos." She got to her feet and walked to the window. "Beneath the waves, the world is vibrant and alive. It's welcoming and peaceful. That wasn't the first time I've swum with that kythi. I've swum with many animals."

A wistful, excited smile curved her lips. Her eyes sparkled in a way he hadn't seen before. Even her voice was different. There was a longing in the tone he hadn't noticed. Likely because he hadn't been paying attention.

"There is music in the water. I've always heard it. Always longed to go to it."

A long-forgotten memory of Kalyani, from when she had just

learned to walk, surfaced. She'd dashed toward the waves the minute their father turned his back, like she was reaching for something. When their dad pulled her from the ocean, she screamed for hours. The only thing that quieted her was the water —and only if she was in it.

"Do you hear it now?" Rohan asked.

She nodded. "It calls to me."

"You've stayed out of the water these past few months since Lata was taken."

Kalyani turned to look at him. "The pull is great. So powerful that I know one of these days I won't leave it. I didn't want to chance that happening, especially after Lata."

Rohan stood and walked to his sister. He pulled her into his arms and held her against him. "Thank you for telling me. Why keep it a secret, though?"

"Father asked me to."

"What?" Rohan questioned and leaned back to look at her.

Kalyani shrugged. "He was upset by it."

"Nay, Kal. He was upset about the idea of the Sea Elves."

"That was one instance, decades before we were born."

Rohan shrugged. "They came, and two of our people died."

"We weren't there. We have no idea what really happened. I'm not saying Father lied," she added when Rohan started to speak, "I'm merely saying that if the Sea Elves were intent on harming us, they've had plenty of time and opportunities to return and do just that."

Rohan couldn't argue with her logic. "I would never stop you from being in the water."

"I know. But you need help here."

"I can get someone else. I want you to be happy."

She gave him a flat look. "Do you want to be rid of me?"

"Never." He pulled her into his arms and embraced her. "Never, Kal. But I also don't want you to long for something and not go after it." That's when it hit him. "Is that why you've not taken a husband?"

She made a sound and pulled out of his arms to return to her stool. "I've not married because there is no one here I wish to share my life with. Before our numbers dropped, I mean."

"I knew what you meant." He scratched his temple. "How would you live underwater, though? You can't breathe like the Sea Elves can."

"I don't know."

Rohan couldn't shake the feeling that she did. She just didn't want to tell him. He didn't press her. Kalyani had shared something very personal, and that was enough for him. "Will you tell me when you decide to follow the music?"

She looked up at him. "Of course. But that isn't going to happen. You have your mission, and I'm going to keep what's left of our people together until you get back with the others. Oh, and also work on the idea of finding a new home."

That in itself would be a feat. "If anyone can, it's you."

"I think your job is easier. Want to change places? I'll go with Farah while you stay behind."

Rohan forced a chuckle. "I think dealing with the elf will be more difficult."

10

It was dark when Farah woke. She stretched her arms over her head and yawned as she gazed out the window. The ocean was beautiful during the day, but it was stunning at night. The moonlight sparkling upon the waves was hypnotic. Even the wind felt different. Like a soft caress, tempting her to explore the water.

The inside of her quarters was dark. She didn't recall Kalyani leaving. After Rohan applied the seaweed, Farah had dozed, lulled by the sound of the crashing waves. Kalyani had brought more broth, along with a section of flat, pale bread. It hadn't looked like bread, but it had tasted amazing.

She pushed herself up to recline against the pillows better and watched the waves move in the dark water. Farah had never wondered where the Sea Elves lived before. They were in the water. That knowledge had been enough. Now, her mind pondered if they had settlements close to shore or if they preferred to keep far away like some of the Wood Elves.

Farah shifted her injured leg. It took a moment for her to realize there was only a slight twinge of pain. She lifted the covers to inspect the bandage. Though tempted to remove it and examine the laceration, she didn't want to interfere with whatever the red leaves were doing to heal her. She was one step closer to escaping.

She lowered the blanket and returned her gaze to the ocean. It wasn't long before her mind wandered between various thoughts. She contemplated her parents. They had tried to persuade her not to go to Rannora, but Farah had ignored their pleas and demands. No one knew she had gone directly to Durga. If Mum had gotten wind of that, she would've locked Farah away.

Nitya's disappearance had changed their family—as well as the village—in profound ways. It had aged her father significantly. Her mother was overly fearful and overbearing, to the point where Farah had to set boundaries in order to continue any sort of relationship with her.

Everyone was devastated about Nitya—Farah included. She had walked around in a fog for weeks, waiting for her sister to come home and say it had all been a joke gone wrong. But she never returned. It wasn't until a few others in their village mysteriously vanished that they had to face the fact that the horrors in the city had finally reached them.

They weren't the only Wood Elves who had believed they would escape the abductions. They soon learned that no place in Shecrish remained untouched. Well, except for maybe the mountains. No one wanted to be there but the Mountain Elves. The peaks were hostile and inhospitable.

Farah hadn't seen her parents in years. She sent messages from time to time—or she *had* during her training before she went undercover. They would undoubtedly be worried. She should've gone to see them before her assignment in Mortham, as Durga had urged, but Farah hadn't wanted to deal with her parents begging her to come home. She had important work to do—work that might include discovering Nitya's location and bringing her home so they could be a family again.

What would her parents think if they learned of the things Farah had done at Mortham? She barely knew what to do with any of it. Facing it, admitting it, was like conceding that she was as unscrupulous as those she pursued. How would she ever face her parents again? Or Durga? Or *anyone*?

Rohan knew what she was. He had seen it clearly. He'd even said the words, branding her.

Even if she got away from the humans, made it to Rannora, and delivered the intel to Durga...what then? She wouldn't be able to go back undercover. Durga might find something for her to do if she remained part of the DIA, but it wasn't as if Farah could return to her village, especially without Nitya. Not after what she had seen—and done. Where did that leave her? Nowhere.

She could go with the human and worm her way back into Mortham somehow. She had time to come up with a story. Once she secured her place there again, she could return to looking for her sister. There was still the issue of Rohan, though. He wouldn't leave without getting what he wanted. She would find some way to give him that. If he got caught in Mortham, that was on him.

Apprehension curled cold, hard fingers around her chest. Had anyone at the fort really trusted her? The fact that Golshan and Amarjeet followed her at all times said they didn't. How would she convince anyone that she hadn't been a part of the explosion? It didn't help that Rohan had taken her from Mortham. That made her look like an accomplice.

Nay. She didn't *look* like one. In their eyes, she *was* an accomplice.

Farah thrust her fingers into her hair, shoving it away from her face. She couldn't give up looking for Nitya, not when she was so close. She'd lost precious weeks and months sinking into the day-to-day at Mortham when she should've been hunting for her sister.

The damage had been done, though. There was no going back, no undoing what had happened. Nothing she could say to Rohan would change his mind. She couldn't tell him that she understood his pain at the disappearance of a sibling, the emptiness that never faded. He intended to take her back to Mortham—to the very place she couldn't go now.

Once she was in the trees and her magic returned, she'd have a chance to escape. Then, she could deliver the information she had to Durga. From there, she didn't know. There wasn't a place for her anywhere. But that was a worry for another day. First, she had to get away from Rohan and his insane plan.

She curled the toes of her left leg, testing her injury. There was only a slight twinge of pain. Apparently, the red leaves *did* heal. It was amazing. She hadn't realized humans had anything like that at their disposal. There was much about them she didn't know.

The sky was turning gray when she heard someone approaching. Farah's gaze slid to the door. Rohan likely wanted an early start. To her surprise, Kalyani's head appeared.

"How are you feeling?" she asked. When she saw Farah sitting up, she walked inside.

Farah shrugged. "Better."

Kalyani rested a hand on the table. "Do you think you can stand?"

"I'd like to find out."

She threw off the blanket and swung her legs over the side of the bed as Kalyani reached her. Farah placed her bare feet on the woven rug. The fibers were cool and soft against her skin. She scooted to the edge of the bed and contracted her thigh muscles as if she were about to stand. Only a dull ache greeted her. That encouraged Farah to push to her feet, though she kept most of her weight on her right leg. She wobbled slightly before quickly gaining her balance.

"Well done," Kalyani stated happily.

Farah grinned and decided to put more weight on her left leg. She did it in increments and had no resistance or pain. It was incredible and not at all what she had expected from humans.

"Care to walk to the back of the room so you can wash?"

Farah's head snapped up in excitement. She would love to bathe. "Please."

"I thought you would say that," Kalyani replied with a smile.

She headed to the back, deeper into the cliff. Farah took her first tentative step. Then another. Each step without pain gave her more confidence as she followed Kalyani around a wall made of stalks to find a hollowed-out area in a small semicircle. She stared in awe at the simple but elegant area. The gray rock was worn smooth on the walls and the floor. Another woven mat, this one thicker, sat next to a stool slightly off to the side.

It would've been dark except for the light pouring in through the wall of stalks. The dim lighting gave the stone a dark look, making it feel relaxing and soothing.

"Pull this string to get the water," Kalyani said as she demonstrated.

Farah watched water pour from one of the hollowed stalks

sticking out of the wall onto the stone floor. It only lasted a short time, which meant she would have to keep pulling the string for water. Still, it was an ingenious design.

Kalyani pointed at the long, narrow stool. "The soap is there." She turned and motioned to a pointed shell protruding from the rock wall. "The drying cloth here. I'll be around the corner if you need me."

"Can I remove the bandages and the seaweed?"

"Aye. I can do it for you if you'd like."

Farah shook her head. "I can handle it."

Kalyani dipped her head before walking away.

Alone, Farah propped her left leg on the stool and unwrapped the bandages before peeling away the layers of red seaweed to reveal a raised, pink scar. She traced a finger along the large, ugly mark.

She shook herself and set her foot on the floor before removing the tunic. Farah tugged on the string, bracing herself for cold water. Instead, she was met with delicious warmth. She stood beneath the spout, pulling the string repeatedly so the water poured over her head. Once her hair was properly soaked, she grabbed the soap to lather her hands. Then she plunged them into her hair and massaged her scalp.

Her fingers moved the soap through the long lengths of her hair. She rinsed and repeated twice more. Only then did she turn her attention to her body, scrubbing it twice. Even after all the soap had been rinsed, she continued to pull the string and enjoy the water.

Finally, Farah wrung out her hair and used the drying towel. That's when she saw the pile of folded clothes, along with some boots. They hadn't been there before, and she hadn't heard anyone come around the corner. She hadn't asked what'd happened to her clothes or her boots when she found them gone. They had most likely been ruined.

She hung up the now damp cloth and dressed. The clothes fit surprisingly well, though their looseness was likely the reason. Even the boots were her size. Farah fastened the belt around her waist and looked down at herself before walking into the main area of the dwelling where Kalyani had fruit and more of the flat bread waiting.

"How was it?" the woman asked.

Farah flashed a smile. "Amazing."

"Thought you might need this," Kalyani said as she slid a comb across the table.

Farah nodded gratefully and slid it through her hair.

Kalyani set the plate of food before her. "Eat."

She popped a piece of the diced red fruit into her mouth. It was soft and sweet, the flavor bursting on her tongue. She continued eating while working through her hair, section by section, until all the tangles were out. Then, she braided it into a single plait.

When Farah finished, Kalyani motioned for her to follow. She set down the comb but grabbed the last bit of bread as she rose, putting too much weight on her leg. Pain brought her up short. Farah held on to the table and waited for the discomfort to pass. The wound might be closed, but she wasn't fully healed. At least not by the standards she was used to.

The next time she put weight on her leg, she was more careful. Kalyani waited at the door, watching the entire episode. Worry glinted in her eyes, but she didn't say anything. There was nothing to say. Rohan intended for them to set out on their journey that day. Nothing would stop him.

The sky was a soft gray now. A few stars could be seen, but they were quickly fading from sight. Farah paused at the door and took in the balcony crafted from more of the sturdy shrava stalks. She followed the handrail to the right and realized they weren't near the top of the mesa as she had believed. They were actually midway down. In the far distance to her right, she could just make out one of the many waterfalls that dotted the plateau. She walked to the balcony's edge and looked down to find dozens of huts hanging against the cliff. She turned and looked up to see even more.

"This way," Kalyani beckoned.

Farah's mind was spinning when she turned and followed Kalyani to a short, narrow, hanging bridge connecting dwellings with ropes and shrava sections. It swung slightly as she crossed. Kalyani took her over three more before she halted on a platform and faced the ocean. Farah turned to do the same. Her breath locked in her throat when she saw the dazzling display of colors from the approaching sunrise.

She had to lean to the side to get a better view of the giant yellow ball cresting the horizon, but it was truly a sight to behold. Maroon, red, orange, and pink painted the sky, and the colors were reflected in the water, giving the ocean a spectacular appearance. The sight, combined with the quiet of the morning, made the entire experience feel sacred. As if she had stumbled upon something divine that was only meant for those worthy enough to witness it.

"No matter how many sunrises I see, they always take my breath away," Kalyani whispered.

Farah had forgotten she wasn't alone. She took a bite of the bread and nodded, unsure if she could find words after such an experience. There weren't such demonstrations within the rain-wood. The thick canopy prevented it.

"This is where I come each morning. Do you have such a place?"

Farah thought back to her village and dragged her gaze from the sunrise to Kalyani. "I did once."

"Many of us used to stand and watch the dawn of each day." Kalyani motioned to the huts. "At one time, our numbers were in the thousands. Now, we are but a few. So many homes left empty, waiting for their owners to return. But no one comes. Only more are taken."

Kalyani had said something similar before, but it wasn't until Farah saw the number of dwellings that she truly grasped the ramifications of what had happened here. It seemed everyone on Shecrish had someone taken, but these humans were hit harder than most.

"Now, do you understand?" Kalyani asked, her dark eyes beseeching.

"I see you've lost people, aye."

Her expression fell. "You don't see."

"What am I supposed to see?" Farah asked in confusion.

Movement above them caught her attention. Farah looked up the cliff to see someone scaling it rapidly. She couldn't make out a form until the sky lightened more, and she found herself staring at a back she was beginning to recognize—Rohan. She watched in shocked amazement as he easily progressed down and to the side before dropping eight feet onto another platform. Then, he used one of the dozens of ladders to reach them.

He stalked toward them, and his pale gaze briefly landed on Farah before sliding to his sister. He strode with purpose and a single-mindedness that warned of what was to come. Their journey—however short or long it might be—would be anything but dull.

11

Rohan had spotted Farah's red hair the moment she exited the hut. The strands glowed like fire in the bright rays of the rising sun. She shimmered as if diamonds had been crushed into her bronze skin. Her thick braid exposed her pointed ears.

He felt Kalyani's gaze. Rohan almost decided to stay at the top of the mesa and wait for Farah to join him, but she would take too long. Besides, he didn't want to start their journey with her believing she was in charge. He blew out a breath and made his way down, all the while steeling himself for what was to come. He had days alone with the elf ahead of him. How quickly before she regained her magic? How much quicker would she try to get away?

If he were in her shoes, it would be immediately. That's why he intended to put things to her plainly once they were out of Siguk. She'd be shocked that he knew her secret. On the heels of that would be anger. She might even try to convince him to remain quiet by stating how knowledge of her being undercover could harm others. When that didn't work, she might try to harm him.

Rohan snorted. She *would* try to kill him. It would be pure instinct, but he was prepared regardless.

He dropped the final few feet to the platform and turned toward Kalyani and the elf. His gaze lingered on Farah for a heartbeat as he walked toward them. The faded gray attire of his people seemed to accentuate her hair. She had rolled up the sleeves and pushed them above her elbows. The clothes hid the curves of her body, but the belt emphasized her small waist.

"I see the seaweed worked," he said.

She raised her brows and looked him over. "It seems so."

"Not completely," Kalyani corrected. "She can stand and walk, but quick movements wouldn't be wise."

Rohan jerked his chin to the cliff. "Can you climb?"

"Like you?" Farah asked with a laugh. "Not even when I wasn't injured."

"There are ladders."

She shrugged, her lips twisting. "I suppose we'll find out."

Rohan swung his gaze to Kalyani. He hoped this wouldn't be the last time he saw her. They'd stayed up most of the night preparing for the future and talking about everything and nothing —something they hadn't done in months. It reinforced his need to find Lata and the others. More than that, it revealed how he had closed himself off to those closest to him when he should've seen Kal was there, waiting to help.

She threw her arms around him and hugged him tightly. "Remember, it's okay to ask for help. You don't have to do it all yourself. Be careful."

Her tears wet his cheek. Rohan gave her a final squeeze and released her. "I'll be back with Lata and the rest as soon as I can."

"We'll be waiting." Kalyani wiped her cheek.

Rohan reached around her for the bags he had prepared for the journey. He gave one to Farah and slipped the other over his head and pushed an arm through. "Ready?" he asked Farah.

"Not even close," she mumbled, then looked at him. "Lead the way."

He exchanged a look with Kalyani before heading to the first ladder. But he didn't go up it. Instead, he waited for her.

"What's wrong?" she asked when she reached him.

"You're not healed. You go first. That way, I can catch you if you slip."

Her eyes widened as she looked up the sheer cliff. "Slip, huh?"

"Just be mindful of your hands and feet. Don't let your mind wander. You need to be focused."

"It's like the trees."

He frowned at her. "What?"

She dismissed him with a shake of her head. "Nothing."

There were several different ladders, each only going up so far on the cliff before the climber had to move to one side to get onto another ladder. However, one main ladder went straight up with a connection in the middle that could be severed to stop someone from getting to them from either direction. Thankfully, it had never needed to be used.

"Here we go," Farah said under her breath and swung the pack around so it hung against her back. She grabbed a rung and put her right foot on a step before hoisting herself up.

He watched her for several minutes to make sure her leg could handle the climb. Then he followed. She was much slower than he was used to, but he had been climbing the ladders since he could walk. He glanced down at Kalyani, who observed them from the platform. She wouldn't leave until they reached the top and were out of sight.

Rohan noticed Farah's ragged breaths after only five minutes. "Pause if you need it," he told her.

"If I do that, I may not move again." But she looped an arm around one of the ropes and stood there, her forehead pressed to a rung.

At this rate, it would take them all day just to get to the top. If there was time, he'd give her another day. But there wasn't. They had to go now. The red seaweed had been a risky decision, but he'd been desperate. They had a long way to go, and if he wore her out now, it would only make things more difficult. He halted to consider his options. Only one made sense.

"Let me get up to you, and you can climb onto my back so I can carry you," he stated.

"I can do it."

She started climbing again before he could reply. Rohan shook his head at her stubbornness and kept a close eye on her. He saw her wince when she pushed off her left leg. Her knuckles turned white as she clasped the rope tightly. He didn't have to tell her to rest again. She halted, making sure to take all the weight off her injury.

"Bet you regret forcing me now," she called down.

He rubbed his forehead on his shoulder. "Things will be easier if I carry you."

Her answer was to continue climbing. The process repeated three more times before her left foot slipped. A startled cry ripped from her lips as she yanked herself against the ladder. There was no getting around it. She was using the leg too much. Even she had to admit it now.

"Hold on," he told her and hurried to climb up beside her.

"Are you crazy?" she demanded. "There isn't room for both of us."

"I know what I'm doing."

Her eyes flashed with anger, but he also saw her fear. "That doesn't comfort me." She looked down and groaned when she saw the distance.

He wound his arm around the rope several times to get a good grip and then repeated the action with his foot before wrapping an arm around her. She was tense, her body trembling from exertion and terror. Her breathing was ragged, her eyes wild.

"Let go of the ladder and hang on to me," he told her.

It seemed she was past listening.

"Farah," he called, loud enough to get her attention.

Hazel eyes jerked to him. He found himself staring, taken off guard by the dark amber burst of color around her pupils that mixed into the brown and gold of her irises. How could such unique eyes exist? Did magic create the color?

"I don't think I can hold on much longer," she whispered, her eyes filled with horror.

It pulled him out of his daze. Look at my arm here," he said, motioning to the one wound around the rope. "Do the same with yours and repeat it with your leg. The rope will hold you."

It took her a few tries, but she got her right arm secured and then her right leg.

"Good. Now, I need you to do exactly as I say, all right?"

She nodded and looked down.

"First, don't do that again."

"Right," she murmured.

He shifted closer so his thigh was positioned under her. Then, he used his free hand to loosen the strips of cord he had attached to his belt for this exact scenario. In seconds, he had tied some quick knots in both ropes. He put them in his left hand and wrapped his right arm around her once more.

"Look at my hand. See those loops? One will go around your ankle so you won't have to use your leg muscles to hold on."

"Okay," she answered shakily.

"The second will wrap around your wrist. Then you'll climb onto my back. That's when I'll secure the bindings to your other arm and leg." He caught her gaze when she tried to look away. "You can do this."

She swallowed loudly, then nodded once.

"Ready?"

"Nay." But she lifted her injured leg so he could loop the rope over her boot and tighten it at her ankle.

He got the cord on her left wrist with relative ease. The hard part would be getting her to release the ladder and move onto his back. It was also the riskiest part. Rohan tested his left side arm and leg that he had wound in the ladder rope one more time.

"Listen closely," he urged. "I'm going to drop my arm from your waist, and I want you to bring your left arm across my back and place it in my hand." He wiggled his fingers to show her."

She started to glance down.

"Farah," he called. Once she met his gaze, he held hers there. "Look at me. Only me. Don't look away. Got it?"

"Got it."

"Now, give me your left arm."

She put out her arm, but her hand only brushed his neck. "It won't reach."

"It will. You need to lean toward me."

Her fingers inched over his left shoulder, then down his biceps.

"More," he urged.

She pressed her lips together and eased to the side.

He had to bend his hand back to finally grasp her wrist. "Good work. I have you. Now, I need you to bring your other arm over so I can tie your wrists together."

"If you wanted me tied up, this would've been easier when I was unconscious."

Rohan bit back a snort at her unexpected dry humor. "I'll remember that for next time."

"There won't be a next time." Then she sucked in a breath and released the ladder to grab his shoulder. Her fingers bit into him, revealing the depths of her fear.

"Well done. Put your hand through the loop there," he directed. When her wrist went through the loop, he grabbed the end with his teeth and pulled it tight. "We're halfway there. The legs will be easier."

She snorted. "I don't think so."

"I'm going to catch your leg with my free hand. All you have to do is unwind your leg from the ladder and swing it over so you can wrap both around my waist. Ready?"

"I wish you'd stop asking me that. The answer hasn't changed."

She gave him no warning but suddenly had both legs around his waist. The rope he had put on her left ankle earlier nearly fell off from her wild movement, but he caught it in time. Within moments, her ankles were tied around his waist.

"I suppose this is where you tell me to let go of the ladder," she said.

"That's right. Once you release the rope, put your arm under my right one. That way, after I tie off the cord, you won't choke me."

She grunted. "That's a thought."

"Ready?" he asked, unable to help himself.

12

Farah closed her eyes, her arms holding Rohan tightly. She was thankful for the cords that held her ankles. Otherwise, her legs would be dangling. Her left one ached terribly, but it was more than that. She was still so weak. It was a new and exasperating experience she never wanted to feel again.

Her arms tensed as Rohan began climbing. She wasn't sure how he would get them up to the top, but she was too exhausted and hadn't thought much about it until now. He moved steadily and carefully up the ladder. If she hampered his motions, he didn't let on.

She didn't look down again. She had never feared heights before, but then again, she had never been so weak that she feared she couldn't hold herself up. His movements became rhythmic and eventually eased her, though she still held on to him with her arms for that small measure of reassurance. The throbbing in her leg began to lessen, but it didn't go away entirely.

Rohan didn't speak again. That gave her time to mull over his quick thinking and reaction to her predicament. He hadn't berated her or made her feel foolish. Instead, he had calmed and reassured her—not something she had anticipated from someone who could barely look at her. Which proved he would do whatever it took to get her to Mortham alive. After that, well, she could imagine how he would treat her once he found his people.

Not that it mattered. She knew he wouldn't find them. He might locate one or two, but even that would be a miracle. And if he was lucky enough to locate more, they wouldn't be the same. No one who spent any time in the compound was ever the same. Her included.

Mortham was an abyss of suffering and misery. It was a void straight to the darkest depths of wickedness. A place which left an imprint that could never be washed away or hidden. It stained anyone who stepped foot inside its gates. And her captor thought to take her back.

Surely, Rohan realized that wouldn't happen. All she needed was a bit of magic to disable him and get away.

She would find an opportunity to free herself of her captor, but Nitya hadn't. Their situations weren't the same, but there *were* parallels Farah couldn't help but see. If her sister had made it through the harvesting—as they called it in Mortham—she would've been sold. Nitya was strong in mind and spirit. She was also intelligent. She would've seen someone's defiance and the beating that followed and kept her mouth shut. She would have found a way to survive.

The problem was, Farah knew nothing about those being sold after they left Mortham or the buyers. That was the information she really needed to find Nitya. She had tried to look for it early on when she arrived in Mortham, but she'd soon discovered that information was only given to certain individuals. She was too new—and too lowly a worker—to gain it. Which is why she hunkered down and tried to move up the ranks. Look what that had gotten her.

Rohan's movements changed. Farah opened her eyes as he crested the top of the mesa and climbed off the ladder. He turned and sat before untying her legs and then her wrists. She scooted back to put some distance between them and breathed a sigh of relief to be on solid ground again.

He rose to his feet and faced her. "How's the leg?"

"Achy."

His lips flattened. "Hmm."

"Maybe the seaweed didn't stay on long enough."

"Perhaps." He looked around, then held out an arm. "Come. I'll help you to a tree."

She took his hand and let him pull her to her feet. It would've been nice if she could walk on her own, but she didn't want to test it just yet. And if he was stupid enough to bring her to something that could restore her magic, that was his problem.

He helped her hop to a tree with large, feather-shaped leaves that swayed above her. She braced her hands against the rough, gray trunk and lowered herself to the ground to lean against it.

Rohan squatted beside her, staring at her thigh. "The red seaweed heals us completely. We've never used it on an elf before, though."

"You're telling me you put something on my wound that might have killed me?"

His celadon eyes lifted to her. "Unlikely."

She was enraged by his pithy reply. "You had no way of knowing that."

"It healed you, didn't it? It just didn't restore you fully."

"Obviously," she bit out, still disconcerted at his willingness to use something untested on elves. Though she had been just as willing to have it used on her.

Rohan straightened and walked to the ladder hidden by the tall grass around it. She wouldn't have known it was there if they hadn't just come from it. The area was empty except for a handful of the same types of trees she was leaning against. One wouldn't fully restore her magic.

Sun Elves only needed the sun for their magic. Mountain Elves needed the mountains. Sea Elves could use any water. And Wood Elves needed the woods. But not just one tree. They required many. Still, one was better than nothing. Farah had been without her magic for too long. She placed her hand at the base of the trunk near the ground and watched Rohan as he lifted a hand, most likely to signal to Kalyani below.

He was the type of man who wouldn't hesitate to kill for those he cared for. He had gone into Mortham. Farah frowned as she thought about the explosion. He had been watched from the ship to the fort. There hadn't been a bomb on him, and even if there had been, he wouldn't have had time to place it anywhere. There were too many eyes on him. Which meant he'd had help.

"Who aided you at Mortham?" she asked.

He turned his head to her. "No one."

"You couldn't have gotten out of the compound alone. It was all planned, and I'm betting you being harvested was also."

"Harvested, huh? Is that what you call it?"

She shrugged, realizing too late that she had resorted to the language from within Mortham's walls. "I'm right, aren't I?"

"So what if you are?"

"Who helped you?"

Rohan walked the short distance to her. "You'll never get the name, so you might as well stop asking. Can you walk? Or am I carrying you? Either way, we're heading out."

Farah glared as she used the trunk to push herself up. He scrutinized her all the while. She waited for him to make some comment about her magic, but he didn't. He had to know the tree would help her. Shecrish had a huge rainwood. There would be more trees.

She tested her leg. It held her, though it still throbbed. She nodded, and he motioned her forward.

"I don't know the way."

"Stay along the edge until we reach the waterfall."

Farah sighed and started walking. It was more of a limp. She wasn't entirely comfortable putting all her weight on the leg yet, but at least she could walk. Strenuous activities like climbing or running were out of the question until she could find a Star Elf or some herbs to complete the healing.

"How long has it been since you took me from Mortham?" she asked.

"Five days."

She grimaced. She didn't need to be in the fort to know what was being said about her. It would behoove her to keep an eye out for anyone who looked like they worked for the Masters.

"How long to get to Mortham?"

"A day and a half if we move quickly." He paused. "Two days if we're lucky."

That meant she would need to recharge her magic soon. "How many left with you?"

Silence greeted her.

"They're going to believe I'm the one who helped you."

"Possibly."

"Not possibly," she retorted angrily and shot him a look over her shoulder. "They've probably already decided it. My body wasn't there. Where else would I have gone?"

"To chase me. Tell them you caught me and are bringing me back."

He had an answer for everything. Most likely because he had been planning this for some time. It irked her that it was a solid plan that might actually work if she got on board. Which she wasn't about to do. But she was curious about how deeply his planning ran.

"There's a problem with that scenario."

"Just one?" he mocked.

Farah blew out a breath. "They'll welcome us back inside Mortham, sure, but once we're there, they'll toss you in a room—likely me, as well—until they can determine if what I say is true."

"I don't think you'll have a problem convincing them of that."

Something in his words made her pause. He spoke as if he knew her. She had only just met him, so that was impossible.

"That's the bigger problem. The smaller one is the issue of my clothing."

He made a sound in the back of his throat. "They were soaked in your blood. Would you rather I had saved them?"

"Of course not."

He had a way of rubbing her raw with everything that came out of his mouth. He was insufferable. The more she thought about his brusque replies and clipped tone, the angrier she got. He had convicted her without knowing a single thing about her.

"You'll come up with a reason to be in those clothes, but I warn you now, if you speak of Siguk, you'll regret it."

That was the last straw. She whirled around, infuriated. "I'll have you know, I..." She trailed off, realizing too late that she had almost spoken about her past. Not a wise move while undercover.

"What?" he pressed.

"Nothing."

Farah turned and resumed walking. There was no more talking between them, which was for the best. She shouldn't have allowed him to get under her skin. She knew better. Without the conversation to focus on, she became aware of the warm sun and the tepid sea breeze. It made her think of Nitya, which turned her thoughts to her village. The air would be cooler there now that autumn had arrived. Had they already made the garlands they draped over all the doors this time of year? It had been Nitya's favorite.

Farah looked to her left and the thick vegetation that began about fifteen feet away. She studied the different trees and flora. She hadn't seen any indication of other Wood Elves yet. Even when she and Nitya had come years ago, there had been no sign of them. What kept their kind from the south? She parted her lips to ask Rohan, then thought better of it. He would likely lie or ignore her. Either way, she wasn't in the mood to engage him in conversation again.

13

Rannora

The shadows didn't just hide him. They were part of him. There was comfort within the darkness that Dain couldn't find anywhere else. He stood wrapped in the shadows, manipulating them as few of his kind could while watching the comings and goings within the city, particularly around The Crossing.

The pub was a favorite of the Dark Elves who ventured from underground to mingle with the other elven races. Probably because it sat half in the Above and half in the Below. A Dark named Sidiq owned the tavern. Dain wouldn't exactly call him a friend—he didn't call many friends—but Sidiq was...an acquaintance.

That wasn't why he was here, though. Dain's gaze moved to the pub's wide, arched entrance, framed by smooth, dark stone. To the right, in plain view of anyone entering from the city or ascending the narrow doorway from below, stood a wall adorned with a colossal painted mandala. Half the geometric symbol representing the elves' universe sat in the sunshine, displaying its vibrant colors. The other half, with its white lines, was bathed in shadow.

Above and Below.

The Crossing was Dain's favorite place for many reasons. He liked that Sidiq had dared to thumb his nose at the unspoken rules by opening a business half in the Above. And there was no better place than the pub for Dain to observe others, especially the elves who dirtied themselves by associating with the Dark, all while never actually venturing belowground.

A different kind of crowd from the city frequented The Crossing. Which made it a good location for meetings when he didn't want to be seen. He was here for such a meeting today, but not with others from the intelligence community. Nay, he was here for someone else.

Reva walked into his line of sight. Her long, brunette locks were gathered behind her head so the length fell down the middle of her back. The petite human wore a smile as she carried drinks to a table. Her beige, short-sleeve shirt skimmed her full breasts and showed off an inch of her stomach. She wore sienna-colored pants with wide legs that gathered at her ankles, and simple black sandals.

He stared at the shoes. They were new. She rarely bought anything that wasn't food. It looked like his money was going to good use.

She turned toward him. Dain found himself staring at her oval face, her pouty lips, and her dainty nose. He had noticed her the moment she began working at the pub. It was his job to discern everything—especially a human within such a place. But it hadn't been until he rescued her from spidorbs in the Below that he'd really paid attention.

Her long ponytail swung out behind her as she whipped her head to the side. She wore a smile, but it was forced, fake. It would drop as soon as she turned away from the customer. Dain had only gleaned a little of her story from his colleague, Arya, when she and Reva had been held as prisoners.

In a world filled with magic, Reva had the biggest secret of all. Magic didn't work on her. That wasn't what had caught his attention, though. She was a fighter, a survivor. She knew how to get herself out of impossible situations. And that's exactly the kind of person he needed. They had come to an agreement: She would listen to conversations while she worked and pass things on to him in exchange for coin.

Elves stupidly ignored humans when they were around. It paid off for Dain since he had human informants all over Shecrish. Dain kept much of what he learned to himself in case he needed to use it in the future.

But things were changing. He didn't show his face as he used to. His scars were too distinctive. With the Masters hunting him and his friends—Ravi, Yasmin, Arya, and Jai—for delivering some massive setbacks, Dain had to be extra careful. His shadows proved useful. He gathered them closer, pushing himself into the corner and away from the sunlight that stretched to reach him.

He would have to move soon. The rising sun would be upon him shortly. Dain glanced inside the tavern again. Reva was headed toward the stock room. He used the shadows to take him there, and when the door closed behind Reva, he dropped them.

She jumped at the sight of him, her brown eyes flashing

dangerously. "You have to stop scaring me," she told him and glanced over her shoulder at the door.

"Things are difficult now."

Her expression softened. "I just don't like being startled."

"That wasn't my intent."

"I know." She crossed her arms over her waist and stepped closer, her voice lowering. "All anyone can talk about is the explosion that happened Below."

He twisted his lips. "Has anyone mentioned a location?"

"I heard someone mention Mortham. Do you know what that is?"

"Unfortunately, I do. What is the talk?"

She shrugged a slim shoulder. "Besides the unease about those who escaped? It's been about the Wood Elf who caused it."

"Did you get a name?"

"Not yet. They've been talking about what will happen to her when she's caught."

That caught his attention. "Her?"

"That's what they're saying."

"I need a name."

She grabbed two bottles of alcohol from the shelf near her. "I'll do what I can. I'm working two shifts."

It was the third time this week. He should caution her about throwing aside her downtime, but he needed the intel. Dain examined her face for signs of exhaustion. He relaxed when he didn't see any. "Are you closing?"

"Aye. Meet me at my flat."

He held out his hand, ready to pay her.

Reva shook her head. "I've not earned it yet."

"You gave me information."

"Nothing relevant." She nodded to his hand with the coins. "Keep those at the ready. I'll have something."

He watched her walk out of the storage room. She always had intel. He tossed the coins into the air and caught them before tucking them into his pocket. Then he considered what to do. He had hours before she got off work. He could visit his other moles, but he didn't want to leave.

The door opened before he could gather his shadows, and he came face-to-face with Sidiq. The tall Dark held Dain's gaze as he softly shut the door behind him. Sidiq crossed his arms over his chest. He'd left his long, white hair down, highlighting the shaved left side and the blue tattoos on his gray skin. Gray eyes looked Dain up and down.

"I have two doors you can use," Sidiq said.

Dain liked Sidiq. Always had. He didn't want to have to fight him. "I know."

"You think I would tell someone you were here?"

"I think everyone has a price. And the Masters have a long reach."

Sidiq nodded thoughtfully. "Maybe so, but you saved Reva. Not many would've done that."

"She's an innocent in all of this."

"She's working for you, isn't she?"

Dain said nothing.

Sidiq blew out a breath and dropped his arms to his sides. "I thought I had gotten away from all of this."

"You're never really out."

"So I'm learning."

They stared at each other for a long moment before Dain said, "All she's doing is gathering information. Nothing more."

"She's a good person. She'll get hurt. We both know it."

"I won't let that happen."

"If she does, I'm coming for you."

Dain hadn't considered that Sidiq might have feelings for Reva. He wasn't sure how he felt about that. "Understood."

Sidiq shook his head and turned toward the door. He put his hand on the knob but hesitated. "If you needed information, you could've come to me."

"As you said, you got out."

Sidiq turned his head and looked at Dain. "Do you know her history?"

"I know she's a fighter."

"Maybe because she's had to be."

Dain shifted on his feet. "Life isn't easy for any of us. I'm trying to help her."

"By putting her in danger?"

"By supplementing her income so she can buy new things like sandals."

Sidiq blew out a breath. "The pub is a safe place for you. I owe you that for what you did for Reva."

The door closed behind Sidiq, yet their conversation hung in the air long after he was gone. Dain had only seen the opportunities in using Reva at first. Maybe he had been living in the shadows for too long. The intelligence community had a way of eating someone up and spitting them out. Too few got to walk away unscathed.

Reva was a survivor. Perhaps he should've seen that as a sign to give her a wide berth and not pull her into his orbit. Sidiq obviously knew more about her past than Dain did, and whatever it was caused Sidiq to question his motives.

Maybe he should question his intentions. It wasn't just listening and passing on information. Those who really had secrets were aware of anyone and everyone. If Reva got too close to something, there wasn't just a chance she would get hurt. It was nearly certain. Just because someone survived one thing didn't mean they wanted to continue doing that every day.

Dain gathered his shadows and went to visit another of his spies. He kept himself busy gathering intel and filing it away, moving from informant to informant. Anything to keep busy. He found himself about to return to The Crossing several times but just stayed out of sight, watching the world pass him by. That was the way it was, the way it had always been. The way it would remain.

It was well past midnight when he finally allowed himself to go to Reva's. Apartment 13 looked the same as it had the few other times he had been inside. It was only one room with a cot along a wall. The kitchen area had a wobbly table. The stool with bricks beneath one of the broken legs to stabilize it had been replaced. A second plant had joined the first next to the window. His gaze moved to the table beside the bed and the book there with the smooth, worn leather cover. It was no bigger than his palm. He wanted to see if the bright pink flower still rested between two of the pages, but he didn't.

He heard the key turning in the lock—something he had gotten for her. Dain turned to face the door as Reva opened it. She smiled in greeting. She should be angry that he'd entered her space uninvited, but she had never said as much. Was it because she was afraid? Or because she really didn't mind?

"I should've waited outside," he told her.

She released the strip holding her hair and shook out the length, massaging her scalp. "I was expecting you."

"I still should've waited outside. And you should demand that of me."

Reva dropped her arms as she eyed him. "What's going on?"

"Nothing."

"Well, I have something that will cheer you up. A name. Farah." When he didn't reply, she licked her lips. "I tried to hear a surname, but that's all I got."

Dain dug the coins out of his coat and put them on the rickety table. "That's more than enough."

"What's going on? Did I make a mistake?"

"Actually, you've been great. I appreciate everything you've done, but I'll no longer be coming to you for information."

Her face fell. "I did do something wrong. Tell me what it was and I'll make sure not to do it again."

"This isn't about you."

"Dain, I want to do this."

He tipped his head to her. "If you need anything, Sidiq is a good man. He'll look out for you. Farewell, Reva."

Dain gathered his shadows but didn't get out quickly enough. He heard her shout his name, and the sound of it echoed in his head.

14

The storm Rohan had feared looked to be headed straight for them. He had kept an eye on it all day. Dusk had swallowed the clouds, preventing him from seeing its approach, but he felt it in the wind. Anyone living on the shore for long enough would sense it. He didn't worry about Kalyani preparing.

He looked over his shoulder at the elf. She sat on the ground, staring off to the side, seemingly lost in thought. They hadn't gone as far as he had hoped, but made it farther than he had anticipated after their rocky start. She hadn't walked sluggishly in an effort to hinder him or tried to use her leg as an excuse to slow them down.

They hadn't exchanged words in hours, either. He had envisioned endless dialogues about how he had been wrong to force her into his plan, or how he would never find his people or his sister. He had even predicted she might attempt to escape. There had been none of that. Not a single word in an attempt to change his mind. Which meant he hadn't had to use her secret against her yet.

Rohan walked over to her and sat. She was so lost in her head that she didn't seem to notice him. He wondered what she pondered so diligently. Yet her pensiveness allowed him to assess her at will.

She had surprised him. He didn't like being caught off guard by others. He had evaluated her and determined her behavior. His mistake was measuring her against the other elves he had interacted with. Was that because she was a Wood Elf, a trained spy, or was it just her nature? He might never know, and he didn't really care. She was a means to an end. Nothing more.

She lifted her head to look where he had been standing. When she didn't see him, her gaze darted about, almost as if she were afraid to be left alone, though he knew that to be false. Her brows snapped together when she found him sitting diagonally to her. Then she smoothed her expression and turned her head away.

Rohan stretched out on his side, straightening his legs to cross them at the ankles, propping himself up on a forearm. "What's your plan?"

"Excuse me?" she asked with a confused expression.

"Did you really think I wouldn't notice that you've not attempted to escape or thwart me in any way? You've not even tried to talk me out of my plan. Haven't even told me there was no way I'd find my people."

"Would any of it have done any good?"

He shook his head once.

"Then there's your answer. A fire would be nice."

"It will draw attention."

She absently rubbed her hand over her left thigh. "What about animals? Shouldn't we have a fire to keep them away?"

"My guess is you'll placate me until we reach Mortham. Once we're inside, you'll turn me over to the guards and wash your hands of me."

"It's not a bad plan. I've been mulling that one over."

She surprised him again by admitting it. "I won't let that happen," he said.

"You wouldn't be able to stop me."

He grinned. Let her think that.

"Even you realize that." Farah moved her braid over her shoulder. "You should return to your sister and save what's left of your village."

"Not an option."

Farah shook her head and huffed. "You have no idea what you're getting into. Do you know how large the compound is? It's eight stories high and twice that in length. Guards are everywhere. They are always watching. The sheer number of rooms where they keep the prisoners would boggle your mind. Even if you were able to look into each of them, you wouldn't want to. Not to mention opening those doors. They're locked by magic, and only certain people can open them."

"Why wouldn't I want to look inside?"

She gaped at him. "*That's* what you took away from what I said?"

"Why?" he pressed.

"What do you think happens to those who are taken?"

The last bit of light was vanishing quickly, leaving her face in shadow. Soon, he would only be able to make out her silhouette. "They're taken and sold."

"Much more happens."

"Like?"

There was a pause before she spoke, almost making him believe she didn't want to tell him the rest. "Had the explosion not happened, your group would've been split up. My job was to look for anyone who believed they could escape. The defiant ones—and there is always at least one—are brought in front of the group and..."

"And?" he urged.

Another stretch of silence fell between them. She drew in a deep breath. "They inevitably try to make their escape. Either by attacking one of us or running for the door. Either way, they're dragged back and tortured with fists, magic, and anything else that can be found. Then they're hauled away to another area, where the beating continues. The goal is to immediately remove any insolence and rebelliousness."

"You need them meek."

"The show works. Whatever fight is left in them, it's abruptly and utterly squashed. They all assume the same posture. Heads down, eyes on the floor, and shoulders stooped. We lead them to rooms, where they await their turn. Until then, they're fed, bathed, and cared for."

Rohan had imagined some of it, but it was far worse than he could have presumed. Cold anger slid through him. "You think taking care of the people you've ripped from their homes and families makes up for what you've done?"

"I'm not asking for your forgiveness."

"Good, because you'll never get it. Not from me or anyone else."

She dug into her bag and took out some of the flat bread and dried fish he'd packed. "That isn't even the worst of it."

There was more? Of course, there was. He didn't want to hear it, but he had asked. If Lata was enduring it, then he would listen to anything the elf had to say.

"Those brought in aren't just stripped of their freedoms, they endure agonizing torture. Not because they did anything, but because they're simply there. Those deemed unable to be sold because they've not learned their place, remain forever in the fort, chained to a wall to be brutalized daily. A few have come off that wall. You'll see them working at Mortham, a shell of who they once were. With all that suffering, you would think wails and shouts would fill the air, yet there is only silence. Because even that small bit of liberty is stolen from them."

"Their tongues are cut out?" he asked.

"Sometimes. Others are stripped of their identities, their minds broken. They can't think for themselves. They only obey."

He clenched his hands into fists, imagining wrapping his fingers around a neck and squeezing the life out of whoever had taken Lata. "The perfect slaves."

"Aye," she said, so low he barely heard it.

"How long are the people held?"

She shrugged. "Depends. Sometimes, a few days. Other times, months."

"And the auctions? Where are they held?"

Farah tore off a piece of the bread and brought it to her mouth. "I don't know, but it isn't at Mortham."

She could be lying. He wanted to believe she was, but he sensed she wasn't. She wanted him to know what he was getting into. Possibly to scare him into giving up his plan. All she had done was reinforce his need to get to Mortham. Lata could still be there.

Rohan rolled onto his back and laced his fingers behind his head to gaze up at the night sky. No matter how he looked at it, he couldn't search the entire complex on his own. He'd be noticed and caught within moments. If by some miracle he found Lata or any of his people, he wouldn't be able to get the doors to their rooms open. The only way his plan might work was with Farah.

"If you continue with this plan," she said, interrupting his thoughts, "you'll leave Kalyani alone. You'll end up inside Mortham. They'll lock on to your strength and resistance, and they will torture you. Your days will be filled with unending pain until you plead for death."

"And I suppose you'll be the one delivering that torture."

"There are specialists for that."

Specialists. By the gods, these individuals had to be stopped. "My duty was to protect my village—"

"Then return to those who remain and do that. Those taken are beyond your help."

He turned his head to her, seeing her dark shadow against the night. "That might be what you would do, but that isn't me."

"I'm trying to help you see the truth."

"The only truth I know is that these Masters, whoever they are, must be stopped."

She turned her head to the side. "It won't be by a human."

"It has to begin somewhere. If that's me, then so be it."

"All you're doing is killing yourself and leaving your people defenseless."

"If that's a threat, I'll take your life right now rather than have you bring others back to Siguk."

She sighed loudly. "You couldn't possibly believe you would be able to manipulate me into doing whatever you wanted. And if you did, you're no better than the Masters."

Rohan sat up and glared in her direction. "Don't you dare compare me to them. You weren't beaten or sold."

"Your definition of being held against my will and mine are two different things. You didn't ask for my help, you demanded it. You threatened and intimidated. The very idea of me in your precious village repulses you."

"Aye, it does. More than you could possibly know."

"If you're so worried about your people, you wouldn't have brought me there, nor would you be heading toward Mortham," she told him.

He rose to his feet and sent her a scathing look. "You've obviously never had someone you loved taken. If you had, you would know the unrelenting weight of that loss, and the persistent need to bring them back because you didn't do enough to protect them. You have no concept of such a tragedy. And you never will. You aren't capable of feeling that kind of anguish."

"You know nothing about me," she bit out.

"Oh, I know you, elf. I know more than I ever wanted."

She tossed aside the food and got to her feet. "What's that supposed to mean?"

"You work for the DIA."

15

Infuriated, her blood running like ice in her veins from shock, Farah faced off against the human. She had expected to fight him eventually, but not this soon. Perhaps it was better this way. How had he discovered her secret? She widened her stance and beckoned him to her. "You don't know what you're talking about."

The night hid his features, but she didn't need to see his face. She watched the outline of his body. He took a step toward her. They both stilled, hearing the approaching footsteps at the same time. Farah swiveled her head toward the sound. She saw the lantern light through the darkness first. It illuminated a grizzled face peering at her.

The man's gray hair was stringy and disheveled, his beard long and unkempt. His clothes had seen better days. When he saw her, his eyes flared, and his mouth widened into a smile, showing several missing teeth.

"Ain't you a surprise?" he said.

She glanced at Rohan, but he was gone. Farah inwardly seethed. Arsehole that he was, he had hidden. She focused on the older human. She was still weak, but she thought she could take the man on her own. "Does that mean you don't often see elves this far south?"

"The occasional Sea Elf, but not one of your kind."

His voice was friendly, and he seemed nice enough, but something about him made Farah's skin crawl. "Now you can say you have."

"Aye, I suppose I can." He raised the lantern and stepped closer.

She instinctively moved back.

He let out a bark of laughter. "An elf afraid of little ol' me? Bless my bones, this is a fine day."

Her strength had improved throughout the day, but her magic hadn't regenerated enough to use more than one good shot.

His smile tightened. "Or is it that you don't want me to get too close? Perhaps the thought of a human touching you repulses you."

"That isn't it at all."

Farah saw something drop into his free hand from beneath his long sleeve. The light glinted off metal. She recognized it as one of the necklaces put on elves at Mortham to impede their magic. The thought had barely registered before he lunged at her and slammed his fist into her jaw.

Her legs buckled as pain radiated outward, dazing her and causing her vision to double. He released the lantern and fell on top of her, the rigid gold band aimed at her throat. She raised her hands to block him, but he straddled her hips, keeping her firmly in place. He leaned back briefly before punching her in the abdomen. All the breath left her in a whoosh. It was instinct to lower her arms to her sides, but she fought to keep them extended and the necklace from locking around her.

"There's a high price for you, elf," he sneered.

She felt the gold metal touch her skin. Without hesitation, she gathered what little magic she had and released it. Green bands shot from her hand and slammed into his throat, knocking his head back. Something crashed into him from the side. The moment she was free, she rolled to her knees and dragged in air, hoping her lungs would stop seizing.

She heard the loud pop of a bone breaking and got to her feet, finding Rohan behind the man, his arms locked around his neck. Rohan hauled the dead body to the edge of the mesa and tossed him over. He then strode to the discarded lantern and blew out the flame before tossing it and the necklace over the side, as well.

"More are coming," he whispered, darting into the brush behind her.

Farah whirled to follow him, not keen on finding out if he was telling the truth. She bent and grabbed her bag as she ran past. Rohan was ahead of her, somewhere in the dark. Her leg twinged with each step she took, but she kept running, the reminder of the necklace at her throat pushing her past the pain.

Large leaves slapped at her face as the brush got denser. She spotted the tall trees in the moonlight and headed for them. Inside the rainwood, she rejoiced. But she couldn't celebrate yet. Not until she was deeper into the woods. Then she remembered the man's words about the price on her head. So much for safe. The Masters would've put out a flyer with her face on it. There was nowhere in all of Shecrish she could go now.

She heard a loud grunt ahead of her and halted to listen. Going deeper into the forest meant running into other elves—some who might be hunting her. She slid to a halt and closed her eyes, tilting her head to listen. She should be able to hear Rohan, but there wasn't anyone ahead of her. Had he doubled back and returned to Siguk? She thought of the sound she had heard. It had been a pained grunt. Maybe it was Rohan.

This was her chance at freedom—whatever kind she might have with a price on her head. Then there was Rohan. Somehow, he had discovered she was an undercover agent. She needed to figure out how. If there was a leak in the intelligence agency, then it needed to be plugged. And quickly before other names were disclosed.

Of course, the human would have something significant to use as blackmail. He was as much the enemy as those at Mortham now. If she ran, she had no doubt he would spread the word about her being DIA to any and all. That would double—if not triple—the price on her head. The reveal would ensure she didn't work undercover again. The DIA would likely cut her loose since she wouldn't be an effective agent any longer. And returning home... well, that wasn't really an option.

She couldn't run, but neither could she remain. If Rohan had his way, they would return to Mortham—the last place she should be.

The image of him tackling the man trying to collar her played in her mind. A little voice in her head also reminded her that Rohan had healed her injury. Though she could also argue that he was the reason she had been hurt in the first place, and that she wouldn't be in her current predicament if he hadn't taken her from Mortham.

Her intuition told her to investigate the sound she had heard.

She carefully picked her way across the ground. She would rather be up in the trees, which was exactly where she would head as soon as she figured out what had grunted like that. It didn't take her long to find Rohan sprawled out on his stomach, unmoving.

She ran her gaze down his body and found his feet tangled in some vines. He must have tripped and fallen. She glanced around, searching the darkness for anyone before sinking to her haunches. She gave him a not-so-gentle shove in the shoulder, but he didn't respond. Farah then rolled him onto his back, spotting the blood trickling from a cut at his hairline. It was as she had suspected. He had struck his head.

Voices carried on the wind, coming from the direction they had run from. Was it coincidence that they were there? Or were they looking for the human who had attempted to collar her? The latter was the most likely answer.

Her eyes returned to Rohan. He still breathed, which meant he was alive and could spread word that she was a DIA agent. He'd do it, too. She would in his place. He didn't believe she understood his desperation to find his sister, but she did. Probably better than most.

There was no easy decision here. Regardless of what she decided, she would be running.

Two people from different worlds, trying to find their kidnapped sisters. What were the odds? Her heart skipped a beat as a thought took root. The voices were getting louder. She had to decide what to do and quickly.

She grabbed one of the thick vines and wrapped it around Rohan's legs, his middle, and under his arms. Then she stood and braced her right leg against the trunk as she pulled on the vine to hoist him up. He was heavier than she had thought he would be.

Her energy stores were mostly depleted, but she had to hide them. The only place she could was in the tree branches. Humans never looked up.

Farah's arms trembled by the time she got Rohan high enough. She hurriedly wound the vine around the trunk a few times before tying it off, then carefully released first one hand and then the other. Thankfully, the vine held. Now, she had to climb. It had never been a problem before, but she had never been so weak or had a leg wound before, either.

She looked up at the limbs. They were too high for her to jump, and she wasn't sure her arms would hold her, even if she could reach them. She scanned the trees around her, searching until she found what she needed. Farah hobbled over to the tree and put her foot in the hollow. She pushed up and grabbed hold of the trunk until she could straighten her leg. From there, she was able to reach the branch and swing herself up.

Farah leaned against the trunk for a moment and soaked in the feel of the forest. Then she took a deep breath and jumped the three branches to get to Rohan. All she wanted to do was sit down and rest, but the men were getting closer. If she didn't get Rohan situated properly between the branches, they would see him, and everything would be for naught.

By the time she grabbed hold of the vine and pulled Rohan toward her, her legs were quivering from the effort. She couldn't get him to her on the first try because she hadn't gotten him quite high enough. That meant she had to swing him—and hope the knot she'd tied in the vine held. All the while, she listened for the men.

Rohan was getting closer, but it wasn't quite enough. She attempted to pull him up the last few inches, but her arms gave out, and she nearly tumbled off the branch. Farah stopped trying to force things and braced herself properly. Finally, she got him close enough to drag him atop the massive limb. It should've been an easy maneuver, but her body had been under too much strain the last few days to do it quickly or efficiently. Her position on the branch—where she needed to place him—made it even more difficult.

Sweat rolled down her face as she struggled to keep Rohan from swinging out while not falling. But she finally got him onto the branch. Just in time, too, because the men's voices grew louder. She couldn't release Rohan because he would tip over. Instead, she lay on top of him, hiding them both. The lanterns came into view first. Then the men.

"I told you not to let him get ahead of us," one of them said.

"Firoz does what Firoz wants. You know that."

A third said, "We don't even know where he went."

"Fuck 'im," the first replied. "If we find the elf, we split the money between us three. Because you know he wouldn't split it with us if he found her first."

The other two muttered in agreement. They were directly below her now. She held her breath when they stopped and looked at something on the ground. If they were good trackers, they would see her footprints as well as the drag marks from Rohan's body. She strained to hear their words as their voices dropped to whispers.

Time stretched for what felt like an eternity before the men straightened and doubled back, returning to the mesa's edge. Farah dropped her head onto Rohan's chest and sent a silent prayer of thanks to the gods. She could fall asleep right here if given the opportunity. She considered that for a heartbeat, but she needed to get Rohan situated better.

Farah sighed and lifted her head. She looked up at his face and found his eyes open and watching her. She pushed off him and put her finger to her lips. He said nothing as she unwound the vines from his body. Then he sat up and slid into a better position on the branch. She let the end of the vine fall to the ground.

Rohan's gaze remained on her, even when she nimbly walked along the limb to the trunk and settled herself for the night. Her eyes were heavy, and she was tired of holding them open. No sooner had she closed them than she heard Rohan moving.

Farah cracked open an eye to see him rising to his feet. They were very high in the tree, and while the limb was large, he wouldn't survive a fall. She watched him stretch out his arms to the sides to balance, then put one foot in front of the other until he reached her. She didn't move to make room for him. Eventually, he got around her to the branch next to her and rested his back against the trunk as she had.

"Thank you," he whispered.

"I bet that was hard to say."

"Can't you just take my gratitude?"

Farah winced at his sharp words. But he was right. "You're welcome."

Two beats went by before he said, "You probably could've left me. They were looking for you, not me."

"I'll keep that in mind next time," she bit out.

"Why *did* you help me?"

She blew out an exasperated breath. All she wanted to do was sleep. At this rate, she wouldn't get any rest. "I had a lapse in judgment as you've so eagerly pointed out."

"Where did the men go?"

"Back toward the edge of the peninsula."

He grunted. "What was that thing the other man tried to put around your neck? I saw it on some of the others on the ship."

"It binds an elf's magic."

"There's a bounty on your head."

Farah opened her eyes and looked out into the woods. "Everyone will be looking for me now."

"Is there somewhere you can go?"

She rolled her head to him. "What? You don't want to use me anymore?" Farah laughed softly at her jest. "To answer your question, nay. There's nowhere anyone can go. That's the kind of hold the Masters have over Shecrish."

16

The throbbing in his head made thinking difficult. Rohan tentatively touched his forehead at his hairline and bit back a curse when pain exploded. His stomach roiled threateningly, and for a moment, he was sure he would be sick. He rested his head back against the tree and lowered his hand. There was no point in making things worse since he couldn't see how badly he was wounded or even see to it. He wasn't sure how far into the rainwood they had gone. It might be farther than he had been before, and that would mean doubling back to the area that he was familiar with to find plants that would help with the pain and nausea.

"I...uh... Thank you," Farah said softly. "For...um...earlier with the man."

Rohan didn't look her way. It hurt to breathe. It was better to keep himself—especially his head—as still as possible. If he was feeling better, he might have replied sarcastically, but he just didn't have it in him. "You're welcome."

"Why did you help me? We were about to...you know..."

"Fight?" he offered.

"Mm-hmm."

He stared out into the trees, watching the play of moonlight filter through the dense foliage to sprinkle throughout the forest. He had never been this high up in a tree before. It gave him a different perspective of the world that would be profound if he weren't hurting. "I don't know," he finally answered.

"If you're thinking of taking me in for the reward money, that isn't going to happen."

Rohan wiped away the blood on his cheek when his skin started to itch. "I hadn't even considered that until you mentioned it."

"You would need one of those slave necklaces, and you tossed it off the mesa."

"Don't worry. I'm not going to try it." Shite, his head hurt.

"So? Why did you help me?"

"A lapse in judgment," he said, throwing her words back at her.

She laughed softly. "I suppose I deserved that. How's the head?"

"Fucking throbbing."

"I was afraid you were going to say that," she replied, resignation in her voice.

He frowned and made the mistake of turning his head to her. "Why?"

"Because that means two things. The first, we can't remain here in case you fall asleep."

The thought of trying to walk was so abhorrent that bile rose in his throat. "And the second?"

"I know where to get some herbs to heal your head injury."

"There's no need for that. I just have to find some..." He frowned as the word he was searching for slipped from his mind.

"And that's why we're getting the herbs," Farah replied as she got to her feet.

He looked up at her silhouette. A beam of moonlight found her hair, but her face remained in shadows. "Why?"

"Because I was wrong. There is one place I will be safe."

"And why does that concern me?"

"Because it's where we were headed."

Rohan couldn't have heard her correctly. It must be the pain. "You want to go to Mortham?"

"No one will be looking for me there." She tugged on his arm to get him to stand.

He rose when she wouldn't stop pulling him. "I don't understand."

"I know. I'll explain once you're feeling better. For now, we need to move."

"I don't think I can."

"You must," she insisted.

Rohan looked over the side of the tree. It was a long way down. He didn't look forward to the descent. He was having trouble following their conversation. How would he climb?

"Don't worry. We're not going that way. Follow me."

Farah moved onto the same branch he was on before stepping to another. Then she walked along the thick limb until it mingled with another from a different tree. There, she crossed over with a small leap.

She paused and looked back at him. It seemed simple enough. And it was better than attempting a descent. This was simply walking. It would be one thing if this was during the day, but he stood on a tree branch hundreds of feet in the air at night. If he fell, he would hit multiple limbs on the way down. But he had to move eventually. It might as well be now. Particularly if it meant finding something that would ease the ache in his head.

"Don't look down," Farah warned.

He scowled as he kept his focus on the dark limb below his feet and slowly put one foot in front of the other. With one arm stretched out for balance, he kept the other on the trunk until he had no choice but to let go. He swayed precariously and held both arms out at his sides as he backed up a step. His heart thudded at the scare, which only made his head throb more.

Rohan calmed his breathing and attempted to follow Farah a second time. He didn't try to hold on to the trunk, which helped him keep his balance. He made his way bit by bit. It wasn't long before the limb began to narrow. That's when he felt it bend beneath his weight.

"Keep coming," Farah urged. "Don't stop."

That was easier said than done. Specifically, when he saw the gap between the two branches. From the trunk, it had seemed a short distance. Now, as he approached, it was much wider than he'd anticipated.

"If you think about it, you won't do it," she told him.

He couldn't spare even a smidge of mental capacity to answer her. All of it had to be focused on staying upright and balanced as he kept walking. His heart lodged in his throat when the limb he was on dipped considerably. Now, he would have to jump up as well as across.

"Stop," Farah told him.

He gritted his teeth. "You told me not to."

"I need you to back up."

Maybe she'd found another way for him to cross. Rohan would gladly take it. Right up until he realized the limb was too narrow for him to turn around. Which meant he had to walk backward. In the dark. On a branch.

The groan of the limb got him moving. He placed his foot behind him and shifted his weight onto it before repeating the movement over and over.

"That's far enough," Farah called out.

The branch no longer bowed under his weight. That was a vast improvement from where he had been. "Now where do I go?"

"The same way you came. I just need you to do it faster."

He glared at her across the distance knowing she couldn't see his face. She had to be joking. "What?" he hissed.

"Faster. As in…well, you need to run."

"Are you insane?"

"This from a man who scales the cliffs as if they're nothing."

Rohan touched his aching head. "I've been climbing them my entire life."

"You got me up the cliff. I'm going to get you over this gap."

"Not quite the same, now, is it? I don't see you carrying me."

She cocked her head. "I got you onto the branch."

He lowered his arm to his side.

"You can do this. Trust your feet to know where to go."

He eyed the gap between the ends of the branches. One wrong step, and it would be over. Farah said nothing more as she waited for him to decide. Rohan briefly closed his eyes against the pounding of his head. Then, he rushed forward.

His gaze was locked on the limb across the way. The gap grew closer. Just as he was about to jump, the limb dipped. Lines of green magic sprang forward and wrapped around him, giving him the lift he needed to cross. He landed next to Farah, and his foot promptly slipped. She righted him. Then, with a pat on his shoulder, turned and continued walking.

Rohan put his hands on his hips and stood there for a heartbeat. He looked over his shoulder. If it hadn't been for her magic, he never would have made it. He'd gotten her up the cliff, and she got him over the gap, just as she had promised.

He followed Farah, his movements still much slower and awkward than hers. They had to cross many more gaps, and he lost count of the number of branches they traversed. He had been so focused on himself that he hadn't paid much attention to her. But when he did, Rohan saw that she was favoring her left leg. Both of them needed healing. Yet despite her injury, Farah fairly floated along the limbs. He even caught her smiling once when the moonlight hit her face just right.

She obviously loved the forest. Why had she left it to become a spy? What could possibly have driven her from her home? Even more curious was why she hadn't left him when he struck his head. She could've been long gone. But she had stayed.

He hadn't cared what her story was because he hadn't believed it would be worth hearing. Now, he wasn't so sure. She had become enraged when he threatened her life, but not because of the threat. Because he had called her evil. She had retorted that he knew nothing about her. She was right. He didn't.

The trees got larger the deeper into the rainwood they went, and he didn't recognize any of them. Suddenly, Farah halted and plastered herself against a tree trunk. She motioned for him to do the same, urgency in her movements. He put his back to the tree next to her and followed her gaze. He didn't see anything at first. Several long moments passed before he spotted a silhouette moving through the branches.

Farah flipped around so her front was against him briefly before she spun again to his other side. Rohan turned his head, looking up and down the enormous trees until he finally saw the second figure. Farah didn't move, even after the two elves were long gone. Were there more he didn't see? It was likely. He stopped looking and allowed himself to rest.

"What now?" he whispered after several quiet minutes.

She startled as if she had forgotten he was there before closely studying the area around them and then looking at him. "We'll have to move quickly and quietly. We're skirting others' territory, and I don't wish to alert these elves to our presence."

"You're a Wood Elf. Would you not be welcomed?"

Instead of answering, she motioned for him to follow. Rohan hoped they got to where they were going soon. Between the headache and the nausea, he didn't know how much longer he could remain upright. Keeping up with Farah proved difficult. She hadn't been joking when she said they needed to move quickly. She was two trees ahead of him when his foot met air instead of a branch.

Rohan pitched to the side, instinctively reaching out. His palm scraped against the bark of a limb, but he couldn't grab hold. Then, he was falling. He frantically grasped at anything he could. His fingers touched something, and he immediately latched on. His body jerked to a halt as he held on with one hand. His stomach churned, and his head hammered to such a degree that the rest of his aches barely registered.

He might have stopped his fall, but now, he had to pull himself up. His fingers were already beginning to slip on the branch. Rohan swung his other arm up and found purchase. It took a few more attempts before he could wrap his legs around the limb. He tried to pull himself up, but his body had stopped listening.

"I've got you," Farah said, clutching his arm.

Relief poured through him. He tried to help her get him up, but his strength was gone, and she ended up doing most of the work herself. He didn't relax until he rested against the trunk. Sweat covered him, and his stomach wouldn't settle. He thought he might be sick at any moment.

"You're not going anywhere else tonight," Farah said as she looked at him. "Stay here. I'll return as swiftly as I can."

He stopped her with a hand on her arm. "Where are you going?"

"To get the herbs. It's vital you stay awake. Can you do that?"

He started to answer her when his stomach rebelled. Rohan leaned over the other side and emptied his stomach. He straightened, only to find his hand empty. The elf was gone. She might have left him, but at the moment, he didn't care. He closed his eyes. Gods, he was so tired. He just needed to rest his eyes for a moment.

"Rohan?"

His lids lifted at Farah's voice. She held something to his lips, but he turned his head away. He didn't want anything. It would likely just come up again.

"Drink this. It'll help with the nausea."

He tried to turn his head away once more, but she somehow

got the liquid into his mouth. Then she placed something round in his hand.

"Drink more as you need it. Remember, don't sleep. I'll be quick."

His eyes blurred, losing focus. All he needed was to rest them for a moment.

17

Farah expected the Nidur tribe to appear at any moment—with every creak of the trees and breath she huffed. Her body wouldn't keep up, no matter how hard she pushed herself. And she still had to make the return trip to Rohan. She thought about how pale he had been, how dark the blood looked against his skin, and ran faster.

Being back in the forest had done more than rejuvenate her magic. It comforted a part of her that she had ignored for far too long. For duty.

For Nitya.

Farah shoved thoughts of her sister aside for the moment. The ache in her leg was constant now and expanding. And she was out of breath. Despite being away from the woods for months, her feet knew where to step. She danced from tree to tree until she reached the village. Like all Wood Elves, their homes were in the trees.

She circled the settlement, keeping to the shadows and out of sight of the sentries, looking for the naturopath who generally distributed the herbs for each village. Their homes were marked with a set of three stars in a triangle and antlers that signified who they were. Farah found the house on the far side of the community.

After another look to make sure no one was near, she crept toward the door. It was shut, but some of the shutters on the windows were open. She stayed low and moved to squat beneath a window to peer inside. There was a table and chairs, so she hurried to the other open window. Frustration mounted when she looked within and found the bed with a form beneath the covers. As she crouched back down, she spotted a table to the right where several bottles of herbs sat.

Farah inched forward to the next closed window. She gave it a gentle push, adding some magic until it unlatched. She kept her excitement contained and reached inside. The instant her fingers brushed one of the jars, she grabbed it and stuffed the bottle between her shirt and belt. Then she turned to scan the trees for sentries.

One came into view just as she was about to creep out. She froze instantly. Luck was on her side because they didn't notice her. The moment they were out of sight, she hurried away. She raced to Rohan, hoping she got there in time.

There was a stitch in her side by the time she reached him. Her knee buckled when she tried to straddle the limb in front of him. She landed hard on her arse, but he didn't so much as stir. Farah gave him a little shake, which earned her a grunt of annoyance. He was alive. For a moment, she feared he had succumbed to the head wound since he hadn't stayed awake as she bade.

Her hands shook from fatigue as she mixed a big pinch of herbs into the water flask and gave it a quick shake. She took several long swallows, then brought the flask to Rohan's lips. He half-heartedly attempted to push it away, and much of the water ran down the corners of his mouth. But he drank.

Was it enough? Only time would tell.

His upper body tipped to the side. She caught him and sat him up before moving onto the nearby branch to rest her back against the trunk. She stretched out her legs in front of her and crossed them at the ankles. Her eyelids fell closed as sleep tugged at her.

Something bumped into her shoulder, rousing her. She blinked several times to wake herself up, instantly on alert, only to realize it was Rohan. He had listed toward her again. She tried to sit him up again, but he wouldn't stay there. Farah had no choice but to let him lean on her. Within moments, she was asleep once more.

Her dreams were plagued by visions of Nitya when they snuck off to the coast. But something was different. Nitya wasn't acting right. The dream took a dark turn when she found herself staring into the man's weathered face. This time, he successfully locked the necklace around her. She called out for Nitya, but her sister was gone.

Farah saw Rohan standing to the side. She yelled his name, but he didn't come to her aid. Instead, he turned away. She fought against her captor, but he just laughed at her piddly attempts to free herself. Then she was in Mortham. Golshan and Amarjeet were there, circling her with predatory smiles until they began beating her.

She screamed, but no sound came out. She fought against them, knowing what would happen. Somehow, she got free. She ran down the halls of Mortham, soaked in blood and looking for a way out, but all the exits had been changed. The doors were differ-ent, too. She tripped and fell hard on her shoulder. Footsteps echoed in the corridor, approaching fast. She pushed to her feet and ran, an eerie laugh following her.

She didn't get far before she fell again. When she lifted her head, she was no longer in the hallway. She was in a room. Inside were various instruments of torture, but it was the see-through, elf-sized box that sent a chill of foreboding down her spine.

"You can't run from me," a voice whispered in her ear.

Farah jerked away, her eyes darting left and right. It took her a second to comprehend that she was awake. The dream—nay, the nightmare—had felt so real. She brought a shaky hand to her forehead to push away strands of hair that had come loose from her braid.

Dawn had broken. Bright morning light streamed through the trees, chasing away the night. It wasn't until she tried to move her leg that she realized something wasn't right. She looked down to find Rohan's head on her lap. Dried blood covered the side of his face and matted his hair, but his coloring looked good, and his breathing was even. She didn't know where the wound had been, and she didn't want to search through his hair for it. Farah yawned and listened to the birdsong as the woods came alive.

Her leg felt better. She was rested, but she wouldn't mind another hour or two of sleep. When she closed her eyes, though, she saw the clear box from her nightmare. That's when she decided she had gotten all the sleep she needed.

She looked down at Rohan. A strand of dark brown hair had curled into his ear. She smoothed it away without thinking, then quickly pulled her hand back. What was she doing? He was the enemy. Or he had been. He wasn't a friend. What did that make him, then? She was the one with a price on her head. With the knowledge he had of her, he could turn on her at any second.

Farah had never thought too much about humans. Her village was remote enough that they hadn't seen many except for the travelers who came their way the same time every year. They were friendly, and her tribe had welcomed them. It wasn't until she traveled to Rannora that she saw the vast divide between the elves and humans. And the hatred among both.

Was it any wonder Rohan and his people preferred the solitude of their village? She couldn't blame him for his animosity toward her kind. Humans didn't have it easy in Shecrish. Those who chose to live in the cities seemed to have it even worse, though. How many more settlements like Rohan's did no one know about?

There was so much corruption and violence in their country. It wasn't as if they could remove everyone and start again, thinking to right mistakes. They would only make new ones. But things needed to change. Starting with the downfall of the Masters and their entire regime. Their foothold in Shecrish went deeper and farther than anyone could have guessed.

It was a reminder that she had intel to get to Durga. She couldn't go into Rannora herself. Everyone would be looking for her. But they wouldn't be looking for Rohan. Maybe she could talk him into delivering a message to Durga so they could meet before she and Rohan went to Mortham.

Farah shook her head and snorted. Here she was, planning on returning to Mortham, where she would live out her days hiding. How different was that from being hunted and brought in? The difference of a slave necklace, that's what. She needed to take a good, long look at the forests because it would likely be the last time she saw them—or had her magic.

Her thoughts drifted to her parents. She should see them, but she couldn't chance even that. A letter was too impersonal, but it was better than nothing. She would leave something with Durga to send on. To think she had left home to find Nitya, and now her parents were losing both of their daughters. She should've remained in her village. She hadn't accomplished anything she had set out to do, and there were no answers, no closure. Nothing but regret and guilt.

And shame.

Rohan drew in a deep breath and shifted. She knew the instant he came awake and realized where he was lying when he stiffened. She remained still, letting him adjust to the day and all that had transpired. He used his hand to push himself up. Pale celadon eyes swung to her.

"Morning," she said. "How do you feel?"

He cleared his throat. "Morn'," he croaked.

She handed him the remaining water that she had saved for him. That hit on the head had really done a number on him. He downed the last of the herbs in a few swallows.

Rohan nodded his thanks. "I feel better." His brows drew together. "Did you leave? Or was that a dream?"

"I left. Do you remember falling?"

He wrinkled his nose in distaste. "That, I do recall."

"You weren't in good shape. I left you here and went to get the herbs. You were supposed to stay awake, but you were out cold when I got back. I managed to get some of the herbs into your system."

"Thank you." He cleared his throat again as he tested the area at his hairline. "I don't feel the laceration anymore. What about your leg?"

She shrugged. "I had some herbs, too. No pain for me."

He looked around, taking in the trees. "I don't think I've been this far north. Where are we?"

"Not somewhere we should stay if we want to remain hidden."

"South? Or west?"

She hesitated as she rubbed her lips together. Then she looked at him. "We need to make a stop before we go to Mortham."

"You're serious, then? You're really going to return?"

"Like I said, no one will look for me there."

His forehead furrowed. "You'll be a prisoner, though."

"Perhaps. But it works out for you."

He stared at her for a long time. "Why do you really want to go back?"

For a brief second, she almost told him about Nitya. Instead, she said, "It's my only option. I thought you'd be happy about this. You did blackmail me, remember?"

He grunted in reply. "What's this stop you want to make?"

"Rannora."

18

Farah wasn't telling him something. Rohan almost called her out on it but changed his mind. Probably because he was still uncomfortable about waking up with his head in her lap. Had she pulled him down? Or had he lay there on his own?

He scrubbed a hand down his face. His head had ached so badly the night before he'd actually prayed for death. Anything to stop the pounding. She had come through for him. He looked sideways at her. Just when he thought he understood who she was, she shocked him.

Rohan stretched his neck and shoulders. He was rejuvenated and refreshed. The little aches and pains that usually greeted him with the dawn were gone. At least for now. No wonder the magical herbs were so sought after. And why the elves were stingy about allowing humans to get their hands on them.

"There's water close by," Farah said. "We can freshen up and refill the flasks."

"Lead the way."

As he climbed to his feet, Rohan viewed the distance to the ground. If he had fallen, he wouldn't have hit the dirt. He would've landed on one of the thick branches below and likely broken his back or cracked his skull well before he hit the ground. And to think he had followed Farah in the dark for miles.

When he walked across the limb this time, his feet knew where to place themselves. He also learned where to jump on a branch before it started to bend under his weight. All of that allowed him to pay attention to what was around him—including Farah. She cast furtive looks at their surroundings every few moments. Wherever they were, she didn't want to be here. Perhaps she was embarrassed to be seen with a human. It could be that she wasn't welcome among the Wood Elves anymore. Or maybe this tribe, as she'd called them, weren't friendly. The reason really didn't matter. He had no wish to encounter other elves, so he willingly followed her lead.

And he was lost. Though not totally. All he needed to do was point himself south, and he'd eventually end up at the coast. But it wasn't just about crossing the land. Tribes of unknown Wood Elves dotted the area along the way. They might allow him to move about freely, but they might not. He wasn't keen on finding out. Not when Farah was giving him exactly what he wanted: Mortham.

She kept close to the trunks as she moved, sprinting across branches and plastering herself against the next tree. He wasn't as nimble as Farah. Or as agile. The way she moved reminded him of Kalyani in the water. Yet he kept up, albeit not nearly as gracefully. Rohan didn't know how to give up. He just kept plowing ahead, figuring things out as he went. That didn't mean much in the world of elves where humans could never keep up. But among his kind, it meant something.

He leapt from one branch onto another and landed solidly. When he took his next step forward, the toe of his boot caught a knob on the limb. Rohan tried to right himself, but he overcompensated. He twisted and missed the branch he reached for. As he fell, he latched onto another limb that stopped his tumble. He couldn't believe he had fallen again. Not to mention the loud ruckus he'd made during the whole debacle.

He looked toward Farah. She motioned for him to hurry before her gaze darted to the side. He didn't wait to see if something was there before he pulled himself up and hastened to reach her. She shook her head and motioned for him to stay. He followed her lead and kept absolutely still and silent. She didn't even swat away the bug that buzzed around her.

It wasn't easy to see through the foliage, but with what little he could make out, he didn't see anything. Nor did he hear anything. Then again, Wood Elves were nearly silent when they moved. Once again, he put his trust in Farah. He wondered at his sanity in that. Sure, she was running for her life, but that didn't mean her decisions would benefit him. Likely just the opposite.

Long minutes passed without anything. Then, he caught sight of the first elf. The male was several feet below them on a tree to their left. His long, brown hair was pulled away from his face. He wore brown clothing that allowed him to blend in, but the quiver of arrows slung over his back, and the bow in his hand, announced him as a warrior.

After the first, Rohan spotted three more. Two were on lower limbs, but the last was nearly even with them. Rohan was sure the elf would see them. He stiffened, ready to react. If they acted now, they could take the four by surprise. He could get to at least one. She, another. It wouldn't be easy, but it could be done.

Farah appeared to think differently. He wanted to look in her direction but didn't take his eyes off the two elves closest to him. They scanned from limb to limb, searching for whatever had caused the noise. Elves likely didn't fall as he had. He couldn't imagine many humans trying to traverse the trees like the Wood Elves, though.

The four didn't make a sound. Rohan watched with interest, taking in the hand gestures exchanged before they shifted positions. He lost sight of one that moved to the side. The only way to track him would be to turn his head, and Rohan wasn't chancing that. He kept his gaze locked on the other elf. Rohan's breath caught when the elf's gaze moved over them. Farah's fingers tightened on him. She must have seen it, too.

The tension mounted moment by moment. Suddenly, the elves exchanged another round of hand signals before turning and leaving. Farah didn't move for another five minutes. Then she released his hand and raced silently across to the next tree. Rohan was right on her heels. They crossed six more trees before she began to descend.

Thankfully, she had found a tree with several branches that made it easy for him to work his way to the bottom. It was a considerable drop to the ground from the last limb even then. Rohan landed on one knee, his hands on the ground. Farah was already gone, slipping through the thick vegetation. He straightened and followed her.

The path—if he could even call it that—was narrow and winding. Huge leaves and branches endeavored to impede his progress. He only knew which way to go by the swaying of the leaves from

Farah's mad dash through them. He was beginning to think she was trying to lose him when he burst into a small clearing and found the pool of water.

She kneeled at the shore, her hands cupping the water and splashing it on her face. Rohan bent at the waist and watched her as he sucked in mouthfuls of air. She hadn't left him last night when she could have. Why did he think she might now?

He walked to the edge of the water and dropped to a knee. The water was cool against his hands as he eagerly splashed his face, head, and neck several times. He braced his hands on the ground and stared into the clear water. The surface rippled before settling back into stillness again.

It seemed odd to look into the still pool and see the many fish swimming around after a lifetime of rolling waves. The fish weren't as brightly colored as those in the ocean, but that didn't make them any less beautiful. He sat back on his haunches and lifted his gaze to the sky. The trees stood over them like guardians, their huge limbs outstretched to the others.

"We need to change."

Farah's voice startled him out of his thoughts. Rohan had forgotten she was there. He glanced at her attire as he recalled what the warriors had worn. The bleached gray stood out in the rainwood. If they wanted to blend, it meant finding different clothes.

"Where can we get more?" he asked.

Her lips twisted as she climbed to her feet. "There is a place."

"You don't sound happy about it."

"I've never been there, but most elves know of it."

He filled the water flask before standing. They only had the one since they'd left his behind. "What's wrong with it?"

"It isn't a place we visit."

"But we can get clothes?"

She nodded but wouldn't meet his gaze.

"What aren't you telling me?" he pressed.

"It's a bit of a hike. East."

Rohan shrugged since they had already been headed east to get to the water. Once more, he knew she wasn't telling him everything. Maybe it was just that, as a spy, she didn't want to share too much. It wasn't as if they were comrades. They were each after something and using the other to get it. Plain and simple.

Farah pivoted and started walking. Rohan fell into step behind her. They traveled for a time in silence.

Finally, he asked, "How did the elves not see us?"

"They were searching for movement."

"I was sure one looked at us."

She glanced at him over her shoulder. "He might have, but, like I said, we weren't moving."

"Hmm. I'm not sure I believe that. I've heard the rumors about how the Wood Elves see everything."

Her laugh caught him unawares. "We're not gods. We know our environment, just as you know yours. If you heard something you knew to be out of the ordinary, what would you do? Say, rocks falling from the top of the mesa."

"I would search the area for something climbing down."

"Exactly. Those elves knew something had fallen. They weren't sure if it was a person, animal, or a tree limb. That's why four came to investigate."

Rohan missed the ocean breeze. The humidity was high this deep in the rainwood. Even with the drop in temperatures, it was uncomfortable. "Keeping with the hypothetical, if I didn't see anything, I would've begun looking for something."

"As they did. You also forget we were shielded by the branches. We couldn't be seen, even with the leaves changing and beginning to fall."

"They should've looked closer."

She snorted. "You wanted us to be found?"

"I'm just saying they didn't do a very good job."

"We can go back and tell them if you'd like."

He glared at the back of her head. Elves, in general, made humans feel as if everything they did was perfect and they never made mistakes—or so his father had taught him. Yet here he was, seeing firsthand that they did, in fact, make errors.

What did this say about him, though? To be so wrapped up in another species that he wanted to point out their faults. It was hard not to be when humans struggled for every little thing in Shecrish. He stared at Farah. She had shown him another side to her kind. It hadn't done more than confirm what he had already believed, but it revealed things he hadn't known about himself.

They walked for hours, endlessly traipsing through thick flora. No one could hear them with the birds and other animals calling out. Suffocating proximity replaced the wide-open spaces he was used to. It was unsettling, so he counted the different leaves he passed to take his mind off it. When it grew tedious, he focused on differentiating birdcalls.

All the while, Farah continued onward. It was hours before she finally stopped. He halted beside a tree and basked in the soft breeze that cooled his heated skin. They didn't remain there long, however, before she continued. Her steps were slower and less confident now. Rohan tried to see what had caught her attention, but there was nothing but trees and more trees.

The next time she halted, he came up beside her. "What is it?"

"We're here."

He followed her finger. Rohan had to look between the leaves of a small tree to make out the outline of a building.

"It's bigger than I thought," she murmured.

He glanced at her. "Are they dangerous?"

"Depends on who you ask."

19

T his was the last place Farah wanted to be. Well. Maybe not the *last*. But it was close. She pulled her gaze away from the dwelling and looked at Rohan. He studied the building as if it might attack.

"Stay here," she told him. "I'm going to have a look around."

He tensed at her suggestion. "Is it a good idea for you to go alone?"

"Absolutely."

His celadon eyes narrowed as his gaze moved to her. "You're not telling me everything again."

It was true. She had been doing that a lot, but she didn't want to tell him certain things. Like exactly where they were. She was second-guessing her decision to come as it was. The farther away she kept him, the better.

"I move quicker than you do. Stay here and keep a lookout while I scout around," she said.

He held her gaze for a long minute before finally tipping his head in acceptance.

She slipped away and waited until she was out of earshot before releasing a sigh. To get a better look at the building, she climbed a tree. The elongated, rectangular structure sat in a natural glade. She moved over a few trees to view the back and spotted some individuals outside the dwelling.

A smile curved her lips when she saw clothes hanging to dry. Exactly what she had hoped for. As she turned to leave, something she saw out of the corner of her eye made her stop. She found a Moon Elf attempting to climb a tree. He wasn't doing a very good job of it either.

Farah moved closer to the wash. The line had been strung between two twisting evergreens, making it perfect for her to reach. She descended several branches while keeping an eye out for anyone coming out of the house. Then she cautiously walked onto the lowest limb and lay on her stomach, stretching her hand down and wiggling her fingers to inch closer to the clothes.

The moment she touched a garment, she pulled it up. After doing that several more times, she got to her feet and hurried to the trunk with the items in hand. Then, it was a matter of making her way back to Rohan. He was just where she'd left him.

She dropped to the ground beside him, startling him. "Sorry," she said as she sorted through the clothes. She handed him a deep green tunic. "This should fit you."

He held up the item and looked at it while she set aside a top and some bottoms for herself. The last two pieces she had were a pair of trousers and another tunic. The pants were far too large for her but too small for Rohan.

"Is this the best you could find?" he asked.

She motioned to the shirt. "At least you have one piece."

He muttered something under his breath before jerking off his shirt. She found herself staring appreciatively at his bare chest as it tapered to a trim waist. She shook herself out of the trance before he noticed and went around the tree to change.

She donned her new attire before digging a hole and stuffing her gray clothes into it. Then she held out her hand to Rohan. "Hand me your old tunic."

He leaned around the tree and tossed it to her. It went in with hers before she covered the items with the soil. She dusted off her hands and straightened, only to turn around and freeze at the sight of Rohan. The deep green shirt looked good on him. Really good. It contoured to his powerful frame and made his eyes stand out even more. She managed to get herself under control as he ran his hands down his chest, looking at the tunic.

"I need pants," he said.

"It'll be fine."

His eyes lifted to her. "If it were fine, we wouldn't be changing clothes, would we?"

"I can't go back. We'll make do. Put some dirt on your trousers."

His lips parted to speak when his face suddenly went blank. Farah looked over her shoulder in time to see a Sun Elf headed toward them, wearing a bright smile.

The female was tall, her golden blond hair cut to her jaw in a riot of curls. Amber eyes crinkled at the corners as she looked from Farah to Rohan. "I thought I heard voices. Why are you two out here? You should come in. We welcome all."

"We were just heading out," Farah said.

The elf tsked and waved a bejeweled hand. "No one here judges. That is our way. It's a safe space for those such as you."

Farah barely held back her groan. This was exactly why she hadn't wanted to bring Rohan this close. "We're not here for that."

The woman pretended not to hear and guided her and Rohan toward the dwelling. "Come now. There's no need to put up such a fuss. You aren't in the city, my dear. You're with friends now."

"What kind of friends?" Rohan asked.

Farah dug in her heels, but the woman released her and focused on Rohan.

"Oh, I see she didn't tell you." The Sun Elf brought her shoulders up to her ears and practically squealed in delight. "I love this part. I'm Rashmi. One of the four founders of Amberstar. It's a sanctuary for those like us."

"Like us?" Rohan repeated.

Farah never should've brought him here.

"Elf and human couples." Rashmi halted and looked from Rohan to Farah. "We've all been where you are. With families who don't understand love that brings two people together. Friends who can't accept facts. Villages and cities that outright cast out elves who dare to love humans. We are left alone here. Not bothered by whatever is going on outside of this glade."

Rohan caught Rashmi's eye. "Nothing?"

"Nothing and no one matters but those who choose to dwell within our walls," she explained.

Rohan turned his gaze to Farah. She knew what he was thinking. It was the same thing that had been running through her mind for the past few seconds. She would be safe here. But not forever. It would only be a brief reprieve. And he was leaving the decision up to her. That was a surprise.

"Why not come and meet the others?" Rashmi offered. "I don't like to stay out here too long. There are all sorts of unsavory individuals roaming the rainwood."

Farah pulled her gaze from Rohan to look at Rashmi. The Sun Elf's smile suddenly vanished as her eyes narrowed to a point over Farah's shoulder.

"Remain here, please. And be quiet. I'll return shortly," Rashmi said in a low voice.

Farah turned as Rashmi walked past her and was immediately swallowed by the dense flora. Unease slid through Farah as she listened for any sounds. There was nothing out of the ordinary. That could mean it was nothing. Or, it could mean Wood Elves were nearby.

"What is it?" Rohan whispered as he came up behind her.

She shook her head, fighting the urge to follow Rashmi and see for herself.

"Halt," Rashmi's firm voice suddenly sliced through the rainwood.

Farah's gaze moved to the right, where the Sun Elf's voice had come from.

"Must we do this every time?" a female asked, the inflection in her words tinged with boredom and irritation.

"You aren't welcome here," Rashmi stated.

The female laughed. "How long do you think your little party will continue?"

"We have a right to live wherever we wish."

"Let me take a look around, and you just might be able to."

Farah didn't like the turn of the conversation. She looked at the tree beside her. As she was getting ready to climb it, Rohan touched her arm. She turned her head as he slipped between the huge, round, dark yellow leaves of a cladrastis bush and the few large, blue-black flowers from the late summer bloom that remained.

He motioned for her to follow. Farah glanced in Rashmi's direction again before ducking between the leaves. Her foot tangled in her hurry to get there, and she somehow found herself plastered against Rohan's chest. She quickly jerked away without looking at him. Her hands tingled from the contact. She curled her fingers into fists and tried to forget the hard feel of him.

"The answer is nay. It has always been nay, and it will remain that way," Rashmi declared.

The female tsked loudly. "Your little sanctuary is just the sort of place those we're looking for might turn to."

Farah closed her eyes. Fear curdled in her stomach.

"Those four aren't here," Rashmi declared. "Just as they weren't two days ago."

There was a tense silence. "Good thing I'm looking for someone new. How about her?"

Farah didn't need to see the picture to know it was of her. She turned to leave, but Rohan grabbed her, holding her still. She looked up at him in disbelief.

"*Wait*," he mouthed.

Surely, even he had to understand that the quicker she put distance between herself and Amberstar, the better. His face remained in shadow, revealing nothing. She tried again to leave, and he once more held her.

"Only couples are allowed here. You know this," Rashmi stated. "No one you're hunting is within Amberstar's walls."

There was another long stretch of silence, then, "If I find out you've lied, I'll personally see to it that the Masters know exactly where to find your little hideaway."

A short time later, Rashmi returned. "You can come out now. She's gone."

Farah hesitated. It could be a trap. Rohan dropped his hands from her and emerged from behind the leaves. She waited to see if he shouted a warning, but there was none. Finally, Farah stepped out.

Rashmi flashed her a smile. "I apologize for that. Threats are something I deal with all the time. I promise it won't be something either of you has to hear as long as you remain at Amberstar."

"Who was that?" Rohan asked.

Rashmi's attention flicked behind her. "An annoyance. The group has grown in size and power and likes to exert its dominance. One such way is hunting individuals they believe have wronged them. It's absurd. And our governing body does nothing. It's another reason we moved out here, away from such violence."

"It doesn't sound like you've escaped things completely," Farah said.

The Sun Elf's lips twisted. "Unfortunately, we haven't. I fear the only way we might be free is if we go into the mountains, but we're already on the edge of the rainwood. Any farther, and those seeking shelter here, like you, might not be able to find us."

No matter how hard Farah searched Rashmi's face, she couldn't determine if the Sun Elf had seen her picture. It was doubtful the threat and sizable payday would keep anyone from handing her over to the Masters—no matter how far removed from civilization they were.

"Our doors are open to you," Rashmi said. "Follow if you wish."

Farah watched as Rashmi turned on her heel and walked down a path toward the building.

"Why do you hesitate?" Rohan asked.

She shrugged, shaking her head as her gaze slid to him. "We should keep moving."

"She's given you sanctuary. And those searching for you are close."

"Maybe. But it'll grow too difficult, and they'll eventually turn me over."

He frowned. "You don't know that."

"And you don't know she won't."

"You would give up a day of rest for a lifetime at Mortham?"

Farah blew out a breath. "Why do you want to stay? You want to find your sister, don't you?"

"Why do you really want to go back?" he pressed.

The sound of a twig snapping silenced them. The hairs on the back of Farah's neck stood on end. It was likely the female returning to have that look she wanted.

"Time to go," Rohan whispered, running down the path to the dwelling.

Farah hesitated for only a heartbeat before falling into step behind him.

20

Lotus River Port

The scrutiny had been unbelievable, but Salil had been prepared for it. No one had questioned him. Not officially, at least. But he'd run into others at the port who got him talking to see if he was involved in the explosion without actually coming out and asking.

It was exhausting. He was used to watching what he said and who he spoke with, but this was a completely different level of surveillance. He would be putting something into motion even if he hadn't already organized his exit.

He stood on the ship deck and looked out over his crew. Each of them served as a slave to the Masters. Some believed his crew and others like them had it easy. He disagreed. Having freedom within reach, tasting it day in and day out, was far from painless. He saw the yearning in his crew's eyes as they moved about the port, remembering when their lives had been their own.

He had already lost two crewmembers. They'd bolted, and he didn't stop them. He never would. Their freedom would be short-lived, but he would let them have whatever time they managed to carve out before he had to report them as missing. Once the report was made, the silver bracelets would be activated, and they would wind up at Mortham. Except they would be in a room instead of a ship.

If it were up to him, Salil would never report them. But some members of his crew willingly spied for the Masters to gain extra privileges. Others did it to find some comfort in a life they had no control over. A few did it purely out of spite.

"Cap'n."

He drew in a breath and turned to the Port Master. The stout Dark Elf wore a constant sneer. He hated everyone who wasn't Dark and despised most of those, too. It seemed he had a particular loathing for Wood Elves because he took every opportunity to make Salil's days miserable. If anyone at the port was actively looking for a way to bring him down, it was the Port Master.

Salil looked into the Dark's gray eyes. He was a head shorter than Salil, which only enraged him more. "Port Master."

"Your next cargo will begin loading within the hour."

"I'm ready."

The Dark's eyes narrowed. He smoothed a hand over his short, white hair. "Lose any crew this time?"

"Since you last inquired thirty minutes ago? Nay."

The Port Master snorted and turned on his heel before exiting the ship via the gangplank. Three other vessels were moored at the port, all being loaded with the newly abducted. Each ship would receive a similar visit from the Port Master. The elf did so love lording his position over others.

Salil turned back to observe his crew as they readied for their upcoming voyage. He put his hands in his pockets and fingered the small vial there. Once he set his plan into motion, there was no turning back. Farah was out there somewhere. He needed to find her before the Masters did. Moreover, he couldn't stomach transporting elves and humans to servitude any longer. Nothing he did took down the organization. It was time he found something that would.

The Port Master's voice boomed over the water. Salil watched him stride onto the next vessel anchored in front of him. The timing had to be perfect. He turned on his heel and made his way down the steps to the cargo hold. He stopped beside one of the small barrels stacked atop some others.

It would be more convincing if he initiated his plan *after* the cargo had been brought on board, but he couldn't take innocent lives. Even if he considered it a mercy compared to what awaited them at Mortham. As it was, some of his crew would die. A few might be happy for the release. They talked about it enough, but talking and actually dying were two different things. The will to live was strong. If given the choice, many would choose life, even if it meant being a prisoner.

He continued to turn the vial over in his pocket. The explosion at the compound had helped his plan. When his ship and the one behind him blew, it would cause a frenzy, thereby making it easier for him to escape.

Salil withdrew a hand and snapped his fingers. Copper magic jumped to the cask. It wrapped around the wooden slats before sinking into the grains and disappearing. The countdown had begun. He retraced his steps and returned to the deck. There, he walked along the railing. In all his years in the rainwood, he had believed the Below was dark and dreary, but he had been wrong. The Lotus River, while underground, had a special appeal. There were dangers, but the bioluminescent animals and vegetation beneath the surface lit up the riverbed to reveal astounding wonders.

And it didn't stop there. The port also had a unique appeal, with the buildings carved out of the rock. The Dark Elves didn't let living underground hinder their artistic flare. It was in everything from the decorative architecture of the buildings to streetlamps and even the docks themselves. Nothing was done simply. There were embellishments and ornamentation everywhere his eye touched.

The slave trade along the Lotus River generated tremendous revenue, particularly at the port. Which had caused the population to swell. Which meant more workers brought in to carve out more living quarters. No one seemed to think about what would happen to Shecrish in the long term. The decline in the population had been noticed, but the governing bodies had yet to do anything about it. The Masters weren't worried about working in the shadows anymore.

As for everyone else, it wouldn't matter if you willingly worked with the Masters or not. They would come for each and every individual, one way or another. It was only a matter of time.

Salil nodded to one of his crewmembers, who called out a greeting. How many of his sailors were innocent? Half? Three-quarters? All? What about the vessel behind him? He hadn't wanted to take innocent lives, but he inevitably would. He tried to tell himself he was freeing them, but even he didn't buy the lie.

Others would die so he could live.

Did that make him as bad as the Masters? Maybe. He made his way back to the helm. The ship bobbed in the water, eager to be taken out. She'd had her last voyage, though. He wasn't just releasing his crew. He was also releasing her. When it was all over, she would rest at the bottom of the river to form a new home for the fish.

He laid a hand on the balustrade and flipped the cap off the vial in his pocket with the other. Salil turned his back to the port and hurriedly emptied the contents into his mouth. The taste was sharp and bitter on his tongue, lingering long after he'd swallowed it. He tucked it back into his pocket.

The effects of the tonic begin working almost instantly. He worried he might have drunk it too soon when the back of the ship suddenly lurched out of the water with the force of a blast. It sent him careening toward the far side of the ship.

Shouts filled the air. The second explosion shot out toward the port. Someone hollered his name. He turned but couldn't see anything through the smoke. The third blast rocked the boards beneath his feet. He slipped over the side and into the river before the fourth detonation happened. He saw it cripple his ship.

Almost immediately, a ripple of explosions took out the vessel moored behind him. Salil removed the fake slave bracelet and let it fall to the bottom of the river before swimming to the front of his ship as others hit the water. By the time he reached the ladder at the dock, his skin was the gray of a Dark Elf. No one noticed him as they rushed to put out the fires dotting the remaining two ships and the dock before they spread.

He even joined in for a time to make it appear as if he lived at the port. Then he slipped away without a backward look. He hid in a small alcove when he heard the sounds of others running toward him and remained long after they passed. Word was already spreading about the explosions.

Slowly, he made his way along the route. His Dark Elf cover would only last for a few hours. He had to reach his destination before then. No one would remark on a Dark walking in the Below. But they would definitely notice of a Wood Elf.

He had never traveled this path, but he memorized it before taking the captain's position in case Farah or he needed an escape. He passed through long sections of nothing between different communities, each more elaborate and extensive than the last. On the surface, everyone wanted to be by the water. In the Below, they kept away from it.

Finally, he found the passageway to The Crossing. His steps quickened as he neared the tavern's door. He made his way inside but didn't go to a table. Instead, he found the stockroom and hid in the back behind some barrels of ale. There, he waited for the effects of the tonic to wear off.

Salil rested his head against the wall and closed his eyes, but he still heard his crewmembers' screams, still smelled burning flesh. How many had died? He hoped none, but the likelihood of that was slim. He had been spared only because he knew where to stand.

He squeezed his eyes shut before opening them. The fires would keep everyone absorbed for a while. Then, they would begin pulling bodies from the water. If he was lucky, they would think he had been blown up. But he wasn't taking any chances. The moment his true appearance returned, he'd make his way out of Rannora—after a quick stop at Durga's—to begin his search for Farah.

An hour later, the gray cast to his skin had vanished. He rose and walked to the door, standing with his hand on the handle and listening for anyone nearby. When he deemed the coast clear, he exited the storeroom. His gaze darted around the inside of the tavern. It was busy, and the noise was loud. He pressed against a wall when he heard the doorway from Below open. Three Dark Elves entered, talking about the port explosion.

Salil fell into step behind the trio to make it look like he had come in with them. They walked to a table, and he headed toward the doorway and out into the city. He kept his head down and blended in with others as he walked the streets on his way to *Twilight,* trading one pub for another.

Once inside, Salil got the nod from the bartender and made his way to the back. He heard Durga's voice before he saw her.

"I need answers!" she shouted.

He turned the corner into the room and saw Durga with a Dark Elf dressed in a long, black leather coat. "Perhaps I can help."

She whirled around to him, and relief filled her face as she softly closed the door. "What happened?"

"What needed to happen," he replied.

The Dark Elf crossed his arms over his chest, his golden yellow eyes still watching Salil. Small, silver metal bands held locks of his long, white hair back on either side of his face, but the scars caught Salil's eye. One dissected the Dark's mouth at an angle from right to left. Another ran from his left temple through his left brow and across his nose to his right cheek. But the deepest was the one running from the inside corner of his left eye diagonally down to his left cheek and jaw. A very distinctive face—and one he had seen on papers circulated by the Masters.

Dain was dressed in all black, the ends of his coat cut into six thick strips, the shoulders bearing armored plating. Salil spotted chest and abdomen armor beneath the jacket, as well. There was armor on the front of his black boots, too.

Durga released a loud sigh. "Salil, this is Dain. He's part of the Dark's CCD. Dain, Salil."

What was an operative from the Counter Corruption Division doing with Durga? Salil nodded at the Dark, and Dain dipped his chin in return.

"Now," Durga said, cocking her head to the side. "I take it you recognize Dain?"

"I do," Salil admitted.

Dain said nothing, merely looked at him.

"He's a friend," Durga said. "And since you're intelligent and acquainted with Ravi, I'm sure you can put two and two together."

"You were with Ravi at Shaldorn," Salil said to Dain.

"I brought Durga intel on Shaldorn."

Durga nodded. "He's risked his life several times for our agents. Now, what happened at the port?"

Salil relaxed a fraction now that he understood who Dain was. "I blew up my ship and the one docked with mine. That way, I wouldn't be looked at."

"Smart. How did you get out of the Below?" Dain asked.

Salil glanced at him. "A tonic. I walked out as a Dark without anyone the wiser."

"You were lucky," Durga bit out.

"You were right that I needed to get out. They watched my every move. I wouldn't get any more intel."

Durga scratched her forehead. "Let's hope your plan worked." She looked at Dain. "Ravi and Yaz are still with Manu, right?"

"Aye. Along with the children," he answered. "They're safe."

Durga blew out a breath. Finally, she pivoted to face Salil. "When can you leave to search for Farah?"

"Right now."

21

Amberstar's interior was nothing like the basic front façade. Pointed-arch windows decorated with elaborate latticework greeted Rohan everywhere he turned. The structure exuded warmth, not just from the rich hue of the wood used but also from the simple, elegant furnishings. The building might be in the middle of a clearing in the rainwood, but plants and potted trees were tucked in corners, hanging from the walls, and sitting on shelves.

Rashmi stood just inside, waiting for them with a smile. "Welcome to Amberstar."

"Thank you," Rohan said. He glanced at Farah, who was busy staring as he had been a moment before.

"We each have duties to see to daily, which is why most everyone is out and about instead of here to greet you," Rashmi said.

A dark-skinned human woman poked her head out of a room to the left. She walked toward them in a long-sleeved, ankle-grazing, soft pink tunic dress with gold embellishments at the neck and wrists. Her hair was shaved, revealing a slender neck and large, bell-shaped earrings hanging from her lobes. Her deep brown eyes radiated warmth.

Rashmi spotted her and returned the smile. She opened her arm to the woman and brought her against her side. "Rohan, Farah, let me introduce you to Halima. My love, we have a new couple joining us."

Halima stood a head taller than Rashmi. She looked from Farah to Rohan and bowed her head. "Welcome. We don't get many new members, so it's very exciting. You're both going to love it here."

"Everyone will return within the hour for the noon meal. Let me show you to your room so you can relax," Rashmi offered.

Rohan was keenly aware that Farah hadn't uttered a word. She wore an easy smile, but he saw the rigidness of her posture as she fell into step behind the couple. Was it the prospect of pretending to be romantically linked with him because he was human? Him specifically? Or was it something else he wasn't aware of?

She didn't trust anyone here. Not that he blamed her. But if Rashmi had seen Farah's picture and didn't turn her in, then that was something. And if Rashmi *hadn't* been shown Farah's picture, they at least had a little time. Regardless, they both needed a few hours to think and plan without worrying about being hunted. Not to mention a decent night's sleep.

"The main areas are in the middle here." Rashmi pointed as they turned left to walk down the hallway. "The kitchens and dining area are to the back. There is a library and another area on either side of the front doors."

Rohan brought up the rear of their group. He looked up to see a second-floor balcony that ran along either side.

Halima glanced back. "Bedrooms are on both sides of the house. Originally, we designed them to be on the second floor, but we soon ran out of room and had to convert a few downstairs areas to private chambers."

"How many rooms do you have?" he asked.

Rashmi called over her shoulder, "Eleven for the moment. We plan to expand. You two are taking our last remaining bedroom."

"There are two stairways, one on either end of the building," Halima explained as they came to the first set hidden behind a wall.

The switchback stairs were crafted with the same care as Rohan had first noticed upon entering the structure. The two women pointed out rooms, naming their occupants as they passed. He wouldn't remember everyone. Farah nodded as though committing it all to memory.

"Here you go," Halima said as they halted next to a door squarely in the middle of the others.

Rashmi opened it and smiled. "We'll let you two freshen up. Just follow your noses to the dining area."

The women waved and walked away hand-in-hand. Farah lingered outside, but Rohan walked past her and entered the room. It was small. Barely big enough for the bed. The view from the window overlooking the back of the property was stunning. It was arched like the others and had a narrow bench along the bottom, perfect for sitting. But his eyes were on the mountains rising through the trees. He had glimpsed the peaks from the ocean, but this vantage point was different, the range closer.

"What are you doing?" Farah asked in a harsh whisper.

He ran a hand down his face and turned toward her. She had closed the door already. "I'm looking at the scenery."

Her eyes blazed as she stalked toward him. She kept her voice at a whisper when she said, "You know what I mean."

"And you know the answer to that. Aren't you trained to pretend to be someone you aren't?"

"Keep your voice down," she hissed angrily.

Rohan drew in a deep breath and turned back to the window before releasing it. "This is a safe place."

"For how long? You heard that woman talking to Rashmi."

"We need a plan."

Farah plopped down on the bed. "We have one."

"We need a better one."

"Fine, but I don't want to be responsible for bringing harm to anyone here. You know that will happen if we remain."

"We'll stay one night."

"If we aren't found out," she whispered.

He cut his eyes to her. "What's that supposed to mean?"

"They'll figure out the truth about us soon enough."

"Not from me."

She snorted and fell back onto the bed. Her eyes closed. The next time she spoke, it wasn't a whisper. "Right."

He studied her, not bothering to answer. How much sleep had she gotten the night before? He didn't know how far she'd had to go for the herbs or even what she had to do to get them. All Rohan remembered was waking up with his head on her legs. He cleared his throat and started to look away when he realized she had fallen asleep.

She was uncomfortable here. Was it because of the lie? Or him? She hadn't even wanted to tell him what Amberstar was. To her, it was nothing but somewhere to get clothes. He hadn't known such a place existed or that there were enough human and elf pairings to necessitate such a location.

The snow-capped mountain peaks drew his gaze again. A person could get lost there. It looked cold and desolate. Untamed and violent. And he wanted a closer look. Needed to see the mountains as they were, not view them through trees.

Rohan let Farah sleep as he continued to stare out the window. Humans and elves emerged from the rainwood and headed toward Amberstar. No one looked nervous or edgy. That might change when he and Farah joined them for the meal.

He turned and spotted a mirror on the wall. He was a sight. He washed his face and hands in the sink and patted his face dry with a cloth. Then he released his hair and combed his fingers through the length before tying it back again. He looked toward Farah in the mirror, but she was no longer on the bed. He found her standing at the window.

"What don't you like about it here?" he asked.

She shook her head. "There have always been rumors about this place. I discovered it was real some years back."

"Why didn't you tell me what it was?"

"I don't know."

He grunted as he moved away from the sink. "Aye, you do."

"It's embarrassing."

"Which part?"

Farah turned her head to look at him. "All of it."

"I thought elves raised human babies."

"They do." She shrugged. "You'd think that would make it easier to accept an interspecies couple, but it doesn't."

He leaned a shoulder against the wall. "We both live in this country, but that's the only thing shared. There are no humans in your village, are there?"

She held his gaze for a long time before she said, "Nay." Her eyes flicked away. "There are some settlements of humans throughout the rainwood, but I've learned that most stay in the cities."

"And you wonder why my people live as we do."

Farah rolled her eyes. "Don't try and be high and mighty. There are no elves in your village."

"Your people outnumber mine, what? Twenty to one? Thirty? Try to imagine if your kind were the ones in the minority." He pushed off the wall. "We should go down."

He went to the door, but she stopped before the mirror and tidied her hair. Rohan waited while she washed her face and hands. Then they made their way downstairs together. Voices reached them as soon as they left their chamber, and by the time they were on the stairs, he could smell the food. They followed both to the center of the building. The dining area sat at the back beneath a soaring, open-air ceiling and arched windows covering three walls, with latticework at the very top. Vines with deep green leaves the size of his hand grew along the arches and the short, two-foot wall.

Six large, amber-colored sconces hung from the beam to illuminate the room. The rectangular table with its live edge was large enough to seat everyone. The chair backs were crafted to look like leaves joined together, and the legs like twisted vines. Sun filtered through the windows, displaying breathtaking patterns on the planked wooden floor.

"You found us," Rashmi said as she entered the room from a side door carrying a bowl. "Please, sit anywhere you like."

Halima hurried out carrying a platter of food. "In the middle so everyone can see you. Right here," she said after setting down the tray.

Rohan walked to the table and waited for Farah to join him. "Is there anything we can do to help?"

"I'll be happy to carry in food," Farah offered.

"Not today. Sit back and enjoy," Rashmi said before disappearing again.

Farah looked at Rohan before she pulled out the chair and sat. He did the same as he looked toward the doorway where all the conversation was coming from. No sooner had he gotten comfortable than others came out carrying more food. Within moments, everyone took their seats. He counted six human women and four men. As for the elves, there were three Sun, three Wood, two Moon, one Star, and one Sea.

Introductions were made, but the names went right out of Rohan's head. He was too busy gauging each couple instead of paying attention to the introductions as they passed the food around.

"So," a male Moon Elf said. "How long have you two been together?"

"Seems like just the other day," Rohan replied.

One of the human women asked, "How did you two meet?"

Farah had just taken a bite of food and shot him a quick glance. He saw the flare of worry in her eyes regarding what he might say.

Rohan bit back a grin and wiped his mouth with the napkin. "Let's just say there were sparks."

She choked on her food. He grinned and lightly patted her on the back as the others *oohed* and *ahhed*.

22

Being undercover was her job, and yet Farah couldn't settle into this new role. Rohan, however, was a natural. She reached for a goblet and some liquid to coat her throat, but as she gulped it, she realized too late it was wine.

Farah found herself coughing again, her eyes watering. Someone took the cup and replaced it with another. This time, she tested the contents. The moment she found it was water, she let the cool liquid slide down her throat. She dared to lift her gaze only when she had herself under control.

She hadn't heard anything as she was hacking up her lungs, but Rohan had obviously said something. Everyone at the table was focused on him. Farah, too, found her gaze locked on his profile. His blinding smile and easy manner mesmerized her, but his laugh took her aback. The sound was warm and genial, so at odds with the man she had seen before. It seemed Rohan had many sides. What other things might he be hiding?

Farah caught herself and looked away. Her eyes clashed with

Rashmi's. She was the only one who looked at her instead of Rohan. Farah was sure she hadn't given anything away, but it was still unsettling. For her part, Rashmi wore a soft, almost wistful smile as if she knew something Farah didn't.

Thankfully, the conversation turned to other things. Farah went back to her food while studying those around the table. Out of everyone, the sight of the male Sea Elf was the most surprising. She wanted to ask how he and the very pretty, petite blonde by his side had met. The adoring looks they shared made something pull in Farah's heart. Their hands were joined on the table like they couldn't get enough of each other.

She knew love existed. She had seen it. But...this was something different. It was unbridled and visceral, electrifying and sweeping. Almost as if their love was so great it couldn't be contained. And they weren't the only ones. She observed the other couples and found varying degrees of the same. The passion, the all-consuming desire.

The longing.

What would it feel like to have a love like that? To crave someone that deeply and have them return that need? When Nitya vanished, Farah had stopped thinking about any kind of life ahead. Everything revolved around finding her sister. Farah had lost more than her future. She had lost friends who hadn't understood why she couldn't accept what had happened. She distanced herself from others—including her family—because it was easier. And if she wasn't close to anyone, then it wouldn't hurt so deeply if she lost them.

What had she gained from such drastic and damaging actions? Absolutely nothing but loneliness and soul-breaking solitude.

A round of boisterous laughter pulled her from her thoughts.

She glanced at Rohan to find his head back as he chuckled. He fit in well, and his ease while pretending was far above hers. He'd make a good agent. Not that he would work for the DIA. He wanted nothing to do with elves, but he didn't seem to hold a grudge against any non-humans at the table.

"Oh, I have it," Halima said. "The first kiss. Remember ours, baby?" she asked Rashmi.

Rashmi caressed her face. "Do I ever."

Farah stilled. Obviously, she should've been paying attention.

"Aye. A kiss means everything," a human man at the other end of the table said.

A male Wood Elf on Farah's left turned to the woman beside him. "After ten years, I still sweep Khushi off her feet."

Then, he promptly demonstrated by pulling her against him and kissing her passionately. It was filled with such yearning that it made Farah uncomfortable to watch them. But she couldn't look away. That longing pulled at her heart again.

The table erupted in cheers when the two ended the kiss, each breathless, their eyes glittering with desire.

As if on cue, each couple took turns kissing. Unease filled Farah as she watched it happen around the table. Rohan's celadon eyes cut to her for a heartbeat. She kicked his foot to get his attention, but he wouldn't look at her. Panic began spreading through her. She would make a scene if she got up and left. But if she stayed, she'd have to kiss Rohan.

An image of hard sinew and broad shoulders flashed in her head, followed by him carrying her up the cliff. Then him falling asleep with his head on her lap.

She realized everyone was looking at her, waiting. Her training told her to just go with it. They were playing characters. If he could so easily slip into his role, so could she. She had done much worse than press her lips against someone else's. But that someone hadn't been Rohan.

Heat stole through her when she felt his gaze. She turned her head to him. He wasn't smiling anymore. She sat frozen, her heart thudding in her chest as he leaned forward. The tips of his fingers touched her neck before sliding around to the back and threading into her hair. Then his mouth was on hers.

His lips were soft as they touched hers once, then twice. The third time he angled her head to the side and ran his tongue along the seam of her mouth. She parted her lips instantly, and his tongue slid inside to tangle with hers. She was unprepared for the riot of emotions that assaulted her, one after the other.

Blood rushed in her ears, silencing the world around her. Passion heated her veins and pooled at her center, turning into a needy ache. She was defenseless against his skilled mouth as he deepened the kiss. She reached for something to hold on to—and found him. Thick shoulders, strapping arms. And a hard chest. Every nerve ending sparked, making her body hum. When she felt him pulling away to end the kiss, she leaned toward him, not wanting the amazing feeling to stop.

Then, suddenly, his lips were gone. She blinked as cheers deafened her ears. But Rohan wasn't looking at her. He had dropped his arm and turned away, causing her hands to fall from him. She righted herself, still dazed and bewildered by her reaction. The couple next to her spoke. She forced a smile but couldn't make out their words. Her brain and body were still locked in that kiss. A kiss she hadn't wanted. A kiss she believed she would regret.

But it was now seared upon her memory.

She wanted to touch her lips, but she kept her hands in her lap, just smiled and nodded. She even managed a laugh to keep up appearances, pretending they shared kisses like that all the time. Yet inside, she was alternatively trying to forget it and relive his touch and taste, over and over.

The meal went on for an eternity. When it finally ended, all she wanted to do was bolt. Instead, she and Rohan joined the others to help with the cleanup. At least with everyone involved, it went quickly. She was in her head and just wanted to be alone.

Drying her hands from the washing, Farah looked around and found Rohan walking outside with some of the men. Just as she was turning to retreat to her bedroom, she found Rashmi standing there.

"Everything all right?" the Sun Elf asked.

Farah nodded, plastering on a smile. "It's just been a long day. I didn't get much sleep last night."

"Then you'll want to retire to your room early. But first, let me show you something."

She wanted to decline, but how could she? They had welcomed her and Rohan into their home. The least she could do was see what Rashmi wanted to show her. "Of course."

They fell into step together as Rashmi led her out of the kitchen. "I hope we didn't overstep. We can be a lively bunch."

"It was fine. Really." It was so far from fine that it was in another universe, but Rashmi didn't need to know that. Neither did Rohan. As a matter of fact, it was better if they never discussed the kiss.

Rashmi shot her a grin. "I'm glad to hear it. I'm also glad you two decided to stay at Amberstar."

One of the things she hated about going undercover was encountering someone she liked but having to lie to keep herself and them safe. Farah couldn't think of a reply, so settled on a smile.

They fell into silence as they left the main building and entered a covered walkway leading to another structure. Large, smooth arches supported by thick columns were adorned with embellishments from the seven elven races as well as those of the humans. She paused beside a column with a winding leafy vine with flowers.

"There are over thirty columns," Rashmi said. "That isn't the only one dedicated to the Wood Elves."

Farah was so enamored with the etching in the stone that she didn't look away for several minutes. When she did, it wasn't to focus on the other columns, the etched walls extending above the arches, or even the carved ceiling. It was to take in the two pools of water and the sunlight spilling in to touch them. The largest was rectangular and sat to her left, surrounded by columns. The smaller was a square to her right. The floor was tiled with stone decorated with geometric patterns. Benches and daybeds overflowing with cushions and pillows were in the back amid more arches. And plants were everywhere she looked.

"The smaller pool is heated by a geothermal spring. I've left some drying towels and soap for you."

Farah swiveled her head to Rashmi. "This place is…"

"I know," the elf said. "Enjoy it for as long as you like. No one will disturb you."

"Thank you."

Rashmi smiled before turning on her heel and leaving. Farah didn't waste time getting out of her clothes. She found a bench near the small pool and placed her garments there so they wouldn't get wet. A tray of woven leaves sat at one corner of the water, filled with various soaps and bottled scents. Next to the tray was a basket with drying cloths.

Farah walked down the steps leading into the pool and descended into the water. The warmth was heavenly. It was a shallow pool, with water that only reached her thighs, but a built-in bench along the inner edge allowed her to sit and submerge herself up to her neck. She rested her head against the stones and let her muscles gradually ease.

Thoughts of Rohan and the kiss tried to invade, but she shoved them away. This was her time. She didn't want to think about the past or the future. She just wanted to be in the now. In the moment. She didn't have to pretend to be someone else or feel a certain way. She didn't have to guard her every word. She was just Farah again.

And that was something to enjoy.

23

ohan tuned out the others, letting his mind drift to the kiss. He still wasn't sure why he had done it. He could've gotten out of it if he wanted. Instead, he had leaned into the kiss. And stopping had taken every ounce of willpower he could muster.

He wanted to forget Farah's hands on his chest. He was desperate to wipe the memory of her taste from his mind. More than anything, he wished to erase the desire that had scorched his blood—and lingered.

The men and elves around him laughed, wrenching him from his musings. He lifted his gaze from the floor and smiled, but he wasn't listening. Soon, he made his excuses and walked away. Though to where, he didn't know. Did he search out Farah and discuss the kiss? Was it better to never speak of it? Maybe he should pretend it had never happened.

He entered the building through the back door and softly

closed it behind him. Halima was coming from the kitchen with a cup of tea.

"If you're looking for Farah, she's in the bathhouse," she said.

He hadn't been looking for her. What he *should* do is get some sleep before Farah returned. Yet even as his mind devised a plan, his mouth chose another. "Where is that?"

"Go around the corner to the hallway. It'll take you outside to a covered path. Follow it to the bathhouse."

Rohan tipped his head. "Thank you."

"You two look good together."

Halima's words drew him up short. He looked at her, unsure of what to say.

She grinned. "Sleep well."

Rohan watched her walk toward the sound of women's voices. He debated seeking Farah out, but in the end, he followed Halima's directions and made his way to the bathhouse. He wasn't sure if it was to talk about the kiss or what, but he had to see her.

His steps slowed as he approached the beautiful structure, listening. No sounds came from within. Maybe she had already left. He walked under one of the giant arches and swept his gaze to the pool. Then he scanned the interior and spotted the second reservoir—and Farah. She sat facing him, her head back and lids closed. His gaze dipped lower and took in the sight of her full breasts through the water.

Rohan turned his head to the side. He shouldn't be here. She likely wanted time alone. His appearance would only disturb whatever peace she had been able to find. Besides, what would he say? They were no longer enemies, but they weren't friends. He wasn't sure what they were. Enemies with a mutual goal? Allies, maybe—though that might be a stretch.

He silently retreated but didn't return to the main building. Instead, he walked off the covered path and along the edge of the glade. Fat drops of water landed on him before the skies opened. Within moments, he was soaked. He didn't withdraw indoors, preferring to remain outside alone with his thoughts and the rainwood.

He examined the various trees around him. How did Wood Elves live? *Where*, exactly? He wanted to see one of their settlements. It might give him some insight into Farah. Particularly why she was so willing to return to Mortham. She made it seem like she had no other options, but there were. Amberstar, for one. And the mountains. Neither might be what she wanted, but it was better than Mortham.

Yet if he talked her out of going back, he might never find Lata or his people. And if he believed Farah, he wouldn't want to locate them. People could overcome such trauma with gentle care, love, and understanding. Having them returned was better than losing them. But he had to admit that not everyone would be willing to go through the necessary—and difficult—steps to heal. He couldn't just let them go, though. He had a duty. One he took seriously.

Could he sacrifice Farah's life for those of his people and sister? A few days ago, the answer had come quickly and easily. Now, there was hesitation. He turned his head toward the mountains. He could no longer see the peaks through the trees. He should bring his people there. It would be a challenging and demanding life, but it had been difficult when the Siguks had first chosen the coast as their home, too. It would be a completely different life in the frigid mountains, and they would have to learn everything anew, but they would be free of the elves. Well, most of them. But he'd heard the Mountain Elves kept to themselves.

It was a better solution than sailing off to find new land. He knew nothing about building a ship or how long it would take to reach a new shore. He hadn't considered the mountains before, but the more he thought about it, the better it sounded.

There was also the option of going over the mountains and finding a new home outside Shecrish.

Rohan shook his head, mentally chiding himself. He would likely never convince his people to leave, no matter what destination he chose. But neither could they stay. Some hard choices would have to be made—particularly by him.

He ran a hand down his face and realized it had stopped raining. Water dripped from the leaves, plopping onto the ground. Animal calls he had never heard before filled the air. He had lumped all elves into the unpleasant category but learned that was shortsighted and small-minded. Time with Farah, as well as seeing humans living with—and loving—elves, had given him a new perspective.

"We were wondering where you went."

He turned and found Rashmi walking toward him. "Just admiring the view."

"It's a good thinking spot. I've used it myself a time or two." She came to stand beside him and admired the towering trees, her hands clasped before her.

He waited for her to say more. When she didn't, he turned his gaze to the rainwood. "You've created a beautiful place."

"I think so. For however long we have it."

"You think you'll have to leave?"

She lifted a shoulder. "I hope not, but we'll do whatever we must."

"Where would you go?"

"I don't know." Rashmi looked at him, her gaze direct and probing. "Where will you go?"

Rohan hesitated, shocked by her question.

She smiled softly. "You've posed two questions, asking what *I* would do. Not what *we* would do."

"I meant nothing by that."

Rashmi faced him and released a breath. "Do not worry yourself about us. We have things well in hand. However, there is another matter we need to discuss."

"What's that?"

"Farah."

Rohan stiffened. He was immediately wary. Maybe she had been right, and they should've stayed away. "What about her?"

"There's no need to get defensive. If I wanted to harm her, I would've turned her over to the elves hunting her."

"You know who she is?" he asked, doing his best to keep his voice calm while attempting to discern what she wanted.

Rashmi nodded. "I do, indeed."

"There's a large reward. I don't know many who would let that go."

"Then you might need to reevaluate who your friends are." Rashmi shook her head. "I'm not in the habit of helping the Masters or anyone affiliated with them."

He looked into her amber eyes and frowned. "Even if it brings them down on you?"

"We might live away from others, but don't let that fool you into thinking we can't—or won't—defend ourselves. We saw you coming our way hours before you reached us."

"Ah," he said as it dawned on him. "Your Wood Elves."

She nodded, grinning. "They are good at what they do."

"Does everyone know who Farah is?"

"We do. It was a mutual decision to allow both of you within our walls."

Rohan briefly looked away. They knew Farah's identity, but that didn't mean they knew their involvement—or lack thereof. "Why? You'd be better off never showing yourselves. Farah didn't want to come inside."

"There comes a time when individuals must take a stand. This was our time. Now, it's your turn. Why did you wish to be at Amberstar?"

"We were chased and had a rough night. I had a bad hit to the head that prevented me from traveling. Farah left me to find some herbs. I wanted to give us time to form a plan and get a decent night's sleep."

"Do you have a plan?"

A brightly colored bird flew overhead. "Sort of."

"Have you considered that perhaps this is where you're supposed to be? You and Farah fit in well."

"I appreciate the invitation, but it isn't possible. I have duties I need to return to."

She quirked a brow. "Is that where you two were headed? Never mind. Don't answer that. I'd rather not be lied to. Do you know why Farah is being hunted?"

"I do."

"And you remain with her instead of leaving her?"

Rohan stared at the Sun Elf, trying to figure out where she was going with these questions. "We have a mutual destination."

"I see."

"I'll leave you to your spot."

He only got a few steps before she said, "Trousers to match your tunic are in your room."

Rohan paused and looked back at her, but there was no censure in her words or expression. He nodded and continued walking. Of course, they had seen Farah steal the clothes. The Wood Elves at Amberstar must be very skilled indeed if Farah hadn't spotted them. He entered the building and headed up the stairs to the room he shared with Farah.

He knocked once before entering. She sat on the bed, braiding her wet hair. Her gaze briefly met his before sliding away. He found the trousers, just as Rashmi had said. Rohan gathered them in his hands, thinking about his conversation with the Sun Elf.

"They know who you are," he said.

Farah's fingers stilled, but she still didn't look at him. "What do you mean?"

"The other Wood Elves tracked us to Amberstar. They agreed to allow us entry."

"Okay."

He cleared his throat and looked at the pants again, then his gaze lifted to her. "Rashmi saw your picture. They know you have a price on your head."

"Then we should leave." Farah tied off the end of the plait with a strip of material before she turned to him. "Immediately. This could be a trap."

"I don't think it is."

She got to her feet. "You said they know the Masters want me. I'm not going to wait around to be taken."

"If it was a trap, why would Rashmi divulge what she knew? From what I gathered while talking to her, they've taken a stand against the Masters. They've offered us refuge."

"They've known all along?" Farah asked softly, her forehead puckered in a frown.

Rohan swallowed and nodded. She was putting things together as he had. He waited for her to bring up the kiss. To his surprise, she didn't.

"We've rested and eaten. We should leave. Now. Before anyone returns."

"You still want to head to the fort?"

Her shoulders dropped as she sighed. "We've been over this."

"I can't figure out why you want to go back. You have a chance to stay hidden here. You could even go into the mountains."

"As I've said, it's the—"

"One place they won't look for you," he said over her. "I know. Now, tell me the real reason. Because I'm having a hard time believing you wouldn't find an alternative to being in Mortham for the rest of your days."

Farah turned to face the window and wrapped her arms around her middle. "I don't like the cold, and that's all there is in the mountains. And this place won't be safe for long. They'll raid it and likely take everyone here."

He nodded. He should've known she wouldn't open up. It still upset him.

"Why do you care?" she retorted. "It's almost as if you're trying to talk me out of going. And that doesn't make sense considering everything you've done to force me to return."

She was right about all of it. He had kidnapped her for the purpose of using her to find Lata. Farah was freely giving him precisely what he had threatened her with and blackmailed her to do. That should be enough.

If only it was.

He turned on his heel and left the room. Being near her was too disruptive. He walked to the bathhouse and, to his delight, found it empty. He stripped and laid his clothes across a bench to dry, then entered the small pool and glided across from one side to the other before ducking under the water. He surfaced and shook the hair from his face before situating himself in the corner.

24

The Crossing

Reva searched the shadows for Dain. She kept hoping he would return to either the pub or her flat, but she hadn't seen him since he suddenly—and unexpectedly—ended their association.

She had disappointed him somehow, and that didn't sit well with her. Dain was...well, he was many things. Mostly, he was difficult to decipher. The elf kept his expressions closely guarded. There was a brashness about him, a certitude that she hadn't encountered before. Not once had he looked at her as inferior. He must have thought she was adept, or he wouldn't have asked her to listen for information.

It would be easy to hate elves for what they had done to her in the past, but then there were those like Sidiq, who had given her a chance and hired her. Arya, who had befriended her when they were both captured. And even Jai, who had helped her escape.

And last but not least, there was Dain. He had rescued her, only to offer her a job.

Sure, there were cruel, depraved elves. But there were also good ones. She had been fortunate to find a few of them. That's why it troubled her to fall short of Dain's expectations.

Reva set down her half-empty mug, but the edge of the cup hit the bar. It slipped from her fingers and banged loudly on the wooden bar, spilling the contents. "Shite," she hissed as she quickly set aside her packed tray to clean up.

Sidiq beat her to it. He casually wiped up the ale before it dribbled onto the floor. She had been clumsy of late, and they both knew it. It was her fault. She needed to stop looking for Dain. The extra coin had been nice, but she had relished the idea of doing something that mattered and being a part of something important instead of just being a server.

"Want to talk about it?"

She looked up into Sidiq's gray eyes. His hands were braced on the bar as he leaned into them. Of all those in Shecrish, he had arguably given her the most. She'd had to convince him, but he had taken a chance on her when no one else would. He never asked about her past or delved into her personal life. Yet he made sure she was safe while inside the walls of the pub. He made sure all his employees were.

Reva shook her head and shoved a wayward strand of hair from her eyes. She shoved it back and adjusted one of the pins that held the mass off her neck. "Nothing to discuss. I'll be more careful."

"Is it one of the customers?" he asked, his voice pitched low so as not to be overheard.

Those in the pub occasionally tried to manhandle her. Some

pubs allowed it, but not Sidiq. It didn't matter if they were human or elf. He put a stop to such things immediately.

She shook her head and gave him a smile. "I'd tell you if there was."

He straightened and tossed down the wet towel before getting another and flipping it over his thick shoulder. A customer sat at the other end of the bar. Sidiq hesitated before dipping his chin to her and walking away. She sighed and put the dirty glasses on the bar to be cleaned, then carefully set the filled mugs on the tray and balanced it on her hand. Her gaze flicked to Sidiq. He poured a drink and scanned the tavern with a look, reminding her of how Dain used to scrutinize the room.

Reva inwardly groaned. She had to stop thinking about him and focus on making her way through the crowded room. It was one of their busiest times of the day, and there wasn't an empty table or chair. She handed out drinks to customers and moved on to the next table to take an order. It was then that she overheard a conversation between two Dark Elves—one male and one female.

"There's nowhere she can run where they won't find her," the female stated.

The male snorted, set down his mug, and swallowed. "Fuckin' Wood Elves don't belong in the Below."

"There's talk that Farah also blew up those two ships yesterday."

"I wish I was out hunting her," the male replied with a smirk. "I'd love to show her how we pay back such wanton destruction."

Reva filed the information away. It was important. Something Dain would want to know. She made her way to the bar and waited for Sidiq to finish serving a customer. He might know where Dain was, or, at the very least, be able to get a message to him so she could pass on what she'd learned.

When Sidiq approached, she saw a muscle jump in his jaw. He was an imposing elf, both in height and muscle. It was rare that he ever raised his voice. His looks stopped others in their tracks, but this quiet, seething rage was something she hadn't witnessed before. It gave her pause.

"What's the order?" he snapped, his eyes looking past her.

She glanced over her shoulder but saw nothing beyond the norm. Unless it was Dain. Hope leapt in her chest. She whirled around and asked, "Is it Dain? Is he here?"

Sidiq's gaze grew frosty. "I've not seen him."

"Oh." Reva regretted her words immediately.

"Why do you want him?"

She shifted uncomfortably under Sidiq's enraged glare. She had obviously made a mistake in mentioning Dain. She'd thought they were friends. Something else she had gotten wrong. So much for asking Sidiq to find Dain. "He's usually around. I haven't seen him in a few days."

Reva quickly spouted off the order in hopes of turning the conversation—and quelling Sidiq's anger. It worked.

She loaded up her tray again and headed onto the floor once more. She purposefully walked past the table with the two Darks, eager to hear more, but they had moved on to another topic. That didn't dissuade her, however. She kept her ears open, listening for anything about Farah, Wood Elves, and explosions. She managed to pick up a few other tidbits. They didn't seem important to her, but they might mean something to Dain.

It seemed the entire pub was tense. She didn't know what had set Sidiq off, but his mood didn't improve much for the rest of the night. It was just the two of them, so they kept busy. An hour before closing, Sidiq suddenly ordered everyone out. She was surprised but also pleased—she was exhausted. She hadn't thought that doing her job and looking for Dain while also eavesdropping on conversations would be so arduous.

She hid her yawn behind a hand as she stood against the wall and waited for the customers to leave. Once the tavern was empty, she began loading up her tray with mugs. She tried to catch Sidiq's eye, but he didn't look her way. He washed the cups with unusual force.

Maybe she wasn't the cause of his anger. He had seemed peeved before she asked about Dain. Someone else could have enraged him. But she couldn't be sure. She wanted to ask. Reva hated when something hung between her and another. It was better to clear the air. The problem was that Sidiq clearly didn't want to talk. If she pushed the matter, it would likely only make things worse. And if he wasn't irritated with her now, he would be if she pried.

She wiped down the tables before starting on the floor. She couldn't stop yawning. Whenever she glanced at Sidiq, he was either cleaning or restocking the liquor from the back room. She walked by the door leading to the Below to lock it. Her hand hovered there as she realized she had a way to find Dain. It wasn't a very good one, but it was a way. If she couldn't ask Sidiq for help, there was Arya and Jai. Though they were hiding somewhere in the Below.

Which didn't do her much good. Besides, she was neither a Dark nor an elf. Walking around in the Below as a human on her own was just asking for trouble, and she'd had enough of that to last four lifetimes. Why risk her life for Dain when he had fired her? She locked the door and turned around. Sidiq stood behind her, watching.

"Everything good?" he asked.

"Aye. Why wouldn't it be?"

"I don't know. You tell me."

She had the distinct feeling he knew exactly what she had been thinking while staring at the door. Reva flashed him a quick grin and walked around him. "What about you? Everything good on your end? You shut down early."

"It was too busy."

His words drew her up short. She spun to look at him, confused. "That's normal for this time of the week."

"I'll be hiring someone else to help out."

There were two other servers besides her. They all worked solo except for a few hours when their shifts overlapped. What he suggested would take away her hours, which meant less money. First, Dain had fired her, and now Sidiq didn't think she could handle the workload.

Distress curdled her stomach. "If you're concerned about me not being able to handle it, don't. I've never had a problem before. I was just a little off tonight. I'll be better tomorrow."

"This isn't about your performance," he replied.

His expression wasn't as rigid, and his words were softer, but she didn't believe him. The timing of it all was suspicious.

Sidiq continued. "Profits have been good. I intend to share that with you and the others beginning tomorrow."

"I'm sorry?"

"I'm giving you a raise."

Reva frowned. "A raise?"

"You've more than earned it." He walked to the bar and finished putting bottles on the shelves along the back wall.

Reva slowly followed, still holding the broom. "Thank you."

"It's just business. When it's good, I reward people," he said, looking at her in the mirror.

She couldn't believe she was getting more money. She should be rejoicing, but something didn't sit right with her. It would be wrong to question him further, though. Sidiq might take it the wrong way. Oh, who was she kidding? There was only one way to take it if she asked.

Her mind turned everything over as she finished sweeping the floor. She put the broom away in the stock room and stared at each of the shadows, hoping Dain would appear in one. But none of them moved. She walked out, hating the dejection swelling in her chest.

"Do you need any help?" she asked Sidiq as she approached the bar.

"I'm almost done. Go ahead and call it a night," he said as he glanced her way.

She waved at him. "See you tomorrow."

Reva collected the small bag she carried that held keys to the lock on the door to her flat, courtesy of Dain. She left the tavern and walked into the night. Rannora's streets always teemed with people. The Crossing was popular, and because of that, people braved the not-so-great part of the city to visit.

She scanned her surroundings, looking for anything and anyone who might try to cause her trouble as she headed toward her building. It was close by, just around the corner, but that didn't mean it was safe. There were dangers everywhere. Even the elite were being abducted, which put everyone on alert.

It hadn't been that long since she and Arya had been taken from right outside the tavern. There were days Reva couldn't believe they had gotten free. She had gone into the Lotus River and braved the terrors of that water, only to face even more on shore. Dain had found her and brought her home before returning to help Arya and Jai.

That wasn't the first time she'd been held against her will, and she swore it wouldn't happen again. But it had. It was also likely to occur a third time. The last time, she'd been taken by mistake. They were after Arya, but she had seen the whole thing, so they took her, too. No amount of protection or magic could keep you safe if someone wanted to take you.

That's why she liked being at the tavern. It was too busy for anyone to grab her. The same couldn't be said about the short distance she walked to and from her flat, or even within her small home. She didn't linger on the streets. She kept a brisk pace and hurried to her building until she heard a grunt behind her.

Reva whirled around, her hand curled into a fist, but there was no one there. She spun and raced to her flat.

Dain let the shadows fall away as he held the Dark against a wall by his throat. He waited until Reva was inside the building before turning his attention to the male. "Your mistake was targeting her."

Dain broke his neck and let him fall to the ground. He gathered his shadows and moved into the building in time to see Reva's key turning the lock. She slipped inside and shut the door, the click of the lock following a second later.

He didn't go inside using his shadows anymore. Not after he'd put wards on her door and the outside of her windows to ensure no Dark Elf could intrude upon her space without her knowing. Dain stared at her door, picturing Reva setting her purse down and then preparing a cup of her favorite herbal tea she drank before bed.

With one final look, he let the shadows close around him and left.

25

Farah woke as the first rays of the morning sun streaked through her window. She rolled onto her back and looked at the other side of the mattress, but it was empty, the covers unmoved. Rohan hadn't returned to the room. She sat up and swung her legs over the side of the bed, a mix of irritation and unease rolling through her.

So what if he slept elsewhere? She hadn't wanted to share a bed with him anyway. Why, then, was she annoyed that he hadn't returned? Had he gone back to Kalyani and his people? Nay. He'd had plenty of chances to leave. He hadn't gone anywhere—not when he wanted to get into Mortham so badly. Yet it was obvious he didn't want to be near her.

Farah released a long breath and rose to her feet. She walked to the window and looked outside to see Rashmi and Halima doing stretching poses together. They moved slowly and in harmony as if they shared one body, one mind. Farah felt that pang in her chest again. She turned away and dressed. She hadn't gotten the restful sleep she had hoped for, but the reprieve at Amberstar had been interesting. It was time to leave, however.

After she washed her face, she loosened her braid and combed her hair. As she looked at her reflection in the mirror, she took in her red hair, pointed ears, hazel eyes, and freckles. When she was younger, she was a dreamer, always imagining the future and its many possibilities. Every scenario had been safe and happy. There hadn't been heartache or danger. There certainly hadn't been any thoughts of running for her life or becoming a spy.

But children knew little of the real world. It had been so long since she had tried to imagine a future of any kind that she could no longer conjure dreams or plans other than finding Nitya. And look where that had gotten her. She wondered what her parents would say if they could see her now. They probably wouldn't recognize her. She certainly didn't.

She parted her hair to one side and gathered the thickest section into a braid. Once that was completed, she gathered some of the other side behind her head and fastened the sections together. It had been Nitya's favorite hairstyle. With one final look in the mirror, Farah walked out of the room.

Amberstar was hushed, the residence just coming awake as others began moving about. She walked silently past on her way to the stairs and descended to the ground floor. Her gaze scanned for Rohan. All the rooms were supposedly taken, so where had he slept?

She headed toward the kitchen and glanced out one of the back windows. That's when she saw him speaking to one of the other human men. They shared a smile and a laugh. She halted to watch him. He was relaxed. Comfortable. Looking almost as if he belonged.

Rohan suddenly looked up. Their eyes met, but he quickly looked away. Farah lowered her gaze to the floor for a heartbeat before continuing on to the kitchen, where she heard voices. She walked in and found several members already there.

"Good morning," Rashmi called in greeting.

Farah smiled. "Morning."

"Did you sleep well?" one of the human females asked.

Farah tried to remember her name but was coming up blank. "I did," she lied. She made her way to Rashmi. "Why didn't you tell me you knew who I was?"

"I already explained to Rohan. If I had, you wouldn't have come inside."

"Thank you for your silence."

Rashmi tilted her head forward.

"And I need to apologize for stealing the clothes."

The Sun Elf grinned and waved away Farah's words. "Think nothing of it. You had a need. We've all been in such situations before."

Farah glanced away. "Thank you." She looked around the kitchen to the others trying not to eavesdrop and raised her voice. "All of you. Your generosity and kindness mean more than you could know. But it's time we left."

"I expected that." Rashmi handed Farah a bag filled with food. "Return anytime. Both of you," she said, looking over Farah's shoulder.

Farah turned and saw Rohan standing at the kitchen's entrance. She faced Rashmi and took the bag, wondering how much Rohan had overheard.

Rashmi turned to her, guiding Farah out a back door. "You're both welcome to stay longer. And I mean it about returning."

"The charity we found here has been incredible. I wish nothing but good things for all of you."

Rashmi stopped and faced Farah, taking one of her hands into hers. "And us, you. Be careful out there. It's a dangerous world we live in."

"Sadly, I'm all too aware."

Rashmi bowed her head, released Farah's hand, and walked away. Farah looked for Rohan but didn't see him. She shifted her feet restlessly. Her attention diverted when she felt a presence above her. She looked up and found one of the Wood Elves descending the tree. She couldn't recall his name either. She should've paid better attention.

He landed silently beside her and shoved long strands of red hair from his face as he straightened. "Things look clear so far."

"I take it you were one of the ones following us yesterday?"

He grinned. "I also distracted the elf warriors."

"Thank you. I thought for sure they were going to find us."

"They keep me on my toes, but I enjoy it. Which direction are you headed?"

A small group of coorodas howled as they swung from tree to tree, using their long arms and tails. She briefly watched them. "Rannora."

"The city is the last place you should be. There'll be many spies there."

"I don't have a choice. I must deliver something."

He quirked a brow. "Will you give Durga a message for me?"

Farah stilled when he mentioned her supervisor.

"She's my cousin," he explained. "We trained together for many years, and you have the look of one of her agents."

Revealing her status within the DIA to anyone went against everything Farah had learned.

"No need to say anything," he told her. "When you see Durga, tell her Jothi is well. She was instrumental in helping us put this place together."

Farah shouldn't have been surprised to hear that.

Jothi handed Farah a small vial. "This is from a stash Durga gave me the last time we saw each other. It will transform you into a human for a time. That should make it easier for you to move about the city."

"Thank you," she said, closing her hand around the pale yellow liquid.

Jothi put his hand on her back and guided her down a narrow path. His voice dipped low, and he grew serious. "Keep close to the mountains and move quickly. When you reach the river, don't cross at the rope bridge."

"It's the safest place to cross. The rapids elsewhere are too strong."

"True, but there's another section that few know about. Head east but keep to the thickest trees. Bands of hunters watch the river. After the second bend, look for the flat boulder. When you get there, it's a tight squeeze through two rocks. Then, you'll see a rope stretched across a narrow channel. I strung it and have traversed it several times. Bear in mind that you'll get wet, but no one watches that area. Keep a hold of the rope because if the water sweeps you away, you'll be in the rapids. I'll track you as far as I can in case you run into trouble."

She nodded and filed his words away. "And after the river?"

"You'll be in Bapun territory. There are rumors they're working with the Masters."

"In other words, we need to get through that area quickly."

Jothi dropped his hand from her back and halted. "You made it here. You can get to the city."

Before she could respond, Rohan walked up. He and Jothi nodded at each other in greeting.

"Good luck," the elf said before climbing the nearest tree.

Farah watched him for a moment, then looped the bag strap over her head and across her chest, tucking the tonic safely inside amid the clothes and food. She settled the sack against her hip so she could adjust it to her front or back as needed. Finally, she looked at Rohan. He had also been given a bag of supplies, and he now had a dagger strapped to his leg.

"Ready?" she asked.

He dipped his chin in reply.

She pressed her lips together. "We're going to move fast and quietly."

"I'll keep up."

He wasn't exactly curt, but he wasn't friendly either. Rohan was his usual self. That shouldn't have come as a surprise, but it somehow did. All because of that damn kiss. That had altered everything, and she didn't like it.

"Whenever you're ready," he said.

Farah looked toward the building and saw the rest of the group gathered there. She lifted a hand in farewell, then found the nearest tree Rohan could scale. He managed well in the trees but couldn't climb like a Wood Elf.

She found one of the thream trees with its big, thick, low-hanging limbs. She got a running start and put her foot on the lowest branch before launching herself to the next. Then she jumped onto the subsequent limb and looked back in time to see Rohan perfectly mimicking her movements.

Farah climbed higher. Some of the branches were close enough that she could step, but she had to jump and grab a few with her arms before pulling herself up. Eventually, they reached the height she wanted. She headed toward the edge of the rainwood to heed Jothi's advice.

She didn't look for him. He would keep hidden unless he had to show himself. She thought of the vial he had given her. It just might be what got her to Durga. Farah halted all thought and looked ahead at the trees. She took a deep breath and set out.

26

Rohan tried to pop his neck before following Farah to the next tree. It had a crick from his long, uncomfortable night sleeping on the sofa. He'd had several of those now. He'd made the decision not to sleep in the cozy bed. Not that Farah missed him. She'd probably slept through the entire night without noticing he wasn't there.

He wobbled on his next landing and lifted his arms to the sides to find his balance. In that time, Farah had gained ground. Or branches. He'd known he would fall behind, but he hadn't thought it would happen so quickly. There was no use struggling to catch up. She was too nimble, and he was as gangly as a baby. Yet he managed to hold his own.

He swept his gaze to the next tree, gauging the distance he needed to jump. The limb hadn't moved beneath Farah, but she weighed nothing. It would likely bend under his weight. That meant he had to leap sooner. All of this went through his head in a split second as he moved around the trunk and took two running steps across the branch before vaulting himself into the air.

This time, he landed solidly. They couldn't run flat out in the trees. That saved his stamina for jumping. Especially the big gaps. He noticed that Farah avoided some he probably wouldn't get across. If she wanted to be rid of him, all she had to do was make him believe he could cross a section and watch him fall to his death.

But she didn't. Just as she hadn't let him die from his head injury or be found by those men.

He gripped the next trunk to move around it and scraped his palm near his thumb. Rohan winced and shook out his hand. He looked ahead to where Farah had paused, waiting for him. She squatted next to a trunk and gazed out at the rainwood. It wouldn't matter how many times he saw her in her element, it would always make him pause and stare.

Rohan hurried to catch up. She straightened and continued as soon as he reached her. They were high enough in the canopy that most birds were below them. A few were curious enough to venture up to see what they were doing, but somehow, he and Farah never startled them.

She diverted around a group of dark-furred coorodas resting in a tree along their path. Some were sleeping, others eating. The ones that were awake watched him and Farah with interest. He knew little about the animals, but they were as skilled in the trees as Farah.

They moved past the primates with ease. Farah didn't slow. She must have known something he didn't. He was breathing heavily, his limbs tiring, when she finally stopped and sat against a large trunk. The bark was smooth beneath his palm as he lowered himself to the limb and leaned back. He drew out a water flask and gulped half the contents, rubbing his forehead against his shoulder to wipe the sweat away.

The mountains were in full view now. He watched the strong wind around one of the peaks drag snow into the air, then looked to the side toward Farah. Her eyes were closed. His gaze dropped to her mouth as memories of their kiss assaulted him. With an internal curse, he yanked his attention away.

After another five minutes, Farah got to her feet. She didn't even look his way before setting out again. Time ceased to exist. It was only the tree he was on and the one he needed to get to, over and over again. Sweat ran down his back and into his eyes. There was no time to look up and see where the sun was. There was only the next branch.

It was only by accident that he looked up in time to see an arrow aimed at Farah. She leaned back and sideways to avoid it, but it put her off balance. Rohan dove as she toppled to the side, landing on his stomach atop the limb to grab her hand. The branch swayed, and the leaves rustled. But no more arrows flew in their direction.

He looked down at Farah. Her eyes were locked on him as she dangled. Rohan felt her slipping. He had to get her up before he lost his grip, but he didn't know if their enemies were waiting to strike. Slowly, after he'd hooked the toe of his boot onto a part of a broken limb, he pulled her up.

She never made a sound. Not when she saw the arrow or when she fell. Nor, he realized, had she used magic to stop her descent. He moved onto his knees when he got her close enough and could finally sit her next to him. That's when he saw the slice in her sleeve by her left shoulder. She had gotten out of the way, but barely.

"Where are they?" he whispered.

Her face was pale as she shrugged. She shifted so she was against the trunk. *"We can't remain here,"* she mouthed.

Rohan looked across the limb she had been on to the next tree. If they stood, they would be exposed. But if they remained, they would likely be found. He pointed down. She shook her head. He pointed up. She followed his finger and stared for a long moment. Her nose wrinkled as she met his gaze. Those were their only choices, and she knew it.

Her head suddenly snapped to the side. He followed her gaze but saw nothing for several seconds. Then he made out someone moving toward them.

"Keep going," she whispered. "I'm going to wait."

And attack. It was a good plan. Usually, he led the assault, but this wasn't his territory. He got to his feet, and she rose with him.

Farah moved closer to keep her voice low and said, "Keep going straight. I'll catch up. Don't stop. Keep moving."

It felt wrong to leave her. The argument died on his tongue when he saw their attacker getting closer. Rohan raced across the limb and jumped. He waited to feel the sting of the arrow puncturing his flesh, but nothing happened. He landed and moved on to the next limb. His ragged breathing kept him from hearing anything behind him, and he wanted to stop and see if Farah had defeated their foe, but he didn't.

He didn't slow until his muscles began to weaken, and he tripped. His legs trembled as he made it to the trunk and pressed his forehead against it. He looked over his shoulder. Someone was following. If it wasn't Farah, he needed to prepare for a fight in the trees.

Rohan turned to wait. As the figure drew closer, he saw Farah's mussed hair and a smear of blood on her cheek. He eyed her when she halted before him, looking for injuries.

"We can't stop," she said in a low voice, even as she bent over and braced her hands on her knees.

"Are you hurt?"

She briefly closed her eyes and shook her head. "I surprised her, but she was a fighter. We're nearing the river. The Masters have many spies in the area."

"Did she recognize you?"

Farah straightened. "Maybe. I didn't ask."

"I take it we're crossing the river?"

"Not the usual way."

Rohan frowned in confusion. "You mean we're not swimming?"

"This river's current is much too swift for that. Large portions of it are nothing but rapids before it feeds into the Ever Reaching River. There's a bridge everyone uses. It's really the only way across."

Now, he understood. "There's another way."

"Apparently. Jothi told me how to get there. It'll be dangerous, but it will keep us away from others."

"Lead the way," he said with a sweep of his arm.

Farah moved around him. As she did, he saw a tear in the back of her shirt. Her clash with the other Wood Elf must have been brutal, but she had come out the victor. It either proved her strength or her ruthlessness. Somehow, in all of this, Rohan had forgotten where he had found Farah.

It didn't take them long to reach the river. He heard the rushing water before he saw it. She didn't take them directly there, though. They deviated to the right at a sharp angle. She took her time looking into the trees and across the ground before jumping to the next branch. It allowed him to peer through the limbs and see the wide river spilling into a small waterfall. The water churned wildly before it surged onward.

He heard voices and looked down to see a group of elves walking beneath them, headed toward the river. Rohan met Farah's gaze. They waited until the group was out of earshot before continuing on for another thirty minutes. Then they began their descent.

The river had appeared imposing from the trees, and it looked even more so from the ground. He grew more dubious about the plan as Farah mumbled under her breath while looking for something.

"Here," she called and waved him over.

Rohan followed her out of the trees toward a grouping of boulders. The river was so loud an army could be barreling toward him, and he'd never know it. Farah disappeared from sight before he reached the boulders. He frantically searched the water, thinking she had fallen in.

"This way!"

He swiveled his head at the sound of her voice and saw her through a narrow slit between two rocks. It was an impossibly tight squeeze. He got wedged in, not able to move either way. The boulders gripped his clothes and pulled, tearing them and scraping his fingers. Rohan wouldn't be stopped now, though. He kept trying to squeeze inside. Farah grabbed his arm and pulled. Together, they eventually got him out.

"This had better be the way," he told her. "Because I won't get through that again."

She twisted her lips. "I guess we'll find out."

They went around another boulder and found themselves at the river's edge. The bridge was a strip of rope that hung over a constricted part of the river. The narrowing only made the water rush quicker.

"Tell me there's another rope somewhere," Rohan said.

Farah shook her head. "Looks like that's it."

"That isn't a bridge."

"I wouldn't have called it that, but it's a way across."

Rohan looked to either side of them. The tapering river helped to shield them, but so did the boulders rising on either side. It was the perfect place to cross if you didn't want to be seen.

He gripped the rope with both hands and entered the cold water. It was over his knees in two steps. It coursed around him, soaking him from the spray and surge. The deeper he got, the stronger the current became. It didn't help that the river bottom was rocky. He fought to stay on his feet and not get his boots twisted between the rocks.

When he got halfway across, he looked back and saw Farah already in the river. He moved carefully, placing one hand and foot after the other, occasionally slipping on the slick rocks, until he reached the opposite shore. Relief filled him as he turned to check on Farah.

She was having a difficult time. The water kept sweeping her legs out from under her. The only reason she hadn't been dashed away was because of her grip on the rope. He watched as she unsuccessfully tried to get her feet onto the bottom. There was only one way she would get across. Him.

Rohan removed his bag and gripped the rope once more.

27

The water was frigid, and the current much stronger than Farah had anticipated. She hadn't gotten far before the rushing river knocked her feet out from under her. She gripped the rope tightly in response. It was the only thing that kept her from being dragged away.

The rope burned her palms as she frantically attempted to put her feet down. The more she tried, the more the rope dug into her hands and irritated the scrapes already there. She couldn't go forward, and she couldn't turn around. Nor could she let go. Her arms were weakening. Worse, her hands were beginning to slip. She looked up and saw red running down the outside of her hand. She called to her magic and watched green wrap around the rope to hold her.

"Farah!"

She looked over and saw Rohan entering the river again. He was too far away. Her magic wouldn't be able to hold out for that long. All she could think about was the information she had that wouldn't get to Durga.

"Don't you dare let go!" Rohan bellowed.

Farah looked at her hands. One had already begun to slip off, only her fingers gripping the rope. The other hand was starting to slide. She was a decent swimmer but not nearly good enough to survive the current or the rapids. Death by drowning. She supposed it was better than being tortured at Mortham.

"Look at me, godsdammit!"

Rohan was somehow standing before her. Her eyes burned with tears. He had come back for her.

His light green gaze held hers, refusing to let her look away. "Wrap your legs around my waist. Do it. Now!"

She tried to lift her legs, but it put too much pressure on her hands. Her magic faded, and one hand slipped off before she could call for more. Her heart hammered wildly, fear turning her blood to ice. Rohan's arm snaked out and grabbed her leg, hauling her against him. She instantly wrapped her legs and her free arm around him. He held her firmly as she buried her head against his neck, but she hadn't released the rope completely.

"You have to let go," he told her.

She couldn't imagine how difficult it was for him to stay standing with just one hand on the rope. The longer she held on, the worse it would be for both of them. She peeled her fingers off the rope and wound that arm around him, too.

"I have to let go of you now," he said.

Her limbs tightened. Then he had both hands on the rope. He didn't turn as she had thought he might. Instead, he walked backward. She locked her gaze on the shore as he methodically—and carefully—placed his feet on the rocky riverbed. She felt his muscles straining as he struggled to remain upright.

"Three more steps," she said as he neared the shore.

And then, they were out. He released the rope, wrapped his arms around her, and carried her to the boulder. He dropped to one knee, but she couldn't seem to make herself release him. He didn't rush her. Finally, she unhooked her ankles and lowered her legs to the ground. Then she loosened her arms. He guided her to sit.

"Bloody hell," he murmured as he grabbed her wrists and looked at the state of her palms. "Where are the herbs?"

She lifted her right hip and leaned back. "In the waistband of my pants."

He said nothing as he lifted her tunic and pulled the bottle from her waist. She missed his warmth the moment he moved away. She began to shiver and pulled her arms and legs against herself, careful to keep her palms up so they wouldn't touch anything. She watched Rohan retrieve his flask.

"How much of the herbs do I add?" he asked.

"A pinch should be fine."

His pinch was big, and then he added a little more before swishing it around in the flask and handing it to her.

Farah gripped it with her wrists and brought it to her lips. She hadn't thought she was thirsty until the water touched her tongue. She ended up drinking what remained, then held it out to him.

"Rest. I'm going to have a look around."

He was gone before she could reply. Farah scooted back against the boulder. The spray of the river continued to hit her, adding to her misery. Her wet clothes stuck to her and made her colder.

There was an itchy strand of hair stuck to her face. She unsuccessfully tried to move it with her shoulder.

First, the near hit with the arrow, then the fall, where Rohan had caught her. She hadn't used her magic, hoping to stay hidden, but that had been a bad decision. Then the fight with the Wood Elf, which had been intense. Farah had gotten in a lucky strike. It had knocked the elf to the side, causing her to hit her head at an odd angle. The sound of the bone breaking had been loud. Then came the river. And they still had much more ground to cover before they reached Rannora.

Rohan jumped from above and landed beside her. He squatted and grabbed his bag. "I found us a place to rest."

"We need to keep going."

"Neither of us is in any condition for that after that crossing. If we keep going, we're more likely to make mistakes."

She reluctantly nodded.

He took her arm and helped her to her feet. "It isn't far."

She leaned close when she felt his heat. It was like she had bathed in solid ice. He hadn't lied about it being close. The alcove of rocks was on the other side of the boulder. The problem was that they had to step into the river to get to it. Rohan never let go of her. He stayed with her, moving farther into the river, but she was glad to have him holding her.

He guided her to the back of the recess. An overhang of rock above her shielded them from the elements. He lowered her to the ground and dropped his bag beside her, then hooked his fingers into her bag's strap and lifted it over her hand and arm. He tossed it to the side with his. She gasped when she heard a clink. The vial was in there. If it broke...

"The bag. Open it," she said urgently. "Please," she added when he hesitated.

He leaned over and cautiously set it before her.

"There's a small vial I stuffed between some clothes. It's no bigger than your pinkie," she explained.

He dug into the pack for several moments as she held her breath. Finally, he lifted it, holding it between his thumb and middle finger. "This?"

"Aye." She sighed with relief.

He studied it as he set it in his palm. "What is it?"

Farah huddled against the rock, wishing the clothes in the bag were dry so she could change.

"Can we chance a fire?" Rohan asked.

She shook her head. "I'll warm up eventually."

He held up the vial again and raised a brow, waiting for an explanation.

"It's magic in liquid form. Well, a kind of magic," she said. "There are several different ones. It allows the person who drinks it to change their appearance."

His brows snapped together as he glanced at the liquid. "How?"

"Some would change me from a Wood Elf to a Sea Elf—any kind of elf, actually."

"How is that possible?"

She brought her legs closer to her center, resting the backs of her hands on her knees. "With magic and science. If a human drank it, it would change them into an elf."

He went utterly still. "You want me to change into an elf?"

"That doesn't hold the brew for an elf. It changes one to a human."

His gaze slid to the vial of pale yellow liquid before he looked at her again. "If it will disguise you, then why haven't you taken it?"

"Because it only lasts for a few hours. I need it for when we reach the city."

"Won't those looking for you suspect that you've used this?" he asked, holding it up.

She began to feel the magical herbs working to repair her palms. "That isn't something just anyone can purchase—or it isn't supposed to be. I heard whispers at Mortham that it was being sold at Shaldorn."

"Shaldorn?"

"It was a secret stronghold in the mountains where the depraved and corrupt went to play. A lot of horrendous things happened there, but that changed recently. Based on the rumors I heard while at Mortham, I believe the DIA had something to do with it."

He grunted. "I'm not sure it hurt the Masters as much as you might think."

"That much is obvious."

"You never considered going to the DIA to hide you," he pointed out.

She blew out a long breath. "Someone leaked my information to you. If you have it, then others will. I can't trust them."

"But you're returning to hand over information?"

"I am. I trust Durga. She wouldn't betray me. Not after what she did to get me inside Mortham."

"Is that why you joined the organization? To take down the Masters?"

Farah leaned her head back and closed her eyes for a heartbeat. "Something like that. My sister was abducted seven years ago. I went undercover to find her."

28

Rohan sat in stunned silence. A sister. It had never dawned on him to ask if anyone from her family had been taken. He'd been too intent on what he had lost to think of anyone else. And now he understood why she wanted to return to Mortham. She was looking for her sister, too. And he had taken her from the compound, threatened to expose her as a spy, and put her in the Masters' crosshairs.

"I'm sorry," he said.

"As am I for those taken from you."

There was a rumble above them. A moment later, it began to rain. He looked up at the dark skies as drops pelted his face.

"Sit here," Farah offered, nodding to the spot beside her. "It'll get you out of the rain."

His clothes were as soaked as hers. It didn't matter if a little rain got on him, but he moved beneath the overhang anyway. Because she'd offered. And maybe because he wanted a reason to sit next to her.

The area was cramped. Their shoulders brushed, even as she made room for him to settle. He pulled his knees up to keep his feet dry and rested his arms on them. The beat of the rain added to the rumble of the river. They sat in silence for long moments. He went over their conversations with the new information and inwardly cringed at how many times he had made an arse of himself.

"I never wanted to leave my village," Farah said suddenly. "I was happy there. The simple life appealed to me. But not Nitya. She was always exploring, always pushing the boundaries. She talked me into going to the coast once."

Rohan turned his head to her. She was staring out at the rain bombarding the river. A soft smile curved her lips.

"We were young. Too young. But where Nitya went, I followed. Even when it went against our parents' wishes. She wanted to see the ocean, and I wasn't about to be left behind. To this day, I still don't know how we made it through the territories without being seen. When we got back, our parents were beside themselves with worry. We were reprimanded, of course. But the sight of my mum's stricken face stamped out any need to do something so foolish again. Not Nitya, though," she finished in a soft voice. "It seemed to spur her on."

He tried to imagine a young Farah at the edge of the mesa, looking out over the coast. Had she seen him and Kalyani swimming? Had they seen any of the Siguks?

Farah glanced at him. "Nitya was always going off after that. Whereas I realized the harm I had done to our parents, our trip seemed to ignite something in her. She couldn't stand to remain at home. She would go off for days at a time without telling anyone.

It's why we didn't realize she was gone at first. We have no idea when she was taken or even where."

"Maybe she found somewhere else to live. Maybe she was never kidnapped," he offered.

"That's what my parents believe, but she wouldn't leave without telling me. She would have said goodbye. Others in our village have also vanished. Everything lined up. I know she was taken."

He released a breath as he leaned his head back to watch the rain. "And you couldn't let it go."

"We were as different as night and day, but we were close. She told me everything. If I had been abducted, I know she would've searched for me."

"What do your parents think about what you're doing?"

She shook her head. "I don't know."

"You didn't tell them?" he asked, rolling his head toward her.

Hazel eyes met his. "I told them I was going to Rannora. They know I'm looking for my sister, but they don't know about me working for the DIA. I was supposed to contact them before I went undercover, but I couldn't bring myself to do it."

"They didn't know about you being in Mortham?"

"They know none of it."

He frowned and returned his gaze to the river. "How close are we to your village?"

"It's days to the north."

"You should see them while you can. One day, they'll be gone."

She made a sound in the back of her throat. "I know. They've lost both their daughters in different ways. I never should've left, but I had to. Nitya is out there somewhere, and I can bring her home. I just need to find her."

"You believe she survived Mortham? Even after what you told me about the place?"

"I have to," she replied softly.

He knew that sentiment. He had been there himself. He was still there.

"Nitya was the strong one, the one who would've made something of herself. This," Farah said, motioning to herself, "is not where I was meant to be. Obviously, I'm not cut out for this kind of profession."

"Could've fooled me. I think you're more than qualified."

She chuckled. "I scrape by on sheer will alone."

"Sometimes, that's all we need."

There was a pause. When she spoke again, her voice was low and filled with despair. "I spent months in Mortham. I wanted to look for Nitya right away, but they scrutinized my every move. Watched me constantly. So, I settled into my role to prove myself to those watching. Days turned into weeks, weeks into months. Do you know what I have to show for my time there?"

Rohan swiveled his head to her. "What?"

"Nothing. Not a bloody thing. I watched innocents like you being led into Mortham and did nothing. I didn't release anyone. I didn't find out about my sister. I did exactly what was expected of me, and it...it changed me."

He waited for her to look at him, but she kept her gaze forward.

Her throat bobbed as she swallowed. "My handler was the captain of your ship. He wanted to get me out that day. He knew something wasn't right, but I couldn't leave. Not before I knew about Nitya. Plus, there were rumors of something big happening, and I wanted to gather more intel. At least that's what I told myself."

"What was the real reason?" he asked.

Her lips pressed together as her eyes closed. "There were two Dark with me, night and day. They said I was done observing. That if I was really part of Mortham, then it was time to prove it. I didn't want to hurt the woman, but I had run out of excuses not to take part in the beatings. She cowered from me afterward. But I can't unsee the blood on my hands."

"If you hadn't done what they asked, the Dark might have done worse to you. You said it yourself: They questioned your loyalties. You did what you had to do. And the woman lived."

"Being in Mortham changed me. If you hadn't taken me, I don't think I would've left."

He scratched his jaw through his beard. "You shouldn't go back."

Her eyes flew open, and she looked at him. "I must. Not just for Nitya, but also for your sister. Your people. I wasn't lying before. They'll never think to search for me there."

"You can't stay undetected forever. Someone will find you. You'd be better off at Amberstar or in the mountains."

"The Masters will find me wherever I go. I want to do some good before that happens."

He shook his head, his anger rising. "Right now, your parents have only lost one daughter. You're still alive. You can keep fighting without returning to the fort."

"What about Nitya? Your sister? The hundreds of others who are missing? This is how I'm fighting. It's just different than what you would do." She searched his face. "You can't sit there and tell me you've done everything you have only to give up now."

"I've not given up. We'll find another way."

"There isn't one."

He couldn't accept that. There had to be another way. Even if it meant somehow finding the elf who had helped him set the explosion.

"Tell me about your sister," Farah urged.

He ran a hand through his damp hair, his thoughts turning to Lata. "Mum died when I was ten and Kalyani was seven. Dad never grieved properly, not with taking care of us and leading our people. Long ago, he found where the infants were being left. He would go there and take any human infants he found."

"The Domestic Ministry wasn't involved?"

"I don't know what that is."

She raised her brows. "The governing body who decides which families get the children."

"Then, nay. My father decided."

"No one ever saw him take the babies?"

Rohan shrugged. "Not that I'm aware."

"I didn't think that was possible."

"All I know is that six months after Mum passed, he carried Lata through our door. She was different right from the start. There was a special quality about her that was hard to miss. She made Dad laugh again. They were very close. I asked him once why he'd chosen her for our family, and he replied that she chose us, not the other way around."

Farah looked at him in confusion. "What did he mean?"

"I never figured it out. He was supposed to show me where he found the infants so I could carry on growing our village, but he fell and struck his head. Not even the red seaweed healed him. He died without ever regaining consciousness."

"That's horrible. I'm so sorry. And you just had a head injury. That must have been frightening."

He twisted his lips. "I was in too much pain to think about it much at the time. Now, though…" He shrugged. "I can't help but make the correlation with Dad. If he would've had the herbs, he would've survived. I'm here because you got me those herbs in time."

She gave him a shy smile. "You loved your father very much."

"Everyone did. His death was a devastating blow to everyone. He was patient and wise. Everyone loved and respected him. He married late in life, and my parents lived alone for many years before Kalyani and I became part of their family."

"He sounds like a good man."

Rohan smiled, nodding. "He was the best. Mum, too. Lata was fourteen when he passed. She was inconsolable. I had moved into my own dwelling years before. Kalyani remained with Dad and Lata, and it seemed natural for Lata to remain with Kalyani. We both believed that keeping things the same was the best for her. But when Dad was gone, Lata grew wild. She had always been a free spirit, but she started acting out. Kalyani asked for my help. I moved Lata in with me, which only seemed to worsen things."

"She was grieving."

"Maybe for the first year. But the second?" He shook his head. "She actively did things to anger us. The sweet child we'd known was gone. She fought me at every turn for every little thing. Like your sister, she wanted to see the rest of Shecrish. Our village was too confining. I begged her to wait until she was older before she struck out on her own, believing she would grow out of it."

Farah wrinkled her nose. "They don't."

"I was tired of arguing, catching her in lies, and having to punish her for disobeying me. Nothing I did or said helped. The worst part is that I would've believed she ran away if someone hadn't seen her and her friends being taken the night they snuck out."

Farah gave him a soft smile. "We'll find her and the others."

"That thought is the only thing that has kept me going. But you said it yourself: It wouldn't be worth looking."

"Forget what I said. I'm going back for my sister, and it's been years."

He sighed and glanced away. "Am I wrong to do this? Kalyani begged me not to go. We're all that's left of our family, and I know there's a chance I won't come out of this alive. She may never know what happened to me or the others."

"Then go back to her."

"I can't do that."

"Aye, you can. I'll look for your people."

He blew out a breath. "You'll have more success with help."

"I can't deny that." She paused. "The abductions must be stopped."

"And you intend to be the one to do it?"

"Someone has to. Why not me?"

He twisted his lips. "I think you can do anything you put your mind to. Especially with someone watching your back."

"You have Kalyani and what's left of your people waiting for you."

"And you have your parents," he quipped.

She flattened her lips and sighed. "You don't have to do this."

"Neither do you. Like you, I want the Masters stopped. I may not have magic, but I have other skills. I'll use them." When she hesitated, he used his secret weapon. "I know an alternate way into Mortham. You're going to need that."

"Looks like we're a team, then," she replied with a frown.

He hid his grin. "You won't regret it."

Enemies to associates to...partners. It certainly wasn't how he'd expected things to turn out.

29

Farah finally stopped shaking at some point during the hour of constant downpour. Partly because Rohan was beside her and put off a lot of heat. She hadn't even tried to fight sleep. She jerked awake when her head began listing toward his shoulder. Things felt different between them now. Rohan's hostility had been tempered, but even she had to admit that'd happened before they reached Amberstar.

The main cause of the shift was likely their openness regarding their sisters. However, there was also an awkwardness that hadn't been there before. That was probably all her. She had kept him at arm's length, too afraid he might want to talk about that kiss.

And desperate to talk about it.

She looked at her hands to see they were nearly healed. The herbs had also returned much of her energy, which would make traveling for the rest of the day easier. They should leave now, but she couldn't make herself say the words or get to her feet. The silence was comfortable, the sounds of the rain and the river soothing.

Yet she couldn't stop thinking about Nitya. Seven years was a long time. Being in Mortham broke people. Even if her sister survived the compound, years spent enslaved could have broken her. On the slim chance Nitya had held on and lived, she wouldn't be the Nitya Farah knew. Her sister had died the day she was taken. In the back of her mind, Farah had always known that. Even if she couldn't admit it.

She was terrified to return to the fort, afraid of what she might become. But she had failed in her mission. Returning and doing what she had been sent to do might bring others peace and give the DIA an advantage in taking down the Masters. She wouldn't have much time there, though. If she stayed hidden, she could have years, but the places she needed to go to for information meant tripling her chances of being discovered.

She looked at Rohan. His head was back, his eyes closed. He appeared peaceful. It was an illusion—the same kind she created daily. Inside, she fought against the onslaught of remorse and regret. Rohan no doubt felt something similar. For him, it was about more than Lata. It was about dozens of his people.

When the rain finally tapered off, and the skies lightened, there was no longer a reason for them to tarry. For every hour she didn't reach Durga, others would be taken. That meant more lives on her head. There were already too many.

"How do they feel?" Rohan asked when she curled her hands into fists.

"There's only a slight pull."

"The storm has passed."

She climbed to her feet and looped her sack over her head. "Shall we?"

He said nothing as he stood and settled the strap of his bag across his chest. She looked back at the alcove as she walked away. It might be the last scrap of peace she ever had.

They had to climb to get over the rocky section. The chances of being spotted grew, which meant they had to stay low. Their green clothes stood out against the pale stone, but they would be back in the forest soon enough. Rohan once more proved how adept he was in navigating the treacherous rocks. He showed her how and where to place her hands and feet and what to look for as she made her way up and then back down. The boulders were slippery from the rain, but they both managed to get down without any injuries.

"Where do we go?" Rohan asked when they hurried into the forest.

"South. If we follow the river, we'll come to Carapid Lake, which turns back into the tributary again. That feeds into the Ever Reaching River that flows straight to Rannora."

He grunted. "We just follow the rivers, then?"

"Once we get to the Ever Reaching River, we'll have to decide whether to stay on this side or cross to the west."

"What difference does it make?"

She looked around to see if anyone was around as she stayed near the trunk of a tree. "On this side, we can head south now, but we'll need to cross three rivers and their lakes. If we cross the Ever Reaching, we only have the west side of the rainwood to deal with."

"That makes it sound like an easy decision, but since you didn't already make that choice, it tells me there's a reason."

"Crossing to the west will bring us close to Silver Falls, where the Asavori Rangers gather."

"And they are?"

She kept forgetting that while he lived on Shecrish, he was isolated from the goings-on of their world. "Elite warriors. As far as I know, the Masters haven't infiltrated them."

"But you don't want to take the chance."

"They're the best of the best for a reason. If even one of them is part of the Masters, and I go into their known territory, I'm just asking to be found."

Rohan's brows drew together. "They don't leave that area?"

"They're everywhere, but the Silver Falls is their home base."

"I see. What do you think? The Rangers or the rivers?"

Farah glanced at her hands, remembering the rapids. Both options were treacherous. Crossing the rivers would expose them. At least the trees would help them hide. "Let's chance the Rangers."

"All right. Lead the way."

She had memorized the map of Shecrish as one of her first assignments as an agent. Durga had blindfolded her and had an agent take her into the rainwood. Farah then had to make her way back to Rannora. While she knew which river was which, she didn't know much about the waterways themselves: like where to cross or which areas to avoid.

Farah climbed a tree and moved toward the top as she had done since the start of her journey with Rohan. Most Wood Elves preferred the middle areas of the trees. Remaining higher gave them an ever-so-slight advantage since elves would be focused lower. They needed every bit of gain they could muster.

She waited for Rohan to catch up. The more he climbed, the better—and faster—he became. Soon, he moved through the trees as easily as a Wood Elf. She watched his shirt tighten across his back as he used his arms to haul himself onto a branch.

"I'm here," he said, slightly out of breath.

She turned west and studied the trees ahead of her. The river would stay on her right this time. They were close to the shore, which meant she needed to take them deeper into the rainwood to keep out of sight. There was a tribe of Wood Elves nearby. They were generally easy-going, but that didn't mean she wanted to run into them.

"Ready?" she asked over her shoulder.

"Ready," Rohan replied.

Farah scooted around the trunk and quickly brought them deeper into the forest before turning west. The river eventually turned into a lake. It was one of the smaller ones, but it still took hours of travel before it became the river again.

She paused when she spotted a carriage and horses below her on the road. Just in time, too, as some Wood Elves came down from a nearby tree to speak to whoever was inside. They waited until the carriage was gone and the elves had returned to the trees and moved away before they continued.

The river took them southwest. She spotted where the river merged with the Ever Reaching as the light of day faded in the sky. They had traveled through the trees before at night, but they were coming up to hirch trees now. Their limbs weren't as wide. Or as sturdy. That meant going slower. Even for her.

Farah didn't like the looks of the trees ahead. They might support her, but they wouldn't hold Rohan comfortably. She stopped against a trunk and turned to wait for Rohan. He landed on the branch easily and made his way to her.

"What is it?" he asked.

She jerked her chin to the trees. "They're not stable. We need to descend and go the rest of the way on land."

He looked past her through the trees to the merging rivers. "Where do we cross?"

"I won't know until we get there."

"In the dark?"

She shrugged. "The night will shield us."

"If we go before the moons rise."

He had a point. Farah nodded and made her way down the tree. It was either cross where the rivers merged or before the river flowed into the next lake. Otherwise, they would have to trek around the lake before making their way back to the Ever Reaching River. It would simply take too long. But she couldn't force things, either. Their last crossing had proven that.

With her feet on the ground and Rohan beside her, she crept to the next tree. Bit by bit, they made it closer to the edge of the rainwood. The sound of the water grew louder the nearer they got. She soon learned why when she saw a dramatic waterfall where the two waterways converged. Her heart dropped. Had they traveled all this way only to have to double back?

"Look there," Rohan said, pointing past her face.

She followed his finger and saw the rope bridge over the waterfall.

"That's our way across."

The trees grew to the river's edge, keeping them covered until they stepped onto the bridge. A short walk across, and they would be back in the safety of the forest. Shadows already enveloped much of the area as the sun was too low to shed its light upon them. Farah started to move forward when Rohan's hand caught her arm. She turned her head to him.

"Let me go first. No one is looking for me. If someone comes out, you know to find another route."

She shook her head. "I'm not leaving you."

"You won't be. We'll meet outside the city."

It was a good plan. "All right," she reluctantly agreed.

Rohan cautiously walked from the tree line to the bridge. He set his hands on the ropes on either side of him and began his trek across. He made it to the other side without incident. She waited as he headed into the trees. A moment later, he popped back out and waved her over.

She sent up a prayer to the gods as she put her foot on the bridge. The scrape of the rope against her palms made her raise her hands slightly above them. The bridge swayed a bit with her movement. She glanced down at the water rushing violently over the side of the waterfall to tumble hundreds of feet into the lake below. Her steps quickened as she glanced over her shoulder to make sure no one followed. She no longer saw Rohan. He must have decided to wait within the forest.

She hurried off the bridge and into the rainwood, where she found Rohan standing between two trees with an odd expression. He looked more aggravated than worried. It was the only reason she wasn't immediately wary.

"What's wrong?" she asked as she stopped before him.

"We should've stayed on the other side," he replied.

The hairs on the back of her neck rose. She whirled around

and found a Sun Elf wearing the distinctive long, white gown and golden belt of a Reader. In the next instant, Asavori Rangers surrounded them.

"Hello, Farah," the Reader said.

Farah looked into the elf's copper eyes. "Who are you?"

"Savita. I'm not here to hurt you. I'm here to help."

30

Rohan eyed the Sun Elf. Savita hadn't bothered to tell him her name. Likely because she had no interest in lowering herself to speak to a human. Her tawny hair was parted down the middle and hung straight and thick down her back. Her sleeveless white gown made her brown skin appear darker, but the gold sash around her waist brought out the golden glints. Intelligent, cunning copper eyes saw everything.

She had markings on her face Rohan had never seen before. A line of gold ran from the outer corners of her lower lashes to her temples. A large golden sun had been painted in the middle of her forehead. There were also five golden dots along each collarbone.

Farah looked at each of the elves surrounding them. They all had the same type of sword strapped somewhere on their bodies. Rohan suspected these were the Asavori Rangers she had spoken of. But who—or what—was Savita?

"What does a Reader want with me?" Farah asked.

The more time Rohan spent away from Siguk, the more he

realized how little he knew about the elves and the inner workings of Shecrish. It was a detriment that needed to be rectified—not just for him but also for his entire village. He had no idea if a Reader was dangerous or if she really could help. For the moment, no one paid much attention to him, so he remained still and listened.

Savita issued a small laugh. "What a silly question when you know the answer. I read the runes. They told me you would be here."

"That still doesn't tell me what you want."

Farah might have told him she didn't want the life she had, but she certainly was good at it. She hadn't backed down from Savita or the warriors. Either she wasn't troubled by their appearance, or she was and hid it well. Either way, he was prepared to jump in and help. He could get in a few good strikes before the elves used their magic.

A small smile played upon Savita's lips. "You know who I am." She motioned to the elves around them. "You know the Rangers. You even came to see me years ago. It wasn't time for us to meet then. It's why I left."

Rohan frowned as the words penetrated his mind. Could Savita have seen everything with the runes she spoke about? Was that even possible? He wished he knew.

"You knew I needed help and withheld it?" Farah asked in disbelief.

Savita drew a bag from her sash. She opened the black velvet pouch and poured several small, irregularly oval-shaped white stones with gold markings into her hand. "The runes see many things."

Rohan tried to see the stones better, but the distance was too great. When he lifted his head, Savita's disconcerting gaze was on him. She grinned as if she knew he was interested in learning more. If what she said was true, then maybe she did.

"You had a journey," Savita said to Farah. "One that is far from complete. The runes showed me this day and our meeting, but none before now."

Farah didn't seem to hear her. "Is my sister alive? Do you know where Nitya is?"

"She's alive."

That gave Rohan hope that Lata and the rest of the villagers might also be among the living.

"Why come to me now?" Farah demanded.

Savita slowly returned the runes to the bag before drawing the string tight and tucking the pouch back into her sash. "I had to wait for Rohan."

A feather could've knocked him over. He blinked at the Reader. "Me?"

"Both of you are searching for someone. Rohan, you might be able to get into Mortham, but you don't know your way around it. Farah does. While she knows the layout, you know your people. The plan only works if you are both involved. Right?"

She posed the question to Farah. Rohan slid his gaze to her.

She glanced at him but didn't reply.

That's when he realized she hadn't intended to bring him inside the compound. "I thought we had a deal."

"If you go in, you'll never come out again," she replied softly. Finally, she looked at him. "I couldn't do that to Kalyani. Or to you."

"He'll get out with your help," Savita said.

Rohan should be angry that Farah had intended to go alone,

but he couldn't be. Not when her reasoning was something he understood. He held her gaze. "I'll do whatever is necessary to keep you alive and free our sisters."

"Glad to hear it." Savita motioned with her hand, and the Rangers melted into the forest.

He watched it all in awe. One moment, they were there. The next, the elves were gone. He looked everywhere but could find no trace of them.

"You won't see them," Savita told him. "None can compare to the skill of a Ranger. Come closer, both of you."

Rohan walked toward her, but Farah hesitated before joining him. Savita squatted and swept her hand over the ground to swipe away some leaves. He and Farah shared a look before dropping to their haunches.

"There are more pressing matters at the moment," Savita whispered as she drew something in the dirt with a stick. Her head was lowered, and her voice was so soft they had to lean close to hear. "The Masters have Durga watched."

"Are you telling me someone within the DIA is a double agent?" Farah asked softly.

Savita paused in her drawing and lifted her gaze to Farah. "That's part of being in the intelligence community. Durga expected it."

"Do you know who it is?" Rohan asked.

The Reader shook her head and returned to her drawing. Long strands of tawny hair fell over her shoulder, the ends lightly sweeping the ground. "They're being hidden from me. It's someone close to Durga, though. If you go to the city and meet with her as you intend, Farah, they'll capture you—and take Durga."

"I have information I need to pass on," Farah whispered.

Savita wrote the letter S in the dirt before she wiped it away. "Good thing the runes showed me another way."

"What other way?" he asked.

"Follow the river as you planned. Someone will meet you."

"I need a name," Farah replied.

Savita kept drawing. "Give your intel to them, but don't tarry. If you want to find your sisters, you must get to Mortham quickly."

"Why?" Rohan asked. The contours Savita drew began to take the shape of a map.

"They don't want the truth to come out." Savita dropped the stick. "Take a good look."

Rohan studied the map and committed it to memory. He was going over it a third time when Farah gasped.

"That's a watch house."

"It is." Savita suddenly stood and wiped the drawing away with her foot. He looked up at her before straightening.

"Did you memorize it?" she asked.

He dipped his head.

"And you?" Savita asked Farah.

Farah nodded. "They're on every level. Why are you sending us there?"

"It's where you'll find answers."

Rohan ran a hand down his face. "Could you be more specific?"

"That isn't how the runes work," Savita replied.

Farah put a hand on his arm and looked at Savita. "All this time, I believed the list to find the missing was in a locked room. Are you telling me they've been at the watch house all along?"

Savita nodded once.

Rohan found himself believing everything she said, which, in itself, was something to be concerned about. Was she using some kind of magic? It wasn't in his nature to accept things so readily. "How do we know you aren't lying? That this isn't all some trick?"

"Readers don't lie," Farah said.

He looked from her to Savita. "Never?"

"We impart what the runes show us," she replied.

Which hadn't really answered his question. "You decipher the stones. That means you interpret them, thereby spinning something to be what you want."

"Rohan," Farah muttered in a shocked whisper.

Savita raised her hand to halt her from saying more. "He doesn't realize that his words are offensive. He and the Siguks have lived separately for too long. They don't know of us, and we don't know of them. Honestly, I would be shocked if he *didn't* question me." She drew in a breath. "I did not choose to become a Reader. I was born thus. The runes show me what they want me to know. It isn't for me to interpret anything."

"And you're telling me you've never lied?" he pressed. By Farah's sharp intake of breath, he realized he might have overstepped.

Savita merely smiled. "Readers do not lie. But not everything shared is truth."

He hated riddles. Why couldn't she just answer the question?

"Now, you must go," Savita said.

Farah nodded and walked away. He followed her to a tree, Savita trailing a few steps behind them.

"Stay high and keep hidden," Savita whispered before changing course.

It wasn't long before the rainwood swallowed her. He swung

his head to Farah and found her halfway up the tree already. He backed up a few steps and adjusted his bag so it lay against his back. Then he got a running start, planted his foot on the trunk, and pushed off. He grabbed hold of the closest branch and pulled himself up.

Farah waited as he got to his feet and steadied himself with his arms. Once he had his balance, he made his way up several more branches and then around the trunk to stand on a limb close to her. She was on a higher branch, forcing him to look up at her.

"Are you all right?" he asked.

"Readers are difficult to get to. Everyone has always known the Rangers have one. I went to her, hoping she would see me and give me information about Nitya. I never told anyone I sought her out."

He glanced through the branches at the ground below.

"I know you don't believe," she continued. "We revere Readers. I'm not saying they never lie, but she knew where we would be. And she waited for us."

"I can't ignore that."

Farah licked her lips. "I trust her. I believe her."

"I understand." It was part of the elven faith. He might not comprehend it, but that didn't mean he would dismiss it out of hand.

"To Mortham?"

Rohan nodded.

Their conversation ended, and they once more moved through the treetops. They kept high again. Dots of light flashed around him. The first few times had been so jarring, he had nearly fallen. It wasn't until he saw a tiny bug on a tree trunk, its bottom half lighting up, that he relaxed. After that, the sight of them didn't set him on edge.

They weren't the only things shimmering. Clumps of moss glowed an iridescent green. This side of the river was almost an entirely new ecosystem. At least, it appeared that way to him. Perhaps what he saw now was found throughout the rainwood. The difference was that he was paying closer attention to discern such wonders now.

No matter how hard he tried, he wasn't as light on his feet as the Wood Elves. The limbs still moved under him, and each time a branch shook, causing the leaves to move, it made him cringe. He managed to stay with Farah, though he suspected she had slowed her pace because it was night. Rohan appreciated the concession, nonetheless. He didn't want to get lost.

The farther south they traveled, the more the knot in his chest tightened. He wasn't afraid to return to the fort. A beam of moonlight broke through the canopy and briefly illuminated Farah as she ran across a branch. Nay, his worry was about someone else entirely.

Everyone would be on the lookout for her with the price on her head—even within Mortham. They would be walking right into the Masters' arms. Savita had said it would take both of them to find their sisters. As he went over Savita's words, he realized she'd never said anything about Farah getting out, only him.

He would gladly trade his life for Lata's or Kalyani's. But could he trade Farah's life for Lata's?

Would he give his life for Nitya to return to Farah? He watched her leap effortlessly across a limb. Aye, he would. He knew what she had suffered because he had lived with the same debilitating pain. One of them should have a happy ending. Somehow, he would make sure Farah got Lata home.

31

The double moons bathed the rainwood in light, though only small portions filtered through the branches and leaves. Salil had spent so much time in the Under that even the night seemed bright. His search for Farah had yielded little. But she was well trained. Which meant she would seek out places to hide that few knew about.

For a Wood Elf, that meant getting lost in the vastness of the rainwood. And there were many places someone could hide for weeks—or even months—without being found. It was where he would go if he were being hunted. The problem was, he could only guess which direction she'd gone.

The odds of locating her before someone willing to turn her over to the Masters did was slim, but he wouldn't give up. He'd known for a while that it was time to pull Farah from Mortham. He'd let her convince him otherwise, and that was his mistake. He was going to make it right.

He moved stealthily through the trees. Unlike most Wood

Elves, he didn't rush. He took his time, scanning the area from top to bottom before moving to the next tree. It might be slower, but his approach allowed him to avoid not just the numerous animals of the rainwood but also other elves.

And that approach was how he soon realized he was being followed.

Whoever it was, was in the trees with him. Salil couldn't make out a figure in the darkness. Either the elf was exceptionally camouflaged—or it was a Dark Elf. He wasn't pleased about either possibility.

Salil leapt across a branch onto another and made his way to the trunk. There, he plastered his back against it and waited. The night was alive with sounds. Wood Elves had perfected the art of moving through the trees, and while it appeared as if they traveled soundlessly, they didn't.

He strained his ears for the soft thump of booted feet landing on a limb. There was no such sound. He clenched his jaw at the confirmation that a Dark was trailing him. Was it Dain? Or one of the Masters' emissaries?

Dark Elves had an advantage. They could cloak themselves in shadows and travel long distances by them. But that didn't mean they were invisible. Salil had learned a lot about the slave trade while captaining his ship, but he had also learned a great deal about the Dark. More than they would be pleased about.

He closed his eyes and turned to his other senses. The eyes could deceive, especially when it came to shadows in the dark of night. He caught a soft *whoosh* as something grew closer. A swish of leaves off to his right helped to detect the direction. The air grew heavier there. He waited another two heartbeats, allowing the Dark to get closer. Then Salil spun and clamped his hand around a neck.

A gray hand shot through the shadows and grabbed his arm before spinning in an attempt to throw him off, but his grip was firm. The shadows fell away to reveal the scarred Dark from Durga's office. He had thought it might be Dain, but it didn't halt the rage that bubbled up.

Dain slipped out of his grasp and came up behind Salil, wrapping an arm around his neck. Salil elbowed the Dark and shoved him off the branch. Dain released him, only to suddenly appear before him. Salil turned just as the punch landed on his jaw. He caught himself with a hand on the limb above him, then dove for the Dark Elf.

Salil didn't attempt to stop his fall. He wrapped his arms around Dain and took the elf down with him. Just as he'd expected, the Dark used shadows to bypass the many branches and land on the ground. Unfortunately for him, Dain shoved him off before they reached the earth. Salil landed hard on his side and felt his shoulder pop out of joint. He jumped to his feet and faced off against the Dark as they circled each other.

"How did you know I was there?" Dain demanded.

Salil sneered. "Why are you following me?"

"You first."

Salil stopped walking and glared. "Durga may trust you, but I have no reason to."

"The fact that she does is all the reason you need."

"That's not how I work."

Dain snorted, a crooked smile forming on his lips. "She said I'd have trouble convincing you."

"Then Durga should've told me you were trailing me."

"I wasn't talking about her."

Salil frowned. He couldn't be speaking of Farah, could he? "Who, then?"

"A Reader named Savita."

He might have dismissed Dain, except he had encountered Savita before. She hadn't done more than look his way, but no elf in Shecrish ever forgot meeting a Reader.

Dain rubbed his neck. "Now, tell me how you knew I was there."

"Something I picked up running the ships on the Lotus. Dark Elves are everywhere."

"Just as Wood Elves are in the rainwood," Dain pointed out.

Salil ignored his comment. "I went into every area expecting the Dark to be cloaked in shadows."

"They probably were."

"They *absolutely* were. After a few days of them parting the shadows to reveal themselves, I endeavored to figure out a way to discern where they were. I couldn't trust my eyes."

Dain nodded. "But you could trust your other senses."

"There is a heaviness in the air close to where a Dark uses the shadows."

"Impressive."

Salil crossed his arms over his chest. "Your turn. Why are you following me?"

"You'll find Farah tonight. She's to pass on the intel she collected, and I'm going to help them get to Mortham."

"Them?"

Dain lifted a shoulder and tilted his head. "She's with a human."

"Where am I supposed to find her."

"I don't know. Savita sent them this way. She told Farah to stay high and move fast."

Salil looked up to the top branches. Now that he knew where Farah would be, it was only a matter of watching and waiting. He began climbing the tree, then found a spot and settled on a limb to wait. The odds of him finding Farah were better if he remained in one location. He grunted when he spotted Dain standing on a branch slightly above him.

"Problem?" the Dark asked.

"Where do I start?"

Dain shook his head of long, white hair. "Not every Dark is like those at Mortham."

Unbidden, the image of the female who had served him in the Below came to mind. Her smile had been shy, her words kind. "I didn't say they were."

"So, it's just *me* you despise?"

"As I said, I don't know you."

Dain made a sound in the back of his throat. "And I don't know you. But you don't see *me* acting like a petulant child."

"Petulant?" Salil repeated in outrage as he swung his head to the Dark.

"You work for your agency. I work for mine. It isn't the first time there has been a joint mission."

Salil returned his attention to scanning the trees for movement. "How did the Masters establish such a hold in the Below? Why didn't the Dark stop them?"

"Don't fool yourself. They have a hold of the Above, too. And I could ask you the same question. You know the answer. There are always bad things going on. There's no telling how long the Masters were operating and growing. Organizations like theirs spread slowly, but once they infect a section, it's too late to stop the sickness. And it spreads uncontrollably. Then you have those who know it's wrong, but the power and money still seduce them over and over. You want to know how we end them? We have to eliminate the infection. We can't just take out one part. It has to be a widespread attack."

"Joint missions," Salil said.

"Exactly."

Salil heard movement and looked up to see Dain climbing onto another branch. The Dark was surprisingly agile. "Do you have a plan?"

"Not yet. We need to know more about them, or we'll waste our opportunity."

"How many of your agents are onboard?"

Dain dusted off his hands and peered out into the night. "Just me and one other. But there is another Dark who will help."

"Oh. Great. Three of you," Salil replied sarcastically.

"We were a small group when we went into Shaldorn."

Salil grunted. "I take that to mean you don't trust your agency?"

"The Masters have invaded everything. They've got their hands in every division of your government as well as ours. To answer your question, nay. I don't trust the CCD."

"Why Durga, then?"

"Farah approaches."

Salil jumped to his feet and skimmed the trees. He moved his gaze from side to side twice before he spotted movement. Two individuals, just as Dain had said. They were closer to the river's edge and moving fast. Salil saw a flick of Farah's red hair as she landed on a branch. He shifted to the right and jumped to the limb beside him. He had to cross two more trees to intercept her. He walked onto the limb and stood near the edge so she would see him.

He knew the instant she caught sight of him. There was a slight jerk of her body, and then she slowed. Salil looked behind her and saw the man. The human had been aboard his ship on the last delivery to the compound. Salil never forgot a face. The man hadn't reacted like most of the people who were taken. His seeming indifference had caught Salil's attention, especially for a man he expected to fight back.

Salil returned his gaze to Farah as she approached. He walked backward toward the trunk when she jumped onto his branch, wariness tightening her face.

"It's good to see you alive. You had me worried," he said.

Her lips curved into a smile as her shoulders drooped with relief. "It's good to see your face."

They shared a quick embrace as the human waited on the other tree, watching the scene play out. Salil leaned back and looked Farah over. "What happened?"

"A lot," she murmured. She turned and waved the human to her.

Salil cut his eyes to the man, watching as he made the leap onto the branch. The human landed hard, but his footing was sure, and he didn't wobble.

"Rohan, this is Salil, my handler. Salil, Rohan," Farah said.

He dipped his chin to the human. "I recognize him."

"And I recognize you," Rohan said.

That's when her words registered. Salil jerked his head to Farah. "You told him?"

"Your secret is safe," Rohan answered.

Salil glared at him. "That might not be up to you if you're caught. You have no clue what can be done to force you to spill secrets. Now, you have not only hers but also mine."

"Why are you here?" Farah asked.

Salil blew out a breath. "I was looking for you."

"Why?" Rohan asked.

Salil was already on edge with Dain there. Discovering that Rohan knew he and Farah were agents only made things worse. And now the human was questioning him? "This has nothing to do with you."

"It does, actually," Farah said.

Salil should've known. He curled his lip and said, "You set off the bomb." He looked at Farah. "Were you in on it? Is that why you didn't leave that day?"

"She had nothing to do with it," Rohan stated. "I'm the one who took her."

"That means you're the one who ensured she now has a price on her head."

Farah stepped between them. "How did you find me, Salil?"

He was taken aback by her question and the heat in her words. But it was the suspicion in her eyes that chilled him.

32

"Don't look at me like that," Farah said to Salil. "It seems odd that you just happened to be out here."

A muscle in his jaw moved. "I didn't just *happen* to be out here. I faked my death to get out of being undercover so I could search for you."

"We were told you would know who it was," Rohan said in a low voice.

Farah glanced at him before returning her attention to Salil. She wanted him to be her contact, but she had been worried ever since Savita told her about the double agent.

"Who told you?" Salil asked, his hazel eyes narrowed.

A Dark Elf suddenly appeared out of the shadows on a branch above them. "Perhaps I can clear this up."

Farah had her arms lifted, palms out, ready to release defensive magic. Salil hadn't made any moves to do the same. The only indication that he knew the Dark was the flare of Salil's nostrils. "Who are you?" she demanded.

"Dain," the Dark answered. "Savita pointed me toward Salil since he was searching for you. I told him which direction you were headed. He's your contact, Farah."

She held back her magic and eyed the elf. "You could've listened to all of that without us knowing."

Dain rolled his eyes. "Savita would've known I was there. The runes would've told her."

He had a point. Farah looked at Rohan, who had moved to a branch on the left. He shrugged at her silent question. How would a Dark know about the Reader unless she had spoken to him? Farah studied Salil's face, but his expression gave nothing away. She had offended him, but that was the price of their current situation.

She had to decide. Did she trust that Salil was who Savita mentioned and share the information? She lowered her arms.

"I take that to mean you spoke with the Reader?" Salil asked.

She glanced at Dain before looking at Salil. "You didn't?"

"It seems she didn't need to speak with me."

Dain leaned an arm against a branch near his head. "Time is of the essence here."

"What's that supposed to mean?" Salil demanded of Dain.

"Exactly what you think it does."

Farah's stomach growled. It dawned on her that she hadn't eaten all day. The herbs had healed her hands and energized her body, but she needed food. She walked closer to the trunk and sat before tugging the bag around to her front and pulling out some bread and fruit. Rohan stayed on his limb but moved closer to the trunk, straddling the branch as he took out the water flask and drank deeply, his eyes still on Salil and Dain.

"Farah," Salil said when she didn't speak.

She swallowed her bite. "Savita warned me there is a double agent around Durga. It's why I can't go to Rannora with my intel. I'll be taken if I show up, and so will Durga."

"Bloody fucking hell," Salil murmured. Louder, he asked, "Have the runes told Savita who is spying on Durga?"

She shrugged. "They did not. Savita told me to travel. Said I'd meet up with someone I knew and could hand over the intel."

"What will you do after?"

She pulled off another section of the soft, sweet bread and popped it into her mouth. "Go to Mortham," she said around her mouthful of food.

"Told you," Dain said to Salil.

Salil blew out a breath, ignoring the Dark. "You can't go back."

"I'm going to find out what happened to my sister, his sister, and the rest of those taken from his village, and gather more information. It could give us the advantage we need."

Dain crossed his arms over his chest. "That's risky."

"Going back is suicide," Salil stated. "Even if you do find something, who will you tell? I'm not there anymore."

"Me," Dain said.

Farah watched the two of them, her gaze moving back and forth as each spoke. She knew what she was risking and was willing to do it if it meant others could be free. It wasn't that she wanted to die. She had already spent months inside the fort. If someone else got in, they would lose all that time. It had to be her.

And Salil knew it.

He crouched next to her. "I don't like it."

"It's part of the job," she answered.

Salil looked past her to Rohan. "And you're fine with all of this?"

"She's not going in alone. I'll be with her," Rohan told him.

Salil shook his head as if he couldn't comprehend what they were saying. "Even with Dain's help, this won't end well."

"The longer we tarry here, the more likely it is that someone will find us," Dain pointed out.

Farah finished the last of the food and drank her fill from the water flask. Then she got to her feet and looked at Salil. He had always had her back, and she hoped that hadn't changed. "They're building another Shaldorn."

"Where?" Dain asked before Salil could.

She shrugged, her lips twisting. "I don't know. Word spread quickly about the new one going up. There have been lots of guesses, but nothing definitive. At least, as far as I know."

"We suspected this," Salil murmured.

She wiped her mouth with her fingers. "I was hesitant to hand this next bit over because it was nothing but a rumor, but there was also talk about those abducted being put on other ships on the ocean."

"What?" Salil asked, his voice pitched higher with shock.

Dain grunted. "That's true. We have one of the ships."

"What?" Salil and Farah asked in unison.

The Dark shrugged. "That was the last mission. Anything else? Even the littlest tidbit might be something."

She searched her mind. "Not that I can think of now."

"What about you?" Dain asked Salil.

He ran a hand down his face and blew out a breath. "Those working for the Masters are very confident they won't be stopped. They look for spies, but not as diligently as they should. They're overconfident."

"It's how I got the bomb in," Rohan said.

The three of them looked his way.

"How *did* you do that?" Salil asked. "You had nothing on you when you were brought aboard my vessel."

Dain cocked his head. "You didn't work alone."

"I did have help," Rohan admitted.

Salil leaned forward. "Who?"

"I didn't get the Star Elf's name," Rohan said.

Dain went utterly still. "Did you say Star Elf?"

Rohan nodded once.

"Male?"

"Aye."

"Long, silver hair?"

Rohan hesitated before nodding.

"Muscular body with hawkish facial features?" Dain pressed.

Rohan's brows rose. "That sounds like him."

Salil straightened and swung his head to Dain. "Do you know this Star Elf?"

"I might, indeed," the Dark answered thoughtfully.

Farah was intrigued. "Who is he?"

"That is the question. I only know him as One," Dain said.

Rohan frowned. "One? That's his name?"

Dain nodded slowly. "It's what they called him at Shaldorn. There were three commanders. A Moon Elf by the name of Gita ruled the stronghold, and she called them One, Two, and Three."

"What happened to Two and Three?" Salil asked.

Dain dropped his arms to his sides. "I killed Three. Ravi took out Two."

"You were there?" Farah asked in shock.

Salil sighed loudly. "According to Durga, he was."

Dain's golden yellow eyes swung to her. "I and another Dark

were backup for a DIA agent and a human who infiltrated the compound."

"It's impressive that you helped bring that place down. It sent shockwaves through Mortham," Farah said.

Salil nodded. "It was talked about by all in the Below."

"Wait." Rohan lifted a hand. "You really think the one who helped me get inside Mortham is One?"

Farah frowned as he spoke. "Rohan has a point. If it *was* One, why would he help?"

"That is the question. One healed one of my agents recently after she was caught in Mortham. She couldn't explain why he did that any more than I can explain why he aided Rohan," Dain said.

Salil asked Rohan, "How did you meet the Star Elf?"

"I was searching for my sister," he began. "She and some other adolescents were taken. Our village has been decimated by abductions. I was looking for tracks when the Star Elf came out from behind a tree. He pointed east and told me I'd find what I was looking for in that direction."

Salil's brows raised. "And you believed him?"

"Of course not. Our village is secluded for a reason." Rohan rubbed the back of his neck. "But I was desperate, and he knew it. He said he had seen others being rounded up in the area. I immediately believed he was part of those responsible until he asked if I had a plan to get my people back. I said I'd do whatever was necessary."

Dain grunted. "And he had a plan?"

"Some of it," Rohan admitted.

"What do you mean?" Farah asked.

Rohan shrugged. "He asked if I meant what I said, and I replied that I did. He then said he might have a way to help."

"He just told you about the bomb?" Dain asked.

Rohan shoved his hand through his hair, moving the strands from his face as he glanced at her. "He said someone working inside could lead me to Lata and the rest of my people."

"Who was he talking about," Salil demanded.

Farah caught Salil's gaze. "Me."

Salil's brows snapped together in a deep frown.

Rohan blew out a breath. "He told me about a female Wood Elf who would be there when I was brought in. I knew her magic would be depleted without the trees. He confirmed that and told me he could place an explosive device near the port. Once it detonated, it would cause enough havoc for me to take her and force her to help."

"How did he find out you were undercover?" Salil asked Farah.

She shrugged. "Your guess is as good as mine."

"We have no idea who else he told." Salil shook his head, unnerved by the information.

It reminded Farah of how she had felt upon learning it. Odd, but it didn't bother her anymore. That might not be a good sign.

"I didn't know Farah would stand so close to the explosive," Rohan continued. "Her wound was too severe. I had no choice but to take her to my village and heal her."

Salil's face was tight with anger. "She could have died. Others *did* die."

"Have most of your village and family taken and tell me what lengths you wouldn't go to for them," Rohan replied indignantly.

Farah put her hand on her thigh where the scar was. "I'm here. Proof of Rohan's skills in healing."

A sound emerged from the back of Salil's throat, and he cut his eyes to Farah. "When did you join him without him forcing you?"

"I had to get back to find Nitya. I spent all my time there trying not to be seen, to fit in, and I let opportunities to look into where she was pass me by. I had to make that right." Farah looked at Rohan. "We wanted the same thing, just for different reasons."

Dain sighed and frowned. "A lot of that is concerning. If it *is* One, he's up to something. And I want to know what it is."

Farah licked her lips. "I know my way around the compound. I know the others' movements. This is my chance to do what I should've done from the very beginning instead of worrying about staying alive."

33

"What do you think about that?" Dain asked.

Rohan looked over to find the Dark Elf's gaze on him. "You're asking my opinion?"

"I am."

Rohan was once more faced with the fact that not all elves could be lumped into one category. He hadn't expected anyone but Farah to consider his thoughts. But he was grateful. "The Masters' time has come to an end."

"Without question," Dain said. "But that isn't what I asked."

Rohan swallowed, the last of the food settling heavily in his stomach as he realized that Dain wanted his thoughts on Farah's statement. "I think Farah is going to do whatever she needs to do. I take responsibility for my part in all of this. It's why I'll be beside her when she enters Mortham."

"You don't understand what they do to people there," Salil stated. He swung his head to Farah. "You need to tell him."

"I did," Farah replied.

Rohan nodded. "Even Savita says I'm to go with Farah. She also said we shouldn't tarry."

"I don't like this. If no one else will point out the obvious, I will. You're human," Salil said.

Rohan might have taken exception to such words before, but he now realized that not everything was meant as a criticism. Salil simply spoke the truth. He knew the horrors that awaited Rohan should he be caught. So did Farah. It was why she had thought to leave him behind.

Maybe Salil found him lacking because he didn't have magic. Maybe he didn't. But Salil's words came from a place of concern. Rohan's outlook had been skewed by the words of his father. Sure, there were elves who did harm. Those who worked with the Masters were proof of that. But others treated him with respect, like those at Amberstar. Even Dain and Salil were decent. The more he was away from Siguk, the more he recognized his biases.

Rohan looked into Salil's eyes. "I may not have magic, but I can fight. They'll never suspect me."

"He has a point," Dain agreed.

Salil's lips twisted. "It's risky."

"Everything we do is uncertain and dangerous. It's what we signed up for," Farah argued.

A noise to the side had everyone swinging their head in that direction.

"We've lingered here too long," Dain whispered.

Rohan looked around at the dark rainwood. He didn't like journeying through the trees at night, but they had ground to make up.

"How are you getting into Mortham?" Salil asked softly.

The hairs on the back of Rohan's neck stood on end. Something was close. He kept his voice at a whisper and said,

"There's an entrance on the east side of the waterfall past Rannora. It's just beyond the edge of the mesa."

"East?" Farah asked, her brow furrowed.

He shrugged. They had been headed to Rannora. There hadn't been a need to tell her where the secret entrance was until after the city.

"I'll find it," Salil said.

Dain used his shadows to move next to Salil. "You have to get to the city. I'll take these two as far as I can."

"The intel is too important. Take Salil," Farah insisted.

Dain's lips flattened, but he said nothing as shadows closed around him and Salil. Then, they were gone.

"Let's go," Farah mumbled.

Rohan rubbed the back of his neck. He'd be happy to put some distance between them and whatever was approaching. They didn't rush through the trees like before, though. Instead, they moved furtively. He thought it would make jumping easier, but it actually made things worse. He was too intent on the sounds around him and trying to be stealthy. He slipped every landing and fought to keep his balance. Each time a limb swayed beneath him, he scowled at the noise that sounded thunderous to his ears.

It took some time, but the feeling of being watched finally faded. That didn't make him feel better as he'd hoped, though. Maybe Farah should've taken Dain up on his offer to travel with the shadows. At least she would have gotten to the entrance without being discovered. But Dain was gone, leaving the two of them as it had been from the start. They had made it through so far. They would make it the rest of the way.

He hoped.

Inside Mortham would be a different story. He didn't allow

himself to think about that place yet. There would be time enough to let apprehension and nervousness chill his blood. He needed to remain focused on landing each jump and remaining hidden. They still had a long way to go.

The food he had eaten helped to keep him going, but he was bone-tired. He thought about the remaining herbs. A little taste would give him a boost. But what if one of them became injured in the fort? The herbs should be kept for that.

Farah stopped ahead of him. He moved silently across the branch to the trunk and rested against it wearily. "What is it?"

"Look."

He leaned to the side and spotted the tree across from them. The distance appeared considerable. Easily twice the distance he had jumped before. Maybe more. He looked to each side for another alternative.

"They're covered with poison cutleaf," she said without looking at him.

Rohan had never heard of it, but the fact that it was toxic, and Farah kept clear of it told him all he needed to know. "All of them?"

"Regrettably. It's why I chose this route." She turned her head to look back at him. "We either double back to find another way or cross."

"Can you get across?"

She nodded once.

He was the reason she hesitated. Rohan assessed the distance to the ground. It was difficult to see through the turning leaves in the dark, but he knew it was far. He'd already fallen a few times, and it wasn't an experience he wanted to repeat. This was worse.

"We'll double back."

He held up a hand to stop her. "You cross. I'll go down and up."

Before she could answer, her face slackened as she looked past his shoulder. "We have to move. *Now.*"

Rohan glanced behind him but didn't see anything. He spun back around just as Farah ran across the limb and launched herself into the air. She caught a branch above her with both hands and used momentum to swing her legs up and in. She released the branch and flipped over to land without a wobble. She immediately spun toward him and waved him over, her eyes wide, her unease clear.

It was all the motivation he needed.

He replayed her actions in his head as he raced across the branch. He locked his eyes on the limb hanging above him and pushed off. Elation spread through his chest when his hands gripped the branch's rough bark. He drew his legs to his chest but realized too late that he didn't have enough momentum to flip as Farah had. Instead, he thrust his legs out hard and arched his back as he pushed off the branch with his hands.

A smile formed when his foot landed on the limb. His heart lurched into his throat when his other foot met only air. He felt himself tipping to the side and tried to find purchase. Farah's mouth opened in shock, and she leaned toward him. But it was too late. He was already falling. He looked around feverishly to find something to grab. Everything was passing in a blur. His shoulder rammed into a branch and sent him spinning. Pain shot through him, but he ignored it as he clutched wildly for something to grab onto.

He hit two more limbs before finally managing to wrap his hands around a branch to stop his descent. His hold was precarious, but at least he wasn't falling anymore. Rohan swung his leg up and hooked it around the branch. He was in the process of pulling himself up when he felt Farah's hands on his body, helping him.

His breath was ragged as he sat up and looked at her. She was perched on her knees, her eyes searching his as her hands cupped his face. He had the overwhelming desire to pull her against him and kiss her again. He craved her taste. Yearned for the heat of passion that had scorched his veins. Death had nearly taken him, and he wanted to feel alive like he had when their lips had met at Amberstar.

Her gaze dropped to his mouth. She was thinking about the kiss, too. He touched her hand on his face, and the spell broke with the sound of a branch breaking. They got to their feet and plastered themselves against the trunk. He tested his injured shoulder and winced at the pain that followed. He would likely have bruises on his arms and legs from the other impacts, too.

"I made too much noise," he whispered.

"It wouldn't have mattered."

"Who's out there?" When she didn't answer, he looked down at her.

Her eyes were directed into the darkness. "Wood Elves. They're tracking us."

"Are we in someone's territory?"

"Aye, but I don't think that's who it is."

Meaning they were after her for the reward. Rohan leaned close to her ear and said, "Take the potion."

Farah fumbled with her bag and drew out the vial before uncorking it and draining it in one gulp. She threw the empty bottle toward the river. "Move," she said urgently.

He glanced in the direction they had come and spotted movement. He had cost them valuable time by falling. She didn't climb up to where they had been but stayed at their current height. The branches were larger and longer, making their travel easier. Now, he understood why most elves remained in the middle of the trees.

They moved so rapidly, they practically flew. There was no time to look behind him to see if the Wood Elves were gaining ground—doing so might make him lose his balance. He didn't hear anything. That had to mean they'd put a fair amount of distance between them. At least, he hoped that was the case.

He did a double take when he expected to see Farah's red hair and found deep brown instead. She looked back at him. He searched for her pointed ears but they were rounded now. She suddenly yelped when someone tackled her from the side. He watched as the two tumbled several branches down before stopping. She fought against whoever held her, throwing punches and kicks instead of magic to maintain her cover.

Before he could go after Farah, a rope dropped over him and painfully cinched his arms to his sides. A presence came up behind him. He threw his head back, connecting with someone who let out a string of curses.

Rohan turned to get in a kick when a punch landed in his kidney. He dropped to his knees as pain blinded him. Someone pushed him aside. He fought against the rope to get his arms loose as the ground rushed to meet him, but there was no getting free. Abruptly, he was yanked to a halt, inches from the ground.

The sudden stop forced the wind out of him, and he struggled to draw in air as he spun with his body in a horizontal position. He looked up when he heard Farah grunt and saw the Wood Elves. He counted six, including the one who had gone after Farah. As he slowly turned, he spotted another coming out of the darkness.

A branch cracked above him. He heard one of the males curse, and then both he and Farah landed unnaturally on the ground. Panic gripped Rohan when she didn't move. Her skin no longer held the coppery sheen he had become accustomed to seeing. The elf jumped up and dusted himself off as he shoved his foot into her shoulder.

Rohan peeled back his lips and growled. The sound seemed to take everyone by surprise, including him. For a moment, no one moved.

The elf who'd walked out of the darkness squatted next to Farah. Her eyes opened, and she looked up at him. "This isn't something we see every day. What are two humans doing in the trees?"

When she didn't answer, the elf looked at Rohan. He stared back.

The elf chuckled. "Or do we have elves attempting to pass for humans? One of my team said the woman had red hair, not brown."

Someone tossed Farah's sack from the tree to the ground. "There's no vial in there," an elf declared.

"She could've gotten rid of it," another elf said.

The leader jerked his chin toward Rohan. Someone cut the strap to his sack to remove it from around him. They dumped the contents onto the ground, but there was nothing there. Rohan chanced a look at Farah to find her gaze on him. Her hazel eyes had been replaced by brown ones.

"What are you doing in the trees?" the leader asked again.

Rohan watched wordlessly as one of the elves suddenly disappeared into the shadows. The leader didn't even notice since he was too intent on Farah.

A muffled cry broke the silence. The lead elf's head snapped up, and his brows drew together as he got to his feet and turned in a circle. As Rohan continued to rotate slowly, he saw the other elves removed, one by one. The leader tried to run but only succeeded in rushing headlong into one of the shadows.

Farah carefully pushed herself into a sitting position as Rohan attempted to get his feet under him. He was about to ask her who was out there when Dain emerged from the shadows with two other Dark Elves.

"Thought you could use some help," Dain stated.

The sight of him sent relief coursing through Farah. "It's good to see you."

They got Rohan loose within moments. After he shook off the ropes, he rubbed his arms. "Nice timing."

"He likes to make an entrance," the female said.

Dain cut his eyes to her, but there was no heat in his expression. "Farah, Rohan, meet Arya. She was with me at Shaldorn."

Arya was tall and slender, her white hair long and straight. Deep gray eyes crinkled at the corners as she gave them a mesmerizing smile. She was gorgeous, and given how Rohan looked at her, even he noticed.

"Glad we made it in time," Arya said. She motioned to the elf beside her. "This is Jai."

Jai's long, white waves were pulled back in a queue at the base of his neck. He had a handsome face with light gray eyes. But it was the loving look he and Arya shared that told Farah they were together.

"Jai was captured years ago and forced to captain a ship along the Lotus," Arya explained.

"You got him out, then?" Rohan asked.

Farah heard the hope in his voice as her gaze moved to him. The fear that froze her blood hadn't been for her but for him when the Wood Elves had put the rope around him. She had almost used her magic. She *should* have. She likely would have if Dain hadn't shown up.

Her gaze dropped to Rohan's lips. They had nearly kissed. She was sure they would have had the elves not arrived. She yearned to feel his lips again. The longing had been so overwhelming that she had forgotten everything but him. Which was why the Wood Elf got to her.

That kind of preoccupation could get her—and others—killed. She had to put an end to whatever feelings were developing. They were bothersome and hindersome. They were, to put it mildly, not something she wanted.

Jai's smile dropped. "Barely."

"You're here, aren't you?" Dain retorted.

Arya waved her hand at the two of them. "Ignore them. Dain filled us in on your plan."

"It sounds dangerous. Count us in," Jai said.

"Dangerous but doable," Arya corrected. "With some help."

Farah looked between the three Dark. "What do you mean?"

"We're going with you," Dain said.

They would be able to move more easily within Mortham than she or Rohan. She had never counted on help but wouldn't turn it away. Not to mention, the Dark would get them to the secret entrance a lot faster. Farah found herself smiling. "Our chances of success just improved."

"We should get moving," Jai urged.

As if propelled by the words, the three Dark encircled her and Rohan, pushing them together until they stood facing each other. Farah held on to his arms while Rohan's hands rested on her hips. When she glanced up, he was looking at her. She could only see the outline of his face in the dark, but she knew every contour of it.

He urged her closer, and she willingly went. Her hands moved up his arms, and then her fingers splayed on his chest. She realized she would go wherever he went. She didn't want to love him. But it was too late. She had fallen for him without knowing it.

Had his kiss sealed her fate? Maybe it was when he braved the churning river to help her across. Or perhaps it had been when he slept with his head in her lap. Or when he so tenderly saw to her wound.

The world was burning all around them. They were about to walk into a hellhole of unspeakable proportions, and all she could think about was him. His hard body, the muscles rippling beneath her palms. He had saved her from more than just a leg injury. He had saved her soul.

"Do not speak," Dain said. "We can pass unseen, but we can still be heard."

Rohan glanced up and dipped his chin in acknowledgment.

She lowered her gaze to his chest to hide the tears flooding her eyes. Shadows rose and closed over them, blocking out the meager moonlight. She had never traveled with a Dark before. She expected to feel like they were moving, but she didn't. Maybe it was because all three were using their shadows together. She wondered how they saw through them or even knew where to go. It had to be instinctive.

Rohan's fingers flexed against her. She closed her eyes and reveled in being so close to him. It might be the last time she had the opportunity, and she wasn't about to pass it up. She had never dreamed of finding someone like him. She wished she was brave enough to kiss him. Nitya would have. Her sister had reached for whatever she wanted without hesitation. Nitya never worried about what might happen or what others thought. That was Farah's problem. She focused on the worst possible outcomes and couldn't consider anything else.

More than any of the others, she knew what awaited them at Mortham. If they were caught, they would wish for death, pray for it. This moment might be the last she had with Rohan. She rested her cheek on his chest. He wound his arms around her, holding her firmly, and she heard the rapid beat of his heart. He would never know of her feelings. Loving someone wasn't in the cards for her—and loving a human was...

The roar of a waterfall grew louder. All too soon, the shadows fell away. She lifted her head. Rohan's hold lingered for another heartbeat before he released her. She dared to look at him, but he had moved away. It was likely for the best. She might say something she would later regret. Farah drew in a breath and put a protective barrier around her heart, then took stock of where they were.

Dain, Arya, and Jai had brought them to the edge of a plateau. If she climbed one of the trees, she would likely be able to make out Rannora to the northwest. She had gotten to Mortham from the Lotus River. She had never known there was another entrance so close to the city. Thanks to Rohan, they had another access point.

Her eyes sought him out. Now that she had labeled her feelings, she couldn't stop looking at him. Without the canopy of the rainwood, moonlight flooded the area. Desire burned in her veins as her eyes roamed the back of Rohan's impressive body. He walked through tall grass to stand on the mesa's rim. Like a string connecting them, she followed.

He glanced at her when she came up beside him before he returned his gaze to the waves crashing onto the shore. She couldn't hear anything over the thunderous waterfall. The five of them stood there for another heartbeat before Rohan turned to the right and started walking toward the cascade.

Within minutes, the waterfall's spray drenched them. It dampened everything around them. Farah looked for a door or something that could be an entrance—to no avail. She wiped the water from her face and slipped on the wet grass. She was able to right herself before falling.

Rohan unexpectedly stopped and dropped to his arse before twisting to the right and pushing off with his hand. Her heart slammed into her ribs in fear, his name on her lips, until she looked over the side and saw him staring up at her. He waved for her to follow. Now that she had a better view, Farah saw the small ridge in the side of the plateau.

Dain followed Rohan next. Farah sat, pushed off, and twisted. She sucked in a quick breath as fear iced her veins when only one foot landed on the ridge. She gained her footing, but her heart thudded painfully against her ribs. Slowly, she turned and moved forward a few inches to make room for Arya and Jai. Water prevented the Dark from using their shadows to travel, which meant they had no choice but to traverse this like anyone else.

Once everyone was down, Rohan led them along some steps so narrow the balls of her feet barely fit. This couldn't be how he had carried her out of Mortham. How could he have possibly done it? Then she recalled how he had scaled the cliffs.

She kept one hand on the side of the mesa, her shoulder scraping rock just so she wouldn't lean too far the other side, where there was nothing but air. The farther they trekked, the wetter they got. There was no rushing down the minuscule steps. Besides being small, they were getting slipperier. One wrong move and it was over. Her thighs burned from creeping down so many steps.

Rocks tumbled behind her. She paused to look over her shoulder where Jai was looking down. Arya had half-turned to put her hand on him. After a moment, the two continued on. Farah made her tired legs start moving. She blinked through the water pelting her face. At first, she thought it was rain, but when she looked up, she realized they were heading toward the waterfall on their way down.

It became difficult to see with the amount of water hitting her face. She slowed considerably to place each foot carefully before shifting her weight. And she wasn't the only one. Just when she didn't think she could take it anymore, Rohan pulled her forward, and she found herself in a cave behind the waterfall.

She walked a few steps before bending forward, her hands braced on her knees as she tried to catch her breath. Her legs wouldn't hold her, though. She ended up lowering herself onto the wet stones, waiting for Arya and Jai to make it inside.

Rohan leaned against the side of the cave, breathing heavily once everyone was inside. They were all exhausted. They needed to be in top form when they entered Mortham. Luckily, she had just the thing.

Farah had taken the jar of herbs and stored them on her just in case. She was glad she had after the Wood Elves searched her bag and ruined Rohan's. The problem was the lack of a water flask or cup. She pulled the jar from the waist of her pants and held it up. Everyone, including Rohan, perked up at the sight of it.

"There's no water flask," he said.

Dain cupped his hands and walked to the waterfall to fill them with water. Then he stopped before Farah. She dropped a pinch of herbs into his hands and watched him drink. Arya was next, then Jai. She raised her brows to Rohan.

"We may need that later," he said.

She motioned to the waterfall with her head. "We need it now. We have to be in top form before we go inside."

Rohan pushed off the wall and got water in his hands. She gave him a bigger pinch than the others and watched him drink it down.

"Your turn," he said and plucked the jar from her hands.

Farah let the water fill her cupped palms and pressed her hands together so none spilled out. She made her way back to Rohan, who sprinkled the herbs into her hands. The water was cold but refreshing, and she drank every bit to make sure she downed all the herbs.

They sat, waiting for the effects to kick in. Rohan sat on the opposite side of the cave. She pulled her eyes away from him to the curtain of water that gushed past. The double moons lit up the falls, creating a mesmerizing effect. The force of the cascade, the sound, and the power was incredible. And this was only one of dozens of waterfalls that fell off the plateau.

Within thirty minutes, the herbs had restored them. There was a curious mix of agitation and anticipation. She looked at each of them, hoping they all made it out again.

Rohan headed toward the back of the grotto. "The way is smooth, so you don't need to worry about tripping on debris, but the tunnel is narrow and pitch-black. The descent is gradual but constant. Use your hands on the walls to help with the descent," he said.

Dain, Jai, and Arya would be fine. It was just her and Rohan who would be all but blind in the tunnel. Rohan paused and looked at her as if he wanted to say something. Instead, he headed deeper into the darkness. Farah fell into formation behind him, followed by Arya, Jai, and then Dain at the rear. It became so dark that Farah had to put her hands out before they even reached the tunnel.

"I'm at the passage now," Rohan said over his shoulder.

The walls narrowed suddenly, and it felt as if everything was closing in around her. It had been dark before, but it got even darker. Within two steps, she couldn't see her hand in front of her face. She stopped trying to see and relied on her hearing, which became easier the farther away from the waterfall she got.

It wasn't long before she could pick out the footsteps of those behind her and even Rohan's breathing. She let her fingers skim along the walls. If she thought about the crawly things that liked such places, it made her want to pull her arms against her body. Instead, she focused on the tunnel.

It had been made, which meant it had served a purpose once. The Star Elf who'd helped Rohan had known about it. And now, four others did, as well. Would it be good for a quick escape? Probably not. But it was a decent way to smuggle agents inside or get others out.

She tried to imagine where the shaft would end. It hadn't been at the port. Though she didn't know why they called it a port. The river didn't reach them, and the ships were docked about a mile away through a long, winding hike. There was very little once the slaves were walked from the ship. Mortham was huge, with areas she hadn't been able to scout. The passage must be in one of them. She could only hope it was someplace that wasn't guarded. Otherwise, this might be a very short trip.

Rohan turned his head and whispered, "Stop."

She halted and told the others. Then, she listened to him feeling around for something. The sound of scraping metal filled the area. A door swung open soundlessly, and light poured in. Rohan stepped out of the tunnel and held the door for her. She followed him into the empty room as the others poured out of the passageway.

"Now what?" Jai asked as Rohan shut the door.

Farah shrugged. "I need to know what floor we're on."

"Two," Rohan said from beside her.

She pulled at her soggy clothing, unsticking it from her skin. "All right. The best bet is for me to get to a watch house. There is one located on each floor. Each station has ledgers with the names of those brought in by date, and records of what rooms they're put into," Farah explained.

Dain grunted. "That will take some time to search."

"Then we'll split up," Arya suggested. "Meet back here in half an hour?"

Jai nodded. "I'll take this floor. What names am I looking for?"

"Nitya. Taken seven years ago," Farah told him.

Rohan blew out a breath. "Lata. Taken five months ago."

"I'll go with Farah and head to level three," Arya said.

Farah frowned. "It would be better if we each took a floor."

"But we can shield you," Dain pointed out.

Right. She had forgotten that part. "Of course."

Dain turned to Rohan. "Ready? We'll take four."

The shadows were closing in around Rohan when he reached out and grabbed her hand. His gaze was intense. "Stay alive."

"You, too," she replied and turned to leave.

Rohan pulled her back, but this time, he brought her against him and claimed her lips in a passionate, toe-curling kiss. Just as suddenly, he released her. Dain's shadows encircled him, and they were gone.

Farah stared at the spot he had been for another few seconds, then turned to Arya and waited for the shadows.

35

Belanore

Rain hung heavily in the air. Most were inside, afraid they might get wet. But he didn't care. He placed his hands on the railing, then leaned in and looked across the city from atop the tower. It wasn't the tallest building in Belanore, but it was close. Only the best would do.

He directed his gaze south. He wished he could be at Mortham to watch what was undoubtedly unfolding at that very moment.

"One!"

Gods, that name. He had been known by many, but he hated that one more than most. He drew in a deep breath and turned to look inside. Gita reclined on the bright turquoise sofa, wearing a long, navy silk gown that left nothing to the imagination. Her blue hair was carefully arranged for seduction. The Moon Elf was a beauty, but he knew what kind of soul lay beneath her pale, silvery skin.

Her ice blue eyes were locked on him. He strode through the balcony doors inside the flat arranged for her to hide out in after the debacle at Shaldorn. Gita wasn't used to being confined. She had been in charge of Shaldorn for years, ordering others about. Sitting idle was not in her nature. Not even when her life was in danger.

"What are you doing?" she demanded.

Oh, the things he could tell her. He wouldn't, of course, but he could well imagine the shock that would darken her face if he did. He dealt in secrets by the hundreds. Few in power across Shecrish didn't have something they sought to hide. But nothing could be kept from him. He uncovered all the appalling, loathsome skeletons—whether buried or locked away.

"It's a pleasant night. I'm looking over the city," he answered.

Gita rolled her eyes. "There's nothing pleasant about the rain. Tell me you have more news on locating Yasmin and Ravi."

"They haven't been seen."

"Impossible!" she retorted.

He stared, remaining calm against her outburst.

"No one can stay hidden forever," she replied in a calmer voice.

"They are at the moment."

Her eyes narrowed as she seethed. "If you can't handle such a task, I will look for them myself."

"You can't leave the tower." He shouldn't get such joy out of reminding her of that, but he did.

Gita huffed, her indignation growing. "Fine," she snapped. "Tell me about New Shaldorn."

Why come up with a different name when they could just slap *new* in front of the old? No one had any imagination anymore. "I would've told you had I anything additional to share beyond what I've already imparted."

"Tell me again," she ordered.

He could refuse. It was on the tip of his tongue. He was tired of being ordered about by her. But he kept control of his ire. It wasn't time to unleash it yet.

"It has to keep me going until the construction is finished," she said as she rolled her ankle, staring appreciatively at her sapphire-adorned blue sandals.

There had been no confirmation that she would head up New Shaldorn, but he kept that little tidbit to himself. For now, anyway. The Masters wanted her hidden, so that's what he would do. Until they figured out what to do with her. They might end up sending him to kill her. Now, *that* was a job he wouldn't mind.

It was better than babysitting.

"The elite have demanded another location to give in to all their...proclivities."

Gita's grin was devious. "I created a playground for those who needed it. Of course, they'd demand its return. Go on. Tell me the rest."

He'd already told it twice. His smile tightened. To hide his irritation, he turned to the bar cart and grabbed the bottle of wine to refill her glass. He chose the cava for himself. It was only after he took a swallow and savored the smoothness that he had himself under control again.

"The need for secrecy is paramount so the DIA and CCD do not uncover its whereabouts," he continued. "Two locations are being considered. The mountains and the sea."

Gita's lips twisted. "The water is ridiculous. It took members a long time to get to the mountains. Traveling under the ocean would take considerable effort. We will lose participants."

"Perhaps that's the point. Your eagerness to grow the membership is likely what led to Shaldorn's downfall. It wasn't so secret any longer."

Her ice blue eyes turned frigid. "How dare you put the blame on me? You, Two, and Three were in charge of security. The responsibility lies with you since Two and Three are no longer here."

"You did dub me One for a reason," he replied.

She sniffed and slid her gaze away as she rearranged herself to recline once more. "Who wants New Shaldorn in the sea? I want to know so I can send over my reasons for why that would be a mistake."

"That information wasn't shared." That was far from the truth, but lies were as plentiful to him as secrets.

"Fine. Where in the mountains?"

"It would be deeper."

Gita sighed dramatically. "Then we'll have to make arrangements so members can arrive easier instead of traveling by carriage. It was already a long journey. And they want to make it longer? That's outrageous."

"Aye. The plan is to make it even farther than before, but I meant *deeper*. As in...inside a mountain."

"Well," she said after a brief pause, "that would keep us hidden. We wouldn't have to worry about anyone escaping again, either. How could they if New Shaldorn's built within a mountain?" Her smile was wide as she took a drink of wine. "I like this idea very much."

It wasn't in his nature to allow her to gloat about something she favored. "Construction underwater would afford the same. Members demand discretion."

Never mind that the members weren't in control of things, even though they acted like they were. They would soon come to find out just who they were dealing with.

Gita's smile vanished. "I don't like the water. I don't want to spend the majority of my time there."

"In the sea, the moonbeams might make it to you, depending on how deeply they choose to build. The same can't be said for inside a mountain."

"I hadn't thought of that," she murmured before sipping again.

He tossed back his drink and set the glass on the cart. His gaze moved through the open double doors. Had Rohan and Farah made it to the compound yet?

"I need something to do," Gita whined.

He had many other things to do, yet he was here. With her. A responsibility he wished he could hand off to someone else. One day, but not tonight.

"Did you hear me?"

He swung his head to her and realized he had an idea that would keep her busy for some time. "You put together Shaldorn's appearance, inside and out. Why not start thinking about how you want New Shaldorn to look?"

"While that is tempting, you know that isn't what I meant. I've been sitting here waiting to be told I can go out and look for Ravi and Yasmin. I want my revenge for what they did to Shaldorn. I want my life back."

It always came back to the Sun Elf and the human. So many other things had happened since he'd gotten Gita out of Shaldorn, but she didn't know about any of them. That was by design. The less she knew, the better.

Dealing with Gita always made him want to drink. He debated whether to pour another splash of cava. In the end, he realized it wouldn't numb his growing annoyance. He focused his attention on her just as she preferred. "You know that isn't possible."

"I'm counting on you to find them, One."

"I have a team of elves searching with me." They were looking, all right, just not for Ravi and Yasmin.

Gita leaned up with a huff and set her glass on the table with enough force that some of the dark liquid spilled over the side. "I know the power of the Masters. I know their reach. How is it possible that those two are still in hiding?" Her eyes narrowed. "Or have they been detained, and you don't want to tell me?"

"Why would I keep that information from you?"

"I'm asking myself the same question."

He'd just about had enough. "You've been ordered to remain here."

"So you say," she said and surged to her feet. "I've heard nothing from the Masters themselves. It's all come from you, and you could be lying."

"Why would I do that?" he asked wearily.

She walked around the table, flashes of silver magic snapping between her fingers. "You want my position."

He threw back his head and laughed. "Your *position* has you locked up here while I can move about freely. I think not." His smile died as he took a menacing step toward her. "Don't think for a second that I wouldn't have gutted you long ago if I wanted Shaldorn for myself."

To her credit, she didn't back down, but he saw her pulse beat rapidly at her throat just the same. His words had hit their mark as intended.

He stepped to the side and swung his arm toward the door. "You want confirmation from the Masters, then go to them."

They stared at each other for several minutes before she whirled around and sank onto the couch once more, swiping the glass into her hand as she settled. "Nice work. I was testing you. The Masters will be pleased to hear how well you've taken care of me."

He almost laughed. Instead, he pivoted to the door. He'd had enough of Gita for the night.

"Return tomorrow," she called just before the door closed behind him.

For a moment, he stood there, listening. Almost immediately, the sound of glass shattering reached him through the door. He grinned as he walked away.

36

ohan's lips still pulsed with the remembered feeling of Farah's mouth against his. He replayed the kiss over and over, focusing on her taste, the way her hands had gripped his tunic, and how her body had melted toward him.

"Focus."

The whisper jerked him out of his thoughts. Rohan realized they'd reached the watch house when Dain's shadows parted. "I'm here."

"Are you?" Dain's yellow eyes were unwavering.

"Is this where you tell me to keep my hands off her?"

The Dark curled his lip, his nostrils flared in anger. "Are you trying to get punched?"

Rohan turned away, wondering that himself. The ledgers were on a set of short bookshelves located under a table. He squatted to get a better look. He never should've kissed Farah. Not this time, and not the first time. Everything had been off-kilter since he'd tasted her. He shook his head, trying to dislodge her from his thoughts. The lights were too dim for him to see properly. He peered closer at the spines.

"Not all elves are against interspecies relationships," Dain said.

Rohan paused in his scan and looked at the Dark over his shoulder. The elf had his back to him, so Rohan returned to searching for the register. He pulled out one and flipped through the pages, but it soon became apparent that he couldn't read the writing. "Fuck."

"Problem?"

He stood and poked Dain in the back with the edge of the ledger. "I can't read it."

Dain took the book and opened the cover. He flipped through a few pages before snapping it shut. "It's in code."

Rohan had expected the Dark to be able to read it. He spun and began pulling out ledger after ledger, hoping to find some he could read. But they were all the same.

"Fuck," Dain bit out from beside him.

"Regroup?"

Dain nodded. "No choice."

Just as they were about to stand, the Dark's hand landed on his shoulder, keeping him down. Dain's brow was furrowed, his head cocked to the side as if he were listening. Rohan remained still.

"Guards," Dain whispered. "Stay low. I'll be back."

The words were barely past his lips before the Dark disappeared. Rohan listened for sounds of an attack but couldn't hear anything. The longer he sat there, the more concerned he became. He had no idea how to get back to the room from his current location. Dain had told him to stay, but something urged him to move before it was too late.

Just as he was about to leave, shadows moved into the watch house. They parted, but it wasn't Dain inside.

37

F arah counted three distinct voices outside Arya's shadows.

"...say it's someone on the inside."

"Fools. They'll be caught. Who blows up the compound and then two ships?"

"They called me in this morning. The interrogation was intense."

Then, suddenly, they were gone. When Arya's shadows opened, Farah found herself back in the room they had just departed.

She turned to the Dark. "Should we try another floor?"

"Not yet," Arya said, her voice trembling.

"What's wrong? What happened?"

Arya shook out her hands. "Something was pushing against my shadows, trying to force them open. It drained my magic. I barely returned us in time."

Farah looked around the room. Neither Jai nor Dain and

Rohan were there. Maybe that meant they'd had better luck. "Has that happened before?"

"Once," she murmured. Something in Arya's eyes spoke of horrors she wouldn't put into words.

"We'll wait for the others and see if they fared better," Farah said.

Arya looked past her. Immediately, her face lost all its color. Farah spun, expecting to see someone. The only thing she saw was the entrance to the access tunnel. It was still shut. Nothing seemed out of place. Until she noticed the thick lock around the latch. Her stomach dropped to her feet when she spotted the wards etched into the metal—markings to specifically keep Dark and Wood Elves from passing without a key. They were stuck inside Mortham now.

"None of that was there when we came in," Arya said.

Farah shook her head. "Nay, it wasn't."

"Someone was here."

They instantly went on guard, spreading out to look around the softly lit room at the shadows. Whoever it was could be waiting for the others to return. Farah turned and met Arya's gaze. The Dark shook her head. Farah did the same.

Something struck the door from the outside. They both jumped at the sound and faced the door. It swung open, and Jai stumbled in, holding on to the handle with everything he had.

"Jai," Arya said and raced to catch him before he hit the floor.

Farah quickly closed the door, and Arya dragged Jai inside as he fell unconscious. Farah pressed one ear against the wood, listening as she eyed the sallow tint to Jai's gray skin and his struggle to breathe.

"He's drained," Arya said as she cradled his head in her lap.

They would have to wait until he woke to learn what'd happened, but Farah had a good idea. Unease slithered through her as she anxiously awaited Dain's and Rohan's return. They might have been caught if Arya hadn't gotten them back when she did. They had all known the risks, but that didn't make what'd happened any easier to accept.

The minutes ticked by with excruciating slowness. Twice, Farah heard footsteps outside the door, but they continued on. She looked at her hand on the latch to see her skin held a coppery tint once more. She reached up to her ears and found them pointed again. Her transformation to human had been mildly painful. She had expected the same when the magic wore off. Maybe she had felt it but was too preoccupied with the current situation to notice.

Jai stirred. Farah turned her head to the couple. Arya helped him sit up. The two embraced, holding each other silently for a long moment. Farah looked away to give them a bit of privacy.

"What happened?" Arya asked softly. "Was something pressing against your shadows?"

"It's, uh…" He swallowed and tried again. "It's the book."

Arya's face went slack.

"What book?" Farah asked in confusion.

Jai ran a hand down his face. "I encountered it recently. I guess you could say it chose me. It's beyond evil."

"You ignored it again," Arya said and smoothed some hair from his face.

But she was unable to hide the quiver in her voice. This was the first Farah had heard about a book, but she wanted to know more. If it had affected Jai in such a way, she wanted to steer clear of it.

"You make it sound like the book is sentient," Farah said.

Arya shuddered. "In a way, it is. Trust me, you don't want any part of it."

"I need to know what it is."

"You'll know," Jai told her. "Did something go after both of you? Are you hurt?"

Arya shook her head. "Something tried to get through my shadows. I got us back here the moment I felt it."

"Any sign of Dain and Rohan?" Jai asked as he stood.

Farah sighed. "Nothing yet."

"They should've returned by now," Arya said.

It was the same thing Farah had been thinking. The longer they remained gone, the more she feared something had happened.

"There's more," Arya told Jai.

He followed her finger as she pointed to the door. He strode to it for a closer look before letting out a string of curses. "Someone was expecting us."

"We'll find another way out. Just like last time," Arya stated.

Farah hoped the Dark was right. Now that she was back within Mortham's walls, she couldn't wait to leave it behind. Something vile and malicious hung in the air. It always had, but she had gotten used to it. She didn't want to become desensitized to it again.

Dark shadows swelled from a corner. They opened, and Dain spilled out onto his hands and knees. But there was no sign of Rohan. The three of them rushed to Dain's side. He tried to stand, but his legs gave out. He toppled over, showing his bloodied and bruised face.

He grabbed Farah's hand and yanked her close. His yellow eyes were wild with fury. "Rohan," he bit out.

"What about him?" Even as Farah asked, she knew.

Dain released her and tried to sit up. "They have him."

Farah dropped onto her butt, inwardly screaming. Arya and Jai attempted to see to Dain's wounds, but he shoved them away. Finally, he managed to sit up.

"They were waiting," Dain said breathlessly.

Jai grunted and pointed at the door to the access tunnel. "We know."

The three shared with Dain what had happened to them.

"How did they know we were coming?" Farah asked.

Dain caught her eye. "There's a double agent within Durga's midst, remember? Could it be Salil?"

"I can't believe that," Farah replied. "Savita?"

Dain shook his head. "Never."

"Then who?" Jai asked.

Farah cut her hand through the air. "I don't care about that right now. I need to find Rohan."

"You *need* to care," Dain said. "If we know who set us up, then we'll know what to expect."

Arya snorted. "We do know what to expect."

Farah saw her rub her neck as if one of the gold necklaces encircled it. She had placed many around elves' necks. Farah might find herself wearing one now.

"What happened, exactly?" Jai asked Dain.

The Dark leaned back on a hand. "We found the watch house and the ledgers, but they were all written in code."

"Code?" Farah repeated. "Not the ones I saw."

"All the ones we looked at were in a language I've never seen. That's when I heard something. I told Rohan to stay hidden while I checked it out." Dain shook his head. "The noise led me into a room, where they ambushed me. Six of them tore through my shadows and attacked. I managed to get free, but when I went back for Rohan, I saw him being pulled into another shadow. My attackers came after me. I had to lose them before I returned here."

Farah dropped her head into her hands. "They were waiting for us."

"No one was in this room when we arrived," Jai said.

Arya added, "We looked for any Dark hiding here."

"What if it was something else?" Dain asked.

Farah lifted her head to look at him. "Like?"

He shrugged. "Your guess is as good as mine. It's one thing to know we planned to come to Mortham. It's another to know every detail."

"Unless it was one of us," Arya said.

Farah surged to her feet, fury making her voice shake. "It isn't Rohan. He wouldn't. Not after what he's lost."

"We know it isn't one of us," Jai told her.

Dain slowly stood and faced her. "We know it isn't you. Arya was with you the entire time. And I was with Rohan. I did leave him, but that didn't give him enough time to warn anyone. Especially when all of us had something happen at the same time."

Farah released a breath. Well, that cleared Rohan. But if it wasn't one of them, then...who?

"They'd know we would meet back here," Arya pointed out.

All four of them looked at the door. No one had come barging inside yet.

Jai shook his head. "None of this feels right."

"You should leave. Now. While you still can." Farah looked at each of them. "If you stay, you may never get out."

Dain wiped the blood from his temple and turned his head to Arya. "She's right. You and Jai need to leave. He should be far away from the book."

"So should you," Arya retorted. "Need I remind you what it did to you."

Farah frowned. "What did it do?"

"Nothing good," Dain answered.

Jai shrugged. "Either we all leave, or we all stay."

"I'm not leaving Rohan." Farah's stomach churned with regret. "He never should've come."

Arya's lips twisted. "It's settled, then. We're staying."

"We need a plan," Dain said.

Farah was relieved that she wasn't doing this alone, but there was also guilt for leading them into this.

"Don't do that," Jai told her. "We knew what we were doing coming here. And we know what we're likely giving up by staying."

Arya smiled slightly. "We do what others cannot or will not."

Farah nodded. "All right."

Dain tapped his ear before motioning them closer. They had been speaking in whispers but only mouthed words now. If someone was listening, they would never know what they were planning.

It took twice as long to sort out the specifics, but they eventually got it hammered out. Since Farah was the only non-Dark, she would be bait while Dain, Jai, and Arya hid in their shadows, watching to see who arrived. It wasn't foolproof. The same anomalies could happen to them again, leaving Farah to fend for herself.

One of them was supposed to get to her if anything happened, but she was confident she could make her way back to the room should something go wrong. She knew Mortham, and she would use that to her advantage.

"*Ready*?" Dain mouthed.

Farah nodded. The three of them called their shadows and hovered, waiting for her. She walked to the door and cracked it open to look outside. She slipped out and crept along the wall to the stairs. A dark shape of shadows moved ahead of her. Arya would scout ahead. If someone was there, she would alert Farah. Jai and Dain stayed behind her.

Farah hurried to the third floor and then onto the fourth, where Rohan had been taken. It was where they would expect her to go. Arya's shadows waited around the corner. She issued no warning, which meant the coast was clear. Farah inched into the hallway. Her gaze immediately went to the watch house. It was empty, just as Dain had said it was when he and Rohan arrived. She walked toward the doorway and looked inside. Several ledgers were on the floor. Had they been in Rohan's hand when they took him?

She drew in a shaky breath and turned her head to look down the long corridor with its many doors. Had they brought him into one of those rooms? Or was he being held elsewhere?

"A human? Really, Farah? You disappoint me."

The voice was one she never thought she'd hear again. She turned around and looked into the green eyes of her sister.

38

Elation at seeing Nitya propelled Farah forward before her mind took control and halted her feet. Disquiet settled in her stomach like a heavy stone. That was Nitya's face staring back at her, but her sister had changed in so many ways that Farah barely recognized her.

Her red hair was cut to her jaw and parted dramatically to the right side. A portion of the left side was shaved to show off her ear. Silver piercings ran from Nitya's lobe all the way up to the point, where a tiny dagger protruded, linked with a chain to a piercing below it. A thick silver filigree choker adorned with diamonds and small pearls dangling around the bottom edge wrapped her neck, and rings adorned each of her long fingers.

Heavy kajal lined Nitya's eyes, drawing attention to them. Just as her all-white ensemble stood out against Mortham's dreary colors. Her long-sleeved jacket brushed the floor and hung open to reveal a scooped-neck shirt that stopped just below her ample breasts. The pants were high-waisted and tapered to her ankles to show off white boots with very high heels.

Nitya had always been beautiful, but her new look was provocative and assertive. The dreamer was gone. Someone else now stood before Farah, and she didn't know who this person was. But whoever this Nitya was, she was here by design. And then her words finally penetrated.

"Ah," Nitya said with a small grin. "You've finally figured it out. Not as dim as I always believed you were."

Farah had so many questions. They clogged her throat, leaving her speechless as she stared.

Nitya released a dramatic sigh. "You're here because I allowed it. I'm the reason you were granted entry to Mortham."

"What?" Farah whispered. She couldn't have heard that right.

"Please. Do you really think I wouldn't know the DIA would try to send someone undercover? And they didn't even try to recruit a Dark. They sent *you*. I was fine with it. I had Golshan and Amarjeet stay with you, not because I worried you might find something but for an entirely different reason."

Farah's stomach soured. She breathed through her mouth in an attempt to keep from getting sick. This couldn't be happening.

"I almost had you, too," Nitya continued. "I saw what you did to the human. How easy it was for you. You were nearly mine. I only needed one more day. But then the explosion happened and changed everything."

This was all just a nightmare. Nitya would never turn against her family. Farah would wake up any moment now.

Nitya's green eyes looked her up and down. "You fought valiantly against the truth of this place. You kept your hands relatively clean for months, considering. But I saw you. The real you.

Stop denying it. Quit fighting it. Things will get so much easier if you do."

"Is that what you did?" Farah demanded.

"It is. Is that so hard to believe?"

Farah couldn't catch her breath. Nothing seemed real, felt real. "You wouldn't have left me."

"Of everyone, you knew how much I hated it there. I told you I would leave one day."

She had, but Farah hadn't believed her. Not really.

Nitya shrugged. "I didn't say anything because you would've tried to stop me. Bigger and better things were waiting for me. Take a look around, little sis. I run Mortham."

"This is why you left?" Farah asked in disbelief. "This...evil?"

"You don't see the bigger picture."

"I see the heartache experienced by those who've lost loved ones. I've seen the horrors of the enslaved firsthand. So, don't you dare tell me I don't see the big picture."

One side of Nitya's lips curled into a smile. "You've only seen bits. If you knew the truth, you'd believe just as I do."

"How can you say that? People are dying. Families have been ripped apart. And for what? Profit? Power?"

"You'll find out soon enough."

Alarms started ringing in Farah's head. Her mind cleared enough for her to remember she wasn't alone. Where were Dain, Jai, and Arya? They must think the intel was worth it if they weren't attacking. Unless...they couldn't.

Nitya had Rohan. But where?

Farah could see no other guards behind Nitya. There might be Dark lurking in the shadows, but she was focused on her sister.

Nitya chuckled. "If you're waiting for the two Dark who came with you to help, don't bother. They've been detained."

Two? One of them must have gotten away.

Or worse, they were working with Nitya.

"What have you done with Rohan?" Farah demanded.

"I wondered when we would get to him. Come," Nitya said and turned on her heel to stride down the hall.

Farah didn't want to go, but she had to find Rohan. She glanced behind her, hoping to see something to confirm that Arya, Dain, or Jai had escaped capture. But there was no movement. She was well and truly alone. Just as she had been for the months she was undercover.

This felt different, though. And not only because of Nitya. Farah had grown...if not comfortable, then accustomed to danger. That had ramped up considerably. It was almost like a cloud of doom hung over her, waiting to bring everything to a tragic and disastrous end.

Nitya's heels clicked on the stone floor, echoing off the walls. Farah didn't make a sound as she trailed behind her, just as she had for most of her life. Big sister leading little. How had it come to this? What had gone so terribly wrong to bring Nitya to Mortham?

The more Farah thought about it, the more she wasn't sure she wanted details. It was bad enough that the image of her sister was forever altered. After everything she had done to find Nitya and return home with her. Her heart squeezed at the thought of their parents. They could never know the truth. It would kill them. They believed Nitya was dead, and that's how Farah would leave it. It was how she should've left it all along, just as her parents had begged her to.

Nitya came to a halt before a door on the right. She watched Farah approach. Only when Farah reached her did she finally open the door. Farah tried to prepare herself as she slowly turned to look inside. The moment she saw Rohan bound to a chair with his chin to his chest, she wanted to run to him. Somehow, Farah kept her feet rooted and her face devoid of expression. But she was screaming his name inside, begging him to look at her.

"It took some doing, but we figured out that he was the one who caused the explosion." Nitya leaned against the doorjamb and crossed her arms over her chest as she observed Rohan. "Brazen for a human. I didn't think they had it in them."

"He's searching for his sister."

Nitya's head swung to her. "We got that out of him, too. Finally. He could barely talk by then, but you know how persuasive we can be."

Farah kept her eyes on her sister. If she looked at Rohan again, she might not be able to hold back her devastation or outrage. It would be pointless to attempt to bargain for his life. They had him, and they weren't letting him go. Her, either. But why wasn't she locked in a room and being tortured, too?

It could only mean one thing: Nitya wanted something.

Whatever it was, it wouldn't be good. And no matter what Nitya demanded, it wouldn't change the situation. It might prolong the inevitable, but Farah knew what the outcome would be.

"This is when you ask what I want," Nitya said.

Farah leaned her shoulder on the other side of the doorjamb and crossed her arms over her chest, mimicking her sister. It used to infuriate Nitya when they were younger. She wanted to know what it would do now.

Nitya's eyes narrowed slightly, but she didn't take the bait. "Still the same old Farah."

"A lot has changed since you left."

"Not that much," Nitya replied icily.

Farah hid her smile. She had gotten to her. "I won't bother asking for Rohan or the Dark to be spared. You won't release them."

"You're right. I won't. They're mine now."

"What do you want?"

Nitya dropped her arms and turned to face her as she leaned back against the doorjamb. "Durga."

"Excuse me?" Surely, Farah had heard her wrong.

"Oh, don't look so shocked. I'm not asking you to kill her."

That didn't make Farah feel any better. "What do you want me to do, then?"

"You, sister, are now a double agent. You're going to feed Durga the information *I* want her to know while giving me everything she tells you. And before you refuse, let me make something very clear. The two Dark Elves and the human can have easy lives. Or they can be...hard. I won't kill them. Instead, I'll make them suffer. Endlessly. Day after day until they are nothing but shells."

Farah could feel her heart beating against her ribs. This whole thing was a ghastly situation, and there was no clear way out of it. She couldn't do anything to free her friends—or herself. She doubted she would even be able to discreetly alert Durga. Savita had warned her that Durga was being watched. Which meant Farah was completely on her own with enemies in every direction. Lives rested upon her shoulders.

It was too much. Durga should've known Farah wasn't ready for undercover work. And that was the rub. Durga *had* known.

Farah was the one who'd said she was going regardless. Durga had merely relented and then given her a crash course, but even decades of training wouldn't have helped Farah in this situation. Because there was no good resolution. No matter what she decided, people would get hurt. It was the opposite of what she had intended.

There had to be a way out. She just needed time to find it. Which meant agreeing to Nitya's demands. "Fine."

"I'm not done," her sister replied.

Of course, there would be more. It wasn't enough that Nitya had already asked for the impossible.

"You're going to track down another DIA agent named Ravi and his human lover, Yasmin. They and one of the Dark Elves I just captured are responsible for the closure of Shaldorn. I want Ravi, Yasmin, and the other Dark."

Nitya purposefully left off the name of the other Dark Elf. It was a test. Her sister wanted her to state the missing Dark's name, but Farah wouldn't be drawn into that, just in case she said the wrong one. If there was a chance that Nitya *hadn't* taken Dain or Arya and whoever it was wasn't a double agent, Farah needed to give them whatever opportunities she could to free themselves and possibly get help.

"You demand a lot," Farah said.

Nitya shrugged. "Apparently, you have an in with the Dark."

"And you don't? You live with them. Besides, I thought the Masters' reach was lengthy?"

"There have been some minor setbacks. I'm righting those."

"You mean you want me to do that while you take the credit."

Nitya chuckled and shook her head. "Little sis has found her backbone."

Farah had found much more than that, but it wasn't time to show Nitya that quite yet.

"I'm going to take credit. It's my plan. I captured you, the human, and the two Dark. And I've made sure you have no alternative but to do as I say."

"Nay."

Nitya's face hardened as she straightened. "Excuse me?"

"You heard me. I'm not doing any of it. You're going to hurt my friends no matter what I do. Even if I somehow accomplish everything you require, there will always be something more you want. It'll never end. So, I'm removing myself from the equation."

39

arah's voice penetrated the darkness, tugging Rohan back to consciousness. Every inch of him hurt. It was so debilitating that he wanted to retreat, but he focused on her. He couldn't make out her words through the haze of agony, yet she grounded him. Gave him an anchor he sorely needed. The more he concentrated on her, the easier he could breathe and keep the worst of his pain at bay. At least for a little while.

One eye was swollen shut, and he could only crack the other open. His hands were bound tightly behind his back, and several fingers were broken or out of joint, preventing him from moving them. His jaw ached so severely he was sure it was broken, too. But none of that mattered now that Farah had come.

The conversation finally became clear. It wasn't until he heard the other woman call Farah *little sis* that it became clear who she spoke with. Nitya. Right after that shock was learning that two Dark had been captured. Which of the trio remained free? And why weren't they helping Farah? Or him?

He wanted to cheer when Farah stood up to Nitya. It took a lot of courage to do that after discovering that Nitya wasn't just alive but running Mortham. It would do nothing but make a statement. Nitya would find another way to force Farah to bend to her will. He wouldn't be there to see it. But they wouldn't kill him. Nay, they had other uses for him.

"Nice try," Nitya told Farah. "Did I forget to mention that I found the human's sister?"

Rohan's heart leapt into his throat. Lata was alive! His baby sister had always been a fighter.

"I had a little conversation with her. She told me the name of her village. Siguk," Nitya said.

Dread sank into his stomach, and he broke out in a cold sweat. If Kalyani and the villagers remained, they would be taken. There was no way for him to warn them, no alert he could send. His throat tightened. He should've expected something like this. He should've planned better. But all he'd been focused on was finding Lata and the others.

There was a slight pause before Farah asked, "So?"

"Quite a few of them are still here. Some died, of course. Not everyone is strong enough to endure. A handful have already been sold. The rest, however, are in rooms on either side of us."

On cue, howls reached him from both sides. Rohan strained against his bindings when he heard Lata's scream. The pain in his body was nothing compared to what he felt in his heart. He was supposed to protect Lata. He had failed.

"Don't pretend you don't care," Nitya stated.

Farah made an indistinct sound. "Nothing you can say will make me agree to anything you want."

"Really?" Nitya asked, a smile in her voice.

Someone grabbed Rohan by the hair and yanked his head back. He caught a flash of white magic before a fist slammed into his stomach. The force of it doubled him over and caused him to retch. He was hauled back up as he struggled to breathe. He looked through his good eye to see Farah watching him. She kept emotion from her face, but her hands were clenched, giving herself away. Nitya noticed. He wanted to warn Farah, but to do so would allow them to know how much she meant to him.

"How much more do you think his body can handle?" Nitya inquired as she stepped closer to Farah. "Herbs are at the ready to heal him so we can do it all over again. And again, and ag—"

"You made your point," Farah said, interrupting her. She cut her gaze to Nitya. "I suppose you'll threaten to do the same to the Dark and those in the other rooms?"

Nitya smiled. "I'm so glad we understand each other. Now, I'll get you fitted for a bracelet and then have Amarjeet take you to the surface so you can begin your work."

"I didn't agree to anything."

This time, Rohan did smile. It tore the scabs on both cuts on his lips and earned him a hit to his broken jaw. The two Dark Elves who had been torturing him went at it again. He blacked out but fought to return. A bellow tore from his throat when something hard landed on his bare toes, breaking them.

He could take anything. But his sister's and friends' screams wore on him.

Dain sidled closer to Farah and Nitya along the ceiling in the hallway. Arya and Jai had been taken almost immediately. He had managed to cloak himself better and stay out of sight. He'd then remained with Farah to hear her exchange with Nitya. It had never dawned on him that Nitya might have joined the Masters, but perhaps it should have. More and more elves were turning to them, thinking it would protect them in the long run. It wouldn't. They would discover that soon enough.

He saw Rohan's beating through a tiny parting of his shadows. Dain had to guard against others coming up behind him. He waited for an opportunity to present itself so he could attack. Part of him wondered if he should leave and get help, but he might miss vital information if he did. Not to mention he might never find them again if they moved anyone to other areas of Mortham. It was better if he remained. At least, for now.

Nitya sighed loudly and looked at her nails as Rohan was beaten. She glanced at Farah. "We both know you'll agree. Why cause your friends unnecessary pain?"

Farah said nothing. Simply watched Rohan.

She wouldn't be able to take much more. Of that, Dain was positive. She was already teetering on the edge of agreeing. Witnessing Rohan's pain and hearing the others was more than Farah could take. Not that Dain blamed her. It would affect anyone who had a heart.

"If it helps, I can threaten Mum and Dad," Nitya said.

Farah's attack was swift and vicious. The punch to Nitya's jaw snapped her head back against the door. Farah then kicked her in the inside of the knee, buckling Nitya's leg. This was the exact opportunity Dain had been waiting for. He swooped into the room and launched himself at the elves beating Rohan.

Dain took the first Dark Elf down by snapping his neck. Black magic shot from Dain's palm and disintegrated the rope holding Rohan. Dain then turned and blocked a blast of white magic from the remaining Dark, but a second struck him in the shoulder, spinning him. He used the wall to brace his foot and kicked off, turning as he did. Dain slammed into the Dark before his opponent could get off another round of magic. They crashed onto the floor, Dain using the impact and magic to finish off the elf. When he looked up, Nitya had Farah against the wall, her elbow at her throat.

Farah looked at him and then at the wall. She was telling him to get the others out. Dain gathered his shadows and hurried away.

"Don't make me do this. You're my sister," Nitya said.

Farah glared. The time for words was finished. Whatever love she'd held for Nitya was gone. Nothing she could say would change Nitya's mind. She had to accept that her sister was past the point of saving. Maybe she had never been redeemable. The truth was there for Farah to see now.

She grabbed Nitya's elbow with her left hand, and her sister's neck with the other. At the same time, she lifted a knee and shoved it between them, pushing Nitya's body away so she lost some of her leverage. Then, Farah turned her head to the left and shoved to the right with her hands. Nitya stumbled to the side, and her hold faltered.

It never entered Farah's mind to run away. She went after her sister with her hands and feet, punching and hitting, only releasing a small bit of magic. She might need it later.

Nitya blocked a couple of blows with her arm and leg before she screamed in rage and violently thrust Farah away. They circled each other as Nitya roughly yanked off her coat. Out of the corner of her eye, Farah saw Rohan in the chair. Only the slightest shift of his head told her he was conscious and watching.

Nitya's blast of copper magic was stronger than it should have been when it struck Farah. She tried to stay on her feet, but her legs wobbled, threatening to buckle. Nitya's magic had gone through hers as if it hadn't been there. There was no way her sister's magic should be that strong, especially in the Below.

Farah held herself up by the wall as Nitya smiled in anticipation. She was enjoying this. Farah couldn't give up yet. She pushed off the wall and widened her stance. Nitya raised her hands, the dim lighting reflecting off her sister's rings. Each held a green stone. How had she missed the stones before? They were imbued to recharge her magic when she couldn't get to the woods. And Nitya had ten of them.

Her sister waggled her fingers. "Just seeing these, I take it? I gave you too much credit earlier."

The screams from the other rooms were silent now. Dain had taken her cue and gone there. Hopefully, he'd freed those he could. She just had to keep Nitya busy until he, Jai, or Arya could come for Rohan.

"You always were full of yourself," Farah replied.

Disdain filled Nitya's eyes. "You don't know the meaning of pain. But you will soon. I gave you an opportunity that others beg for, and you threw it aside."

Farah was ready when the attack came. They had sparred often enough that she knew her sister would aim high while Farah usually dodged. Instead, she dropped down and swung out her leg, swiping Nitya's from under her. Her sister landed hard on her back but immediately jumped up. They got to their feet at the same time.

Three strikes of magic struck Farah in quick succession. One in each arm, and the third in her chest. She dragged in an agonizing breath. The pain was immense. She wanted to retreat, but this wasn't the game they used to play. This was real.

This was life or death.

Farah saw Rohan get to his feet—albeit uneasily—keeping his weight on one side. He grabbed the chair and swung it around to hold it before him. She met his gaze. He nodded. That's when Farah rushed Nitya, using every ounce of strength and magic she had to propel her sister backward. Nitya laughed until she ended up impaled on a chair leg.

Blood bubbled from Nitya's mouth. Farah released her, but her sister remained on her feet. She swayed as she looked down at the wooden leg poking out of her chest. Then, her knees buckled.

"Farah," she whispered before toppling to the side.

Farah rushed to Rohan. She bit back a cry of pain when she wrapped her arms around him to keep him on his feet. The wounds in her arms made it difficult to hold him as tightly as she wanted, but he was alive. That's what mattered.

"Go," Rohan whispered in a pained voice. "Save yourself."

"I'm not leaving without you."

Farah helped him to a wall before running to the two dead Dark. She searched them for herbs but found nothing. She even searched her sister. She wanted to scream in frustration. She was about to stand when she caught sight of Nitya's hand. Farah removed the rings and put them on her fingers, just in case. Then she hurried to Rohan.

She molded herself to his side after he wrapped an arm around her neck. "Ready?"

She took his grunt as affirmation and guided him to the door. Farah took the brunt of his weight. She knew he was in tremendous pain, given the sweat dotting his face and his labored breathing. They'd barely gotten into the corridor when Amarjeet rounded a corner. His eyes flared at the sight of her.

"Farah," Rohan murmured.

She looked in the other direction and saw three more guards. The sight made her glad she had taken Nitya's rings. She had few choices left. They wouldn't get far with her and Rohan's injuries. Her only option was to fight.

"Can you get to the wall?" she asked.

He released her and hobbled the short distance to the doorway of the room they had just exited. She walked into the middle of the corridor and stood to the side, turning her head one way and then the other to look at her opponents. Her magic was depleted, she had no idea how much was left in the rings, and she could barely lift her arms. Not good odds facing four Dark Elves.

Her thoughts ceased when Amarjeet came for her, throwing black magic as he did. She dodged and ducked, but one strike caught her in the thigh. It thrust her leg back, so she went down hard, her cheek slamming onto the stone floor. Pain radiated down the side of her face, but she quickly rolled twice and got to her feet in time to see black magic land where she had been.

It wasn't a killing strike, but it would have stunned her and allowed Amarjeet to catch her. He sneered as he pivoted and strode angrily toward her. The guards fell into step after him. They were too intent on her to notice the shadows forming behind them. Farah smiled because she knew what was coming.

"Something funny?" Amarjeet asked.

The three guards were taken out simultaneously without a sound. Then, one shadow barreled straight for Amarjeet.

"Farewell," she said right before the shadows parted, and Dain snapped his neck.

40

I f only it was over. But they still had to get out of Mortham.

"Farah?"

She blinked and found Dain in front of her. It took her a moment to bring his scarred face into focus. His brow was furrowed, and his golden gaze was filled with worry. Did she look that bad? She certainly felt it.

"I'll get you out," he said.

Savita's words about Rohan came back to her then. Farah took a step back and shook her head. "I can stand."

"Barely."

"But that means I can walk. Where are the others?"

"See for yourself," Dain said and moved aside.

Farah saw several humans of all ages huddled together in the corridor. A young, dark-haired girl broke from the pack and rushed into Rohan's arms. The relief on his face said it all. Farah smiled at the sight of the brother and sister reunion. Beyond them, she spotted Nitya's arm where it had fallen after Farah had yanked off the rings, and her smile faded. She and Rohan had ventured into Mortham for their sisters. At least he was able to leave with his.

Suddenly, she stiffened and hurriedly looked around. "We need to get them out. Now. Before more guards come. Are you, Jai, and Arya able to take the wounded?"

Dain glanced at Rohan before his eyes locked on her. "Aye. They sustained a few injuries, but we should be able to cover it. And you?"

"I'll lead the ones who are able to walk back through the tunnel."

"Have you forgotten it's warded against us?"

Farah suddenly felt very depleted, as if every ounce of her energy had been drained. "The humans can get it open with the right tools."

"We don't have time to look for those tools."

"We don't have time to argue," she reminded him.

His lips flattened. "You don't look well. You've lost a lot of blood."

"I'll make it. Just get Rohan and the others who can't walk."

Dain hesitated before whirling around, his long, black coat billowing out behind him as he stalked down the hall. Everyone was silent and looked terrified. It wouldn't be long before more guards came—if they weren't already on the way. She took a careful step forward, praying she remained on her feet. Her leg ached from Amarjeet's strike, but it still held her. That injury was nothing like her arms or her chest. She felt the blood rolling down her arm and along her fingers before dripping from her fingertips. She wouldn't look. It wouldn't do any good to see the severity of the wounds.

As long as she could remain standing, she was fine. She was getting out of Mortham if she had to crawl. The abhorrent place had already taken one member of her family. It wasn't getting another. She tried not to think of the hundreds of other rooms and the individuals locked inside. She wanted to free everyone, but no one would make it out now if they tried.

Rohan's eyes swung to her after Dain reached him. Lata looked from her brother to Farah and then back at Rohan before taking a purposeful step out of his arms. She was hurt, but like Farah, she could still walk. That meant she would remain behind. Rohan and Dain exchanged words before Rohan shook his head. Thankfully, the Dark ignored him. A heartbeat later, shadows moved around them, and they were gone.

Unexpected tears filled Farah's eyes. She couldn't shake the feeling that it might be the last time she saw Rohan. Her heart felt as if it had been ripped out of her chest. She didn't want to love him. She'd even tried to tell herself she didn't. But she did. Deeply. Passionately.

Completely.

He would survive the horrors of Mortham and live to tell the tale. To his family. That was more than she could've hoped for.

The room spun. Farah tried to reach out for a wall to hold herself up and swallowed a cry of pain. But the agony pulled her out of her thoughts and back to the present. Arya shot a troubled look at Jai as he took a couple of the injured. She then enveloped the remaining hurt with shadows and vanished.

Farah shook herself. It was up to her now to get the rest of the Siguks out. She walked as fast as she dared to the eleven who'd remained behind, including Lata. Her lip was busted, one of her eyes was blackened, and there was a trail of blood down her face from a broken nose. Her clothes were torn in places and bloodied, but she stood ready and eager to leave. Farah looked at the group. This was all that was left of Rohan's people. The number was shocking, but at least she could get them home.

"We must move soundlessly. Stay together and move swiftly," Farah whispered as she led them to the stairway.

No shadows led or followed her this time. She was on her own with eleven other souls to think about. Lata was two steps behind her, and the others lined up behind *her*. Farah reached the first landing without incident. She was fine as long as she didn't try to move her arms or take a deep breath. She turned the corner to continue down the switchback stairs when the floor suddenly tilted.

She grabbed the banister on instinct. Pain exploded through her arm, drawing her to a halt. She bit her tongue to keep from crying out as her stomach roiled. Fresh blood gushed down her arm to drip onto the steps—enough that she heard it splatter. Her breathing was deafening, and nothing she did could slow it. It was surprising that she heard approaching footsteps coming up the stairs. She looked at Lata over her shoulder and jerked her chin for them to stay hidden. Lata quickly backed up and had the others do the same.

Farah swallowed and bit down hard on her tongue as she bent her elbows, drawing her arms up at her waist. It was either suffer a little pain now or never-ending torment if she were caught. She chose to deal with a little now. Tears welled in her eyes from the agony of that small movement. Blood flowed freely down both arms now. Too freely. She was growing weaker by the second. She thought about Lata and the others and refused to give up.

A Dark female came around the corner and looked up to find

her. Surprise flashed on the guard's face. Farah didn't hesitate to call to her magic. Hers was depleted, but there was still some in the rings. The magic was so repugnant that she wanted to recoil from the feel of it, but it had already left her hands and struck the guard. The female fell back, dead before she hit the ground.

"Come," Farah whispered.

She didn't look back to see if Lata followed. There wasn't time. She had to get down both flights of stairs and to the room before the last of her strength disappeared. She kept her elbows bent because she couldn't handle any more pain. The humans moved as stealthily as she had asked. Her throat tightened with gratitude when they reached the second floor without encountering anyone else. Her joy plummeted when she heard movement outside the stairwell in the hallway.

Farah flattened herself against the stair wall, and the others immediately did the same. She listened for footsteps, trying to discern how many she had to go through to get to the room. Her eyes dropped to the rings. Of the eight, only two still glowed with magic, but even they were dim. They had one, maybe two uses left. It had to be enough to get the group into the room and give the humans time to open the lock. No other moment in her life had meant more than this one.

She looked over at Lata. "We need to get to the first door on the left."

"I can do it," the girl said.

"On my mark."

Lata nodded.

Farah peeked around the corner and saw an empty corridor. "Now."

Lata moved around her with the others right on her heels. Half got through before Farah heard footsteps and halted them while the first group reached the room safely. Lata had the door open a crack, looking at her.

Farah waited another moment to ensure the hallway was quiet before she urged the others forward. She moved in behind the last one and glanced furtively around until Lata shut the door softly behind her. They'd made it. Just a little farther to go. She leaned against the door and briefly closed her eyes. When she opened them, the humans were staring at her. They were waiting for her to tell them what to do next, she realized. She had wasted precious seconds when they could've been opening the lock.

She licked her lips, her mouth suddenly dry. "We need to open the small access door in the back."

"It's locked," a woman said.

Lata shouldered through the others to the back. "I can get it."

The need to slide down the wall to the floor was overwhelming, but Farah knew she wouldn't get back up if she gave in. It would take too much energy. She propped herself up as best she could and kept one ear at the door in case someone tried to open it. She hadn't asked Dain where he planned to take Rohan. There hadn't been time. She could find out later, after they got out of the tunnel. Dain would be in the cave behind the waterfall. She was sure of it.

Her eyes closed on their own. Before she knew it, she was sliding down the door. She gasped in agony when she stopped herself. She bit her lip and squeezed her eyes closed to fight the anguish that seemed to go on forever.

"Farah?"

The feminine voice punctured the haze of pain. She opened her eyes to find Lata standing before her.

"I got it," the girl said with pride.

Farah held back a grunt and straightened when she spotted the access door ajar. "Good job. Get everyone inside. It's going to be dark. They'll need to use their hands on the wall to guide them on the ascent."

Lata nodded and passed on the information to the others. Farah watched how easily the young girl took over. She was a natural leader, just like her siblings. Lata quickly got the others into the tunnel before turning to her.

Farah made her way over. "Go on. I'll follow."

"I think it'd be best if I followed you."

Did she look that bad? Farah didn't have the energy to argue. She ducked under the low door and into the tunnel. The meager light shining into the passageway was quickly doused when Lata closed the door behind her. Farah carefully turned her hand out until she felt one side of the wall. It was all she could manage.

They trudged upward for what felt like an eternity. She wanted to stop so many times, but knowing Lata was behind her kept her going. She heard the waterfall's thunderous rumble long before she exited into the murky cave. Farah stumbled without the wall's aid, and Lata moved quickly to steady her.

"What now?" the girl asked.

No matter how hard Farah looked, there was no sign of Dain, Arya, or Jai. No one was there. She was comforted that guards from Mortham weren't waiting for them, but the disappointment she felt in the absence of her friends overshadowed it.

"Farah?"

"There are stairs there," she said, nodding to the left. "They go up the face of the mesa to the top. It's a dangerous climb, but the sooner we get up there, the better."

Lata bit her lip. "We can't stay here?"

"We shouldn't."

"You won't make it."

Farah grinned at the girl's frank assessment. "I will. I just need to rest."

"Then we'll rest with you."

"Rohan risked everything for you and the others. Go, be reunited with everyone. I'll be right behind you after a brief respite."

Lata hesitated. "I don't know."

"Please. I promise I'm just going to catch my breath. I'll be right behind you."

"Rohan wouldn't leave you."

Farah faced the girl. Lata's face went out of focus, and it took Farah several blinks before her eyesight cleared. "You aren't leaving me. Go, please. The steps are tricky. I need to regain my strength before I attempt them."

"All right. I'll be looking for you, though. If you aren't there, I'm coming back."

She sounded just like Rohan. Farah nodded and somehow remained standing until Lata found the stairs and got the group headed up them. She nodded again when Lata waved before following the last of her people. That's when Farah's legs gave out. She landed heavily, but she barely noticed. She was so tired. Her eyes kept going unfocused.

She leaned to the side, thinking she was near a wall, but there was nothing there to break her fall to the floor. Once on her side, she stared at the waterfall, thinking of the last time she had been here with Rohan before letting her eyes close.

"I swear to the fucking gods," Rohan growled to Dain after the Dark sat him on a chair in a room he didn't recognize. "Get to Farah!"

"Dain?"

Rohan's head snapped to the side to find an elegantly dressed female Wood Elf. She raised a dark brow, and slowly set a pen on her desk.

"Rohan will fill you in. He needs a Healer immediately," Dain said before he vanished.

There was no mention of him returning to Farah, but Rohan hoped Dain would go there.

"Well, then," the elf said, pushing to her feet. "It looks like there is a story to tell, but Dain was right. You need healing. You look a fright."

Rohan watched her through his one good eye as she stopped before him.

"Rohan, is it? I'm Durga. If Dain brought you to my private residence, things went badly."

This was Farah's supervisor. One of the high-ranking officials in the DIA.

"Don't talk now," Durga told him as she walked to the door. When she opened it, she whispered something to someone before closing it and turning back to him. "There will be plenty of time for speaking after."

"After?" he murmured.

He heard two light knocks on the door. When Durga opened it, a Star Elf walked in. The female was petite with fair skin and violet eyes. Her lavender curls brushed the tops of her shoulders.

"Lila, this is Rohan. As you can see, he's had an ordeal," Durga said.

The Healer ran her gaze over him. "Indeed." She stopped before Rohan. "It will be better if you're lying down."

Rohan glanced at the expensive rug. He didn't want to get blood on it.

"Not there, dear man. Here," Durga said.

She stood next to an ornate sofa covered in light green fabric. That was even worse than the rug. "I'd rather not."

"Don't be ridiculous. Durga grabbed a throw from over the couch's arm and spread it on top of the cushions. "Come. Time is wasting."

"Farah," he began.

"Leave her to Dain. We need to get you fixed up."

Lila held out a hand. Rohan sighed as the Star Elf helped him to the couch. He grimaced when he sat. Lila's touch was gentle when she lifted his feet after he swung his legs up. Then he was on his back, staring at the ceiling. He couldn't get the image of Farah's blood-soaked front out of his mind. Maybe the injuries weren't as bad as they looked.

Or maybe they were worse.

"Close your eyes," Lila urged.

Rohan shook his head. "I'm waiting for someone."

Lila pulled up a chair as Durga carried over a glass. "Drink this."

"What is it?" he asked, eyeing the liquid inside.

"Something to help with the pain," Durga replied.

Rohan sniffed it before downing the slightly bitter-tasting liquid. The moment it hit his stomach, his limbs began to feel heavy, and he couldn't keep his eyes open. Then, the room faded into darkness.

His lips twisted ruefully when he squatted next to Farah. He gently rolled her onto her back and looked over the ghastly wounds.

"Nitya got you good," he murmured.

He glanced up and sighed. The poison was already working through her system. If he didn't do something, she would die long before one of her friends found her. He rubbed his fingers along his thumb. The best course of action would be for him to heal her, but it would take much more time than he had. He was already late.

"Good thing I'm always prepared."

He delicately pulled Farah's tunic away from the wounds. Then he tugged out a packet from the inside chest pocket of his coat. After he balanced it on his knee, he carefully opened it. He placed the narrow, finger-length white leaves into each lesion, one by one.

It was up to them to do their work now. Hopefully, it would be enough until someone got her to a Healer. He folded the packet and returned it to his pocket before straightening.

"See you soon," he told Farah before entering the tunnel.

41

"**F**uck," Dain muttered when he entered the cave and spotted Farah on the floor with blood pooled around her.

He rushed to her. She was breathing, but barely. He'd been afraid she was injured worse than she had let on. It was why he had brought herbs and already had them mixed in a flask. He held her head as he brought the flask to her lips. Most of the liquid spilled out of her mouth.

"Come on, Farah. Fight," Dain urged.

He kept trying. Eventually, he saw her swallow, indicating that she'd gotten some of the herbed water. Next, he cut open her tunic since it was drenched in blood and searched her wounds. Dain's jaw went slack when he saw her right shoulder. The flesh was puckered, and the bone looked nearly pulverized. The left shoulder hadn't fared much better. The wound on her upper torso was a massive bruise that likely meant internal injuries.

"Rohan will be fine. He's demanding to see you. Don't make

me go to him without you," he said, pulling a length of bandage from one of his long coat's inside pockets to stanch the blood flow in one shoulder before turning to the other.

He tied off the second bandage before carefully lifting her to lay her over his right shoulder. Dain got to his feet and headed toward the steps. Arya and Jai were making sure the rest of Rohan's people returned to their village. All three of them were exhausted from transporting everyone, and he was far from finished.

Dain couldn't take Farah to CCD headquarters, and he didn't trust the DIA. Taking Rohan to Durga's residence was one thing. The Masters weren't looking for him. If Dain had enough strength, he'd take her to Manu, but he'd never make it to the mountains. That left only one place. Even then, he wasn't sure he would make it.

The climb to the top of the mesa was trickier while carrying Farah. He tried to call his shadows twice, but the spray from the waterfall was too powerful, and he couldn't manifest them. Dawn had broken, and the piercing sunlight made him squint to protect his eyes. He kept one hand on Farah to keep her steady in case she woke, and trudged up the unending steps. Someone called his name. He looked up to discover Arya leaning over the side of the plateau. His legs burned as he reached the final few steps.

"How bad is she?" Arya asked, jumping down to meet him on the slim ledge.

"Bad. She needs immediate healing."

"Where are you taking her?"

Dain leaned against the cliff. "Sundar."

"Can you make it?"

"I don't know."

Arya nodded. "Then we'll help."

"Where is Jai? Were his injuries that bad?" Dain asked when he saw no sign of him.

Her eyes darted away. "It was the book. It was nearly on the fourth level when you helped us escape. Being that close to it distressed him."

The book that had chosen Jai when they infiltrated Mortham just weeks earlier. The same tome that had cut Dain's finger and caused him to become someone else until the wound was treated. "Is he all right?"

"He will be," she confirmed. "I'll get him."

Dain shifted Farah to cradle her in his arms as Arya jumped atop the mesa. Farah's bandages were already stained red. Had the herbs not stopped the bleeding yet? Something was very wrong. Within seconds, Arya and Jai were on the ledge with him.

"We're ready," Arya said.

Dain was grateful for their help as shadows closed around them. It became apparent immediately that he was more fatigued than he realized. He wouldn't have gotten far on his own. He steered the group away from the city deep into the rainwood to a building set away from others. Songbirds sang loudly in the quiet morning as the shadows fell away. Arya and Jai stood off to the side within the building as Dain carried Farah to the table and laid her on it. There was a slight squeak of a hinge as the door opened. Dain turned to face the Star Elf.

As usual, Sundar's straight, purple hair hung down to his arse. He kept it parted down the middle and tucked behind his ears to show off the points. A brightly hued, loose-fitting robe dragged on the floor behind him and hung open to reveal a lean, bare chest.

The floor-length wrap skirt was fastened at the side with a silver clasp and sat precariously low on the elf's slim hips.

Sundar's bright purple eyes regarded Dain before he looked at Farah on the table. "I thought you collected favors, Dain, not owed them."

"I had no other choice," Dain replied.

Sundar glanced at Arya. "Glad it isn't you on my table again."

"Me, too," she said with a quick smile.

"Now, what have we here?" Sundar asked and strode barefoot to Farah.

Dain stood at the foot of the table as Sundar unwrapped the bandages and let out a hiss. "What is it?"

"Poison."

"Poison?" Dain, Arya, and Jai repeated in unison.

Sundar sliced his hands through the air, then leaned close to a wound and dug around in Farah's shoulder before withdrawing something black. He held it up and pinned Dain with a look. "Since when did you learn about drood leaves?"

"What?" Dain asked with a frown.

"You don't know what this is?" Sundar demanded.

Dain drew in a breath as he held the Star Elf's gaze. "I do not."

"They didn't get there by accident. Especially given they were tucked in that deep. That means someone put them there." Sundar set it aside and looked into Farah's other shoulder. "It isn't knowledge we Healers share with other elven races." He dug around for a moment and pulled out a second leaf. "When plucked from the tree, they're white. They change color when leaching poison. If you didn't put this inside your friend's injuries, someone did. You should thank them because they likely saved her life."

Dain parted his lips to speak.

Sundar turned his head away. "Shh. I need quiet."

There was nothing for them to do while he worked, and there was no telling how long it would take. The poison troubled Dain. That wasn't something elves used. As far as Dain knew, Farah hadn't been struck by a weapon. That meant the poison had come from magic. Specifically, Nitya's.

Then there were the drood leaves. Who could have done that? He had an idea, but he didn't like it. He motioned for Jai and Arya to follow him outside. Normally, Dain stayed inside, but he didn't want to disturb Sundar. He kept to the tree line near the building in case any others were around.

"How was Farah poisoned?" Jai asked.

Dain ran a hand down his face. "She battled Nitya, but only with magic. The only other weapons there were fists and feet."

"You can't think Nitya passed it to her through magic. That isn't possible, is it?" Arya asked, her brow furrowed deeply.

Dain shrugged. "I don't know."

"What about the leaves? If you didn't put them there, who did?" Jai asked.

Arya bit her lip. "Could it have been One?"

"Maybe." There was much about One that Dain didn't know, and he didn't like it. He'd done a little digging and found nothing. That was damning. If it was him, he had helped them three times now, when he supposedly worked for the Masters.

Jai crossed his arms over his chest. "Perhaps he's a double agent for the DIA."

"Durga would've told me," Dain said.

Arya wrinkled her nose. "Not if she doesn't know."

"True. We may never know who put the leaves in Farah's wounds. Honestly, I don't care right now. They bought her time so

I could get her to Sundar." Dain looked toward the building. At least he hoped the leaves had done enough so Sundar could save her. He didn't want to have to tell Rohan that Farah had died.

"You have enough to deal with. Let us look into the poisoning," Jai said.

Dain shook his head. "You two risked a lot by entering Mortham again. Go home. Rest. I'll let you know how this all works out."

Arya regarded him with a cool look. "Hiding isn't helping anyone, and it certainly won't end the Masters. We're here to help. Let us."

"What she said," Jai added.

Dain blew out a breath. "All right. But discreetly. See if you learn anything about poison mixing with magic. I'll drop by your house for an update."

"Stay safe," Arya said.

"Both of you, as well." Dain waited until they were gone before he returned inside the building.

He settled into the same chair he had used when Sundar had healed Arya's injuries. The Healer had his hands over Farah's shoulder. It would be a long day.

42

Rohan ran along the wet sand after a red-haired woman as foaming waves stretched for him. He was almost to her, his arm extended to grab her shoulder when the voices intruded and severed the dream. He drew in a shaky breath as a feeling of profound loss settled in his chest. His eyes opened to stare at the ceiling as the events of what'd happened came crashing back, one after the other.

Farah.

Where was she? Had she made it out? He had to find her.

The voices came again, dragging his gaze to the side as he rolled his head. He spotted Dain and Durga talking in low voices.

Durga spotted him and smiled. "About time you woke. I worried I'd given you too much."

"What was that?" he asked as he recalled the drink that had knocked him out.

"Just a little something I keep handy. How do you feel?"

There wasn't a trace of pain anywhere. He pushed himself up

and wiggled the toes that had been smashed. "I feel great." His gaze slid to Dain. "Where's Farah?"

"That's a little complicated," Durga answered.

Dain stepped forward, his hands clasped behind his back. "She got your sister and the others safely out of the compound. They're at your village now."

"That's good. But that doesn't tell me about her." Rohan braced himself for the worst, even as he prayed to any gods who were listening.

"Her injuries were worse than she let on." Dain paused and drew in a breath. "She was poisoned."

"Poisoned?" Rohan repeated in confusion. "Is that something elves use?"

Durga's lips flattened as her face lined with regret. "It is not. And before you ask, we don't know how it happened. We're trying to sort it out."

Rohan had known she needed to get out of Mortham. He should've insisted that she leave with him. "Will she live?"

"The infection spread. She's being cared for by one of the best Healers," Dain explained.

That was his way of saying they weren't sure. Rohan swung his legs over the side of the sofa and dropped his head into his hands. He should've made her leave with him.

"She's a fighter. She'll pull through. I'll tell you the moment I know anything," Durga promised.

Rohan raised his head and sat up straight. "What do you need from me?"

"I have a change of clothes and some food waiting. While you're eating, I'd like you to recount what happened, starting from the very beginning when your sister was taken." Durga walked to the closed door and stood, waiting for him.

Rohan glanced at Dain, who dipped his head, telling him to trust Durga. Rohan pushed to his feet and followed the elf out the door.

Three hours later, after a very long conversation where Durga asked the same questions in twenty different ways, Rohan found himself standing on the edge of the plateau, looking out at the sea.

"It's a beautiful place," Dain said from beneath the shade of a tree.

Rohan nodded slowly. "It certainly is. Thank you for bringing me home."

"Of course. When they brought your people home, Arya and Jai left some herbs with Lata."

"We're grateful for that." He eyed the shoreline, hoping to see red hair—and knowing he wouldn't. "It feels weird to be back after everything."

Dain grunted. "You'll fall back into things soon enough."

Rohan blew out a breath. He wasn't so sure of that. He looked over to say the words out loud, but Dain was already gone. He smiled to himself and began the climb down the cliffside.

He heard his name and glanced down to see Lata running to him. He scrambled down faster, dropping the last ten feet to the platform. When he turned, both Lata and Kalyani threw themselves at him. He caught his sisters in his arms and held them tightly, thankful he had his family once again.

An image of Nitya's dead body filled his mind. He couldn't imagine Farah's pain at learning who—and what—her sister was. After everything Farah had endured, she hadn't gotten the happy ending she hoped for. And without her, he wouldn't have his.

But he had lost, too. It was only after being parted from Farah that the depths of his feelings became clear. Perhaps it was better that they parted this way. There was no need for false words or hurtful excuses. He had seen for himself the lengths humans and elves went to in order to be together. Farah wouldn't leave the DIA, and he had his people. They came from two different worlds and wanted different things. Even if she felt as he did, it probably wouldn't have worked.

But what if it did...?

Rohan shut down such thoughts and leaned back to look at his sisters. Kalyani was radiant. The herbs had healed Lata's injuries, but she looked older than her young years. There was healing to do by more than just his family.

"Now what?" Lata asked.

"We leave," Kalyani said. "Just as Rohan wanted. Not everyone wants to go, but they all understand we must."

He blinked, taken aback. "You talked them into it?"

"You asked it of me," Kalyani replied with a grin.

Lata shrugged. "I guess that means we learn to build boats to sail."

Rohan looked at Lata, who watched him with dark eyes. "I don't know if we should go. This is our home. And, Kal, you love the ocean. I don't want to take that from you."

"You won't if we sail off. I'll have water all around me," Kalyani replied.

Rohan looked at the shore again. "We know nothing about building boats or sailing. Or even if there *is* more land out there."

"There has to be somewhere out there we could disappear," Lata said.

He thought about the mountains. "Maybe."

Kalyani swept her arm wide. "Everyone has been packing. Just tell us when to go."

Lata took his hand and pulled him after her. Rohan glanced back at Kalyani and saw her gaze lingering on the water.

Four days later, Rohan watched thirteen Siguks strike out for Rannora. It turned out his sisters were right. It was time for a change. There had been too much heartache in their village. He searched the trees for signs of Dain or even Farah, but he hadn't seen anyone. There had been no word from anyone about her condition.

The time of seclusion for the Siguks was over. It would be a slow process of seeking trade with others, including the elves, for the forty-two who remained. His adventure through Shecrish had opened a new world for him—one the others needed to learn. But they would do it in a new location.

Rohan waited until the thirteen were out of sight before he led the remainder of his people away. He set his sisters on a heading and took to the trees. He stood on a branch high above them and looked into the distance. Then he turned back. He could just make out the sea through the turning leaves. Farah had shown him a different world within the trees, and he wouldn't forget it. He jumped from tree to tree, scouting ahead for danger.

43

Farah faced the vast sea, watching the waves crest and break before rolling against her feet. The birds squawked around her as the breeze lifted her hair and brushed against her cheek. After two trips to the coast, she was finally standing at the water. It was everything she had imagined it would be. The sun warmed her despite the chilly wind and cool water. Her feet sank into the wet sand that pushed between her toes. Only one thing was missing.

Two weeks of intense treatments from Sundar had rid her of the poison. She had ignored his wishes for her to remain another few days, but he had stated the poison was out of her system. She had hidden away for long enough. It was time to face the world— and her decisions.

She hadn't intended to return to Siguk, but her feet had taken her straight to the coast. No amount of telling herself she didn't want to love Rohan had worked. Her heart already belonged to him. It always would. He had opened her eyes to a world she hadn't believed had anything left to give her. How very wrong she had been.

Even if she wanted to talk to him, it was too late. She glanced over her shoulder at the cliffside and the vacant dwellings. Everyone was gone. She wasn't surprised after all they had suffered. A fresh start was just what they needed.

What hurt was that he hadn't tried to find her. At least not that she was aware of. Dain would've told her. After all, the moment she woke, he was the one who revealed that everyone was healed and at Siguk. She had relived her two kisses with Rohan hundreds of times as she lay at Sundar's. Especially the second one. That hadn't been for show. Rohan had meant it. Had his feelings changed? Maybe he realized how difficult a relationship with an elf would be. Their time at Amberstar had shown them that. Or maybe his feelings didn't run as deep as hers.

Things between them felt incomplete. There hadn't been a farewell, no well wishes for a happy future, just a separation that she had instigated because she feared what loving someone meant.

Rohan could be anywhere. She could spend a lifetime searching and never find him. She'd made the mistake of entering the hut she had used when Rohan brought her to Siguk. Everything was just as they'd left it. Memories of Rohan were everywhere she looked. They were in the very air. Those recollections played out before her, allowing her to see his expressions again, hear his voice. The dam of tears cracked. She wept as she had never wept before.

For a future that might have been.

For what she'd had for a short while.

For Nitya.

She cried until there were no more tears. Then she came down to the shore. Finally, she knew what the sea felt like. This had been Rohan's world, and she had been a part of it for a brief time.

She wrapped her arms around her middle and allowed herself to dream of a future. It was the first time she had dared such a thing since Nitya left. Farah conjured a make-believe life with Rohan. It was so beautiful she wanted to remain in her fantasy. But life didn't work that way—no matter how much she wished it could.

All her tears had dried, and fate had decided Rohan wasn't to be hers. It was time for her to move forward. That meant a trip home. It was time she saw her parents. She intended to tell them she had confirmed Nitya was dead, but she wouldn't tell them the rest. She wanted them to hold on to the good memories of their daughter.

Farah dropped her arms and turned to walk to the ladder. She did a double take when she saw a man standing at the top of the cliff. Her heart skipped a beat, and she halted. She knew that stance. The man stared for a moment more before he began the climb down the rock face of the mesa. Farah started running across the vast expanse of thick sand that kept tangling her feet.

Rohan shouted her name as she reached the ladder. She looked up to find him already off the cliff and jumping from one platform to another without even using the ladders. She backed up a few steps to watch his muscular body as he drew closer. The climb down the final ladder to the sand was almost too much.

Then, he was standing before her.

He was breathing hard, his celadon eyes moving over her face as if she were the most precious thing he had ever seen. "I saw you at the water like I had so many times in my dreams. I thought you were a figment of my imagination. Then you turned."

Her mind buzzed with a thousand different questions as she drank in the sight of him. She wanted to touch him, hug him, and kiss him all at once. "What are you doing here? I thought everyone had left."

"We did." He swallowed, his throat bobbing. "I was taking them to the mountains, but it didn't feel right. We turned around to come back. What are you doing here?"

"I came for you. I thought I was too late."

"Never," he said.

They reached for each other at the same time, their lips crashing together in a fevered frenzy, each frantic for a taste of the other. He stole her breath as his kisses aroused and enthralled her. Her body melted against his, her lips eagerly parting for him. His hard body trapped hers as he deepened the kiss.

She dug her fingers into his shoulder muscles to remain upright. Her world was spinning out of control, and at the center was Rohan—steady and solid. Never had a kiss been such sweet seduction, such tantalizing persuasion. He unleashed all his intoxicating virility upon her. She was no match for his commanding potency, his masterful touch.

Her chest heaved when he lifted his head, and his celadon gaze speared hers. His eyes burned with desire. Scorched her with the intensity of his need. Chills of anticipation raced over her skin. She had longed for his touch, craved his kisses. Ached for something she hadn't dared to voice, something she thought could never be hers.

Farah couldn't keep her hands off him. She traced the hard line of his jaw and his square chin. And, finally, she gave in to the need and slid her fingers into the cool strands of his long, dark hair.

"Come with me," he urged in a voice roughened by desire.

She would go anywhere he asked. He released her, went to the ladder, and began climbing. She watched him, mesmerized by his movements. Her legs shook as she followed him to the middle level. Once there, he took her hand and led her across several bridges to a hut near the one she had used. He shoved open the door and yanked her inside, moving her against the door before claiming her mouth again.

There were no words between them.

There was no need.

Everything could be felt, sensed...*shared.*

Chills raced down her arm when his hand skimmed her flesh. His caress was tender and possessive, gentle and sensual. He pulled a moan from her when his mouth found her neck. She turned her head to the side to give him better access. While his lips worked their magic, he took her hands and pinned them over her head. She arched her back, rubbing her breasts against him and wringing a groan from him.

He held her wrists as he lifted his head, giving them a slight squeeze—a silent command for her to keep them there. Then, he leisurely glided his palms down her arms and sides to the hem of her tunic. Her body was primed for him. She was about to rip the shirt off herself, but she kept her arms above her head, impatient and ravenous with desire.

He didn't yank off her shirt. That wasn't his style. Instead, he slid his hands beneath the hem and rested them on her waist.

With her shirt gathered at his wrists, he stroked his hands up her sides. She sucked in a breath when he paused to rub his thumbs along the undersides of her breasts. A small smile played at his lips, but it was the darkening of his eyes that made her knees weak.

He continued his upward movement so his hands slid over her breasts in a frustratingly slow glide. She bit her lip and groaned when he passed over her nipples. They were instantly hard, her breasts swelling and aching for more. He persisted in his unhurried removal of her tunic until his hands reached her shoulders, moved up her raised arms, and finally over her head.

He casually cast her shirt aside as his gaze lowered to her chest, where he could see the outline of her turgid nipples through the thin, tight shirt made to hold her breasts. She lowered her arms and gripped the wall as he moved a finger around her nipples, never touching them, teasing her mercilessly.

She was quickly becoming a puddle of need, and she hadn't even gotten to touch him yet. That had to change. She grabbed the hem of his shirt. His eyes crinkled at the corners as if daring her. She laid both hands flat on the warm skin of his waist. There was steel beneath her fingertips, and she wanted a good look at it. She wasn't as slow in her removal of his shirt—a quick push up to his shoulders and then over his head before tossing it aside.

The hard sinew of his chest lay before her, begging to be explored. Her palms flattened on his pecs. His delicious heat met her skin. She caressed over hard muscle and a dusting of hair, feeling every tremor, every twitch that went through him. Just as she reached for the waist of his trousers, he kissed her again and again until she couldn't remember her name.

Only then did he kneel before her and remove her boots. She

couldn't take her eyes off him. No male—mortal or elf—had ever shown her such care, such attention. She smoothed away a lock of hair that fell into his eyes. A smile pulled at her lips when he neatly set aside her boots before looking up at her. She felt beautiful and...wanted. Desired like never before. It wasn't until that moment that she knew she had been searching for just such a look in someone's eyes.

Her breath caught in her chest when his fingers slid between the waist of her pants and her skin. With their gazes locked and the flames of desire mounting with each heartbeat, he gradually tugged her pants over her hips and down her legs until they pooled at her feet. He grasped one leg at a time and freed them.

When he straightened, she rose onto her toes and kissed him. His arms were bands of steel as they came around her, locking her against him. His arousal pressed against her stomach, causing desire to pool between her legs. An urgency filled her, a hunger to have him inside her in that instant.

Her hands shook when she grasped the fastening of his pants. This time, he didn't stop her when she loosened them. She pushed the opening wider and caught a glimpse of his cock. Her sex throbbed with need.

Within moments, he was nude. She stared in wonder at the beautiful man before her. His hand slid around her neck and dragged her against him for another scorching kiss. The longer they kissed, the wilder their passion became. He bent and tightened his arms around her, lifting her and walking them to the bed. He gently lowered her onto the mattress, never breaking their kiss.

Rohan had never been so consumed by anyone before Farah. He couldn't get enough of her delightful lips, sweet taste, or passionate responses. She was fire and softness in his arms. Her feminine curves were pleasing, as was the toned muscle he felt beneath her silky skin.

He rocked his hips against her and moaned at the incredible feeling. Her nails dug into his back as she opened her legs wider, cushioning him against her core. Need, craving...*hunger* slammed into him. He fisted a hand in the blanket and fought to rein in the insistent yearning. Rohan ended the kiss and rose onto his hands, his arms straightening. When he loomed over her, she blinked up at him with heavy-lidded eyes and kiss-swollen lips.

She was a sight to behold. He had dreamed of this moment so many times. He gazed at firm breasts that were a perfect handful, and pink-tipped nipples. They were too much to resist. He bent his arms and flicked his tongue over one hard peak. Her moan made his balls tighten with need. He settled between her legs and suckled the nipple while teasing the other with his fingers.

Her hips rocked against him, and her moans grew louder, causing a sheen of sweat to break out over his skin. He moved from one breast to the other, teasing, fondling, and licking each tight bud until small cries fell from her lips.

He kissed the valley between her breasts and moved over her stomach to her hips. His gaze briefly lifted to her face as he kneeled on the floor. Her chest heaved, and her lips parted. He finally looked down at the triangle of red curls and her sex that glistened with desire. He stroked his palms up her shapely legs, pushing them wider, then gently tugged her to the edge of the bed.

When he leaned close and slowly licked her, her moan filled the room. He used his thumbs to lightly caress the junction of her thighs as he found her clit and leisurely rolled his tongue around it. Her hips bucked against him as her soft cries turned to shouts of pleasure the more he licked and laved her swollen clit. Only when she was writhing on the bed, her head thrashing from side to side, did he slide a finger inside her.

She came apart with a scream.

44

Farah was sailing, floating, soaring on a cloud of incomparable bliss. Radiant, luminous rapture took her. She had never experienced such euphoria before, had never known she could be taken to such heights of ecstasy.

Her body shuddered with the climax as Rohan rose over her. She reached for him, needing to feel his weight atop her. As soon as her hands met his skin, she opened her eyes. His face was a breath from hers. And in his eyes she saw a raw, visceral need. Her stomach fluttered at the sight of it. She urged him to her and gasped when his cock grazed her swollen, sensitive flesh.

His jaw clenched when the thick head of his arousal found her entrance. Her back arched as he slowly slid inside her, filling her, stretching her. She bit her lip when he pulled out, only to plunge inside her once more—harder, deeper.

He filled her over and over again. She matched his tempo, their bodies moving together. Sweat glistened on their skin as the rhythm increased. She was rapidly descending into a tempest of desire she knew would change her forever. And in the middle of the storm was Rohan. He was all that held her steady, all that kept her anchored.

The familiar ache settled low in her stomach, tightening, constricting as the passion built with each thrust of his hips, each plunge of his shaft. Her legs wrapped around him. One of his hands slid beneath her buttocks and angled her hips higher. As soon as he did, he drove inside her, filling her deeper than before. She cried out from the exquisite feel of him moving within her as if she were finally whole. Their gazes clashed, held as his hips pumped savagely, relentlessly, each stroke taking her closer and closer to another climax.

She was unable to look away, even as her body stiffened, and the orgasm struck. She shouted his name, her nails digging into his flesh as she was taken higher, swept farther than before.

Rohan was enthralled as he watched pleasure spread across her face. Each time her body clamped around his cock, it brought him closer. There was no holding back his orgasm, not after seeing and feeling her climax twice.

He couldn't look away from her hazel eyes. He was trapped, caught within her beguiling gaze. With his hips pumping rapidly, he gave in to the orgasm, his seed pouring inside her. The attraction he tried to deny, the need he couldn't ignore, was strengthened, deepened into a thick thread that bound them.

Their breaths were ragged, their bodies pulsing from their shared climax. With limbs still entwined, he pulled out of her and rolled to the side, nestling her against him.

Farah didn't know how long she lay on his chest, drifting between that curious state of sleep and wakefulness when she felt his cock thicken against the leg she had thrown over him. She grinned and leaned up on her elbow to find his eyes open. She straddled him, rising onto her knees until her sex hovered over his arousal.

Approval flashed in his celadon eyes. She took hold of his rod, enjoying the hard steel encased in soft skin. She ran her hand up and down his length, watching his gaze darken, and desire quicken his breath. Then she slowly lowered herself onto his shaft until she had taken all of his impressive length. Only then did she rock her hips.

A low, deep moan rumbled from his chest. She had never felt such decadence, such hedonism. She was needy, desire burning within her that only he could quench. His large hands massaged her breasts, tweaking her nipples until they were hard and swollen. She rotated her hips, her movements quickening the more their desire escalated.

Suddenly, he sat up and wrapped an arm around her. She ran her hands over the thick sinew of his chest and shoulders, marveling at his gorgeous physique and the power she felt just beneath her palms. He leaned her back over his arm, one hand on her hip to keep her moving, then clamped his lips over a nipple and drew it deep into his mouth.

She cried out, passion causing her blood to scorch her veins. He pushed her higher, daring her to follow as he tongued the tiny peak. She was powerless to refuse. Her body was an instrument he knew how to play to perfection.

He shifted to her other breast and gently bit down on the

turgid bud before his tongue swirled around it. Another climax was coming, fast and hard. She screamed his name as the orgasm rolled through her, tossing her about on the ocean of ecstasy.

With tremors still coursing through her body, she found herself on her stomach with Rohan behind her. He lifted her hips and entered her in one smooth thrust. She moaned, her fingers digging into the covers. His engorged cock pounded into her. With the blanket rubbing against her cheek, she moved back against him, wanting more—needing more.

Rohan ran his hands over her perfectly formed ass. Every time he filled her, he wanted more. She was completely delectable with her arse in the air, rocking against him. Her responsive body only fueled his already ravenous need.

That need, the devastating yearning to claim her, besieged him again. There was no holding back, no gentleness as he mercilessly pounded into her tight sheath. Her cries of pleasure only pushed him further until another orgasm claimed him. He threw back his head and shouted, digging his fingers into her hips until they were both spent.

They fell sideways together, and he tucked his body next to hers, surprised to find a small measure of satisfaction filling him. But he knew he wouldn't stay sated for long—not with Farah in his arms.

Even as he thought about checking the perimeter, the way she tucked his hand against her chest lulled him. He closed his eyes to the feel of her heart beating.

She woke to Rohan kissing her back, his tongue and lips teasing her skin, arousing her with his skilled mouth. His erection pressed against her. There was no stopping the hot, wet rush of anticipation that filled her. He wanted more.

He wanted *her*.

"I can't stop kissing you," he murmured with his lips against her skin.

She turned to face him. "I don't want you to."

"There was a moment when I woke that I feared this had all been a dream."

She touched his face, loving the scratch of his beard against her palm. "It isn't. I'm here. This is real."

"As much as I'd love to continue pleasuring you—and I will later—we need to talk."

"I know."

He gently moved a lock of hair from her face to tuck behind her ear. "Our journey brought a lot of realities to my attention. Some, I never could have imagined."

She wanted to stop him, but the words had to be said. No matter what happened next, she didn't regret her time with Rohan.

"My preconceived notions about elves were wrong. Well," he corrected, "mostly wrong. This is me apologizing for putting you in danger by using the bomb and taking you from the compound. And for blackmailing you. This is me thanking you for saving me countless times. This is me saying that I saw Shecrish through your eyes, and you made me want to see and experience more. This is me telling you that I love you."

Farah gasped, never expecting to hear such words.

"I know we come from two different worlds. I don't know how it would work or if you even want to try, but I had to tell you how I feel. Dain and Durga promised to tell me if you were getting better, but I've not seen anyone. I feared you were gone, and they didn't want to tell me. I..." He paused and licked his lips. "I realized the many times I should have told you about my feelings that I couldn't get back. I promised myself that if I got the chance again, I would take it."

His speech had taken her aback. She searched his eyes as she digested everything.

"Say something. Anything. Please," he begged.

She pressed her lips to his for a brief kiss. "You were the enemy turned ally turned friend. It was so unexpected and...well, beautiful, how it all fell into place. I told myself not to fall in love with you. I even tried to pretend that I hadn't. But it was a lie. From the moment of our first kiss, you stole my heart."

"Farah," he murmured and pulled her against him.

They held each other for a long time, simply relishing their shared feelings and everything they had survived together. What they had prevailed against.

Footsteps sounded on the bridge near the hut. They jumped up and hurriedly dressed. Rohan poked his head out and called to someone, then came inside and shut the door.

"The others have arrived," he told her.

She nodded. "How do we go forward?"

"I don't know."

"Me either."

He shoved a hand through his hair. "Are you still working for the DIA?"

"I am. At least, I think I am. There is more work to be done against the Masters."

"I can help."

She raised a brow, not at all surprised by his offer. "What about your people?"

"Kalyani is a great leader."

"Where would we live?"

He walked to her and took her hands in his. "We could split time between here and wherever you want to be."

"Even with my tribe to the north?" she teased.

He grinned. "Even there. I'm getting pretty good at traveling by trees."

"That you are."

He cupped her face, growing serious. "I love you."

"And I love you," she whispered before their lips met.

EPILOGUE

Two days later...

Rohan nodded to Farah, who was below and to the left of him on the cliff. "You're doing great. Stay vigilant."

"And don't look down," she replied tartly. "I know. You say it every few minutes."

He chuckled and remained where he was as he waited to make sure she had the next handhold. She had taken to rock climbing just as easily as he had thought she would. Her arm strength was building rapidly, too. Soon, he wouldn't have to wait for her. But they weren't there yet, which was why he still had a rope connecting them.

She made her next two moves with ease. He climbed higher and glanced up. They were near the top of the mesa. Farah didn't look down, but she also didn't look up. She kept her attention directly around her. The next time she placed her hand, she moved it twice before finding the right hold and pulling herself up. That gave him enough rope to get over the top. He kneeled at the edge, watching as she easily scaled the last few feet. She wore a huge smile when he helped her over the ledge.

"I did it!" she shouted with a laugh.

He got to his feet and tugged her up before wrapping his arms around her. Shadows moving out of the trees into the sun caught his attention. "Farah."

She tensed and turned around as they watched the shadows part and Dain step out. They both relaxed at the sight of him.

"You could've announced yourself," she stated.

The Dark grinned. "What would be the fun in that?"

"What brings you here?" Rohan asked.

Dain shrugged. "You two."

"How did you know where I'd be?" Farah demanded.

Dain gave her a flat look. "You two were obvious with your affections. We just had to sit back and wait."

"We?" Rohan asked.

Farah grunted. "He's talking about Durga."

"That's right," Dain said. "We have a proposition."

Rohan glanced at Farah. "We're listening."

"Several of us now have landed strikes against the Masters. Each of us also has a price on our head. The problem is, we're all over Shecrish. We want to gather in one location. Somewhere no one would think to look," Dain explained.

Farah shook her head. "The Masters know about Siguk, remember?"

"I'm not talking about Siguk itself. But perhaps somewhere close by." Dain turned and pointed down the coast to the east.

Rohan grinned. "I think I know just the place. It's secluded and difficult to get to. How many of us are we talking?"

"Ravi and Yasmin are leaving the kids hidden, but they both have exceptional skills they want to put to use. Then there is Arya and Jai, along with me and Salil. Plus, the two of you. If you're both up for it."

Farah slid her hand into Rohan's. "We're definitely up for it."

"Count me in," Kalyani said as she popped up from the ladder. "I saw we had company and wanted to say hello. And I mean it. I want to help. They struck my family and village, remember? I won't sit back and wait for it to happen again."

"Kal..." Rohan began. Farah and Dain looked at him, waiting for him to finish the sentence.

The Masters were a large and powerful group. They needed as many supporters as possible.

Rohan blew out a breath. "All right."

Salil squatted on a branch and peered through the limbs of an evergreen as he followed two elves hunting for the ever-growing list of people the Masters wanted. He and Durga had had a long talk about what he should do next. She had sensed his need to take direct action instead of sitting by and gathering intel.

He eyed the female Sun Elf and her male Moon Elf companion. The male deferred to the female on everything. By the way she sneered at him, they weren't lovers. Nay, their relationship was purely mercenary. And Salil would bet the savings he had stashed that she planned to kill the Moon Elf if they captured anyone on the Masters' list.

Salil waited until the Moon Elf walked away before silently dropping down several branches until he stood directly over the Sun Elf. He didn't use magic. Instead, he dropped a noose over her head and yanked her up.

She gasped and struggled. She even attempted to call to her magic, but she couldn't concentrate enough to use it as she fought for breath. He wound the rope around the branch and left her hanging until she no longer moved.

When he heard the Moon Elf coming back, he grabbed the next noose.

Dain knew it was wrong, but he just wanted to get a glimpse of Reva to make sure she was all right. He waited until nightfall and used his shadows to get as close to The Crossing as he dared before looking inside. He heard her laugh before he saw her.

Then she came into view. Her smile was bright, her eyes shining. She had on new clothes. The dark circles under her eyes were gone. She walked to the bar and talked to someone. Dain slid his gaze to where she looked, expecting to find Sidiq. Instead, he spotted a blond man behind it with Sidiq. Reva and the man shared a few words before she laughed again. She walked away with a tray of drinks. The blond watched her.

Dain growled, not liking the human at all. And he wasn't the only one. The man had no idea that Sidiq was glaring in his direction, too.

Thank you for reading **STORM WOOD**. I hope you enjoyed Farah and Rohan's story as much as I loved writing it.

There's a bonus short story featuring Rohan and Farah.
Grab it here: https://mailchi.mp/donnagrant.com/stormwood

If you want more Elven Kingdom stories, I'm pleased to announce that **MOUNTAIN FIRE** is up next in the series.

BUY MOUNTAIN FIRE NOW
at www.DonnaGrant.com

* * *

If you love the elves, you'll love the next Dark Universe book set in the Dragon King series, **DRAGON FORGED**.

BUY BUY DRAGON FORGED NOW
at www.DonnaGrant.com

To find out when new books release
SIGN UP FOR MY NEWSLETTER today at
https://www.tinyurl.com/DonnaGrantNews

Join my Facebook group, Donna Grant Groupies, for exclusive giveaways and sneak peeks of future books.
https://bit.ly/DGGroupies

Keep reading for a glimpse of MOUNTAIN FIRE and a sneak peek at DRAGON FORGED…

GLIMPSE AT THE NEXT
ELVEN KINGDOMS BOOK

MOUNTAIN FIRE, ELVEN KINGDOMS, BOOK 4

New York Times and *USA Today* bestselling author Donna Grant returns for the next Elven Kingdoms story.

* * *

BUY MOUNTAIN FIRE NOW
at www.DonnaGrant.com

SNEAK PEEK AT DRAGON FORGED

DRAGON KINGS SERIES, BOOK 10

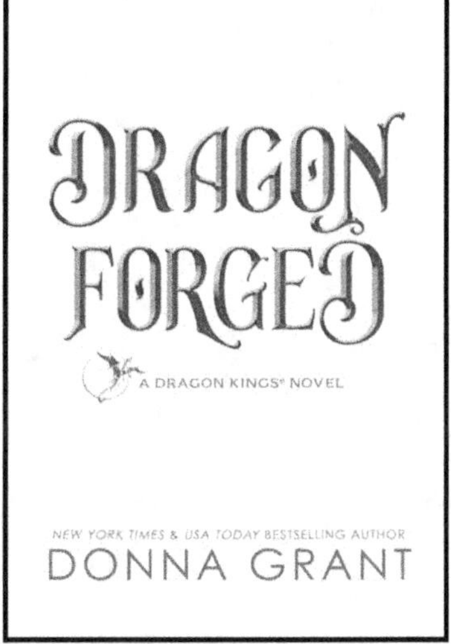

The next book in the Dragon King series by *New York Times* and *USA Today* bestselling author Donna Grant.

* * *

BUY DRAGON FORGED NOW
at www.DonnaGrant.com

Keep reading for an excerpt of DRAGON FORGED…

Last days of Autumn
Iron Hall

Boredom had never been a good companion for Hector. He was a man of action and deed. Not that he didn't enjoy some downtime. After everything he and the other Dragon Kings had endured of late, a little respite was agreeable. But after a week of twiddling his thumbs, he was restless. He needed something to occupy him, and he wasn't due for his patrol rotation along the border for another six days. That was too long to wait.

His boot heels thumped softly on Iron Hall's stone floors. The underground city was enormous, and every time they thought they had explored all there was to see, they discovered more. For the most part, the city had survived relatively well. However, some sections had some damage or had even caved in, making them impassable.

Hector had been exploring an area of devastation found weeks earlier. A few blocked corridors had already been cleared, but there was one he could focus on. He needed a project to curb his irritation and keep him from getting on anyone's nerves.

He paused inside the atrium, finding Marcus where he had left him three hours earlier. Hector grinned as he took in his friend leaning on a table, staring at blueprints. Marcus was in his element bringing the city back to its original glory, piece by piece. And he was doing a great job.

Hector lifted his gaze to the arched dome ceiling, and the large, white six-pointed star with its starry blue middle. Each of the points correlated to one of the six hallways branching off from the anteroom. The room was like every other part of Iron Hall, simple and elegant in its construction and decoration. A lot of emphasis had been placed in the atrium, which made everyone—especially Marcus—believe the entire area was important.

The corridor Hector had just traversed connected a city wing to the antechamber. All four smaller, flanking hallways had suffered damage, but the two closest to the corridor directly across from him had the most. Marcus specialized in architecture—every aspect of it. He had designed and built Dreagan Manor, the distillery, and every other building on their estate in Scotland on Earth. Then, he came to Zora to construct another manor at Cairnkeep, in the heart of dragon land, but his focus had since deviated to Iron Hall. Hector grinned and leaned a shoulder against the wall when he recalled how Marcus's eyes had lit up at the sight of the underground city.

"Tell me again why you doona just use magic to clear this last hall?" Hector asked, looking at the remaining blockage.

Marcus didn't lift his head from the blueprints as he said, "That takes the fun out of it."

This was far from Hector's idea of enjoyable. He was a warrior, a fighter. Give him wide-open skies and an enemy to vanquish over ruins to be put back together any day. He wasn't made to be stuck inside. Yet he never hesitated to lend a hand when needed—or when he had nothing else to occupy him.

He pushed away from the wall and walked across the atrium to the blocked corridor. He only saw rocks and debris, but Marcus viewed things in ways no one else could. It was why building and rebuilding were his fortes. It was also why, if they wanted a spectacular meal, they turned to Keltan, who could make a feast out of nothing. If someone needed healing, Con stepped in. All the Kings had unique skills. Even him. Though he wouldn't call his skill at battle all that special. He picked up battle tactics and fighting styles as easily as breathing. Sometimes, he wished he had something more meaningful or fun.

When the Kings first came to Zora, all that mattered to them was the discovery of their dragons. Enemies had soon emerged, and it seemed they had been fighting one foe after another ever since. It kept them from exploring more of this new world than the bit of land the dragons had claimed. Most of the Kings' time had been spent at Stonemore, a mountainside city near dragon land, where they'd fought multiple battles.

From what the Kings had seen of Zora so far, the realm was stuck in a medievalesque era. Stonemore had many striking buildings, especially the palace at the very top of the mountain. They had glass windows, plumbing, and even heated water. Yet they still used horses and carriages for travel.

Iron Hall was different in more than its architecture. The

stones used for the floor glowed from within, but not with magic. Sconces of flames that never went out hung along the walls. The aqueducts would've made the Romans weep with envy. Everything about the city, from the very design to the murals and lighting, made a person forget they were deep beneath the earth. Yet for all Iron Hall's wonders, they had yet to discover the builders, how long they might have lived here, or what had happened to them. He was beginning to wonder if they ever would.

"The debris looks different in here," Hector called out as he walked to the entrance of the blocked corridor. "The floor tiles aren't cracked. They're smashed."

He walked the last few feet into the hall where the rubble began. Squatting, Hector picked up a small piece of broken rock. The edges were burnt as if from a blast of some kind. Or fire. He tossed the rock into the air and caught it. Scanning from one side of the wide passage to the other, he saw deep into the darkness beyond as well as he would have if it were lit. His enhanced dragon senses stretched out, though searching for what, he wasn't sure. *Something* wasn't right.

It occurred to him that Marcus hadn't replied to his previous comment. He looked over his shoulder at his friend, whose dark head was still bent over the designs.

"Did you hear me?" Hector asked.

"What?" Marcus briefly lifted his head and speared him with a perturbed green gaze. "Of course."

Hector grinned. "Did you now? What did I say?"

"Fine. I wasna listening. I have to…"

Hector didn't wait for Marcus to finish, because he wouldn't. Whatever was going on happened inside Marcus's head and never made it past his lips. It was better to leave him to his musings and only interrupt if it was life or death.

Hector faced the debris field once more. The blackened stone bothered him. The few areas that needed work, like shoring up a few cracks, was nothing compared to this section or the two beside it. The hall was situated far from the city's main hub and only connected by the corridors, which explained why the damage was so contained. They hadn't discovered what it had been used for yet. It would likely take the reconstruction of the last hall before they could piece it all together. The other four hallways that branched off the atrium had one or two rooms along the sides, but all had a room at the end. Each was a different size and shape, with nothing inside that might tell them what it was for.

Hector straightened and carefully picked his way around the rubble, moving deeper into the corridor. It led him to more scorch marks on the rocks littering the floor. That confirmed that something—or someone—had blown up this hallway, either by accident or on purpose. It would explain why the others had sustained damage.

It wasn't long before Hector had to duck under the collapsing ceiling. There was no telling how much dirt was above him. With their magic, the Kings could survive a cave-in, but others wouldn't be so lucky. He needed to mention that to Marcus in case he hadn't inspected the areas back here. They needed to set up a barrier, at least to make sure none of the bairns accidentally found their way to this section.

He reached a wall of rock and was about to turn back when he spotted a small opening through a pile of rocks. He did a double take and leaned to the side, trying to get a better look into the gap.

"Fuck," Hector mumbled when he struck his head on a rock.

The indescribable, overpowering need to see inside gripped him. Without a second thought, he dropped to his hands and knees to crawl around and over the large rocks. He cut his palms and arms numerous times on the sharp edges, but his body healed instantly. If it wasn't for Marcus, he would've already reached for his magic to clear his way, but he respected his friend enough not to do that.

It took some time before Hector reached the cavity. His elation was short-lived. When he peered inside, he only found more debris. But even with nothing visible to his dragon vision, he couldn't turn away. The overwhelming need he'd felt earlier intensified, pushing him to investigate further. There was space enough for someone to stand upright, but beyond that was a solid wall of rock.

He continued to scan the space, trying to decipher what had made him want to remain and get inside. The pull was so persuasive that he jerked away from the gap. Hector tried to leave, but found he couldn't. He *had* to know what was inside that room.

Something was in there and luring him. He looked down the hall to the antechamber and briefly thought about calling Marcus. As soon as the thought crossed his mind and passed, he realized he would have to share whatever he found. Hector was at the opening in the next heartbeat. He eyed the width and height, comparing it to his body. It would be tight, especially since he couldn't use magic.

He stuck one arm through the gap, and then squeezed a shoulder and his head inside. When he tried to pull himself the rest of the way through, he got stuck. He had to contort himself to get his other shoulder through. Dirt rained down around him, the ceiling groaning ominously. He flipped onto his back and stared above him, his magic at the ready, just in case.

But it held. When he was sure nothing would fall, he pulled himself through the gap and got to his feet. He had to lean his head to the side so he didn't bonk it. Again. The room was about eight feet square and, remarkably, didn't have as much debris as the rest of the corridor. Hector skimmed the walls and floor, trying to find what had drawn him in. He found himself turning left and walking toward a wall.

He squatted and rolled away a rock the size of a beach ball, finding a slowly blinking turquoise light. The color was vivid, but not bright enough to sear his eyes. He reached for it before he could stop himself. Even as he made contact with the light, he tried to pull back.

One moment, he was in the scorched corridor. The next, he stood in an all-white stone room. A salty breeze caressed his cheek as waves crashed against rocks nearby, and gulls squawked loudly. He turned his head toward the open window and the brilliant sunlight flooding through it. He moved toward it, only to spin around at the sound of an opening door. Hector found himself staring into vibrant blue eyes as bright as a summer sky.

The woman drew up short at the sight of him. He shook himself, unsure if he was dreaming or if the stunning female staring back at him was real. For a moment, she so arrested him that he couldn't move. She had an oval face, a delicate nose, and a mouth that made him think of long nights with their bodies tangled in sheets.

Her airy, white dress was clasped at the shoulders with bands of leather, while a simple leather belt gathered the material against her waist, showing shapely curves before stopping at her ankles to reveal leather sandals. Her blond curls were gathered away from her face and hung past her shoulders, revealing darker strands underneath.

Hector started to reach out to touch her, only to stop himself in time. He couldn't remember the last time someone had mesmerized him so. He had to know her. In every way possible.

"Who are you?" he asked.

As if his words had broken the spell between them, she shut the door behind her and hurried past him. "There isn't time. You must come with me now."

He turned with her. "Just hold on a damn minute. You've no' told me your name. I need to know how I got here. And where is *here*, anyway?"

"I'll show you. Come," she urged as she motioned to another door he hadn't noticed.

He hesitated, then sighed and trailed after her, moving through the doorway. Hector found himself in a narrow hall. "Can you at least tell me your name?"

"All the answers are just ahead."

Why wouldn't she give him her name? It irritated him. He intended to get it from her. He warily followed her, eyeing the doors on either side of him. Everything within him threw up red flags. His lips parted to pose another question, when she halted and spun to face him. She barely spared him a glance, not even meeting his eyes. She hadn't been able to look away when she first saw him. Now, she wouldn't look at him. What was going on?

Hector dipped his chin and caught her gaze. She swung her attention to the opposite side. "Lass? What's going on?"

"I'm sorry," she said.

"Sorry?" he repeated. "For what?"

She walked to the side, and he turned to face her. Her eyes briefly met his. Hector glanced down the hall in both directions. When he looked back at her, he noticed the pulse in her throat was erratic.

"I'm no' hearing any of those answers you promised, lass."

"You will."

Hector planted his feet, refusing to budge. "I think it's time for you to at least tell me your name."

"I'm no one of consequence," she said, at the same time she reached around him and opened the door.

He turned to see what was inside, not realizing he was so close to the threshold. He lost his balance and tumbled through the air. He was about to shift when he landed on the hard ground with a loud grunt. Hector rolled to a stop and gingerly sat up, his legs bent as he shook his head. The room was gone. Now, he was in a field beneath a dazzling sun and big, fluffy clouds.

Hector scrubbed a hand over his jaw. There hadn't been any malice or anger in the woman's words. Nor had she touched him. But there was little doubt she knew exactly what the door was and that it would take him away. The problem was, *why* had she done it? He also had to figure out where he was. He couldn't see the door he had fallen through anywhere. He got to his feet and dusted off his hands. That's when he noticed the man leaning on a shovel, watching him.

BUY DRAGON FORGED NOW

at www.DonnaGrant.com

ABOUT THE AUTHOR

New York Times and *USA Today* bestselling author Donna Grant® has been praised for her "totally addictive" and "unique and sensual" stories.

She's written more than one hundred novels spanning multiple genres of romance including the bestselling Dragon Kings® series that features a thrilling combination of Druids, Fae, and immortal Highlanders who are dark, dangerous, and irresistible. She lives in Texas with her dog and a cat.

www.DonnaGrant.com
www.MotherofDragonsBooks.com

facebook.com/AuthorDonnaGrant
instagram.com/dgauthor
tiktok.com/@donnagrant_author
bookbub.com/authors/donna-grant
goodreads.com/donna_grant
pinterest.com/donnagrant1

www.ingramcontent.com/pod-product-compliance
Lightning Source LLC
Chambersburg PA
CBHW072006190726
48293CB00001B/173